THE WENCH IS DEAD . . .

Dene is on vacation, staying with her married friends
Vera and Sam at their Long Island summer retreat.
It is here she meets Paul Debrulet, a tall, handsome
and somewhat mysterious man who lives on the
estate. The attraction is immediate. But Paul seems
to be a man with a secret, and try as she can, Dene
can't figure out what it is. Then Lt. Gridley Nelson's
wife, Kyrie, joins the group for a dinner party, and
she recognizes Debrulet—he looks just like an
accused wife-killer whose picture she'd seen in one of
her son's true crime magazines. When an accidental
hit-and-run death occurs at party's end, it begins to
look like Paul is involved… in fact, it begins to look a
lot like murder.

MISCAST FOR MURDER

Bess Rohan had lived a sheltered life with her
divorced mother, so when she moves to New York
City, nothing prepares her for Link Bassett, the TV
and radio personality who finagles her into lunch
with him. Nor is she prepared to see Kevin Culhane,
the once-famous singer, seated with an attractive
young lady nearby. Culhane is the father who left her
as a child. The day becomes stranger still as she
stands outside her father's hotel room… unaware
that inside, lying face down on the bed, is the body of
the young lady Culhane had been having lunch
with—strangled to death. And now it becomes the
task of Lt. Gridley Nelson to determine whether her
estranged father is as guilty of murder as he
appears!

Ruth Fenisong Bibliography (1904-1978)

Gridley Nelson Mysteries:
Murder Needs a Name (1942; UK edition, 1950)
Murder Needs a Face (1942)
The Butler Died in Brooklyn (1943; UK edition, 1946)
Murder Runs a Fever (1943)
Grim Rehearsal (1950; UK edition, 1951)
Dead Yesterday (1951)
Deadlock (1952)
The Wench Is Dead (1953)
Miscast for Murder (1954; reprinted in PB, 1956, as *Too Lovely to Live*)
Bite the Hand (1956; UK edition, 1958, as *The Blackmailer*)
Death of the Party (1958)
But Not Forgotten (1960; UK edition, 1960, as *Sinister Assignment*)
Dead Weight (1962; UK edition, 1964)

Unrelated Mysteries:
Jenny Kissed Me (1944; reprinted in PB as *Death is a Lovely Lady*, 1944)
The Lost Caesar (1945; reprinted in PB, 1950, and UK edition, 1946, both as *Death is a Gold Coin*)
Desperate Cure (1946)
Snare for Sinners (1949; UK edition, 1951)
Ill Wind (1950; UK edition, 1952)
Boy Wanted (1953; juvenile)
Widows' Plight (1955; UK edition, 1957, as *Widows Blackmail*)
The Schemers (1957; UK edition, 1958, as *The Case of the Gloating Landlord*)
Villainous Company (1967; UK edition, 1968)
The Drop of a Hat (1970; UK edition, 1971)

Plays
The Boiled Eggs: A Federal Theatre Project Play for Young People (1937)
Katcha and the Devil (1938)
The Speckled Band
The Mighty Mikko
A Valiant Little Tailor
The Totem
Babar the Elephant
The Children of Salem

THE WENCH IS DEAD...

MISCAST FOR MURDER

RUTH FENISONG

Introduction by
Curtis Evans

Stark House Press • Eureka California

THE WENCH IS DEAD... / MISCAST FOR MURDER

Published by Stark House Press
1315 H Street
Eureka, CA 95501, USA
griffinskye3@sbcglobal.net
www.starkhousepress.com

ISBN: 979-8-88601-090-9

Book design by Jeff Vorzimmer, ¡caliente!design
Cover art by Shootelkora
Proofreading by Bill Kelly

First Stark House Press Edition: July 2024

Ruth Fenisong

By Curtis Evans

Ruth Fenisong, a popular and prolific twentieth-century American mystery novelist hailed in her day as a "virtually faultless pro" by Anthony Boucher, dean of American crime fiction critics, published twenty of her twenty-two crime novels in the very heart of the mid-century, during the two decades falling between 1942 and 1962, beginning with *Murder Needs a Name* and ending with *Dead Weight*. Only a poignant children's story, *Boy Wanted* (1964), and a couple of additional crime novels, *Villainous Company* (1967) and *The Drop of a Hat* (1970), appeared from the author's hand in her later years; and, even before Ruth's death in 1978, her name had almost fully faded from the mystery field, with all of her books having gone out of print. Yet in her heyday as a crime writer, from the early Forties to the early Sixties, Ruth Fenisong was a component part of that remarkable corps of women mystery authors who flourished in America, right alongside the more attention-grabbing hard-boiled boys, during World War Two and the early years of the Cold War.

Over these creatively fertile years Ruth Fenisong published non-series mystery novels as well as her Gridley Nelson detective series, the latter detailing the murder cases of an empathetic, prematurely white-haired and Princeton-educated New York City police investigator, Sergeant (later Lieutenant and Captain) Gridley "Grid" Nelson. During the course of the thirteen novel series, Nelson acquires an indomitable housekeeper and cook named Sammy (a black woman who is closely involved in his earliest cases), a lovely wife named Kyrie (first encountered in the fourth novel in the series, *Murder Runs a Fever*) and a lively son named Junie (Sammy's nickname for the boy, derived from Junior); yet as Nelson rises up life's ladder of success he never loses his intelligent sympathy for the unfortunate individuals thrown willy-nilly into the monstrous maelstrom of murder. Although Ruth Fenisong somewhat romanticizes Grid Nelson, who as one of fortune's favorites is even blessed with an independent income in the fashion of the charming aristocratic gentleman sleuths associated with the British Crime Queens Dorothy L. Sayers (Lord Peter Wimsey), Margery Allingham (Albert Campion) and Ngaio Marsh (Roderick Alleyn, himself a cop too, however improbably), the world which Nelson inhabits nevertheless is a grittier one than that of Wimsey and his gang, more akin to that which one finds in the American mid-century police procedurals of Ed McBain and Hillary Waugh. Fans of American police procedurals and British manners mysteries alike should find much to their taste in Ruth Fenisong's appealing crime fiction.

Ruth Fenisong was born on April 29, 1904 in New York City, under the name Ruth *Feinsong*. Although the author's deliberate transposition, later in life, of two letters in her surname obscured the telltale traces of her actual ethnic identity, Ruth in fact was one of two children of immigrant Jews: Maurice Feinsong, a tailor and clothes designer originally from Russian Poland, and his wife Janie (or Jennie), who had been born in Whitechapel, London to Simon Bobbe, a cloth cap maker, and his wife Martha, both of whom came originally from the Netherlands. (Janie would have been nineteen at the time of the Jack the Ripper murders that terrorized the East End of London.) As a child Janie had attended a charity school housed in a great three-story Jacobean Revival structure, the Jews' Hospital and Orphan Asylum (later the Norwood Home for Jewish Children), indicating that her parents were possessed of no great means. In New York in the 1890s Janie joined her elder brothers Samuel, a tailor, and Louis, an advertising manager for the department store Koch & Co. and wed Maurice Feinsong, a successful clothing shop owner, in 1895.

Ruth's sole sibling, her elder sister Martha, married Edmund Theise, a movie theater projectionist, and with him had one son. Ruth herself never wed, although for some four decades she resided in Greenwich Village with her life partner, native Irish schoolteacher Kathleen Gallagher (1901-1980), the daughter of a lace importer. In the first years of their relationship, Ruth and Kay, as Kathleen was known, lodged with Phil Berry (aka Sverre Filberg), a prominent popular women's magazine illustrator originally from Norway, and his wife, Evelyn, but from the 1940s onward they resided at an apartment in a five-story, turn-of-the-century row house at 227 Sullivan Street. "I have many fond memories of my Aunt Ruth and her dear friend 'Aunt Kay'," recalled a great-niece of Ruth's (although unfortunately she to date has never related any of these memories to me).

How Ruth supported herself in her twenties is unclear. Throughout the 1930s she traveled in Europe, to England

(1930), France (1932) and Italy (1937), on the latter trip in company with Kay Gallagher. This suggests she enjoyed either her own independent means or the indulgent support of her father Maurice, or "Pop" as she called him. (Her mother had passed away in 1928.) After the Second World War, Ruth and Kay resumed traveling, though to Bermuda and the Bahamas rather than the war-ravaged nations of Europe. By this time Ruth was enjoying a steady income from the sales of her popular crime novels, many of which were published not only in hardcover but in paperback. Before she began writing crime fiction in the Forties, however, Ruth in the Thirties found herself, as the Depression tightened its dreary grip in the United States, rewardingly (if not necessarily remuneratively) employed with the Federal Theater Project (FTP).

Launched under the Works Progress Administration in 1935, the FTP at its peak provided creative work to over 13,000 jobless actors, artists, writers, directors and stage workers. Despite the success it enjoyed with the public, the FTP was terminated in 1939 after the organization came under blistering attack from the House Un-American Activities Committee (HUAC), an investigative arm of the United States House of Representatives that was tasked with rooting out political "subversion" in the United States. (In practice this came to mean anything, in the eyes of the reactionary gentlemen who led this committee, deemed critical of capitalism and sympathetic to racial integration.) As far as I know, Ruth Fenisong was never singled out for attack by notorious red-baiting HUAC committee chairman Martin Dies, as was future one-shot mystery writer Irving Mendell (who hid under a playful anagrammatic pen name, "Amen Dell"), then head of the FTP's "Living Newspaper" (an innovative theatrical form designed to present factual information on current events to a popular audience). However, during the few short years that she worked with the FTP, Ruth did much interesting work, and her political perspective in that work, when it is discernible, is discernably Left.

As one of the more than three hundred and fifty people in the FTP who worked with marionettes, Ruth wrote and staged Puppet Theater in collaboration with such notable artists as the great Puppeteer Remo Bufano, Director of the FTP's marionette projects. Ruth's marionette plays included *Katcha and the Devil*, *The Mighty Mikko* and *A Valiant Little Tailor*, all adaptations of European folk tales (the last of which her father should have particularly enjoyed); *The Totem*, concocted from Iroquois tribal legend; *Babar the Elephant*, based on the beloved (and then contemporary) children's books by French writer Jean de Brunhoff; and classic English tales by literary giants Charles Dickens (*Oliver Twist*) and Arthur Conan Doyle ("The Speckled Band"), the latter of which of course is one of Sherlock Holmes' most famous and thrilling adventures. More provocative to the likes of Martin Dies, no doubt, were the allegorical *The Children of Salem*, about two children who nearly provoke the killing of a purported witch (the play was billed as "a strong indictment of superstition"), and *The Boiled Eggs*, in which a ruthlessly scheming restaurant owner ("Landlord") and his equally atrocious Wife, attempting to fleece a simple Farmer of $2000 for a meal of a dozen boiled (and very rotten) eggs, have the tables deftly turned on them by a wily Lawyer and a goodhearted Waiter. By the end of the play, the waiter has joined a union and is picketing the Landlord's restaurant, which in a burst of poetic justice is destroyed when the remaining rotten eggs explode. Evident throughout these works is Ruth Fenisong's ardent sympathy for the different and the downtrodden.

With the demise of the FTP in 1939, Ruth, now thirty-five years old, launched out on a second career, one suggested by her composition of the puppet play *The Speckled Band*: writing mystery fiction. In 1942, she published two Gridley Nelson detective novels, *Murder Needs a Name* (dedicated to "Pop") and *Murder Needs a Face*, the latter of which makes estimable use of her background in Puppet Theater. Two more Gridley Nelson novels, the cleverly titled *The Butler Died in Brooklyn* and *Murder Runs a Fever*, appeared the next year, followed by the non-series *Jenny Kissed Me* (1944), *The Lost Caesar* (1945), *Desperate Cure* (1946), *Snare for Sinners* (1949) and *Ill Wind* (1950), rounding off a prolific and highly praised decade for the author. 1950 also marked the welcome return, after a seven years absence, of Gridley Nelson, in the novel *Grim Rehearsal*, which also made excellent use of the author's theatrical background. Eight more Gridley Nelson mysteries followed over the next dozen years, which would prove the perceptive policeman's busiest period: *Dead Yesterday* (1951), *Deadlock* (1952), The *Wench Is Dead* (1953), *Miscast for Murder* (1954), *Bite the Hand* (1956), *Death of the Party* (1958), *But Not Forgotten* (1960) and *Dead Weight* (1962). Interspersed among these winning works was a fetching pair of non-series crime novels, *Widows' Plight* (1955) and *The Schemers* (1957).

In addition to clever mystery plots, Ruth Fenisong's impressive crime corpus offers readers sensitively rendered portraits of people from a variety of social and ethnic/racial backgrounds—or, as an admiring Anthony Boucher in his 1952 review of *Deadlock*, the seventh Gridley Nelson mystery, memorably put it, "beautifully realized [characters], on every level of Manhattan from café glitter to basement sordidness."

Dead Weight, the final Gridley Nelson novel, takes readers back to a milieu which has more in common with the murderous comedies of manners of the British Crime Queens, though there is seriousness at its heart. The last pages, which take place in the Nelsons' cozy living room as Grid and Kyrie discuss the recent case, have the feeling of a coda, as indeed they were, *Dead Weight* turning out to have been Grid's last recorded case. "Capt. Gridley Nelson is as quietly perceptive a detective as ever," noted Anthony Boucher in his review of the final Nelson novel, neatly bookending his 1943 observation, in his review of *Murder Runs a Fever*, that then Sgt. Gridley Nelson was "one of this department's favorite gentlemen coppers."

Over his twenty-year recorded career Grid Nelson remained one of the most likeable and appealing of fictional American detectives, a testament to the admirable creative vision of his idealistic and kindhearted creator. "Will you please stop trying to remake the world?" a lovingly exasperated Kyrie asks Grid, in the novel's closing lines. "Sometimes you seem to have a sneaking idea that you can change it singlehanded." There doubtlessly was a limit to what Grid Nelson—or Ruth Fenisong for that matter—could accomplish in society singlehanded, but in their mysteries, at any rate, Grid and Ruth made pieces of it better for a time, giving Ruth's readers a reassuring feeling that there could yet be some measure of justice meted in an unjust world, to both the guilty and the innocent.

—August 2019/May 2024

Curtis Evans received a PhD in American history in 1998. He is the author of *Masters of the "Humdrum" Mystery: Cecil John Charles Street, Freeman Wills Crofts, Alfred Walter Stewart and British Detective Fiction, 1920-1961* (2012), *Clues and Corpses: The Detective Fiction and Mystery Criticism of*

Todd Downing (2013), *The Spectrum of English Murder: The Detective Fiction of Henry Lancelot Aubrey-Fletcher and G. D. H. and Margaret Cole* (2015) and editor of the Edgar nominated *Murder in the Closet: Essays on Queer Clues in Crime Fiction Before Stonewall* (2017). He writes about vintage crime fiction at his blog The Passing Tramp and at Crimereads.

THE WENCH IS DEAD . . . .

RUTH FENISONG

Nadine Cameron and Paul Debrulet were past thirty when they met. Up to that time they believed that they had led full lives. Each had made conquests along the way with very little effort. Each had an almost childlike singleness of purpose and rarely glanced to the right or the left when moving toward a set goal. And each could be charming, and thoroughly confident of the power of that charm when it was used. Yet in Nadine's case, at least, a new note was sounded with the meeting. Paul Debrulet was her first love. She hoped, but could not be quite sure, that she was his.

She had returned from England after a settlement of accounts with her second husband. She was a woman of exceeding physical attraction, with poise and wit enough to inject vitality into any social gathering. Her acquaintances in New York were pleased to welcome her.

For a while she was content with the entertainment they provided, savoring the taste of her new freedom, the meals that presented no view of a hurt or sullen face, the heady knowledge that she could turn herself on full blast for anyone's benefit without incurring a jealous aftermath from "Mistake the Second."

In company that extracted nothing but surface grace she attended parties, visited the shops, the theaters, and the smart restaurants. And she was careful to spend relaxing interludes in her small suite in the hotel on the park. There she read a bit, but most of her time alone was dedicated to her mirror. If she took anything seriously it was her beauty. She gave unstinting devotion to its maintenance, and the results were rewarding.

She was of average height, slim-legged, but inclined to overweight at hips and breast. This tendency she considered her only flaw and exercised daily to keep it in check. Actually it was an arresting contradiction to the hollows beneath her cheekbones and at the base of her sculptured neck.

The skin on her face and body was white and fine, and she nourished it with expensive creams. Her hair was a soft smoky black and it prospered under the precise routine of the brush. Throughout the changing modes of wind-blown and page-boy and poodle cut and horse's tail she wore it like a coronet.

Her eyes were a deep, vivid blue with dark lashes lengthened by subtle artifice. Her nostrils flared delicately. Her mouth in its natural state might have been drawn by a great artist. Accentuated, it became an objective for most men. Humor relieved its perfection and out of it issued a warm, rich voice which added light, color, and unification to the canvas she presented.

Her mental equipment was on the less positive side, largely because it had received less attention. As a child she had traveled too much to acquire the formal education that might have served to discipline her brain. And what reading she did was less to slake intellectual thirst than to enrich her conversation. In full swing she could leap from profundity to cliché with such acrobatic ease as to bemuse any critical faculties her listeners might possess. Usually they classified her as "brilliant," and since she seldom explored behind her own facade she inclined to the general opinion.

The latter half of a cool, uncertain May passed smoothly. Dene, as she preferred to be called, did not intend to continue indefinitely in a manless state, but she could afford to take her time, and her survey of a somewhat sparse field held no urgency. She met a few men who pleased her mildly, but they had been preempted, and none was sufficiently tempting to engage her in the business of breaking up a marriage. She was not, she told herself, a predatory woman, and only if the need arose would she enter into what was at best a complicated undertaking. She did not know exactly what she meant by need; a strong urge, probably, or financial embarrassment. She could not have meant love because she had never more than touched the tips of its wings.

The month of June broke in upon her well-being. It brought a stretch of almost perfect weather which fed the germs of restlessness in the people who surrounded her and set them to making vacation plans. She too became infected with the seasonal fever, but although she received several invitations to join the exodus from New York, her enthusiasm was not aroused. She did not like the role of house guest for more than a few days at a stretch. She had been at both the giving and receiving ends of hospitality and she believed the axiom that guests and fish stank after three days. Moreover, she resented the petty rules and regulations imposed by even the best host; the necessity dictated by good manners for conforming to patterns other than her own. Yet she could not help feeling excluded from the preparations for departure. It seemed to her that everyone was part of a family unit except herself.

For the first time she began to have doubts concerning her

future, and to dwell upon the fact that youth was passing and with it the zest that had always been hers for any new venture. Her gregarious temperament made it unthinkable to remain behind in a city where it was difficult and perhaps dangerous for an unattached woman to acquire companionship. Besides, briefly in the past she had suffered the heat of Manhattan pavements, and she had no wish to repeat the experience. She could, of course, stop at some country inn where new associations were easily formed, but for some reason the idea did not appeal to her. Nor did any other, and she was troubled that with no ties, and with money enough to follow her fancy, none of the places in the world she had visited or intended to visit seemed worth a voyage, a train trip, or a plane flight. This was as close to inertia as she had ever been. Impatiently she backed away from it by accepting the most promising of the invitations, and quite frankly admitting to the reason for her first refusal.

She was not particularly drawn to Vera and Sam Curtis, her hosts to be, but they lived well and entertained well, and if the choice proved unwise, she could leave. She was, after all, signing no contract to stay. She had met them through mutual friends during their one and only summer tour through Europe, and Vera had pressed their address upon her and begged that she look them up when she came to America. She had done so, to be received by Vera as a cherished friend.

The older woman, plain, guileless, and garrulous, had conceived a sort of wistful admiration for her. She said, "I'm glad you changed your mind, Dene, I know exactly how you feel and I've thought of a way for you to be absolutely independent. You can stay at the new gatehouse. We had the original one torn down a year or so ago and put up a completely modern structure. You'll love it. It's a quarter of a mile or less from the main building, and Bridie, a woman who's been with Sam's family for years will keep it in running order for you. You can get up when you like and sleep when you like—and if there are times when you don't want to come over for meals you needn't. Bridie's a good cook and will jump at the chance to keep her hand in. But of course I hope you'll join us more often than not. Sam needs stimulating company. He's been grumpy ever since we decided to let Patsy go to Europe with her schoolmates."

Dene agreed silently that Sam could do with stimulation. He was a fussy, middle-aged man. Aside from golf and the stock market his interests were limited to his wife and daughter. She suspected that if he approved of her, Dene Cameron, twice divorced, it was against his better judgment, but she said warmly that Vera and Sam were too kind, and that the gatehouse at Sandy Crest, Long Island, was the perfect solution to her problem.

The Curtises left the city in the middle of June. They wanted her to drive out with them, but there were still a few engagements to keep her occupied. She postponed the move until ten days later when her social life came to a full stop.

She, who had visited so many places, had never been to Long Island, and no one had thought to mention the singular lack of comfort on its railroad or that on the Sandy Crest route a transfer had to be effected at Jamaica. She swore at herself for not having hired a car, and at Vera and Sam Curtis for not having cautioned her. The station at Jamaica was crowded and porterless. Only by giving several strong men the impact of her eyes did she manage to board the Sandy Crest train, complete with smart, heavy luggage. Her destination appeared to be at the far end of Long Island, and she discovered that Long Island was well named. For several hours the train was propelled at a dusty crawl punctuated by convulsive stops and starts. The air of the smoker she had inadvertently chosen was as stiff as jelly. Its fumes seemed to penetrate her hair and the invisible pores of her smooth flesh, and when at last she stepped onto the platform at Sandy Crest, it was with the feeling that her own scent had been plowed under and that she smelled like a cheap cigar.

There was no welcoming committee. Surrounded by her bags, she stood outside the rude shed that marked the station and waited crossly for more than ten minutes. She had sent a telegram announcing her arrival, and she supposed that either it had not been received or that the Curtises were being unpardonably casual. She was about to go in search of a telephone when a Cadillac pulled up in the station yard and Sam Curtis called her name.

He waved stiffly and she waved back although her mood demanded a less polite return. He was not behind the wheel, and he did not, as she naturally expected, get out to greet her and apologize for being late. Instead, the man in the driver's seat unfolded more than six feet of muscular power and used it sparingly. Watching his leisurely approach, she thought that she would give short shrift to a chauffeur who looked and walked so arrogantly. She noted further that his clothes were more disreputable than even the law of informal country living should allow. He wore shapeless moccasins, maroon sailcloth slacks hitched to his narrow waist by a piece of twine, and a white sports shirt that had protested the strain of his great shoulders. Her irritation was replaced by interest before he reached her.

His eyes went to the luggage first, and the first sound he made was a sigh. He said, "Mrs. Cameron—I'm Paul Debrulet—"

"*Miss* Cameron," she said, and caught herself on the verge of explaining that it was her custom to reassume her maiden name between marriages. To cover the impulse to translate herself for this reluctant hireling, she indicated the small case that contained the glassed paraphernalia of her dressing table. Her voice was as brusque as she could make it. "Please handle that one with extra care, Paul." He had given "Debrulet" a full Gallic rendition. She could not imagine Sam wrapping his tongue around it.

He bestowed upon her his full attention. He did have a most insolent face, strong-featured under cropped black hair. Permitted to grow longer the hair might have curled. His lips and nostrils did.

She knew a curious moment of misgiving as he stood staring at her. "You *are* the Curtis chauffeur, aren't you?"

"No," he said abruptly. Then, still staring at her, his gray eyes squinted as though he might be measuring. He nodded. His smile was like sudden illumination on a darkened stage. "Paintable," he said. His voice was a husky baritone. "Beautiful women often aren't."

She was accustomed to admiration. She blossomed under it. "You're a painter?"

He shook his head. The smile disappeared. He delivered an expressionless recital. "I live near the Curtis place. The poor squire hasn't had a very happy day. His wife rushed away this morning to visit a sick relative and as soon as she'd gone he swung a golf club and did something peculiar to his sacroiliac. It happens to be the chauffeur's day off—and aside from a butler who can't be expected to heft anything heavier than a teaspoon—the rest of the help is female. So Curtis asked me to help out."

She laughed. She checked it and said, "I'm sorry."

"Why? That's a very pleasant noise."

"Thank you. But Sam's troubles don't rate a pleasant

noise—nor does the fact that I mistook you for a chauffeur."

"Quite flattering from my point of view." He stowed bags under each arm. His hands were enormous and sure. "I've never been anything half so useful as a chauffeur."

But, oh, how decorative, she thought, walking beside him to the car. She wondered what, if anything, his occupation was, and decided it must be lucrative because none but an extremely wealthy man could afford to be seen in such attire.

He loaded the bags in the luggage compartment. "You'll sit in the back, of course," he said, and held the door for her with a kind of good-humored mockery. When she was settled he went back to the platform for the leftovers.

Sam Curtis, meanwhile, had swiveled his thick neck around and was well into his apology for keeping her waiting. "Nothing but an emergency would have dragged Vera away," he said, "although why a rotten-spoiled aunt who can afford a battalion of trained nurses should be considered an emergency is beyond me." A touch of pride won out over the petulance in his high-pitched voice. "But that's Vera for you—as soft-hearted as they come. After we got Patsy off she spent a whole week supervising operations to make the gatehouse ready for you, and she'd be sunk if she knew you had to wait at the station—but it couldn't be helped—"

"Of course it couldn't, Sam. And I haven't been waiting more than a quarter of an hour."

"Twelve minutes," he said gloomily.

"Yes—well—I haven't a mathematical mind."

"You've got what it takes," he said unexpectedly, and at once skimmed the compliment of any suspicion of impurity. "That's what Vera always says. Vera thinks a lot of you. Even in her hurry to leave she kept giving me last-minute instructions about seeing that you were made comfortable. Warm, isn't it?"

She regarded, without actually recording, his round, undistinguished face, the small, surprisingly shrewd brown eyes behind horn-rims, the moist brow extended by a deserting hairline. "Mr. Debrulet must be a good neighbor," she said.

"Truth is he's a newcomer to Sandy Crest and I've no more than a nodding acquaintance with him. But Patsy developed some kind of a kid crush on him—she's been here since her school closed in May. She loves it and she's safe enough in Bridie's care—well—Vera's run into him several times in the village and keeps saying we ought to ask him over for cocktails. I guess we'll have to now. I called him because I couldn't think of anyone else to turn to. Our closest neighbors are in Mexico for the summer and the town's one taxi driver hasn't answered his phone all day. Of course we've plenty of friends nearby—but most of them are busy settling in for the summer and I sort of hated to impose ..."

Debrulet was strolling toward the back of the car with the heavy dressing case suspended like a featherweight from his large hand. Dene craned her neck a little for the pleasure of observing the way he coordinated.

"The biggest Frenchman I ever saw," Sam said. "Never know he was anything but one hundred per cent American except for his name and the way he rolls it out."

"He certainly hasn't any other trace of accent," Dene said.

"And no trace of a decent wardrobe, either. Patsy told us he was a painter or something—which might account for that outfit."

"That's strange ..."

"I don't know. It takes all kinds. Anyway I shouldn't think it would seem strange to you. You must have met plenty of eccentric artists in your travels."

"I meant that he seemed insulted when I asked him if he were a painter."

"Maybe Patsy got it wrong. But whatever he is he probably doesn't count on it to support him. He's rented the Tate place, which is a pretty sizable property. True, it's run-down because it's been empty for some time—but I guess a man alone doesn't mind...."

They heard the luggage compartment close. Debrulet, the man alone, reappeared and folded himself behind the wheel.

Sam said, "Well—I guess we're all set. I'll do the same for you sometime." He groaned as he brought his eyes front. "This damned back—any wrong move and it kicks up. Mind stopping at the post office? I didn't get a chance to collect the mail today."

"Have you seen a doctor?" Dene sounded as though she cared deeply. She almost convinced herself, but Debrulet, as he started the car, flung her a quick, skeptical look over his shoulder.

Sam took her concern for granted. "No—it's an old story with me—it has to run its course. If Vera knew she'd be back like a flash—aunt or not. Patsy and I always come first with Vera."

A few minutes later Debrulet stopped the car before a frame building on Sandy Crest's main street. He went in. When he came out he was stuffing an open letter back into its envelope.

That seemed to be all the mail there was for him. He handed Sam a small stack as he climbed into the car.

"Most of them for Vera," Sam said, glancing through them. He placed them in a dashboard compartment.

"You must miss her frightfully. How long does she intend to stay away?" Again the deep, caring note was in Dene's voice. Amused by Debrulet's reaction, she had placed it there deliberately. She would not have been surprised to see the ears that lay small and flat to his head twitch knowingly, but he made neither that nor any other manifestation of having heard. He seemed to be concentrating upon his driving.

"Not a minute longer than she can help," Sam was saying. "Depend on that. Meanwhile we'll have to do the best we can...."

"If it's awkward for you to have me, Sam, I could stay at some hotel until things are normal again."

"Not a bit of it. In the first place there's no hotel within miles I'd board a dog at—and in the second place Vera would divorce me if I let you get away—and I don't hold with—" He gave an embarrassed laugh. "Seriously—you're not inconveniencing anybody and I promise that when Vera does get back she'll start things rolling for your entertainment. So if you can just hold on without getting bored ..."

"Don't worry, Sam. I won't be bored."

"Do you play golf?"

"I don't play any games."

Sam said obscurely, "Well—I guess you don't have to. What about you, Debrulet?" He stressed the name's syllables equally and sounded its final consonant.

"I play all games," Debrulet said.

"You've got the build all right." Sam's attention wandered. He gestured toward the open window at his right. "The Tate house, Dene. It's set too far back to see much of it from the road. How did you come to rent a place of that size, Debrulet?"

"There wasn't a small one available." Debrulet's tone consigned it to the foolish-question department. He added with more grace, "I got it for a song on the realtor's theory that a house is apt to hold up better when it's lived in."

Dene's eyes traveled over the spread of shaggy grass to the scrawled outlines of the house. As they passed, she saw or thought she saw a human figure sprinting toward its rear.

Sam said apologetically, "If I'd known you had company I'd have hesitated to—" He groaned as the car swerved sharply. "Look out—mind that ditch—"

Debrulet swore. He righted the car and said in his normal, very male voice. "Excuse it—I shouldn't be carrying passengers—too absentminded."

Gingerly Sam reached around to clasp the aching region of his back. "Lucky you've got good reflexes. I guess being absentminded goes with the artistic temperament. I hear you're a painter."

"Me?"

"My young daughter, Patsy, gave me to understand—"

"Patsy's romantic. She can't bear to associate with just ordinary people. To pass muster, I had to be some kind of genius. I guess that's how the painter myth started."

Sam laughed. "I hope she wasn't a pest. I'm told they all go through that romantic phase—and it's pretty trying at times—but no man could ask for a nicer kid that Patsy."

"Delightful," Debrulet said.

"Just what is your line?"

"I'm retired." He said it politely, but Dene could almost hear a lid banging down on the subject.

About a half mile down the road he turned in at a long, tree-lined driveway and braked several yards from its start beside a cottage built of upright cedar logs. The front lawn of the cottage was a scarf hung toward the calm waters of the bay. Its sides were terraced in dull blue tile.

"Your castle, Dene," Sam said. "Wonderful view of the bay if I do say so. This late afternoon sun doesn't do it justice. You want to get up early in the morning to see it at its best."

She got out of the car and stood, head raised, inhaling air that was seasoned with salt and new-cut grass. She said, "In the city I'd almost forgotten how to breathe."

Sam was pleased with her genuine pleasure. "Hard to believe it's only ninety miles or so out of Manhattan isn't it."

"Yes." She canceled out the long and dirty train trip. "I'm going to love it here, Sam."

"Wait till you see the inside." He had eased himself out of the car. His round face was a little drawn.

For the first time she showed real sympathy. "You should be resting, Sam."

"Will do as soon as I see you settled in." He turned from her to watch Debrulet enter the cottage with bags under each arm. "Kind of hate to be under obligation to a stranger. Do you like the fellow, Dene?"

She was quite unprepared for the question. "I've only just

met him."

"Yes—but you've met so many people I thought you might have formed some sort of opinion."

"He seems pleasant enough." It sounded inadequate to her.

Obviously Sam found it inadequate too. "Well—I don't know. I guess Vera's got something when she accused me of being suspicious of every new—" Incautiously he shrugged. "Hell's bells!"

"Poor Sam—perhaps a chiropractor ..."

He was not listening. He said, "I know what I'll do. Baching it the way he is, he's probably got a lot of accumulated laundry and mending and cleaning that needs to be done. I'll send one of the maids around tomorrow to put in some work for him. That should even things up."

Debrulet came out of the cottage, followed by a short, sturdy woman. Her thick gray hair had been set in rigid waves, but her freckled skin was beholden only to soap and the haphazard slap of a powder puff. She had probably removed her glasses to receive the company. The mark of them was plain on her blunt nose. Her faded blue eyes, however, seemed keen enough to take in every aspect of Dene.

When she had completed her scrutiny she said with such volume as might be expected to issue from a man's deep chest, "This will be the lady we've waited for."

Sam said, "You'll take good care of Miss Cameron, won't you, Bridie?"

"I will. But it's you who needs care from the look of you. I've some liniment—"

"How many times must I tell you that liniment has no effect on—"

Debrulet broke in. "If there are no more chores—" His moccasined feet were firmly planted, but he created the illusion of being poised for a takeoff.

Dene held out her hand to him. He accepted and relinquished it in what seemed like a fraction of an instant and yet was long enough for her to feel a hard roughened palm. Not so useful as a chauffeur, she thought, puzzled. She said, "A noble rescue. I hope we meet again."

He smiled briefly, but did not second the hope. "Want me to drive you up to the house, Curtis. I might as well. My car's there."

Sam hesitated. "Perhaps I'd better hang around here and see that—"

"Do go along, Sam. I'm going to be busy unpacking—and after that I expect to spend a full hour in the tub."

"You take the lady's advice and go along, Mr. Curtis," Bridie said. "You're not wanted here."

"Well—if you're sure ..."

"Of course." Dene ended it by turning toward the cottage. The car had started off before she reached the front door.

II

The new gatehouse was a dwelling of luxury and utility. There was a small entrance hall. There was a well-proportioned living room featuring predominantly a color scheme of chartreuse and gray, a central fireplace, a dining alcove, a television screen, and chairs and tables fashioned of walnut and sycamore. There were two bedrooms, two baths, and a bright square of kitchen. The floors throughout were sleek with wax. The drapes, furniture, and mechanical appointments mated happily with the setting, and Dene Cameron was amused to note that the whole showed orthodox adherence to a spread in one of the best magazines. But she granted that if Vera's clothes were an example of her own taste she had been wise not to rely upon it. She praised everything to Bridie, and Bridie remarked in powerful tones that there were many who could make do with such quarters and not feel put upon.

Dene observed silently that if she could become accustomed to the woman's terrible voice she might grow rather fond of her. She said, "What was the original gatehouse like, Bridie?"

"Well—it hadn't so many windows for one thing—and the fireplace was against the wall." Where any self-respecting fireplace should be, her tone implied. "And there were more rooms and it had a cozy look to it...." Briskly she washed the criticism from her voice. "But everyone to his taste. Mrs. Curtis wanted it this way and you're the lucky lady to be the first to tenant it—the excuse, so to speak, for putting the finishing touches to it. Not," she added sternly, "that Mrs. Curtis doesn't wear herself out for all and sundry—and sometimes with small thanks."

They had reached the room where Dene would sleep. "Mrs. Curtis is for what they call the modern," Bridie said unnecessarily. "There's some who might want things more homelike without being thought too set in their ways."

"It will be homelike as soon as it's been lived in a bit." Dene removed the jacket of her smart light suit and flung it over the back of a chair.

Bridie watched the original hat sail in another direction and said, "I shouldn't wonder." Eyeing Dene doubtfully, she continued to play cicerone. "If you're the reading kind you couldn't ask for more." She nodded toward the headboard of the wide, low bed that extended on either side to provide shelves of brightly jacketed books. "Mrs. Curtis had the decorator himself stretch out to see was that lamp placed right—and didn't she even sit down there at the dressing table mirrors to test out could she catch sight of her rear end if need be."

Dene laughed. She too tested the semicircle of mirrors and found them adequate. She thought that she looked less travel-stained than might be expected. She thought of Paul Debrulet. She walked over to the wall of windows that gave on to a terrace. Absently she started to strip, moved by a slight, pleasurable shiver as the soft air touched her shoulders.

Bridie said, "It's well there's only the bay outside. But doubtless you'll want your robe against the evening's chill. I had the Frenchman line up your bags where they'd be easiest to manage. Will I help you unpack now or—"

"Just open the bags so that I can get at what I need when I come out of the bath." Leaving a trail of blouse and skirt and slip, she went to the bed, where she had dropped her purse. She extracted the keys and handed them to Bridie.

Bridie glanced at the castoff clothes and said flatly, "It's more homelike by the minute."

Dene thought it might be time to take a firm stand. She said pleasantly, "I'm afraid you'll have to put up with me, Bridie, for as long as I stay. Since you're to do the cooking and general housekeeping perhaps I'd better speak to Mrs. Curtis about arranging for a personal maid."

Bridie said, "Save yourself the bother. There's no great work to an establishment of this size." She gathered up the discarded clothes and went into one of the closets to hang the jacket and skirt. She emerged and said, "Another here will only make a crowd—not to mention that the right kind is hard to come by—and Mrs. Curtis has trouble enough with what the agency sends."

"Well—we'll see. Meanwhile I'll try to remember to pick up after myself."

"Mrs. Curtis says you've been living on the other side." Bridie was making grudging allowance for her.

"Yes—on and off ever since I can remember." She had lived in Europe and in North Africa and in South Asia, and everywhere servants had been plentiful, seldom showing that they considered extraordinary the most extraordinary behavior on the part of their employers. Her marriages had carried out the pattern of her childhood. Her first husband was, as her father had been, a career diplomat. Her second husband's interests or lack of interests had led him to wander over the face of the earth. America was almost as alien as any country to her, especially when she was confronted by the need for classifying its people. It was evident, for example, that the outspoken, independent Bridie did not intend to be classified as a servant.

"But you're American born," Bridie said.

She nodded. "Of Scots extraction."

"Scots, is it? I'm Irish myself, though you might not notice it—for I said goodbye to the old country before I was turned fifteen and became a citizen as soon as ever I could." She slapped her thigh. "Scots, is it?" she repeated. "And haven't you brought to mind the thing I was searching for. He's the image of a man named Mr. Jock Fraser, who used to come visiting the old Mr. Curtis. He looks no more French than I do myself."

"Are you talking about Mr. Debrulet?"

"I am."

"He was probably born in this country too. He may be second- or third-generation French."

Bridie shook her head. "I'd mislaid his name for the moment—though how I could with young Patsy speaking of no one else I'm sure I don't know—and when I asked him what it was didn't he say it as only a foreigner could?"

"Debrulet," Dene said experimentally. "Paul Debrulet."

Bridie nodded. "You give it the same curl and twist—or near enough as makes no difference. Still—you've the excuse of living away so much—but there's something queer about the man—and I for one am glad that Patsy's been removed, though I didn't hold with her going when first the subject came up."

"Patsy's only a child—surely you don't think he—" She tried to visualize Patsy, and received a vague picture of a fresh-faced youngster whose hands and feet had outdistanced her body's growth. She visualized Paul Debrulet. His picture was much clearer.

"Who's to know what lurks in a man like that," Bridie said portentously, "him being the image of Mr. Jock Fraser and all."

She went into the bathroom.

Dene followed her, intent on tracing to its source the elusive quality of Bridie's mental processes. "Was there something wrong with this Jock Fraser?"

"There was not—but then he didn't call himself by some outlandish name, either," Bridie said triumphantly. For her that seemed to end the matter. She turned on the bath water. "You'd best get in as fast as you can. As I've mentioned the evenings are cool here and walking around in your pelt is asking for trouble."

"All right," Dene said meekly. The last person who had spoken to her like that was the "Nanny" who saw her through her childhood after her mother's death.

A little less than an hour later she came out of the bathroom wrapped in a great towel and saw that Bridie had done the unpacking. She exchanged the towel for a blue and silver robe and sat down at the mirrors to perform the ritual of face and hair.

Bridie entered the room and stared at her.

"Thanks for unpacking, Bridie."

"You're welcome. I'll stow the bags away in the morning. My mother, rest her soul, had hair like that. She could sit on it if the fancy took her. You being so fashionable I wonder you never cut it."

"It suits me this way."

"I make no doubt it would suit you any old way. What came to tell you is that Mr. Curtis telephoned." She pointed to the extension set that occupied a niche in the all-purpose headboard. "You can call him back on that. The number written on the pad. He asks will you be having dinner with him at the big house?"

"I don't know." An intimate dinner with Sam did not appeal to her. He would be certain to dither on endlessly about Vera and Patsy. "Under the circumstances wouldn't it be better for him to have a tray in bed?"

Bridie nodded approvingly. "You tell him that. He'll take it coming from you. And you won't lose by it, for I've started a fine meal going just on the chance. Now I'll be getting on with it."

Dene felt as though she had won a good-conduct medal by foul means. She went to the telephone.

Sam seemed more relieved than disappointed, although he made an effort to be gallant. "I would come up with something like this the first time I get to dine alone with a pretty woman other than my wife. It seems a shame that your visit had to start so badly. You're sure you won't be lonely?"

"Not a bit. There's plenty to read—and I have Bridie."

"Is she looking after you properly?"

"She's being all things to me—including nursemaid."

"Well—just don't let her get the upper hand. Her heart's in the right place, but she can be as stubborn as a mule." He said as an afterthought, "She doesn't sleep in the gatehouse, you know. She has a room here."

"Oh?"

"She used to live in the old building winter and summer. She and her husband acted as caretakers until he died a few years ago—and then she stayed on alone until we had it remodeled. But she doesn't share Vera's enthusiasm for modern architecture, so she moved herself out bag and baggage. You can't teach an old dog new tricks. Anyway, for some reason or other, Vera insisted you'd prefer to be entirely alone, but if you're nervous and would like one of the maids—"

"I'm not nervous—and this isn't exactly a place that starts the imagination working on ghoulies and ghosties. Good night, Sam. Sleep well. I'll probably make an early night of it too."

She hung up, a bit annoyed at that "for some reason or other." She thought that Vera was interpreting her expressed desire for privacy a bit too freely.

She dressed as carefully as though her appearance would be appraised by many pairs of eyes. She went to the living room, where a place had been set for her in the dining alcove fronting the television screen. Again Vera had looked to the magazines for inspiration. The woven gray napery was Mexican, the chartreuse pottery dishes, Californian, the glassware, Italian, and the flat silver, Danish. The tight bunch of red and yellow and pink roses painfully crammed into two tall vases were pure Bridie.

"Mr. Curtis sent them over fresh picked," Bridie said from the doorway. "The stems being too long for any of the vases here I packed the girl off to fetch a pair of my own."

Dene thanked her and said tactfully, "I'll cut the stems later so you can have your beautiful vases back. The roses will do well enough in those squat—"

"That would be wasteful. The longer the stems the more they charge for them in the city." She looked with suspicion at the neckline of Dene's black dress. "You wouldn't be expecting a visitor? No—I didn't think so—with you new in these parts—and Mrs. Curtis away and all. Start on your nice fresh shrimps till I serve the rest of the meal."

Dene ate with appetite the shrimps, the broiled chicken, the grilled tomatoes, the green salad, and the large native strawberries. The program Bridie had summoned to the television screen was not so tempting. Bridie, coming to clear the table, found her searching for the switch that would exorcise it.

When the screen was blank again, Bridie said in surprise, "Don't you like wrestling?"

"I don't like fat men. Perhaps if I'd been around when the Greeks went in for it—"

"Greeks? It's the Turks who have the name for it now. Perhaps you've some favorite program you'd want to see instead."

"No, I haven't had much experience with television. I expect it will grow on me, but right now I'd rather concentrate on what I'm sure will be excellent coffee."

Bridie looked at her pityingly. "I guess there's a lot you've missed wandering hither and you. Would you care for music then? This set has a radio too—and a record player."

"I'll save it for later."

Bridie piled the dishes onto an outsized tea cart. "Well—at least you don't pick at your food."

"It was delicious, Bridie. You never learned to cook that way in the old country."

"No, I did not—though you wouldn't turn up your nose at my mother's soda bread and colcannon. It was old Mrs. Curtis who taught me. She had a taste for good simple food with its own flavor and would more often than not wave away the fancy messes the chef dished up for the company. I'll brim the coffee now. Would you like a bit of cheese and—"

"Just coffee, please."

Dene took a cigarette and smoked it through one of the elegant little holders she used to protect her teeth. She sipped coffee. With the exception of breakfasts this was the first meal she had eaten alone since her arrival in America. She told herself that she had enjoyed it and would enjoy the solitary evening ahead. The bay breathed salt through the opened windows. She was vaguely disturbed by the intimacy of its steady whispering. She got up and walked the room, stopping here and there to finger an ornament, a smooth surface, a glossy magazine. She went to a window and leaned out. The moon was a flat yellow daub set off by a busy pattern of stars. Outside seemed as stagy and unreal as inside. Unsatisfied, she turned away.

She thought that as soon as Bridie left she would rearrange the roses. That would help. It would give her something to do. It was a project that would take at least twenty minutes. She tried to laugh at poor Dene Cameron, so cruelly committed to her own resources with nothing but rows of new books and television and records and radio between her and boredom. Ritchie, who had been Mistake the Second, always turned on the radio the moment he entered a house. He knew all the words to all of the popular songs. He would be junketing about Paris by this time, telling his tale of woe to anyone he could fix with his slightly bloodshot eyes. He had accused her of aggravating his drinking habits. But that was …

She sat down at the table again and poured more coffee but did not drink it. She wondered if there was any liquor in the house. Bridie had not offered her a cocktail, and dinner would have been improved by wine. She must remember to order some. She could hardly expect the Curtises, who, barring special occasions, were not wine-drinking people, to supply it. Of course she could do without, but some form of alcohol might have tided her over what was beginning to seem like a touch of depression. No more than a letdown from the round of activities in New York.

Certainly it had nothing to do with the divorce. It was firm part of her credo to regret nothing once it was done. She had gone as far as she could with Ritchie Hildebrand. The qualities that had drawn her to him, the good looks, the air of suppressed vitality, the disarming boyishness, and yes, face it, his money, had been swamped in a very short time by the qualities he had kept hidden until after marriage. The vitality, she discovered, was manifest only when he could do exactly what he wished to do, without concession to other wills. The boyishness settled into the form of sulky brooding or bursts of undisciplined rage. Even the good looks …

She raised her lovely shoulders. She put him away. His sole use to her now was as a guide to future relationships. She must be careful in choosing— She turned her head in response to Bridie's sturdy march across the room.

"If you've finished—and there's nothing else you want," Bridie said, "I'll give the coffee things a wash and be off."

Dene nodded, her dark blue eyes remote.

Bridie cleared her throat. "I'm not so set in my ways I couldn't spend a night or two here until the strangeness of it wears off for you."

Dene focused upon her. "That's good of you, Bridie, but not necessary."

"Well—you couldn't be safer than held in the arms of your own mother. I've lived here in the dead of winter—when it was the old gatehouse, I mean—and there were more nooks and crannies for creatures to hide in that you could shake a stick at—yet nothing ever happened to cause me a moment's alarm except maybe the wind howling or—"

"I'll be quite all right."

"Of course you will. If you should hear screaming now and again it will only be a gull—"

Dene said a little impatiently, "I'm accustomed to sea sounds. I've spent a good part of my life on the Mediterranean."

"Then that's all right. I was born near the sea, myself, in a place called Rathglass. Do you know—you've the most beautiful Irish voice that should by rights be mine." She showed a row of too regular teeth. "Didn't my man always say I'd be fitting mate for a banshee."

Dene said impulsively, "Do you miss him, Bridie?"

"Not so much now as I did at first." Bridie was matter-of-fact about it. "Which is not to say Mulvey wasn't as fine as they come. But we all go sooner or later—and one of these days it will be my turn—so wouldn't I be foolish to waste the meanwhile in sorrowing? Besides—there's something to be said for the single state. I mind Mrs. Curtis telling me you'd been married yourself—"

"Bridie, is there any liquor in the house?"

Bridie struck herself on the brow with a businesslike fist. "I'm glad you asked. Did I forget all about it—and Mrs. Curtis drumming it into me you'd want a cocktail or two before your meal—though the mixing of them is not my strong point. Never mind. Tomorrow's another day—and if you should be a lady who likes her nip before going to bed you'll find the bottles in that cabinet near the big couch. Good night to you. I'll sing out when I'm leaving—and I'll lock the kitchen door behind me. The rest of the doors and windows have strong bolts to them and there's no harm in seeing they're fixed when you're ready for sleep—for it's just as well to be on the safe side." She gathered up the coffee service, repeated her good night, and went from the room.

Dene's spirits slipped a notch lower, whether at the mention of death or the emphasis on locks and bolts she could not say. She knew that Bridie's intentions were kindly. Bridie was mothering her. Women, she had often noticed, wanted to mother her or to do her injury. She herself had never been prey to either impulse. She supposed that she had hurt many women, but only because it had been unavoidable, and not out of envy or malice. And if she possessed any maternal instinct at all, no one had ever aroused it. Edward had accused her of being completely lacking. Edward. The name jumped to the foreground of her mind. Edward Roper. Mistake the First. He had tried to father her, had been old enough for the role, too. Now remarried, he was probably a father at last. He had always wanted children. But she had not. At least, not his. Perhaps he had been right. Perhaps she had failed him in a sense. Perhaps she had failed Ritchie ...

She made a small disgruntled sound. She had not thought of Edward Roper in years, and did not mean to think of him if she could help it. Or of Ritchie either. Or of possible sins of omission or commission that might have been hers in the past.

There must be something in the American climate that encouraged introspectiveness, she thought half seriously. The word had an almost foul connotation for her. So many members of the group in which she had moved were constantly fishing in their innermost depths and hauling out the catch for all to see. She found it a shocking practice. She would as soon have bared her body to an audience. Sooner. It struck her that since her last voyage home the place of Frigidaires and washing machines in the American scheme had been usurped by psychiatrists and chlorophyll. The juxtaposition cheered her a little, made her smile. One to counteract the other, she thought.

Bridie sang out vigorously, and a moment after, the slamming of the kitchen door underlined her departure. Almost at once Dene became very busy. She carried three squat and angular containers to the kitchen and filled them with water. She released the roses from their cramped quarters, cut their stems, and divided them into three unequal groups. She arranged them loosely and carelessly and when she had finished the effect seemed one of planned grace. Even the kitchen looked better; not quite so aseptic, with stems and stray petals giving color to the stainless steel drainboard, and water splashed about, and the towel she had used for her hands outstandingly limp among its stiff fellows. Back in the living room she tried the roses out in different places until she was satisfied. Then she looked at her watch. It was nine o'clock of an endless tiresome day.

She walked the room again, absently shifting a chair from its invisible chalk mark, opening a magazine and leaving it open, moving an ash tray off precise center, where Bridie had undoubtedly placed it. She caught herself at it and thought, Dene Cameron, Homemaker, yet continued her activities until she reached the liquor cabinet. It was, of course, the last word, complete with an automatic champagne cooler and trays that manufactured ice. She poured a scotch over ice cubes and sat with it in the vicinity of the television screen, which could, it appeared, be viewed from almost every point in the room. She toyed with the idea of turning it on, but the knobs looked mysterious and she would probably succeed only in calling forth more fat men. She thought of investigating the record supply, and stirred herself to do so. The neat albums held only popular songs. She put a Rodgers and Hammerstein medley on the turntable and settled back to listen. But the sentimental tunes rubbed raw her needs. She turned the record off. Wiser, she thought, to down her drink and put the homemaker to bed with a book.

She sat on. The blank television screen became peopled with familiar images moving among familiar backgrounds, herself the star player running the gamut of the lesser emotions from pleasure to annoyance, but most characteristically offering a pliant devil-may-care attitude to the changing winds of her existence. No, she thought, that's not true. Whenever things got out of hand I called a halt. I'm here because I called a halt.

It was small comfort. She closed her eyes and leaned against the chair's foam rubber upholstery. That will do, she told herself. When and if you round eighty you may sit alone with your memories. And if Vera does not return tomorrow to "start things rolling," the guest of honor will have departed to where things *are* rolling. Because it's becoming more and more obvious that the guest of honor's own society does not amuse her in the slightest. Privacy is all very well when it's a matter of free choice but—

She did not know how long the knocking had been going on. She thought at first that it was a loose shutter until she realized that the house had no shutters. She rose, thinking almost affectionately, Sam—good conscientious Sam. He's dragged himself over to see how I'm getting on.

"Coming," she called on a welcoming note of unquestionable

sincerity. She could not find the light switch in the entrance hall although moonlight streaked through the windows on either side of the door. Impatiently she pulled the door wide.

A voice said, "Are you the caretaker? Everyone seems to be sleeping in the main house."

"I'm not the caretaker," she said, and thought of Bridie's nooks and crannies and creatures because the creature under the moon reminded her of a leprechaun. "What is it you want?" Once more her hand passed over the wall and this time found the switch.

The creature was human. He blinked his eyes at the sudden radiance, a small tightly built man dressed in slacks and a jersey, a lock of fair hair fallen over his forehead.

"I'm sorry to bother you," he said. "I don't suppose you'll know anything about it."

"What won't I know anything about?" His face looked young in the moonlight, young and anxious. "I'll be glad to help if I can."

"That's kind of you but—you see—my friend lost a letter. He was doing some driving for Mr. Curtis and he thinks he may have left it in the car."

"Your friend—Mr. Debrulet?"

"That's right. Do you know him?"

"Not really—I just happen to be the reason for Mr. Curtis asking him to act as chauffeur today. He met my train."

"He didn't mention that. Then maybe you know if the letter's been found."

"No—I'm sorry. I did see him collect one at the post office—I think he put it in his back pocket. If Mr. Curtis had found it I'm sure he'd have telephoned to let him know."

"Oh." It was a sound of defeat. Then he rallied. "It might still be in the car. Is there any way I could get into the garage …?"

"Can't it wait until morning?"

"It shouldn't—it's important." He had a reedy voice "Something that must be answered by the first mail."

Dene weighed the man's intense, almost feverish manner, and thought that if it was all that important, Debrulet should have come to make inquiry himself. She thought it even stranger that he had not mentioned her arrival to his emissary. Still, Sam owed him something. And so did she. And time hung heavy and the night air was pleasant. She said, "I don't like to disturb Mr. Curtis because he hasn't been feeling too well. I'll walk over to the garage with you to see if it's open—and if it isn't I'll telephone."

"Thank you." He was staring at her, and a look of discovery had gained brief ascendance over his anxiety. "Do you—won't you want a coat?"

"No—I'm warm enough." She experimented with the door's latch, fixed it, and crossed the threshold. He was no more than a half inch taller than she, and she was not a tall woman. Side by side they crossed the lawn to the tree-lined driveway.

As they neared the Curtis house she observed that its lines were rather imposing. It seemed to have three stories, and only in the top one were any lights visible. She supposed that they came from the servants' rooms. The house spread long wings on either side, and set back from them were the shapes of the out-buildings.

She said, "I don't even know where the garage is."

"We'll find it," he said absently. "People go to bed early in the country, don't they. You'd think with a place like that there'd be plenty of entertaining going on."

"Mrs. Curtis is away."

"Well—all the more reason." He laughed reedily. She could almost feel the touch of his oblique gaze. "You're kind to take this trouble," he said, and again it was as though he had mislaid his anxiety, as though normally he might be an experienced lady's man. "The sea air's deceptive. I'd hate to catch cold ..."

She had a feeling that he would not improve upon closer acquaintance, but the exclamation she uttered had nothing to do with that. A bit of the driveway's gravel had entered one of the openings in her fragile high-heeled shoes.

He missed the exclamation. "That one on the left," he said, "that's the garage," and quickened his pace.

Involuntarily she placed a restraining hand upon his forearm. "It won't run away."

He stood still. He looked at the hand, white against the tan of his own flesh. She removed it, and he said in the accomplished voice of the lady's man, "I didn't mean to rush you. I should have guessed that only high heels would go with that dress you're wearing. There's a bench over there if you'd like to sit down while I investigate."

It occurred to her that she might be doing Sam a disservice by allowing a stranger the run of his garage. For all she knew he could be a car thief. She had only his word that Debrulet had sent him.

"Mr. Curtis keeps several cars," she said. "Did Mr. Debrulet tell which one was used today—so you'll know where to look?"

"Yes—a Cadillac."

She dismissed her fears. It was unlikely that a thief would take pains to make his presence known to the caretaker. And he *did* know the name of the car.

She permitted him to lead her to the bench. If he came racing out in the Cadillac she could not only give the alarm but furnish the police with a detailed description.

"I won't be long one way or the other," he said, "unless your Mr. Curtis has an oversupply of Cadillacs." He sprinted off.

The garage had not been locked. She heard a door slide back on its rollers. She took off her shoe and shook the gravel from it. As she replaced it a gnat bit her shoulder. She resisted the impulse to scratch for fear of leaving a mark. She began to wish that she had brought a wrap or cigarettes to keep the insects at bay.

Abruptly she sat forward, then rose to her feet. Bridie had said, "If you hear screaming it will only be a gull." But no gull had been responsible for that sharp cry of alarm. She took a few tentative steps toward the garage. The cry was not repeated. She glimpsed what appeared to be a flashlight turned on and off, and heard a voice raised in anger. It was nipped hurriedly by a "shhhh" and a muffled flow of syllables.

Before she could decide whether to storm the Curtis house, to retreat to her own sanctuary and bolt the doors and use the telephone, or to stand her ground and hope for the best, two figures emerged from the garage. The smaller of them raised an arm. The larger took direction from it and strode toward her. He said with ominous control, "I'll walk you back to the gatehouse, Miss Cameron."

"I don't need an escort, Mr. Debrulet." She thought that Bridie was probably right. There was something wrong with the man. He was looking at her as though she had committed an unnamable crime.

He addressed his companion. "Go home—I'll see you later."

The slight figure hesitated. Then he said jauntily, "Okay. So long, m-mug," and started to walk away.

Her most social voice went after him. "Good night, Mr. ...?"

He muttered something without stopping, tacked on, "Thanks," and broke into a run.

She turned toward the lights of the gatehouse. Fingers curved strongly around her cool bare arm, and should have steadied her but did not. She let them stay, telling herself that protest would be undignified. She expected him to make some attempt at conversation. He said nothing at all. But as they walked, the tension went out of his supporting hand.

When they reached the gatehouse it was she who found it necessary to end the silence. "You don't deserve to be asked, but did you find the letter?"

"No," he said calmly. "It wasn't in the car. It doesn't matter."

"Your friend seemed to think it mattered a great deal."

"Masters?"

"If that's his name."

"Didn't I introduce you? I've rotten manners." The rage she had heard in his voice, seen on his face, might never have been. "Tim Masters. He has an enlarged sense of the dramatic, has Tim. Aside from which he seems to think he owes me something because I'm putting him up for a night or two. That nonsense about the letter was his idea of being helpful."

"I had an idea of being helpful too when I went to the garage with him. His manner led me to believe that it was a matter of life and death."

"And I haven't thanked you. What an oaf I am." The fingers on her arm exerted pressure. She was swung off balance and caught. He hurt her lips.

Released, the delicate flare of her nostrils was more pronounced. She managed to say evenly, "As a connoisseur, I must admit that your technique has rare flavor. But don't ever bother to demonstrate it again because I doubt if I could acquire a taste for it." She went into the house.

She closed the door quietly. She turned off the light in the entrance hall and looked through the glass panel. In the moonlight she saw him take a step toward the house, shake his head, and walk away. She had no conviction that he was walking out of her life.

III

Lieutenant Gridley Nelson, acting captain of homicide, reached his Lexington Avenue apartment in time for dinner that night. Sammy, his cook, ushered him into the colorful living room with the air of one who had unexpectedly been awarded the grand prize. Kyrie, his wife, said, "Grid," making the syllable a comprehensive statement of love and welcome. His little son, aged two and a fraction, rushed from some inner fastness to tackle his straight long legs. Nelson grunted and pretended to fold. Grid, Junior, laughed, stretched his arms up, and was hoisted to his father's shoulder. He grabbed a handful of curly white hair.

Tall Sammy, whose skin had the tinge of ripe apricots, looked on, her handsome dignified face not entirely approving. She said in her dark rich voice, "Mr. Grid-dely—Junie just had his bath—and you all covered with them police station germs. You get washed while I fix some drinks."

Nelson set Grid, Junior, down. The little boy opened his mouth to protest, changed his mind, and trotted after Sammy. Nelson went into the bedroom, shedding his coat en route. Kyrie followed him. She sat on the bed waiting until he had showered and shaved. When he reappeared, she watched him dress. He had width in all the right places, to his brow, to the space between his eyes, to his shoulders, and to his outlook. She hoped that Junie would grow up to be a reasonable facsimile.

"You're not very talkative," he said.

"I thought I'd wait until you'd relaxed a bit."

He put down his hairbrushes. He knotted his tie and reached for his coat.

She shook her ash-blond head. "No—it's too hot. Anyway you're prettier without than most men with."

He walked over to the bed. He pulled her to her feet and hugged her. "Too hot for this?"

"That will be the day," she said.

"I deduce you like me."

"You're a detective sure enough."

"Oh yes," he said. He released her. Under the curly white hair his smooth olive-skinned face was somber.

"Grid—it's such a nice surprise having you home. I hope Sammy rises to the occasion. This morning you didn't think you could make it."

"I know. But I didn't get anywhere today so I decided that I might as well not get anywhere in comfort."

"Don't worry. You'll get somewhere. You almost always do."

"Almost," he said, "but not always."

"Is it a very tough case?"

"It's over now. It was a tough case, but not in the sense you mean." He knew the motive for the crime. He even knew the criminals. Usually that was sufficient. But usually the criminals did not have influence or money enough to retain clever, twisted sorcerers who employed black magic that transformed prison bars into butter so that no interval worth mentioning passed between the arrest and release of their clients.

"The Cascone thing?"

He nodded. "We brought them in and barely had time to discuss the weather before they were out again."

"Poor Grid—I know how you hated the whole business."

He hated it as much as he loved his country. He hated it as much as he would have hated to see some blatant disfigurement on Kyrie's lovely face. He had been working to round up not one murderer but a group of murderers who had brought about the death of an unsavory associate. The man had not been killed because he was unsavory, but because he might, under questioning, curtail the activities of the group. Its wealthy members were ambitious citizens, according to their lights. They took an inordinate interest in government and were frequently seen arm in arm with elastic-moraled holders of office.

"Do you want to talk about it?" It was a question Kyrie always asked when he was troubled, but one she never pressed. Sometimes he talked. Sometimes a comment from her, or just the sound of his own voice would clarify a problem.

Now he shook his head because the problem was only too clear. "Talking won't do any good," he said. Only time would, he thought, and a general surge toward decency. "Let's go see what Sammy has for us."

Junie sat in the middle of the living room floor surrounded by a sea of dilapidated magazines. He was turning pages busily.

"Work he brought home from the office?" Nelson asked.

Kyrie laughed. "He has an amazing span of interest for a child of his age—but I've been meaning to speak to you about those—"

Junie had stopped turning pages. He shouted triumphantly, "Daddy—Daddy—" and slammed his little fist down on a picture.

"He calls them all 'Daddy,'" Kyrie said. "It would be awfully embarrassing for me if I chanced to meet one of the originals."

"Daddy—" Junie bounced on his sturdy little bottom. Nelson dropped to the floor beside him. There was astonishment on his face as he looked at the picture. "That's not very flattering. Kyrie—where did he—"

Sammy came in bearing frosted daiquiris and smoked salmon on thin black bread. Sammy said, "This going to start up your appetites while I give Junie his supper and put him in bed. No—you sit still, Miss Kyrie. Ain't often you got such nice company. Funny how something tell me to buy those squabs in the market this morning. You coming, Junie?"

Junie was a man of few words. He said, "No." But it was only a token rebellion. After a tussle involving both his parents, he went amiably, lugging one of the magazines.

Nelson sat back in his chair. He sipped his drink and ate a few *canapés*. His deep-set brown eyes roamed the room. The rugs had been taken up for summer, and cool summer drapes hung from the windows. Daisies were massed in a bean pot on the long ash table, which Sammy had set with yellow linen place mats. He returned his eyes to Kyrie. He sighed.

"Grid—you're feeling better."

"I'm going to miss you—you and Junie."

"Then we won't go."

"Yes—you'll go. I'm not going to miss you. I was just making polite conversation. Are you all packed?"

"I can unpack. I'm not making polite conversation. I mean it."

"There's Junie."

"I know. The city's no place for a child in summer. But it's no place for you either. Damn the Cascones—and come with us."

"I wish I could—not damn the Cascones—because they're damned—but come with you. Perhaps later I might be able to get away for a few days. Anyway—it's not the Cascones. I've said that's finished. The powers have so decreed—but there are other matters wanting attention. We're understaffed—and things have been piling up ..."

She said something she had never said before. "Have you ever considered getting out for good? You could. It isn't as though you depend upon it for a livelihood. We've plenty of money—the money your mother left—the money I—"

"Do you want me to give it up?"

Almost at once she shook her head. "No—of course not—put it down to the heat."

He tried to put it down to the heat. After Princeton had granted him its seal of approval he had worked at a number of jobs, ranging from little theater to the laboratory of a criminologist. Even the laboratory had not completely held his interest, but it was there he discovered that what he wanted was not theories but actual contact with those who had caused the theories to be formed. Then step by step be had reached his present position. In the police department he had achieved full release for his peculiar talents, for his emphatic identification with his fellow men, the deviators as well as those whose lives had been affected by them. He said lamely, "It does eat into our domestic life—doesn't it? And I suppose there is some job I could take with regular hours so that we'd see more of each other—"

She made a decisive interruption. "Maybe you'd see more of me—but I'd see less of you. Even if we were to have breakfast, lunch, and dinner together for the rest of our lives I'd see less of you." She went to sit on the arm of his chair. "I wish I hadn't said such a nonsensical thing. Amputate your work and what would I have?" She answered herself. "A great deal—a great deal more than most women have—but I'm greedy. I want everything—the whole Nelson—the one who's all of a piece with his precious department and me and Junie."

"You haven't got it quite in the right order."

"I know. Junie and I come first—the department after. She smiled down at him, a tall supple girl with a strength of character that was masked by her deceptive, fragile appearance. "It's just," she said, "that I don't like to see you worried and not be able to help you."

"You do help—a lot." He was still subject to wonder at the miracle that had transformed the skinny little scourge of his childhood into Kyrie. He added, "Never think that if it comes to a showdown—a choice between you and—"

"It will never come to a showdown. I love your work. If it hadn't been for your work we might never have met again. Now let's talk about sensible matters."

He drew her down to him. Sammy found them that way. She showed no surprise because she often found them that way. She called them to the table.

Nelson ate well, at first to please Sammy, who made of his unexpected homecoming a small celebration, and then to please himself because her squab and wild rice and avocado salad were not to be resisted. Except, he thought, by the mad or the very sick. And he was neither. He was merely temporarily discouraged, and after he had put a period to dinner with clear strong coffee his discouragement was diluted enough to have lost its dirty flavor. Sammy too, he thought, had come to him by way of a case. It was not every man's work that provided such premiums. His wide, expressive mouth lifted. He got up from the table and did a little jig step to flex his long legs. He walked over to Junie's disreputable pile of magazines.

"Isn't this carrying progressive education a bit too far?" he said. "And what about the germs someone mentioned while back?"

Sammy had started to clear the table. She turned toward him. "Junie can't catch no germs from them. They fumigated. Maybe if he could read what they say it make a difference—but this way they ain't going to harm him." Sammy seemed to be suffering from embarrassment, an unusual state for her. She went on earnestly, "They same as fairy books to Junie—only he don't like no fairy books and he sure do like these. It easier to take swill from a pig than pry him loose from—"

Kyrie intervened. "Your son has a will of his own." Behind Sammy's back she sent him a warning look.

Sammy smiled her slow smile. "He got plenty of will. When he want a story he get it—only Miss Kyrie and me don't read him what's there—we read him something we make up in our heads." She turned back to the table.

Kyrie said, "Let me help you with the washing up."

"Not tonight. When you at Long Island I ain't going to have nothing to do but take care of Mr. Grid-dely. You sit still." With no waste motion she stacked the last of the dishes, lifted the heavy tray, and carried it to the kitchen.

"Why is Sammy so sensitive about the magazines?" Nelson asked.

"She feels responsible for them. She isn't really. You know how Junie follows her around? Well—a few days ago he tagged her to the incinerator and there they were. The original owner hadn't bothered to burn them—and for some reason or other they attracted Junie. He refused to be parted from them and he can produce some pretty resonant chest tones when he's frustrated. Unknit your brow. Sammy doesn't spoil him any more than you do—or I do. As a rule he's as reasonable and charming as his old man—but there are times when he feels the need to assert his rights."

Nelson said, "Like his old man." He stood looking down at the magazines.

"Yes. Anyway—Sammy gave in because she didn't think it was very important. She thought he'd forget about them—but he hasn't. He trots them out whenever he has a free moment—and every night he insists that one or the other of us read him a story from them."

"Which you make up in your heads." Nelson scooped up the

magazines and dumped them on a table near the couch.

Kyrie said, "Careful. Sammy put them through some sort of antiseptic process that loosened the pages." She came over and sat down on the couch.

He dropped beside her. He offered her a cigarette, lit it, and took one for himself. She watched him pick up a magazine, rifle through it, set it aside, and start on the next one. She said, "You're going at it just like Junie. Will you set up a howl if I take them away from you?"

He grunted absently.

"Grid—I shouldn't have thought they'd be your speed at all—unsolved cases—the ones who got away—"

"My speed exactly—at the moment."

"Quit—that's not like you."

"Sorry." He grinned. "I was fishing for vehement denials."

"That's even less like you, but I'll give you all the vehement denials there are—unexpressed—because if I expressed them it would carry us into next winter." She moved closer so that she could scan the magazines with him. She said, "They're mostly murders that happened out of your jurisdiction—men who held up banks in Mississippi or Wyoming, and killed tellers or guards in the process—men who killed their wives in Connecticut or California—and managed to disappear without leaving a trace."

Nelson was studying one of the photographs. He said, "We've had calls for cooperation from states as far away as California if the suspect is thought to have headed our way."

She glanced down at the photograph. "He doesn't look like anybody's concept of a criminal, does he?"

"Very few criminals do look like anybody's concept."

"Grid—are these really true cases?"

"Essentially. They might be embroidered a bit, depending on who did the reporting. Why?"

"Because the most unlikely men seem to murder their wives."

"Maybe their wives are unlikely." He closed the magazine, put it back on the table, and did not reach for another.

"Well—what's the verdict? Do you think the magazines will hurt Junie?"

"If they're a fertilizer for the fruits of your imagination and Sammy's they'll provide him with a liberal education. Kyrie—are you sure you don't want to persuade Sammy to go with you?"

"And leave you completely deserted? The only reason I've agreed to go is that I know you'll be well taken care of. Besides, Sammy hates the country and her loyalties are torn enough as it is without adding any further stress." She sighed.

"Kyrie—would you prefer to go somewhere else?"

"It isn't that. I'm very fond of Louise and Charles and if I have to go away their setup is perfect. Louise has a wonderful nurse for her own two and she wrote and said she'd be more than willing to take on Junie, but—"

"What time are they calling for you tomorrow?"

"After lunch. About three."

"Good. While Junie's having his you meet me for a gala celebration."

"What's there to celebrate?" But she brightened. "I'm making time at last. At long last my boyfriend is dating me for lunch. Now if I can only find some way to lure him to the wilds of Long Island ..."

IV

The blast seemed to be pounding against her eardrums. Dene whimpered a little. She opened her eyes, fully expecting to see an armed intruder bending over her. It took her a moment for orientation, a moment to realize that the blast was Bridie calling from outside the bedroom door. She made outraged response.

Bridie came into the room. "I was asking if you were still asleep."

Dene said crossly, "There could be only one answer. What time is it?"

"Nine o'clock. Last night you forgot to mention when you wanted to be called."

"I don't ever want to be called. I want to wake when I wake."

"And waste the beautiful day away?" Bridie pulled a cord and drapes slid back. Sunlight rushed into the room.

Dene burrowed under the satin quilt. Bridie said inexorably, "What do you want for breakfast?"

"Milk and poison."

Bridie eyed her, hands on hips. "Were you after having a nightmare when I called you?"

"I don't have nightmares. Oh well." Dene sat up, flinging the smoky hair back from her face. She scowled. "I don't think you quite understand. I'm staying here rather than in the main house so that I can do exactly as I choose."

"Of course," Bridie said solemnly. "Mrs. Curtis herself made that plain to me—and I mean to see you have everything your heart desires. Fix your nightgown. Is it to be ham and eggs, or something a bit more out of the way—and will you have it on the terrace, or where?"

Dene glanced at the windows and stopped scowling. She said in a pleased voice, "It is a beautiful day, isn't it? I'll have coffee and toast on the terrace. That's all I ever take."

She had grapefruit, and ham and eggs, too, because Bridie brought them. When she had eaten she lit a cigarette and sat with her elbows on the table. No trace of last night's depression remained. The sun touched her companionably, birds sang, and beyond the terrace the bay shone like clean glass. As Bridie stacked the empty plates on her cart, Dene said, "You've got to stop tempting me or I'll put on weight."

"They tell me swimming's a fine way to take it off again. And you'll get no better swimming anywhere. It is said that to drown in the bay you would have to stand on your head—and you'd not be likely to try that for fear of washing away the stuff in the jars and bottles—though I was giving you a good look this morning before you went to work and I can't see that improvement's so needful."

Dene smiled at her. "That's one of the nicest compliments I've ever had."

"It's the truth. You can set your clock by it. When you're ready I'll show you the steps to the beach."

"Have you seen Mr. Curtis this morning?"

"Yes—he was up before I left. He had an easy night he said—though by the stiffness of him he's still in pain. I'm to let him know how you slept."

"Never better," Dene said. She had gone to bed right after Debrulet walked away. She had been disturbed, unable to focus her attention upon the book she chose. So she had turned out the light and surrendered herself to a review of the incident. She had tried quite honestly to determine whether or not she was responsible for the crudeness of Debrulet's tactics. She had tricks, so much a part of her, that the initial calculation had long ago been absorbed by constant practice. She did not need to produce intimacy by dusting a man's lapel or straightening his tie. She could generate a special kind of excitement with her eyes or the expressive curve of her mouth. She asked herself if she had invited that almost contemptuous onslaught, and came to no conclusion except the resentful one that Debrulet had been unnecessarily rude. She had been attracted to him from the first moment. Kissing him, really kissing him, might have been sheer delight. At that point her thoughts had taken a decidedly pleasant twist, had eased her into dreamless slumber.

She got up and followed Bridie to the house. "Has there been any word from Mrs. Curtis?"

"Not yet. Now never you mind. There's plenty to keep you busy."

She had not thought that she could be so eager for Vera's company. But Vera would have a woman's view of Debrulet, and she was curious to know what Vera's eyes had made of him.

Bridie said, "Will I get your bathing things for you?"

Yes, Nanny, and don't forget my bucket and spade. But she did not say it aloud. "I'll get them, Bridie."

She decided to take her writing case down to the beach and catch up on neglected correspondence. Bridie escorted her along a path that ended in a steep flight of wooden steps. She pointed out the large gaily painted cabaña below. "There's where you undress and here's the key to it. You'll find a place to hang your things to dry so you won't need to be bringing them back and forth and tracking sand into the house. If Mr. Curtis should come asking for you I'll yell."

"Naturally," Dene said.

She walked down the almost perpendicular steps. Several heavy iron tables and chairs had been grouped in the vicinity of the cabaña. Their look of waiting emphasized the emptiness of the long sandy stretch. With the exception of a pair of sandpipers doing a Chaplinesque strut at the water's edge, the beach was all hers. She wished it otherwise.

She unlocked the cabaña with the key that Bridie had given her. She went into a dressing room, dropped her clothes, and put on one of the bathing suits she had bought for its audience appeal. A full-length mirror gave it back, renewing her desire for spectators, although she was certain that Bridie would have given pious thanks for the lack of them.

She selected an aluminum beach chair and set it up in the shade of the cabaña's awning. She reclined. The deep blue of her suit matched and merged with the chair's cloth. Her eyes might have been a decorator's touch for carrying out the color scheme. She glanced down at the silky white flesh of her midriff, admired it, and thought lazily that the general passion for a darker skin in summer was nonsense and that she would make no deliberate attempt to subscribe to it. She speculated upon the temperature of the water but felt too comfortable to test it. She wondered if the cabin cruiser bobbing at anchor belonged to Sam. She thought that being alone was not so bad. She might even acquire a taste for it in time. It was just that all her life she had been surrounded by people, without opportunity or necessity for calling upon her own resources. Bridie was right. There was plenty to keep her busy. Determinedly she stretched out an arm for the leather writing case she had dropped at the chair's side.

She pressed the little spring lock and took out a packet of unanswered letters. She started to go through them to see which should be tackled first, but got no further than the top envelope.

It was addressed in a large, rather immature hand to Paul Debrulet, Esquire, Post Office Box 162, Sandy Crest, Long Island, and, judging by the date of the California postmark, it was undoubtedly the letter that had caused last night's commotion. She stared at it incredulously, seeking a reasonable explanation for its presence in her writing case.

He had come out of the post office with the letter in his hand. He had stuffed it into the back pocket of his slacks. And it must have fallen out when he set her luggage down in the gatehouse. Probably under one of the bags. The rest was simple. Bridie had found it during the unpacking, assumed it was hers without bothering to confirm the assumption, and, since for Bridie all things had their proper place, she had slipped it into the writing case.

With a small feeling of excitement Dene started to draw the folded sheets from the envelope. This might be better than anything Vera could tell her. And it was not, she assured herself virtuously, that she was violating the United States mails. The letter had been opened and read by its intended recipient. Even if she were to return it without a glance the man would be sure to question her innocence. So she might as well provide him with a basis for doubt.

Ethics did not stay her. Company did. Her hands were quick. When she looked up at Tim Masters, the letter was safely enclosed in the leather case. "Hello—I didn't hear you coming."

"Commando tactics," he said, "not to mention the way the sand absorbs footsteps." In the full sun he looked neither boyish nor even particularly young. He was just a small man in dark green sports attire so obviously new that Dene would not have been surprised to see a dangling price tag. The short-sleeved shirt exposed tight muscular arms, the open collar a thin but strong brown neck.

She said, "Is this an accidental meeting?"

"Not exactly. I knocked at your door like a gentleman, and the housekeeper asked for my pedigree. Then she said you were out—making it sound final."

"She couldn't have liked your pedigree."

He grinned, showing sharp white teeth. "I haven't one, Miss Cameron. I'm known far and wide as a mongrel."

Dene thought it quite possible. "But you must have softened Bridie or she wouldn't have told you where to find me."

"She didn't. Her manner was so sharp I couldn't get up the courage to ask. So I said to myself, If I were a raving beauty summering at the shore where would I be on a sunny morning?" He dropped to the sand. He hugged his knees, and again Dene thought of a leprechaun. The eyes that looked up at her resembled the eyes of a goat, almost yellow, and thickly fringed. His small nose was pugged, his bracketed mouth a wide red slash.

"I take it you've come on your own this time," Dene said, "and not as a messenger."

"That's right. I left the gentleman working. He was much too busy to want my company, so I took myself off."

Dene did not utter the question that came to her lips. She hoped her face did not ask it. Masters unclasped his knees. He scooped up sand and dribbled it through his fingers. "That house he rented is a steady job," he said. "Not that he seems to be making much progress with it. It would take an army to put it into any kind of shape—what with the state of the grounds and the number of rooms to be dusted and scrubbed."

The goat eyes were just a little too candid, Dene thought. He had been on the verge of revealing Debrulet's occupation before he checked himself. She found herself making a mental list of illegal pursuits from counterfeiting to white slavery. She said with studied disinterest, "Last night I got the impression that you were an extremely thoughtful guest. Doesn't your conscience bother you for deserting when there's so much to be done?"

"Not a bit. I put in a stint with the broom and the dishcloth before I lit out. But when it came to mowing and weeding I left him to it. I'd be less of a help than a hindrance at that sort of thing. It's not my speed."

"I shouldn't have thought it was Mr. Debrulet's either."

"He likes anything that keeps him outdoors—in fact there's very little that can hold him to four walls, including—if you don't mind my saying so—the fair sex." He went on confidingly, "Now you'd think that a fellow of his build and style would be a regular Don Juan. But not Paul. You might almost put him down as a—a what-you-call-it—misanthrope ...?"

"I expect you mean misogynist." Dene yawned. She said in a bored voice, "I'm not bored—just pleasantly relaxed." She thought with surprise, he's warning me—it's unmistakable. He's warning me not to pin my hopes to Debrulet. Either he wants a clear field for his own fun and games, or there's a less obvious reason. She said, "Was there anything special you wanted to see me about?" and smiled ravishingly into the too candid eyes.

"Why, yes—I came to apologize for taking you off on that wild-goose chase last night."

"You needn't apologize. I found it quite entertaining."

He dribbled more sand through his fingers. "Well—it's decent of you to say so, Miss Cameron, and the least I can do is explain what it was all about. You see—the missing letter had to do with some property Paul's been trying to sell. It involves a large sum of money—and between you and me, Paul needs looking after when it comes to money. He's the most impractical man I ever came across—and, being his best friend, I often feel it's up to me to protect him from his own carelessness." Ruefully he added, "Not that I've ever been thanked for it. All I got for my pains last night was a bawling out for raising a fuss about nothing."

Dene believed nothing of it, and unbelief served to renew her curiosity. She patted the leather case in her lap. She said, "Thank you for telling me, although it really wasn't necessary." The wisest procedure, she thought, was to rediscover the letter in Bridie's presence and make it seem natural for her to assume the burden of returning it. That way she need not be implicated at all.

Masters seemed intent upon the play of her fingers. At least he seemed intent. She said, "Would you mind getting my robe. I hung it over the cabaña railing."

"Glad to do anything for you—anything." He jumped up, dusted himself fastidiously, and went to the railing. He returned, holding the robe at ready.

"Thank you, I'll manage." She took it from him.

"You couldn't be cold," he said, "if you weren't last

night—and you won't burn because you're not exposed to the sun."

Not to the sun, she thought. She covered herself, making a deliberate process of it.

A brief look of deprivation crossed his features. He rallied immediately. "I'm wondering," he said, "if you'd honor a lonely man by dining with him—preferably tonight."

"At least I can put an end to your wondering. I'm here at the invitation of the Curtises, and it would be discourteous to make any plans that didn't include them."

"But I thought you said Mrs. Curtis was away! Oh—excuse me—I didn't mean to be obtuse ..." He dropped to the sand again, as though embarrassment had weakened his knees.

Dene said, "People never mean to be obtuse. I expect it's rather like a disease—and perhaps I'm catching it from you because I can't quite grasp what you're being particularly obtuse about." Some women, she thought, might find the compact little man attractive, but she was not one of them. She would suffer no loss if he took his elfin face and his elfin grin elsewhere.

He said, "Ouch!" Then he said, "Well—wouldn't you say the conclusion I've jumped to is a natural one?" And answered himself. "No—I guess it isn't at that. I caught a glimpse of Mr. Curtis a little while ago and he's hardly the type you'd fall for—even taking the financial picture into consideration—which you don't have to because there must be thousands of rich men who—"

She was gazing over his head at the bay. The tide was coming in, moving with slow and gentle undulations. Her voice sounded lazy. "Why don't you go for a swim, Mr. Masters?"

He responded to the interruption automatically. "I didn't bring my—" He broke off with a laugh. "Look—what's your first name? I can't go on calling you Miss Cameron."

"You needn't," she said.

He looked hurt. "Are you angry with me? I didn't mean to put my foot in it. The moment I saw you in the moonlight I had a hunch that at last the fates had decided to come across. You couldn't call this a lively place—but there's no reason why we—"

She held up a silencing hand. She said, "Bridie's shouting for me. If you're going up the steps please tell her I'll be along as soon as I've dressed." She clasped the writing case firmly, swung her legs over the chair, and went into the cabaña.

Tim Masters seemed to be snub-proof. She pretended not to hear him call after her, "Sure you won't change your mind about dinner? I rented a car this morning. We could—"

She shut the door upon his voice. She spread the letter to read while she dressed, and found it to be a frustrating bit of composition. It was signed, "Mothy," and Mothy called Paul Debrulet, "Mac, "and hoped he could spare that extra contribution at such an awkward time. He assured Mac that everything was going well and that there was nothing to worry about. He said that so far as could be figured, you-know-who had given up in disgust and stopped leaning all over everybody who had so much as passed the time of day with Mac. He said he knew he had agreed not to write but a guy had to blow off steam once in a while or bust. Then he went on to complain about leading a damn dull life—longing for the good old days—headaches and all—but Mac could depend on it—he would do nothing to stir things up and Mac was guaranteed peace and privacy to complete the job on hand. And maybe it seemed a wrong thing to say—and maybe it wasn't in the best of taste—but Mac was to be congratulated on the way the matter had turned out and he had Mothy's blessing.

Dene folded the sheets of paper thoughtfully and restored them to the envelope. Nothing was clarified except that Paul Debrulet lived in a decidedly shady climate and seemed a man to be avoided. She felt cheated. It had always been easy for her to accept or renounce people on the basis of their potential in entertainment value or general usefulness. Now she tried to dismiss Debrulet, but found it difficult, in spite of the fact that as recently as the day before yesterday he had not existed for her.

Tim Masters was not in sight when she came out of the cabaña. She climbed the steps dwelling on what a stupid piece of business it had been for him to offer her that gratuitous lie about the contents of the letter. But perhaps the property deal was the tale Debrulet had told him. With surprising fervor she hoped so, hoped that he was not in Debrulet's confidence no matter what Debrulet had done or was about to do. For Tim Masters, in her opinion, was as subtle as cabbage. Furthermore, that other friend, Mothy, gave off an even stronger effluvium. If he and Masters were typical of Debrulet's associates, she doubted that "the job on hand' would ever see completion.

She touched her lips. She remembered watching Debrulet through the glass panel in the entrance hall, seeing him take a step toward the house, shake his head, and walk away. She had thought at the time that the headshaking was one of the helpless gestures men make when confronted with the unpredictable behavior of women. But in the light of the letter she put another interpretation upon it. About to add a sequel to the unsatisfactory kiss, he had recalled "the job on hand" and the possibility that it might be endangered by complications attendant upon a romantic episode. And he had made up his mind not to take the risk.

She did not like that. It negated her assurance that even the slightest dalliance with her was worth any man's risk. It caused her ego to tremble.

She rearranged her features for the benefit of Sam Curtis, who met her at the top of the steps. "Good morning, Sam."

"Good morning, Dene." He did not sound cheerful. "Excuse me for not joining you on the beach. Ordinarily I take a swim before breakfast, but I don't dare try it with this back—"

"Isn't it any better?" They walked to the terrace and she sat down. Cautiously he lowered himself to a facing chair. "Some—but I might take a run into the city tomorrow to see if my doctor has any new ideas."

"Do that, Sam. It always helps to get a professional opinion."

"Well—I could consult Freystadt. He's the local practitioner—but he never shows any interest unless a man's practically on his deathbed—only I don't like to leave you to your own resources—and Vera's just wired she can't get home until a week from tomorrow."

"Oh ...?"

"I know how you feel. You can't imagine what a difference her presence here makes—but there it is. Her aunt's had an attack of asthma—and Vera's about the only one who can manage her even when she's up and around. She sends her love and apologies and says you're to get out your best bib and tucker for the dinner on the Fourth. She'll arrive that morning."

Dene said dutifully, "That sounds exciting. How ever did she find time to plan a dinner?"

"It was arranged for in advance. We always have some sort of a celebration on July Fourth. Think you can stick it out?"

"Stop being concerned about me. Just attend to that back of yours."

"Well—" Then he said, "At least the chauffeur's on tap. He stopped for the mail on his way through town and brought a nice fat letter from Patsy. Nothing for you as yet. If you've anything to mail just give it to Bridie to leave at the house and it will go out with our stuff. And in case you should want to do any shopping or gallivanting there'll always be a car at your disposal."

"Thank you, Sam. Is Patsy having a good time?"

"Wonderful." He sighed. "I suppose you can't hold on to kids forever, but I sure miss her."

"How old *is* Patsy?"

"She'll be sixteen in October." He smiled. "But, judging by her letter, you'd guess she was at least a world-weary twenty. I shouldn't be surprised if she turns into quite a heartbreaker—but naturally I'm prejudiced."

"Bridie says she's started by making a conquest of Mr. Debrulet."

"Him?" Sam's face darkened. "If you ask me that man's as crazy as a coot. I sent one of the maids over first thing this morning to offer her services and she hotfooted it back in an awful state. From what I could make out another fellow came to the door first—then Debrulet appeared and used every means short of physical violence to send her packing. Not so much as a thank you from him for my good intentions. What do you make of that?"

Dene said, "Nothing—except that his manners aren't out of the top drawer and that he prefers to fend for himself."

"Well—he could have said so without scaring the girl out of her wits. Damned if I'm going to attempt any other means of repaying him if that's the way he acts—and you can bet I'll warn Vera to steer clear. I've a good mind to ask that real-estate agent what kind of tenants he rents to—"

Dene said temperately, "It does seem a bit odd. Did the man who's staying with him give you my message?"

"Message?"

"I met him on the beach—and when Bridie shouted I asked him to say I'd be up as soon as I'd dressed."

"I didn't lay eyes on him. What the hell did he think he was doing anyway—on my private beach?"

"I don't know—out for a walk I suppose."

"Well—from now on the less I see of Debrulet or his friends the better I'll like it." He changed the subject. "I took the liberty of telling Bridie you'd have lunch with me at the house. Does that suit you?"

"Of course, Sam."

"Fine. I hope the cook has something fit to eat. It's about

noon, isn't it? By the time we've had a drink or so— You don't want to change or anything, do you?"

She smiled. "Not unless you insist."

He said weightily, "That dress you're wearing reminds me of strawberry ice cream."

"Then I hope you like strawberry ice cream. I won't be a moment. I just want to put my writing case away."

She located Bridie in the kitchen. "I've accepted a luncheon invitation from Mr. Curtis, Bridie. I thought I'd better tell you."

Bridie had her glasses on and was reading the morning paper. She looked at Dene over the thick lenses and said absently, "Run along and have a good time." Then she said, "Watch out, now!"

The writing case the lock of which Dene had unfastened, fell from her hand, spilling its contents on the kitchen floor. Grumbling, Bridie took off her glasses and stooped to retrieve letters, blank envelopes, pens, and pencils.

Dene said, "Sorry—how clumsy—oh—this isn't mine—"

Bridie put on her glasses again. She took the envelope from Dene's hand and scrutinized it. "That would be the name of the Frenchman," she said. "There it is—as plain as day."

Dene nodded. "I wonder how it got into my case."

Bridie thought. "Well," she said, "I do seem to remember picking up some sort of a letter last evening and putting it where it belonged—but what with all I had on my mind I can't say was it this or another—"

"Never mind—I expect the important thing is to get it back to Mr. Debrulet."

Bridie hesitated before she put the letter into her apron pocket. "I'll attend to it, myself. There's no great hurry—him having opened it and knowing what's inside. This afternoon will do." Her face brightened. "As a rule I'm not one to poke my nose where it's not wanted—but with Patsy's talk and all I've nothing against seeing with my own eyes what the man's like when he's at home—which reminds me—there was a scrap of a fellow came by this morning passing himself off as his guest. I was on the phone talking to my lady friend in Quintogue when he interrupted bold as brass to ask for you by name. But since he didn't make it clear what business he was on I—"

Dene said, "Perhaps Mr. Debrulet missed the letter and sent him to inquire about it. I'll see you later, Bridie."

She joined Sam and they walked over to the main house. With daylight upon it the building exhibited at least three styles of architecture in a wealth of afterthoughts tacked on as they had occurred to the owners. A table was set on a screened porch overlooking the rose garden, Sam explaining that whenever he and Vera were at Sandy Crest they spent as much time as possible in the air.

Very good martinis preceded lunch, which was rather heavy for a midday meal. She would have chosen to sit back and aid digestion with conversation rather than physical exercise. But Sam, trying earnestly to be a perfect host, suggested a tour of the grounds, and she had not the heart to thwart him.

"Vera will show you over the house," he said. "That's entirely her province and I don't want to muscle in on it—but she left the landscaping to me—loosely speaking of course—because I acted only in a supervisory capacity—"

"Sam—should you be doing so much walking?"

"Walking's all right. It's sitting down and getting up that's painful. As I was saying—you wouldn't believe it, but every year it takes a crew of nurserymen to put things in shape. You've no idea of the amount of work and fertilizer involved to get this sandy soil to—"

There certainly was a great deal of landscaping. Trees, shrubbery, and flower beds had been pruned within an inch of their lives, and where they ended tennis courts and artificial ponds and birdbaths and barbecue arrangements sprouted. "We considered a swimming pool," Sam said apologetically, "but we don't really need it—"

Dene listened somnolently to his monologue, and long before it was over she had stopped punctuating it with, "Is that so," or "How interesting." Trying to follow a particularly dreary dissertation on compost heaps, she worked up a hearty distaste for even such gay inoffensive blooms as portulaca and larkspur, and wished that gardening had never been added to the brief catalogue of Sam's interests, since unfortunately he was incapable of retailing it in a manner designed to arouse enthusiasm.

She balked when at the very end of the property they came upon a small wooden cabin that seemed to hold promise of shade and rest. "What's this, Sam?"

"We call it Patsy's hideaway. Up until she was about eight or so she held her dolls' parties here—and many's the cup of calico tea I had to drink. Recently, as far as I can make out, it's become a storage bin for the overflow from her room—stuff she's outgrown and is too sentimental to throw away." He laughed.

"Vera and I have the notion she comes here to think very private thoughts. It's quite a walk from the house—which makes her safe from interruptions. Want to have a look? It will probably be as messy as all get out." He took a key ring from his pocket. "I should have something here to fit that old padlock. There—this one ought to do it." The lock opened and he pushed the door inward. "Well—imagine that," he said. "The kid's getting tidy in her old age." He stood aside to let her pass. "Step in."

The one-room interior was cool. Shrubbery, partially obscuring the two small windows, lent it a green dimness. Dene crossed the threshold and sat down in the nearest chair. It showed its age by creaking in protest. She said, "I really must be putting on weight."

Sam said, "Wasn't there some German philosopher who held that a skinny woman was no woman at all?"

"I think it was Nietzsche—airing his opinion of a small woman."

"Whoever it was—personally I think he had rocks in his head. Not that you're exactly a small woman." He fairly snatched his eyes away from where they dwelt. She could have sworn that he reddened. "Rocks in the head is one of Patsy's expressions," he said heavily.

She was pleased to find that Sam was not entirely a stuffed shirt, and that his attitude toward her was not so rigid as to provide him with complete armor. She sat back, anticipating a leisurely discussion that would give her own neglected voice a workout. "I didn't know you went in for the philosophers."

But Sam had shot his bolt. "I don't. I misquoted that at second hand. I guess I must have heard it somewhere. Anyway, it's not your weight but the furniture that's responsible for the creaks. Patsy chose it herself—hand-picked from the attic—and she seemed so satisfied that we never bothered to do anything about it. But this European jaunt is bound to give her more sophisticated tastes." He looked around. "Maybe I'll have it redecorated as a surprise for her."

"Shouldn't you consult her first? Perhaps she prefers it this way."

"Maybe she does at that. She put this light green paint on the walls herself—last year. As I remember they were only plastered. Still—being her mother's daughter, she won't object to a few modern refinements. The place isn't even wired for electricity—and that foliage outside must have sprung up overnight. It sure cuts off what light there is—"

Dene's eyes, adjusting to the dimness, glanced off a walnut sofa with its original upholstery amateurishly covered with flowered cretonne, moved to a display of books on brick-supported planks, to a child's play chest, its contents guarded by a prim rag doll, to a rickety bridge table which obviously served Patsy as a desk, its orderly surface holding a block of writing paper, an inkstand, a line-up of pencils, and a large penknife. Here and there on the painted walls were faded squares and oblongs to show where pictures had been tacked. Only one remained. It was centered above the bridge table, a charcoal sketch on a torn sheet of drawing paper. Dene left her chair to get a closer view of it.

Sam said, "First it was comic strip panels—then movie stars—and now this." He stood behind her, craning over her head. "No accounting for kids' tastes—is there? I suppose one of her schoolmates did it."

"She must have very talented schoolmates," Dene said.

"You think so? I don't. Not if it's supposed to be Patsy. I'll grant that the jeans and the shirt and the way the hair falls look kind of familiar but—"

"Sam—can't you see? It's every jean-clad adolescent in the whole wide world—it's a study of youth and the very special animation of youth—and the inner workings responsible for that sort of sprung, ready-to-fly look."

Sam said grudgingly, "Well—maybe—but—" His round face lighted. "Say—if you want to see something really beautiful we had pictures taken of Patsy just before she sailed. Remind me to show them to you."

V

Sam needed no reminder. Later, on one of the terraces of the main house, Dene responded gamely while he exhibited the studio portraits of Patsy. "How sweet," she said, or, "What a delightful smile she has," as Sam delivered stereotype after stereotype into her hands.

Sam devoured her comments, quite unaware that her mind was not upon them. "The one where she's playing with the kitten is my favorite," he said at last. "If you'd like a copy I'll have it framed for you."

She became present long enough to protest. "Oh no. If you can spare it I'll take it as it is." Framed, it presented more of a disposal problem since she had no intention of adding conventional photographs of other people's daughters to her luggage. If Sam had offered her the charcoal sketch ...? Debrulet? Damn the man for his effrontery. Her mind seemed well on the way toward becoming a stopping-off place for his unannounced exits and entrances. He had denied being an artist. He had said that Patsy was responsible for that rumor. Well, he was responsible for the charcoal sketch, and let him deny it until the moon dropped out of the sky. It followed, didn't it? Patsy's crush on him had been mentioned by both her father and Bridie. For whom but a current flame would she have discarded the previous record of her tastes? Artist? Crook? How did the crookedness tie in? The economy of those sure and telling strokes was no tyro's essay. She knew a little about art just as she knew a little about a great many things. Additionally, she had a true feeling for it that went beyond the glib patter she had garnered here and there. Debrulet aside, no schoolmate of Patsy's, not even a budding genius, could have mastered—

Sam, aware at last of her wandering attention, stopped saying whatever it was he had been saying. "Dene—I'm afraid I've tired you out."

"Not at all." She strengthened the polite disclaimer with a vivid smile. She stretched gracefully. "I still haven't recovered from the effects of that good lunch. It made me sleepy."

"You should have said so. Living on the Mediterranean so long I guess you're accustomed to an afternoon siesta."

"Yes—that's true." She thought of the siesta hour—of many siesta hours—alone or companioned....

Sam arose. "It isn't too late to get in a few winks. I'll take you back to the gatehouse. What's your pleasure for this evening? We could go for a drive and stop at one of those roadside inns for dinner. I might ask someone to join the party. There's Neddy Parks, who lives in East Hampton—"

"Neddy Parks?"

"You'll like Neddy. He's got a great sense of humor—and a lot besides. He's turned the East Hampton estate into a gentleman-farming proposition and he can tell you more about crops than—"

"I don't particularly want to go out," Dene said, "and it would be a good idea for you to conserve your energy for your trip to New York tomorrow."

"I know but—well—whatever you say. Of course it isn't as

though you won't meet Neddy sooner or later. He's one of our standbys."

Hurray, she thought. Good old Neddy. She could not resist saying, "If he's as interesting on the subject of crops as you are on gardening, I have something to look forward to."

Sam said gloomily, "Well—unless it rains soon we'll have no garden to speak of—" Belatedly he caught the flavor of her remark and gave her a disconcerting look.

She felt a little ashamed. Sam was a very decent person, she thought, and it was a pity that very decent people were often so tiresome. To counteract her words and their unexpected reception, she was her charming best on the way back to the gatehouse. There she extended herself still further by urging him to come in and chat for a while. In the living room she called his attention to the roses and thanked him prettily for having sent them. And she completed her penance by propping Patsy's photograph in a prominent spot. Sam seemed well thawed by the time he departed.

Bridie had put in no appearance during his visit. Dene went in search of her, but the kitchen was empty. Resolutely she chose a book and stretched out on a couch in the living room.

At first she read as though the printed words were medicine to cure some strange malady contracted heaven knew where or how. She read with ears attuned for the sound of Bridie's return, an inventive account of Bridie's adventures with the missing letter taking easy precedence over the pages she turned. But presently her interest was captured. The author had obviously intended to extract tears. Dene's reaction was opposite.

The heroine was called Sandra. She was a soft, luscious divorcée, a strawberry blonde, so thoroughly innocent in spite of strenuous sessions on the marital couch that she simply could not help inviting every prowling male to become her natural enemy. Naturally, therefore, she was mouse to the hero's cat. And the hero, a marauder named Sebastian, kept batting her from one paw to the other until she was knocked so silly that she would have welcomed the death bite. Then love entered his black heart and—

Dene had read the mawkish tale under many titles. She could have foretold each last witless, will-less action of the protagonists. But the pretentious literary style of the current version contrasted so ridiculously with the content that Bridie, entering the room, found her giggling like a schoolgirl.

Bridie said, "I thought for a moment it was Patsy come home from her trip."

Dene put the book aside. "Did you have a pleasant afternoon?"

"I did and I didn't." Her disgruntled face gave a more straightforward answer. She looked everywhere but at Dene. "Are you here for dinner? If so I'll see about it. It's getting on toward six."

"There's no hurry. I ate a whacking-big lunch."

Bridie nodded. "I sampled it myself. Much too heavy for a heat like this. But that new cook doesn't know is it summer or Christmas. I'll be fixing something light for you."

Dene glanced at the region where Bridie's apron pocket had been, the pocket that had held the letter. But Bridie wore no apron now. "Were you in the main house all afternoon?"

"On and off—as I am most afternoons. Mrs. Curtis gave me a television set for my own—and my room is cool—so I sit enjoying myself with a bit of mending. It's sinful the way the laundress will drop everything into those washing machines with no mind for the wear and tear on buttons and all. One of these days she'll be losing the use of her scrubbing arm—"

Dene scrapped the indirect approach. "Did you get a chance to return Mr. Debrulet's letter?"

"I did. That is to say I got the chauffeur to run me over. But it was the little man—the same I had words with this morning—who answered my knock at the door—and taking his good time about it too. I had to go around to the kitchen before I could raise him at all and even then I waited my feet off. I guess with the arguing and the hammering going on inside they couldn't hear a thing. Enough to split your head it was. Not wanting to lower myself by listening, I was taking a look in the barn to see if old Mr. Tate's collection of saddles was still there when the little man came and shouted to me." She frowned. "Now what would they be keeping a truck in the barn for—except they're scheming to run off with old Mr. Tate's furniture?"

"Perhaps the truck belongs to Mr. Tate too."

"He never owned the sign of one."

"Did Masters thank you for bringing the letter?"

"His manners don't come easy. He snatched it from my hand inquiring to know how I came to find it and if I'd read it. The impudence of him. I could see it was far from his mind to ask me in for so much as a drink of water, so I wasted few words on him."

"Then you didn't see Mr. Debrulet at all?" Dene could not have said why it mattered, except that all day she had been expecting some evidence of his interest in her.

"Nor hide nor hair of him—nor the inside of the place either." Bridie went on regretfully, "It was a beautiful home when the Tates had it—and I'm thinking they should be notified—because from the sound of that hammering the Frenchman is after wrecking it entirely."

The evening promised little variation from its predecessor. Dene bathed and changed and ate. A short while after Bridie's departure Sam telephoned to ask if she would like to come over and play gin rummy or canasta. When she professed ignorance of both games, he surprised her by pressing the invitation. "We could just talk," he said. "Or you could." He cleared his throat. "Gardening will not be on the agenda."

She was amused. "Sam—you've been more than a perfect host. I'll see you when you get back from the city—and I hope the doctor's able to do something for you." She hung up, thinking that Sam was more vulnerable than he appeared.

No breeze stirred the air of the living room. It was heavy with the scent of the great full-blown roses. She gave them fresh water, thinking sadly that they would not last the night, and *sic transit* and all that. And she smiled because philosophizing about flowers reminded her of the heroine, Sandra, who often indulged in just such flights of fancy.

With scotch and cigarettes at hand she settled down to read the remaining pages of Sandra's saga, or tried to settle down. But somewhere along the way Sandra had lost the power to entertain her, and coupled with her feeling that she had read the book before was that most disturbing of all sensations, the feeling that she had lived this night before, this place, this chair, this drink, this sequence of events in which presently there would be a knock at the door and she would hurry to answer and see the little man silhouetted against the glass panel. He would give his reason for intruding and she would walk to the garage with him, and the larger man would walk back with her—

So she kept listening for the knock at the door, and at last catching herself at it, dropped the book to the floor, took a deep swallow of scotch, and went to the television set. No fat men came. That much was different. The two who appeared on the screen were wrestling only with passion. The man's smirking face was carefully turned toward the cameras. The woman's face was hidden on his chest, doubtless, Dene thought, because she was ashamed to be caught in the arms of such a lover. Then, suddenly, the screen was peppered with machine-gun fire, and the woman added to the din by screaming her last scream and sliding to the floor. The man registered stock horror, immediately superseded by a stock expression of revenge. The shots banged on and he began to rock backward and forward and sidewise, riddled, but hammily game. Dene said, "Heavens!" and consigned him to oblivion, her final view being of his fat rear as he climbed through a backstage window to pursue the villain.

The telephone added a shrill aftermath to the din. She located a handset in the dining alcove and addressed the mouthpiece with no finesse. "Yes, Sam—what is it?"

The very male voice was like a remembered song. "I can't answer for Sam—but I can tell you what it is with me."

She said without too long a pause, "I beg your pardon?"

"That's a coincidence. I called to beg yours."

"I'm afraid you have the wrong number."

"I have the right number, Miss Cameron. This is Paul Debrulet." His tone said, "As if you didn't know."

"Very well, Mr. Debrulet. I accept your apology. Good night."

"Hold on. Once I'm convinced of the error of my ways I have the compulsion to atone handsomely. And I don't consider a telephone apology adequate to the seriousness of the offense I've committed. This is to give you notice that when the doorbell rings it will be me." He waited briefly. "Do I hear a dissenting voice?"

She said, "No, I like life well enough to welcome any new experience. And from past encounters, I judge that your conduct in a drawing room will be quite out of the ordinary."

He said, laughing, "I hate to disappoint you, but I was housebroken at an early age. In a drawing room I'm just like anyone else."

"And whom do you imagine you're like at other times?"

"I can't think of an answer to that on the spur of the moment."

"Bridie has it that you're like a Mr. Jock Fraser." She said it on impulse.

"Who?" He sounded startled.

"Never mind. I'll expect you." She broke the connection.

She went to the semicircle of mirrors in the bedroom. She

had on a low-cut dinner dress, worn to please herself or perhaps to evoke one of Bridie's suspicious comments. She discarded it for a chaste white silk with full, tightly cuffed sleeves and a neck that buttoned under her chin. She girded the dress with a wide blue velvet belt and fastened star sapphires to her ears. When she was ready she gave the mirror's cool, chaste version of Dene Cameron a satisfied nod, switched on the light in the entrance hall, and returned to the living cabinet. There she took survey, made a few changes, and with malice aforethought, placed Patsy's portrait on the liquor cabinet. Sandra kept her company until she heard gravel spattering under the tires of a car.

Her nature could not sustain the role of reluctant maiden. She had opened the front door before Debrulet reached it.

He seemed taken aback to see her. He halted on the lawn and called a rather lame, "Hello." Then he said, "I didn't exactly hope for a reception committee."

"I heard the car and decided to investigate. I'd rather expected you to arrive on foot." He had come within the radius of the entrance light, but it gave her no clue as to what might be happening behind his strong, insolent features.

"Oh—then the reception wasn't for me?"

She clung to her poise. "Yes, it was. I couldn't bear to have you suffer that awful contrition a moment longer than necessary. I wanted you to know at once that I harbor no grudge. Please come in."

She had turned on every lamp in the living room. She saw his curled mouth twitch as he crossed the threshold. He said, "You're being very kind. Somehow I shouldn't have tagged you as an essentially kind woman."

"You don't know me."

"Yes—I know you." He gave her no time to reply. He sniffed the warm air and said quickly, "Those roses are out of keeping."

She raised the dark arches of her brows. "Presumably you're speaking English but—"

"Too lush for the fine, wholesome atmosphere you've created—the smell of them conjures up—"

"Sam's garden," she said. "You must get him to show it to you." She dealt sternly with the urge to smile.

He went on as though he had not heard, "Your own perfume is out of keeping too—very heady stuff."

"I like perfume. I like all the niceties of civilization. You don't—do you?" Deliberately she measured him. He wore no jacket. The frayed shirt was very white against his tanned throat. "Do sit down for a moment, Mr. Debrulet." She herself sat down. "About gardening—"

He stood, taking her in, looking almost sleepily relaxed. "Detail for a group of angels," he said, "complete with touches of blue—"

"There's no doubt you have the true artist's flair, Mr. Debrulet." She took note of the way his absurd outfit seemed to tighten on his stiffening frame.

His voice was casual enough. "You'd bring out the artist in any man."

"But we were talking of gardening, weren't we?"

"Gardening—flowers—you. Allied subjects—"

"Your friend said something about having left you to cope with the weeds this morning."

Abruptly he turned his head away. He seemed to be staring directly at Patsy's photograph. He said, "You saw Masters this morning?"

"On the beach. We had quite a chat."

"Look here—"

"Yes?"

"Masters is—he's an erratic little devil. He had a rugged time of it in the war—and as a result he—he's apt to say more than his prayers. It doesn't do to pay too much attention to him."

"Now that's extraordinary. Women have the reputation for doing each other down—yet I come to a place as a stranger—and before two days have passed two strange men who share a roof go out of their way to warn me about each other."

He shed all pretense at ease. His back and voice were rigid. "What did he— Hell!"

She had thought to extract enjoyment from the visit, but there was nothing enjoyable about seeing so large a man so much at loss. She said, "That curious piece of furniture over there contains stimulants. If the apology is still troubling you a drink might help you to get it off your chest."

He walked over to the liquor cabinet. He picked up Patsy's photograph and handled it absently.

Dene reverted to planned tactics. "Yes—I suppose that should stimulate you too, in a sense. Although it isn't a patch on the sketch you did of her—the one she keeps in her hideaway. I expect you've been there—"

He said in mimicry, "Presumably you're speaking English but ...?" and made a deliberate business of setting the picture down. It toppled on its face as he opened the doors of the cabinet, but he did not right it. He turned and glanced questioningly at her glass. "Scotch?"

"I've enough to go on with. Just help yourself."

He brought a bottle of scotch and a shot glass over to her chair. Still standing, he filled the shot glass.

"So you're that kind of drinker," she said. "Or is it my fault for not telling you where to find the ice?"

"Maybe I do need ice." He raised his glass, stared down at her, and muttered, "To years from now."

"What a curious toast." She wanted to say, What's wrong with now?

He drank. He set glass and bottle down on the table beside her. He said, "The not too near future should settle things one way or another."

"Am I expected to grasp the significance of that?"

"No—and an explanation would take us far into the night."

"Well ...?" Her lips closed upon the rest of it, the Why not? She made almost angry substitution, the anger being directed at the abnormal quickening of her heartbeat. "Well—since obviously you don't intend to sit down I'll consider your apology as rendered." She arose.

His eyes held to her. "The polite hostess," he said, "speeding the parting guest."

"Let's say I'm tired of straining to look up at that guest."

He said expressionlessly, "It would be even more of a strain to look up to him."

"Many years ago," she said, "I went through the phase of wallowing in cross-purpose conversation and DOUBLE ENTENDRE but—"

"But now—tonight—you find yourself too old to enjoy that adolescent form of entertainment."

She did not find herself too old. That was the trouble. She felt too young, catapulted back through the years to her first awakening. Paul Debrulet was larger than life as he stood over her, dwarfing not only that first blind seeking, but all that had come after, dwarfing the precious DECOR of the room, dwarfing her and everything she had ever felt or whipped herself into believing she had felt.

Suddenly, and without warning, she stood on the edge of panic. Get him out of the house, her mind said. Let him go his way, whatever way it is. And thank heaven it's not too late. Think of something. Think of Sandra—

Her smile was spontaneous. For a moment it shut off the current in the room, and the giant dwindled to no more than a tall good-looking man, one among the many tall good-looking men who had fringed her life. She held out a hand to him in what was meant to be a formal gesture of dismissal.

He took the hand and kept it. She had either to pull away or stand quite still and wait until he chose to release it. She waited. That was another mistake. The current went on again. Artist—crook—doctor—lawyer—Indian chief—rich man—poor man—beggerman— There was a button missing from his shirt. There was— When had he dropped her hand!

Her head was pressed against his shirt, pressed against a hard wall with behind it the thudding drum. His fingers touched her chin, forced her head up. She saw his eyes before she closed her own. She tried to speak and was stifled, and it was too late. Her arms in their chaste white sleeves reached out and banded around him.

<h2 style="text-align:center">VI</h2>

There were days of fair weather, but the morning of the Fourth threatened an end to them. Shortly after the sun's feeble rising, Dene sat up in the wide bed with the niched headboard. She said, "Vera's coming home today."

"Damn Vera."

"And Bridie said something about coming over earlier than usual."

"Damn Bridie. God, how beautiful you are."

"You're beautiful too. I think I love you."

"Don't think."

"But Bridie— Oh!"

A while later she lay quietly in the curve of his arm. "Paul?"

"Yes?"

"You know that sooner or later we've got to talk."

He smoothed her hair back from her brow. "Whoever started the bob had an all-time grudge against men."

"Do you think it's serious—this thing that's happened to us? Do you think it will wear itself out?"

"I don't know."

"What are we going to do about it?"

"Are you asking me to declare my intentions?"

"No. I'm rather expensive. I'm afraid what money I have wouldn't carry us both. I couldn't marry you unless you were rich. You aren't—are you?"

"Beautiful *and* practical."

She made still another of the attempts that had so far come to nothing. "Do you want to tell me about yourself?"

"It isn't a question of wanting."

She turned her head. His mouth was tormented. She said, "Darling."

He achieved a fairly convincing smile. "You've had a lot of practice with that word. You give it everything."

"I've had nothing but practice—nothing but rehearsals until you opened the show. Paul—that night—that night it started—did you mean it to?"

"I swear I didn't. My better nature got the worst of me. I really meant to apologize and leave. I should have left. It wasn't as though I didn't hear the warning signal."

"When?"

"At the station."

"I heard it too."

"You should have heeded it."

She said sleepily, "Are you sorry I didn't?"

"Yes."

"Paul—I want more of you than this. Why don't we ever see each other during the day? What do you do—" Then she stopped. "Did you say, 'yes'?"

"I did." He groaned. "I wish I'd never seen you. It can't work out. I wish you'd never smiled at me or—"

"That's enough." She moved to the edge of the bed. She told him he was free to go—to stay away. Bitterly hurt, she closed her eyes. When she awoke he was gone. She had, as always, a faint memory of the comforter gently tucked around her, of a softness on her lips. And as always, she thought she had dreamed it. Because when they made love to each other it was with savage dedication and no tenderness at all. As though each time was the last time. This morning, in the face of the quarrel, it seemed doubly strange.

She dressed, heard Bridie moving about, and went to the terrace. The sun had completely disappeared after a half-hearted attempt to blot the moisture from the oppressive air.

Bridie, wheeling out the laden cart, said, "You're improving in your ways—getting up without me calling you—and making your bed as well these mornings. And it doesn't seem to do you a bit of harm. I've seen many come and go here—but never any who took more kindly to the country life."

"It has its points," Dene said. Or had, she thought bleakly. She sipped coffee.

"Will you be driving to the station to meet Mrs. Curtis?"

"What time does her train get in?"

"On the stroke of noon—barring it being tardy as always."

"I think I'll stay here. I don't want to intrude on the Curtises' reunion. I imagine they haven't been apart very often."

"They haven't. But then, they're comfortable married folks—gone far beyond where a third would make the difference. However, no doubt you'll suit yourself."

"No doubt," Dene said. She wondered idly if anyone had ever succeeded in fooling Bridie.

The peal of the telephone rolled onto the terrace. Bridie turned automatically. Dene's chair scraped. She cried, "Wait."

"It's only the telephone."

"I know—I'll answer it."

About three minutes later she returned to the terrace. She sat down like a disappointed child.

Birdie found her staring over the bay. Birdie said, "Well?"

"It was Mr. Curtis."

"And who else would it be? You've hardly eaten a thing."

"I can't go on stuffing myself forever and it's easiest for me to draw the line at breakfast. I do look awful when I'm fat. Your cooking's hard to resist but—"

"I'm not out for the blarney. What I wanted to ask is did Mr. Curtis mention how you'll be passing the day. I know about the dinner tonight—but meanwhile it's no weather for the beach—and there's lunch ..."

"I'm to lunch at the main house too. He said Mrs. Curtis would expect it since I'm not meeting her."

Bridie hesitated. "Then after I've seen to my cleaning would it be a matter for your inconvenience if I was to make myself scarce until tomorrow?"

Dene roused herself. She smiled. "No inconvenience—except that I'll miss you."

"Didn't I tell you I wasn't asking for blarney?" But Bridie answered the smile with a free showing of dentures.

"I wasn't giving you blarney. Have a good time—and tell him he's to treat you well."

"Him?" Bridie looked scornful. "That foolishness is far

behind me—thanks be."

"Thanks be?"

"That's what I said and that's what I meant—and one of these days you'll be understanding why—though I shouldn't wonder you'll put up more of a fight—you with beauty enough to take the fine words and the kiss-your-hand as no more than your natural due. You won't want to notice when the bright bait you are starts to dry—"

"Bridie!" Dene pushed her coffee cup away.

Bridie went on in her loud matter-of-fact voice, "For you've more to lose than ever I had." She nodded cheerfully. "Yes—it's women like me have the better of it in the end—little to start with and little to miss when the years suck the juice away. I mind how glad I was to catch one man—though I never could see what tempted him—and if I'm not glad now, I'm satisfied. When you're my age—"

Dene said desperately, "What are you going to do today—or is it a secret?"

"No secret at all. I'll spend it with my lady friend who lives in Quintogue—the next town away—and if she's added a few more wrinkles since last visited I'll take more kindly to her—and roundabout—neither of us being a threat to the other—and we'll have a comfortable gossip—with a bite to eat and the play to come—and when we say good night we'll each trot home to our beds and I doubt that either of us will give so much as a thought to the one who lay alongside for nights on end—barring a prayer for his soul—her being a widow too." Her teeth flashed again. "For it wasn't always my poor Mulvey got his full rest on earth—not to speak ill of the dead. And if you want the truth—after the terrible shock of it has worn away there's a bit of relief sets in. You having been married yourself—and married still depending on how you look at it—I can speak this way, though maybe you're still too young to relish the ease that comes with not dancing to another's—"

Dene managed to wriggle off the pin. "Did you say you were going to a play?"

Bridie patted her apron pocket. "I did—and I am. I've the tickets right here to prove it. The summer theater in Quintogue is giving a fine Irish musical called *Finian's Rainbow* and I happened to let the word slip to Mr. Curtis that I'd like to see it. Of course when he got them he didn't know for sure that Mrs. Curtis would be home in time for the Fourth—but now he says it makes no matter and I'm to go anyway." She broke off to look at the man's watch on her wrist. She said reprovingly, "You letting me go on as if I'd all the time in the world—with only an hour to finish my chores and change my dress and catch the bus. Then I can tell Mr. Curtis you'll spare me? Of course it hangs on that."

"Yes, I'll spare you," Dene said. And would have spared you happily some yards of wordage back, her thoughts added.

Bridie misinterpreted her troubled face. "You haven't been bothered here while I'm away, have you?"

"Bothered? No."

"Well, I was only asking. A couple of times I've caught sight of that little man—the Frenchman's friend—making free of the property. And yesterday—or was it the day before—when Mr. Curtis asked me to take the electrician down to Patsy's little house to see could it be wired, I glimpsed the tail end of him scuttling off through the bushes. I've been meaning to speak to Mr. Curtis about it," she added dourly, "about that and the other things too—"

Dene said inattentively, "He was probably bird-watching or something."

"Bird-watching is it? He's a bird will bear watching himself—"

"Bridie—didn't you say you had to catch a bus?"

She continued to sit on the terrace, the memory of the quarrel hot and strong within her. Paul was probably going about his business, his nefarious business. Quite unconcerned, he would be. Men, the consensus had it, did not react to sex as women did. And damn the consensus, because she, herself, had never before reacted in the manner ascribed to women, had experienced no silly, sentimental carry over, or waited for some symbol of continuity, say, the ringing of the telephone, or a note expressing contrition or reassurance. On the contrary, the look of complicity, the quarreling, and making up, the need to reaffirm by touch of hand, by words, had been no part of her behavior until—

She recalled a poem she had read when she was Patsy's age. "I find this frenzy insufficient reason for conversation when we meet again." She tried to lift the corners of her lips. But they were weighted. Edna St. Vincent Millay—poet. Dead poet. Bridie—squawking like a bird of ill omen, squawking of age—aridity—death....

Every time I asked him questions, she thought, "this frenzy" interfered to cancel out the need for conversation. I should have clung to my wits. It was while I held him that I should have demanded an accounting. It was then I should have said, "I read that letter, Paul. Who are you? What have you done? Tell me and I'll share it." While I held him he must have answered. He could not have turned away—not with all the power of his will and body. I should have said, "It makes no difference to me, Paul. There isn't room between us for any separating wedge." I should have said, "What have you in common with a man like Tim Masters? You!"

I'm in love, she thought wonderingly, and it's the most uncomfortable thing that has ever happened to me. She looked up at the laden sky and thought, Start raining—storming—do something—get it over with.

Bridie marched sturdily down the road that led to the main house. Her roar more than covered the distance between them. "I'm lucky the grocer's truck comes by at this time. If I catch him he'll give me a lift to the bus stop—otherwise what with the chauffeur being occupied—and me never getting the hang of driving through my skull—"

"Hurry then—or you'll miss him."

But Bridie had halted and turned. "You'll make my explanations to Mrs. Curtis should the mister forget? I wouldn't want her to take it amiss that I'm not on the premises to welcome her—but with the tickets—and not being required to assist at the dinner—and the cook giving me black looks if I so much as—"

"I'll tell her," Dene said. "She'll understand."

"Well then—goodbye for now. I've laid your raincoat out in case—"

"Thanks—have a lovely time."

Presently Dene left the terrace and went into the house. At once she felt more cheerful. Cultivated heavy-headed daisies had been placed in the squat vases, with a noticeable bow to her taste in arrangement. And the fireplace glowed cozily against the threat of rain. She was able to smile without effort. Bridie had redeemed herself. She was no longer a bird of ill omen. She was a darling, and Dene wished that she could wrap her up and take her wherever the future might lead.

It would be a bright future because Dene Cameron's confidence in Dene Cameron had never been seriously shaken. Everyone was entitled to an occasional aberration. She had suffered no more than that. Naturally, Paul had not telephoned. As usual he would assume Bridie's presence, and he would wait, as on previous days he had waited, until night fell and she was alone. Night was the time for Paul.

But why? Why?

All the unasked, unanswered questions rushed back to torment her. She sat down. The clock in the dining alcove ticked time away. Presently she heard the thin far-off sound of a train whistle. She sighed. How long ago was it that she had looked forward to Vera's homecoming? Now she wanted no one except Paul. And phenomenon in the midst of phenomena, if she could not have Paul she wanted—she really wanted—to be alone.

Outside a car braked. So did her heart. But it resumed its steady beat as she heard voices. Sam's voice. Vera's voice. Vera rushed into the house calling her name. Dene submitted to embrace and scrutiny.

Vera said breathlessly, "Why—you look absolutely marvelous—I simply love those Italian silk shirting dresses—" She laughed. "I think I expected to find you a mass of twitching nerves. I can't tell you how sorry I am—"

"Sorry for what? You've a charming place. I wouldn't have missed being here for anything."

Vera looked skeptical. She also looked tired and travel-stained. "You're just being polite—"

"Not me. But you are. You should have gone straight home and rested. Didn't we agree I wasn't to be treated as company?"

"I couldn't have rested until I'd reassured myself about you. Tell the truth—weren't you bored sick—especially with poor Sam not at his best and—"

"Sam was noble. How is your aunt?"

"Better. I think most of it's psychosomatic. She wants attention—poor soul. She's lonely—no husband—no kids—nothing but herself to worry about—and of course she's getting old."

It appeared to be Dene's morning for inviting dissertations on lone old women. She said, "Isn't Sam waiting in the car for you?"

"Yes—come on." She linked her arm in Dene's. "We can talk while I'm getting cleaned up. You look so band-boxy you make me feel like something out of a jungle—which about describes that disgusting train. Never again. I hadn't taken it in years. If I had I'd have made other arrangements for your trip here. That's another thing you can hold against me—but train or no train it's good to be back. Tell me—what have you been doing to pass ...?"

Dene had forgotten that Vera was quite so garrulous. She hoped that fatigue was responsible, because fatigue could be overcome. She disengaged her arm. "You go on ahead, Vera. You'll want to give yourself a thorough going-over and I'll only be in the way." Seldom, if she could help it, did she lend herself to the confidential exchanges that took place among women in the privacy of their bedrooms. And this one was certainly to be avoided. She had no wish to confide in Vera, and she wanted to hear no more talk about childless, husbandless women.

The horn on the car honked several times.

Vera said, "Sam shouldn't let the chauffeur do that. He knows I don't like it. Well—all right. We're having lunch at one-thirty. Try to come earlier, though. Oh—it's going to be such fun having you here—" She glanced around the room. "Do you know—this place has turned out even better than I thought it would. Did Bridie do those flowers? How are you getting on with her? I realize she isn't the sort of help you're accustomed to but—"

"She's more than anyone deserves," Dene said. She steered Vera to the door.

After the car had pulled away, she remembered her promise to make Bridie's excuses to Vera. She resolved to do so at lunch. She had also neglected to show decent appreciation for the trouble Vera had taken on her behalf. She must remedy that too. Lack of enthusiasm was the worst sin a guest could commit short of upsetting a hostess's plans—oh hell—the dinner tonight!

How could she bear it? No—not how could she bear it but how could she get out of it? Because she had no intention of wasting her light upon Neddy So-and-so, and all the other so-and-sos collected by Vera, when Paul might— Might?

Yes—might. And then again might not.

Decidedly, she thought, the time had come to take a firm hand with herself. She took it. She walked out of the house and shut the door behind her.

The dark sky was still all threat and no implementation. She frowned at it. The humidity was almost past endurance. That, or the fact that she had been racing, forced her to remove the light matching jacket of her dress. Her bared arms were unpleasantly damp. Deliberately she slowed her pace, only half aware that she had been hurrying to get beyond earshot of a telephone's possible ring. She saw that she was nearing the main house. She looked at her watch and shook her head. Let

Vera get lonely aunts out of her system before she made her appearance. She redirected her course, taking one of the paths that she and Sam had covered in their tour of the grounds.

The prescribed "firm hand" became dangerously flaccid. She walked to the beat of a one-sided conversation. "Vera, your visit to your aunt followed by that long train trip must have taken quite a lot out of you. Why not postpone the dinner tonight? The guests will understand. They're all close friends, aren't they?" Or, "Vera—I haven't been sleeping as much as I should lately. Would you mind very much if ...?"

She passed, without seeing, the neat flower beds, the birdbaths, the tennis court. She did see the small structure that was Patsy's hideaway. It brought her to a halt.

The padlock hung open, an invitation to anyone who might want to intrude. Dene did not want to intrude, but she did want to take a longer look at the charcoal sketch. She wanted to determine if it was as good as her initial glimpse had proclaimed it, or if her judgment had been clouded by strong cocktails and too much food. She pushed the door open and stepped inside.

Because of the pall outside her eyes took less time to adjust to the dimness. She nodded companionably at the prim rag doll on the wooden chest, laid her jacket beside it, and went to the improvised desk. Above it the green wall was bare. Tiny thumbtack perforations marked the place where the sketch had been.

Her first reaction was anger. This was how he went about his business. The business that left no room for even a courtesy phone call. A wonder he had not closed the account by leaving a small payment on the mantelpiece. The rude, pompous, one-track fool. The artist who denied being an artist and then went to extreme lengths to recover the precious fruit of his genius—or sent his precious friend to recover it. Hadn't Bridie said something about seeing Masters in the vicinity of that cabin? Was Paul actually so well known that even the unsigned sketch might serve to unmask him? Or was he an egomaniac who merely fancied his renown and so took ridiculous precautions to keep his identity hidden? And was the thing he hid from fancied too? Some petty misdemeanor inflated by his ego to criminal proportions? The fool—the—

But she could call him names until there were no names left to call, and nothing would be achieved or altered. She was in love with him. She loved him.

On her way to the main house she attempted to piece into some working whole the fragmentary words they had exchanged. *Are you asking me to declare my intentions? ... No—I couldn't marry you ... What money I have wouldn't carry us both ... I'm not exactly poor ...*

Thoughtfully she reviewed her financial situation. The alimony—the hard-earned alimony from Ritchie would cease. But there was still a portion of the money inherited from her father. She nodded slowly, as though she had made an important and irrevocable decision.

Vera and Sam were waiting for her on the front terrace. Vera looked fresh but dowdy in an over-trimmed print dress. She said, "Oh—there you are. We were beginning to worry. We thought you'd lost your way."

"I almost did," Dene said. Sam looked annoyed, nor did he brighten as she developed her pretty excuse. "I simply had to take another look at the gardens—and I've such a rotten sense of direction that I strayed off the path. I'm terribly sorry."

Sam said ungraciously, "It doesn't matter." But his ill-humor, it appeared, had other source than her tardiness. He maintained it through lunch.

They ate indoors, in what Vera called the morning room. She explained that the day was too dismal to make an alfresco meal enjoyable; and that the dining room was being prepared for the evening's festivities.

Dene told her that the morning room was delightful. She said it had a lovely, familiar atmosphere, and elaborated. "The first house I remember living in had heart-backed Hepplewhite chairs like these—and almost identical wallpaper. I'm glad you haven't modernized it."

"But I wanted to—in fact I wanted to do the whole place over—only Sam wouldn't hear of it. We compromised by remodeling the gatehouse. I hope you—"

Dene said enthusiastically, "Oh—I like modern too. I think you did a wonderful job." She took pains to praise every detail of the gatehouse. She did a wonderful job herself of portraying the perfect guest, considering that she worked with only the top of her mind.

They drifted into a general discussion of furniture, of clothes, of the weather. They went on to talk with the same amount of interest of the state of the world, of Sam's back, of the possible influence of the weather upon it, and inevitably of Patsy.

Up to that point Sam had eaten busily and contributed little.

Dene was not surprised that Patsy's name acted upon him as a catalyst. Her surprise came a moment later.

He set his demitasse down. He said heavily, "By the way—I was telling Vera about that sketch. You wouldn't happen to know what became of it?"

"You mean the sketch of Patsy—the one that was in the cabin?" Dene was thankful that she seldom, if ever, blushed.

"Now how on earth would Dene know what happened to it, Sam? Really!" She turned to Dene. "He doesn't like to admit it, Dene, but he was very much impressed by your reaction to it—so he walked over to the cabin early this morning to get it to show to me. He thought maybe I'd know which of Patsy's friends was a budding genius. Only it wasn't there—"

"Well—it's a funny thing," Sam said. He added sourly, "Not that it matters."

Vera said, "Didn't you tell me you'd sent Bridie over with the electrician? Maybe he knocked it down and it was thrown away."

"He wasn't supposed to do a thing but look the place over and give me an estimate, so how—"

"Anyway," Vera said, "Patsy's friends seem to me to be all budding scientists. If they drew anything it would be rocket bombs and space ships. No—I'm pretty sure I know who did it. Patsy said he was an artist. For goodness' sake, Sam, stop scowling. Dene, I can't imagine what's got into him. Usually he's the sweetest-tempered man in the world—and now he's in an absolutely poisonous mood simply because I invited Mr. Debrulet and his house guest to the dinner tonight."

"You should have consulted me," Sam said angrily. "I always consult you when—"

"But Sam—you always leave the entertaining to me, and I was upstairs dressing when it occurred to me, and you were somewhere on the grounds, and it seemed like a perfectly reasonable thing to do—especially after you'd said that Neddy Parks' cousin couldn't come—and Mr. Debrulet's so much more attractive. Besides, you'd only got around to telling me he'd driven you to the station to meet Dene. You hadn't even mentioned what happened when you sent Genevieve over to clean for him—and if you want my opinion, Genevieve's inclined to exaggerate—so I called, and naturally I had to include his house guest in the invitation—not that I minded—an extra man is always welcome."

"For Pete's sake," Sam said, "you act as though we're giving a formal dinner. It's an outdoor shindig. What's the difference how many men or women there are?"

"Mr. Debrulet didn't ask whether it was formal or informal—and unless the weather clears I won't risk having it outdoors. Why do you think I'm having the dining room decorated? Also—for your information, Mr. Sam Curtis—an extra man can make all the difference between success and failure—"

Dene not only produced her voice, she subjected it to her will, infusing it with light and air. "May I have more coffee, please? Cheer up, Sam. He won't come."

Vera said, "Of course he'll come. He was a little hesitant at first—but then he accepted very cordially." She looked from one to the other. "After all—people don't accept dinner invitations unless they mean to come. Everyone knows that a hostess has to make certain arrangements." Her belief in the rules of Emily Post was firm. The doubt that seized her suddenly and obviously was another matter. She wailed. "Oh, Dene—please don't tell me I've committed a social boner. Don't tell me you took a dislike to Mr. Debrulet?"

Sam glowered at the ceiling. Dene said calmly, "Not at all. I'm looking forward to seeing him again." She was thinking, He does want to make amends for what he said. Nothing else would bring him into the open. She forgot about the sketch, about everything else that had troubled her. I didn't even give him the benefit of the doubt. But from now on I will. Her lips curved. I'll give him more than that—whether he wants it or not. She became aware that Sam was staring at her. The expression in his round eyes was such that she glanced down to see if there was something amiss with her attire. But before she had time to become really uneasy, he had turned to Vera.

Vera rose. "Dene—would you like to see the rest of the house now or ..."

Dene said she would prefer to wait. She said that Vera must have a great many things to attend to, and that she herself must return to the gatehouse to answer some letters. Otherwise, she said, she might be in danger of becoming a social outcast.

VII

Dene went back to the gatehouse, but did not answer letters. She slept the afternoon away and awoke refreshed. She made a pleasurable process of bathing and dressing, and presently, glowing in strapless sherry voile, stood in the archway of the Curtis living room.

Quickly she took in the pre-dinner assemblage, and quickly noted that except for huddles of Queen Anne sofas and chairs and tables squatting under a storm of red, white, and blue nothing marked Vera's party from countless other parties. Nothing.

Vera, circulating among the guests, saw her and seized upon her. "Dene, you should have let me send a car for you. You might have ruined your shoes."

"It's perfectly dry out," Dene said.

"I know. Darn those weather reports. They've been predicting rain all day. If only I'd been sure it would hold off we could have dined outside as usual. It's so much more fun. Last year we had perfect weather."

"You've done an amazing job for indoors," Dene said truthfully.

"Wait till you see the dining room. Is that a Jacques Fath model? It's out of this world—at least it is on you." She patted the blue cotton of her summer evening dress. "Mine's supposed to be a Balenciaga. At least I bought it from a friend who said it was, only it didn't suit her."

"It suits you."

"Well—I hope so." Vera's freshly waved hair was a bit shaggy. She looked rather like a good-tempered pony.

Sam, in a white mess jacket, emerged from the pool of unfamiliar faces. He gave Dene an almost glacial greeting and flashed a signal to his wife. Vera became aware that quiet had descended upon the room, and went into a flurry of presentations.

Dene said, "How do you do," to a pretty red-haired girl dressed somewhat obviously in sea green, exchanged pleasantries with the girl's husband, a young man defiantly informal in a Palm Beach suit, acknowledged that she had probably caught a British accent while living in England to a severe white-haired woman who commented upon her diction, submitted her hand to the over fervent clasp of the woman's elderly mate, and took three more couples, a lovely, lone ash blonde, and Neddy Parks in stride.

Usually above average in social adeptness, she discovered when the introductions had been performed that Neddy Parks' name was the only one she could couple with its owner. Sam's preview had led her to expect little of Neddy Parks. At first glance she revised her concept. At second she returned and adhered to it. He was slim and immaculate, and tall enough, and a slightly recessive hairline lent him a scholarly look which was enhanced by fine dark eyes. But the eyes sparked with the same old light as soon as they lit upon her, and commonplace words in a commonplace voice unraveled his initial effect. He actually said, "Where have you been all my life?"

He asked her what she would like to drink, and she expressed a desire for a pink gin in order to make life more difficult for him. He returned with it quicker than she could have wished, and complained about the inefficiency of Vera's hired bartender, who had been caught in the act of adding the bitters instead of rinsing out the glass with them. He went on to boast that he knew every drink under the sun, and that until this night he thought he had known every variation of womankind, but never, so help him until this night, had his eyes been blessed with such a vision as herself. Dene, who could digest almost any form of flattery, began to feel queasy when he produced for the third time his opening gambit of "Where have you been all my life?"

She glanced about her for rescue. What she got was Vera's approving eye and something that might have been sympathy in the eyes of the lovely ash blonde. It made her suspect that the blonde had been through Neddy Parks' grinding mill prior to her own arrival. She tried to divert him by bringing up the subject of crops, but obviously Sam had overestimated the gentleman farmer aspect of Neddy Parks. He was not much of either. She blanked out her mind to him and wondered what could be the matter with Sam. After his visit to the New York doctor she had spent quite a few daytime hours with him, and he had seemed to scrap entirely his first conventional disapproval of her. What could she have done to offend him …? Her warm, all but blatantly beckoning smile intercepted the young man in the Palm Beach suit, who was bearing drinks toward his redheaded wife. She willed him to halt and he halted. His wife took the broken twosome as signal or a threat, and drifted over. Others were sucked into the group. Dene held forth, produced laughter, and Vera's party awoke and breathed a little.

But not for her. She began to entertain serious doubts that either Paul Debrulet or his house guest would appear. And until the last moment they did not. Out of the corner of her eye she saw the butler come to the archway. Obviously, he was there to announce dinner, but a negative headshake from Vera caused him to retreat.

Admiring Vera's faith, Dene talked some more. Neddy Parks produced a small firecracker and set it off at her feet. It left a scorch mark on the polished floor. Dene lost the thread of the story she was telling and said with control that Neddy Parks had discovered the one way for him to get attention. She suggested that he patent it for the lean years ahead. Neddy Parks looked sulky. Vera laughed falsely and said, "Now, Neddy, save the fireworks for later." Even before the incident Sam's lips had been grimly set. It seemed, when he drew Vera aside for conference, that he had another type of fireworks in mind. Vera looked distressed. The young man in the Palm Beach suit wondered aloud if cook had burned the roast. His redheaded wife advised him to think occasionally of something beside his stomach. He answered, staring at Dene, that occasionally he did. Neddy Parks, probably to prove that he had more than one string to his bow, exercised his personality upon the ash blonde. She seemed unimpressed. Dene heard him say, "I'd better watch my step with you, Mrs. Nelson. I'd call you Kyrie, but there's a rumor afoot that your husband's a cop." Kyrie Nelson nodded, and said in a pleasant, husky voice that her son was going to be a cop too if she knew the signs. Dene glanced at the girl's figure, which was a really enviable example of—well—a girl's figure, and clothed far beyond the salary of a policeman. Neddy Parks was incredulous too. "You have a son?" He bellowed to a couple on the other side of the room, "Hey—Louise—Charles—is this sylphlike creature the mother of a man-child?" An exclamation from Vera compelled Dene's attention. Along with everyone else she followed the turn of Vera's head. And there was Paul complete with leprechaun. Paul did not, as she had done, pause in the archway to take survey. He advanced toward the center of the room, looking more insolent and even more comfortable in his dinner jacket than he had looked in the rope-tied slacks and the frayed shirt. The leprechaun, whose attire might have been furnished by Hollywood, seemed to dance in his wake.

Vera, the hostess, went halfway to meet them. Sam joined

her. Vera's greeting sounded effusive. Sam's was more of a growl than a welcome. The redheaded girl broke the group's concerted trance with a rapt, "I'll buy that." She glanced at her husband and added, "Except that I probably wouldn't get much off for turning in the old model." Dene laughed, so easing the tension of her facial muscles, and everyone joined in.

It was Sam who did the honors. Vera had disappeared, perhaps to carry a soothing message to the kitchen staff.

Sam said hurriedly and without finesse. "Debrulet—Masters, you've met Miss Cameron." Then he reeled off a list of names, making it hopeless for the two men to sort them out, "If you want a drink," he said, "you'd better have it right away. We've been holding dinner for you."

Everyone began to talk. Paul Debrulet's voice rose above the rest. He said, "Sorry," expressing no sorrow at all. Tim Masters said, "It was just one of those things," and applied himself to the glass that someone had placed in his hand. Paul had done no more than nod at Dene, and she had not quite dared to look at him. Her eyes happened to wander to the ash blonde. She kept them upon her, because the ash blonde was not only looking at Paul, but looking at him as though she knew him.

He hasn't been a recluse after all, Dene thought. They've met. It was true that Paul seemed unconscious of Kyrie Nelson's stare, even of her presence. But that meant nothing, because he seemed unconscious of—of everyone. She heard him say, "No, thanks—I don't drink martinis," and then she did look, and saw him striding toward the bar.

She became aware that Neddy Parks was bending over her chair, obscuring her view. She said impatiently, "I can't hear you."

"I said I'd never run into those two before—and I thought I knew everybody on Vera's and Sam's list. Oh well—summer people, I suppose." His tone evidenced what he thought of summer people.

Dene said, "Excuse me." She arose and went to where the ash blonde was standing. "Mrs. Nelson, we seem to have something in common."

Kyrie was following Paul's progress to the bar. She said absently, "Really?" Then she turned to Dene and smiled. "That sounded uninterested, didn't it? It wasn't meant to be. Have we mutual friends? I know I haven't met you before, because I should remember."

Dene said, "I too. It isn't often a room holds—well—to put it modestly—two such distinctive types of beauty." She noted that the ash blonde was amused rather than flattered by the compliment. She went on, "No—we haven't met—and, barring the Curtises, I doubt if we've mutual acquaintances. Do you live near here?"

"I'm staying with the Cotters." She gestured in the direction of a statuesque brunette, whose name Dene had missed. "Louise Cotter is my cousin. She and Charles have a place at Quintogue. That's Charles standing near the bar." But her eyes glanced off the man who was Charles Cotter, and went to Paul Debrulet again, and lingered upon him until Dene called her back.

"They look like very pleasant people."

"They are. Were you referring to Mr. Parks when you said we had something in common? I'm hoping we've more than that."

"More or less—depending on the point of view. I meant we're the only unattached women present."

"But I can't even claim that bond with you. I'm completely attached—even though my husband's in New York."

How nice for you, Dene thought. She shivered inwardly. It was an ugly sensation to make the sudden discovery that she was equipped with a full set of sharp claws. In the moment it took her to sheathe them, Kyrie Nelson spoke again.

"You're a stranger in these parts, aren't you?" Her voice was friendly. "At least I got that impression when Mrs. Curtis was introducing you."

"And I gather that you're not a stranger—that you've met most of these people before."

Kyrie looked surprised. "No, I haven't—not any of them—except Louise and Charles—not even the Curtises. My invitation tonight was purely one of courtesy. Junie and I arrived only a few days ago."

"Junie?"

"My young son. That's his nickname—he ..."

Dene thought that she could wait indefinitely to hear his real name. She said, "I find the fact of your motherhood as hard to believe as Mr. Parks did." But she found it still harder to believe that this willowy Mrs. Nelson—Kyrie?—and Paul Debrulet were unacquainted. Given another moment, she would have said so quite bluntly, but the play was taken away from her.

Kyrie said, "Is Mr. Debrulet—the large, handsome man who

just came in—is he a celebrity?"

Dene was startled out of her aplomb. "I— Perhaps. I don't know too much about American celebrities, unless they're international as well. You see, I've lived in Europe for so long that I'm out of touch with my homeland." Then she said, "No—I'm sure he isn't—or at least not celebrated enough to have been recognized by Vera and Sam. He's here because he happens to have settled down in the neighborhood."

"That's strange. I could have sworn I'd seen him or—" She raised her slim shoulders.

Dene could have sworn it too. Yet the girl had no given reason to lie to her. With some relief she felt the claws drop off. "Are you a New Yorker?"

"Not a born one, but I've been living there for quite a while."

"Well then—it's such a large city, and you encounter so any people—in the streets—in the theater."

"That's true—and I'll admit the man's enough above ordinary in appearance to—" She shook her head. "Would just seeing him in passing give me such a strong impression of—of— Things like that can be awfully annoying, can't they? It will probably develop that he faintly resembles some actor I've—"

Neddy Parks was there at Dene's side. He said, "Aha, my proud beauty—you're in my power. Vera tells me I'm to have the honor of taking you to dinner."

Once more Kyrie Nelson sent her a look of sympathy. Dene was able to return it in full measure because it appeared that Kyrie was not doing so well either. Tim Masters had come prancing up to claim her with an unmistakably alcoholic bow. "From the description given by my charming hostess," he said, slurring the words, "you'd be Kyrie Nelson—for no one else is so divinely fair." He reached only to Kyrie's shoulder, and she was looking down at him with a baffled expression in her eyes. Dene could not help smiling, and Neddy Parks, watching her, took the smile as a belated tribute to himself. He said, "Hold it," and pretended to snap her picture. "Something told me we'd get with it sooner or later. Come on—let's join the parade."

She looked around for Paul, but did not see him until after the party reached the dining room. There she observed that Vera's house held infinite variety. The dining room was Early American, circa eighteenth century, and contained a museum's worth of colonial pine. She observed further that, outdoors or in, Vera had determined to make the occasion as rustic as possible. A star-studded blue cloth had been draped across the beamed ceiling. Beneath it fruit, foliage, and flowers sprouted everywhere, illuminated by flickering lanterns.

"What—no ants?" said Neddy Parks. "Look ma—no ants."

He drew back Dene's chair and she sat down, half expecting to have it jerked from under her. Delivered of that hazard, she continued her observations.

Vera was not, after all, one of Emily Post's brightest pupils. If there was any plan for the seating of her guests it did not meet the eye. Dene herself had been placed well above the salt, which was as it should be, but so far as she could see, no protocol had been practiced in disposing of the others, either by order of age, beauty, or possible importance. Or could it be that the Palm Beach suit at her left hand was more important than either his wife or the severe white-haired lady, both of them almost the length of the trestle table away. Sam was right. Since there were no arrangements to be upset, Vera's excuse for inviting Paul was of the flimsiest. Probably she had just liked his looks. And why not? Vera was human. But where was …?

Then she saw him, sitting diagonally opposite, sitting, damn him, next to Kyrie Nelson, and not it seemed, impervious to her divine fairness. He was being quite charming, Dene thought viciously, holding the fort against Tim Masters, who sat at Kyrie's right. How attentively he listened to the pearls that dropped from those shapely lips. He must be hearing some really remarkable exploit concerning the precious little son with the precious nickname. Or perhaps, together, he and this—this "completely attached" siren were attempting to track down the source of her conviction that they had met before.

Tim Masters was raising his wineglass, making a bid for notice. Kyrie Nelson looked his way, and Dene willed that Paul should look her way. He did.

Their eyes met and locked for a space, and the room was a distant planet inhabited by two. It was Dene who returned to earth first, casting some witless words at Neddy Parks, who picked them up and plunged with them to conversational depths. She did not wince. The quarrel was ended. She felt appeased and warm. She felt like Dene Cameron, beautiful and loved.

She spread her warmth to the Palm Beach suit. He was attacking a slice of melon stuffed with black grapes, but he suspended operations to bask. She looked down at her own plate and saw that she too had been served, had even automatically partaken. She began to eat again, tasting the food, finding it sweet and cool to her tongue. Throughout the long meal she ate and drank and talked to the men who flanked her, joining now and then in some general discussion that swept the length and breadth of the table, and once exchanging an opinion with poor Kyrie Nelson, who had a stuffy husband in New York. Paul's eyes did not meet hers again, nor did she seek such meeting. There was time enough for Paul, an inexhaustible roll of time.

While dessert was being served a mishap occurred. She and the Palm Beach suit had progressed to terms of Dene and Joe. He had asked her whether Europeans were as concerned about the current world situation as Americans. She said she thought not. The horrors of the past, she thought, had numbed them to the future. They seemed to her to live from day to day. Neddy Parks intruded with an extremely isolationist statement. Joe changed the subject by saying that for all the strides made by science, the mortality rate was as high as it had ever been, and you couldn't win, because if you didn't die of disease you died of tension. You had only to look at the obituaries. Clever young men and women giving up the ghost for no more reason than that they had been unable to stand the pace. It took lunatics, he said moodily, or unimaginative dopes to eke out a normal, happy existence in this day and age. Dene was framing a reply when she realized that his attention had wandered. She heard him mutter, "Poor guy. I'm the one who usually pulls a stunt like that—just ask my wife." He wore an embarrassed commiserating expression. She followed his eyes.

Kyrie Nelson was looking at Paul, distressed at his distress, saying, "Please—it doesn't matter."

And what did not matter was the dark stain spreading downward from the *décolletage* of her pewter-colored dress.

"Good grief—the girl's been moidered," shouted Neddy Parks.

Paul, in that moment, looked capable of murder. The butler had swooped behind his chair to pick the emptied wineglass from the floor, and Dene saw that Vera was trying not to glance at it, or at the spattered tablecloth. Vera's loyalties were obviously divided between concern for Kyrie's dress and a desire to be the perfect hostess. Furthering neither objective, her high voice dropped inepitudes. "Mr. Debrulet, if it will put you at your ease I'll turn my wineglass over. Mrs. Nelson—Kyrie—would you like to go upstairs and—"

"Salt," Tim Masters said thickly. "Salt will take the spots out of anything." He dipped into the cellar at his place and held forefinger and thumb over Kyrie's breast. "Of course," he said, "if you were a bird I wanted to catch I'd aim for your—"

"Be quiet." Paul's intention might have been to reach across Kyrie to implement the command with a blow, but the butler was there, setting another wineglass before him.

Kyrie's laugh was the breath of sanity. "My husband will be so pleased. He doesn't like this dress." She picked up her dessert spoon, all poise and calm.

Tim Masters grinned loosely. "The lady's a gent if ever I met one." He flicked the salt from his fingers and sent an unfocused beam around the table, but all present were intent upon minding their manners. The rain came opportunely. The sharpness of it against the panes cut through the stilted attempts at conversation.

Vera wailed, "Now we can't even have our coffee outside—and all those wonderful rockets and candles gone to waste."

They had their coffee in the living room. Preoccupied, Dene was hardly conscious of how she came to be sitting in a Queen Anne chair, nursing the little cup in her hand, letting the talk swirl around her. The mishap in itself was unimportant. Versions of it happened at the best of parties among the best of guests. The importance was that it had happened to Paul.

She knew the shape and texture of Paul's hands, their sureness, the way they touched and held and lifted. She found it incredible that they had been guilty of clumsiness, but more incredible that Paul had been unable to pass the clumsiness off with anything like grace. Something, she thought, must have been said to unnerve him, something that produced both cause and effect.

Kyrie Nelson was not in the room. Neither was Vera, nor Tim Masters, unless he lay sleeping it off beneath a table. The wretched little brute. How understandable if he had spilled the wine.

She saw Paul on the other side of the room. He was talking to Sam. She wondered if the stiff set of his neck and shoulders meant that he was still brooding, or simply that he did not like what his host was saying. She wondered if it would be impolite to join them.

She heard the white-haired lady suggesting bridge, heard the pros and cons of the suggestion debated until someone placed a stack of records on the gramophone and a dance band swamped the voices. Then Neddy Parks stood before her. He held out his arms and started to jig to the music. Before he could say the word, "Dance," she murmured, "I think Vera wants me," and arose, and walked to the archway.

Vera did want her. She drew her out of the room. "Dene, I feel terrible about Mrs. Nelson. That expensive dress ruined ..."

"Don't fuss. Haven't you some cleaning fluid?"

"That's just it. Bridie's a whiz at removing stains, but she seems to have gone off somewhere and I don't even know where she keeps the stuff. Funny her disappearing without—"

"She hasn't disappeared. She—"

Vera said crossly, "She has too. That's why I wanted to talk to you. I phoned the gatehouse twice and there's no answer."

"Of course there isn't. Bridie went to the summer theater. As a matter of fact I was to give you a message of welcome from her, but I forgot. Didn't Sam mention getting her the tickets?"

"He didn't say a word. What is the matter with that man?"

"I expect he was so pleased to have you home it slipped his mind."

"Pleased! He doesn't seem a bit pleased—about my being home or about anything. Frankly, though, it turned out he was right to be annoyed at my asking Mr. Debrulet and his friend. I must say—"

She was restrained from saying it, not by Dene, but by Paul himself. He came stalking into the hall to stand before his hostess. He may have ignored Dene because he did not see her. His eyes looked blind.

He said tonelessly, "Thank you for your hospitality. I hate to go, but I'm committed to a previous engagement. Good night." He headed straight for the front door. The sound of it closing was as loud as a shot in the hall's silence.

Dene was unaware that she had called after him until she saw Vera's face. It was lumpy with surprise.

VIII

Vera said, "I didn't realize you knew him that well."

"What well?"

"Using his first name as though you'd been bosom friends for years. This is only your second meeting, isn't it? And tonight—so far as I could see you scarcely exchanged a word."

Dene sounded amused. "I used his first name the moment I met him because I mistook him for Sam's chauffeur." She went on quickly, "It doesn't suit him, does it? Not the way Neddy suits the life of your party—or the way Joe suits that young man in—"

"I'm sure I don't know what suits him. He's certainly a sad disappointment." She was diverted for a moment. "Isn't he stunning in a dinner jacket?" She shook her head. "It's just too bad. First he holds up dinner and—"

"Did his friend leave too?"

"He did not. He's fallen asleep in the library. Honestly! I suppose he meant well with that business of the salt, but— Well—of course everybody drinks too much once in a while and— Oh dear, why am I standing here? I've simply got to do something about Kyrie Nelson's dress. I offered her one of mine but she refuses to ..."

Dene, looking at Vera's large bony frame, and thinking of Kyrie's figure, could understand the refusal. She said, "She behaved so well when it happened. Is she being a bitch in private?"

"Not at all—but it's spoiled her evening. She'll have to leave because she can't be expected to walk around with—"

"She won't have to leave. I've an almost foolproof cleaning fluid that I brought from Paris. I'll take her to the gatehouse and see what can be done. Where is she?"

"Upstairs—in my room. Do you really think— But you needn't go. So far you've been the only bright spot of the evening and I can't spare you even for a little while. Tell me where you keep the stuff and I'll send one of the maids."

"I don't exactly know. I'll have to hunt for it because I haven't quite got onto Bridie's system for putting things away."

Vera said indignantly, "Why Sam gave Bridie tickets for tonight is more than—well—I don't want to be unreasonable. I had told him that I might have to postpone the dinner—and it's true she doesn't get on with the kitchen staff. Dene if you're sure you don't mind—you're being very kind...."

"Don't be silly." She was not being kind. She was more interested in Kyrie Nelson than in saving Kyrie Nelson's dress, and this seemed a providential means of discovering what, if anything, had led to the wine-spilling. Two of the girls, she thought wryly, sharing confidences over a bottle of cleaning fluid. She was also certain that Paul would seek her out in the gatehouse, and after she had disposed of Kyrie she did not mean to return to the party.

"You can't walk in the rain," Vera said. "The chauffeur will drive you—or perhaps Neddy—"

"Not Neddy," Dene said firmly.

"Why? Don't you like him? I did so hope—you both have such a wonderful sense of humor and—well ..." She sighed, and led the way upstairs.

Kyrie Nelson was sitting on the edge of a chaise longue in the large, frilly bedroom. The ash tray at her side contained several half-smoked cigarettes. She was lighting another as Dene and Vera entered. She put it down and smiled at them. Dene thought it was rather a strained smile. Perhaps the poor girl had scrimped and saved to buy the dress, and perhaps, in spite of her gallant assurance to Paul, the policeman-husband would make life miserable for her when he discovered the damage done to it. Policeman! Paul ...? Her heart seemed to lurch. That misbegotten letter shrieking of Paul versus the law.

She addressed Kyrie determinedly. "You're to come along with me—" She broke off because it occurred to her that the words had an odd ring, almost as though she herself were making an arrest.

Vera said, "Dene is the rescue squad, Kyrie. You won't have to leave after all. At least you won't have to go any further than the gatehouse because—"

Kyrie said, "Please—"

"I'm not offering to lend you a dress," Dene said. "You're taller than I am—and not so ostentatious in key places—so my clothes wouldn't be much good to you, but I've a cleaning fluid that's guaranteed to work on most materials. We'll give it a try."

"Wouldn't it be much simpler all around if I went back to the Cotters? Charles says I'm to take his car and he and Louise will beg a lift when it's time for them to go."

"If it comes to that," Vera said, "you can drive home in one of our cars, but I don't intend to part with you so easily."

"I'll never be missed. I'd have slipped out quietly before you returned only I didn't want to seek you out among the guests to say my good night and my thanks—for fear it might a stir."

It was not just a coy protest, a "don't let little me be a nuisance" kind of thing. She meant it. And a less persistent hostess than Vera, Dene thought, would have accepted it and given her Godspeed. But Vera would have none of it, and was unnecessary for Dene to add anything to the blast of persuasion that followed. She almost felt sorry for Kyrie, whose capitulation was the only means of shutting off the blast.

The chauffeur brought a car to the front entrance, and the

two women wearing raincoats provided by Vera, ducked into it. Kyrie dismissed the chauffeur, saying that there was no point in keeping him waiting at the gatehouse since she could handle the car. From the way she handled it Dene suspected that she was badly in need of an outlet.

Dene said experimentally, "You seem all set for a journey far into the night. A pity the gatehouse is such a short distance away. See—where those lights are. I left them on purposely. I'm not a very economical guest."

Kyrie said ambiguously, "Yes—I see." Then, like a dutiful child remembering to be polite, she said, "Do you drive?"

"I did once—when I lived in England. I keep thinking that the wheel ought to be where I'm sitting now. Have you been in Europe?"

"Not recently."

"Rotten luck."

"I don't know. Traveling's exciting, but—"

"I didn't mean that—I meant about your dress."

"Oh." She could not have expressed less interest.

Dene thought that she was probably the daughter of wealthy parents, had married out of her class, and was not yet adjusted to penny-pinching.

Kyrie made another effort at conversation. "It seems a shame to take you away from the party."

"I don't mind a bit."

The rain was steady and hard. Kyrie parked as near to the gatehouse as she could get, and in the helter-skelter rush for cover dropped some of her constraint. She said, as Dene pushed the door inward, "New Yorkers don't dare to do the shortest errand without padlocking everything."

"As a matter of fact I don't know whether Sandy Cresters dare. I wasn't thinking when I walked out and left the door open." In the light of the entrance hall she saw that even in the shapeless coat, Kyrie looked damnably attractive. The rain had beaded her curling eyelashes, which were a few shades darker than her hair, and worked color beneath her almost translucent skin.

When they had shed the coats, Dene led her into the bedroom, switched on a few lamps, and was pleased to note as she passed the mirrors that the rain had played no favorites. She went to the closet, plucked a robe from a hanger, and tossed it to her guest. "Make yourself comfortable. The stain will be easier to manage if you take the dress off." And it will be more difficult, she thought, for you to get away when I start probing.

Kyrie looked at her. She said, "Must we bother? Nobody will believe it, but the dress isn't at all important to me."

Dene smiled. "But it's important to me. It's provided me with a reprieve—and perhaps I won't go back at all if I can think of a decent excuse to give Vera. For one thing, since fireworks are out they're getting set to play bridge—and for another, there's Neddy Parks' personality."

"I don't like bridge either," Kyrie said. She added reflectively, "Or Mr. Parks."

Dene laughed. "Well, then—let me have the dress. My conscience says I must at least take a stab at it."

"All right—if you promise to botch it so completely that I never have to think about it again."

"I'll probably do that without trying."

Kyrie dropped the small evening bag she was holding to a chair near the bed, manipulated a side zipper, lowered the dress, and stepped out of it. She put on Dene's silver robe. It might have been a bargain basement item for the notice she paid it. She was accustomed to beautiful things, all right, Dene decided, policeman's wife or not. And she was nice, too. It might be pleasant to have her for a friend.

But what Dene said next was not in the interests of friendship. "Upstairs—in Vera's room—you looked a bit upset. Was it because you were in a hurry to get back to your little boy?"

"Did I look upset? Perhaps I was embarrassed at being fussed over. No—I'm not worried about Junie. If he misses anyone it's Sammy."

"Your husband?"

"Our cook. Grid's home so little that Junie hasn't got around to missing him."

Except that having a cook confirmed the aura of wealth, it seemed an unproductive line to pursue. Dene went into the bathroom, scanned the shelves, and came out bearing the bottle of cleaning fluid. She sat down near a lamp and started to read the directions.

Kyrie said in half-serious protest. "That's not fair. You don't need directions to do a botch job."

"I'm just easing my conscience. The results will be the same, but I've a Scots grandmother who haunts me, given the slightest provocation. Anyway you've no cause for alarm. I neglected to tell Vera that this stuff has a frightful stink which needs a full day's airing. I could have told her too that I've a fancy blouse and skirt which can be adjusted to fit almost anyone. So if you really do want to get back to bridge and Neddy Parks—"

Kyrie said, "That sounds almost like blackmail." She sat down on the evening bag, fished for it, and played with its clasp. "Since I've served my purpose as an excuse for your own exit, I can't understand why you don't just send me on my way."

"Put it down to the fact that I'm enjoying your company." Dene looked up from the directions. "It says we're to add some of this to a gallon of water and then dip the entire garment in it."

"That really would cut off my escape. If you don't mind I'll take a stained, dry dress in preference to a wet, smelly one."

Dene wondered if she knew that Paul had left. She said, "My offer of the blouse and skirt still holds—and of course there are compensations to going back—the handsome Mr. Debrulet, for example. Did you discover where you'd met him?"

Kyrie took a few moments to reply. "I discovered that I hadn't. I only thought so because he—he reminded me of someone." She looked down at her lap. She opened the evening bag.

"Would you like a cigarette? Try that box in the headboard."

"I have some, thank you." She drew out a small jeweled cylinder.

Dene stared at it absently, some part of her mind associating it with a showcase at a Fifth Avenue jewelers. She said, "But at least you traced the resemblance."

Kyrie was lighting a cigarette. She nodded vaguely.

Dene said, "I should think that to meet two such striking male specimens in a lifetime was better than any girl deserved." It sounded heavily obvious to her. She thought that Kyrie Nelson must surely realize that her interest was something more than normal curiosity. Kyrie Nelson did not look like a fool.

"I've always had better than I deserved," Kyrie said, "all along the way."

"If I were you I'd touch wood after a statement like that."

"My husband wouldn't approve."

"A realist, is he? I expect policemen are bound to be."

"Grid's not what the word 'policeman' conjures up. I wouldn't exactly call him a realist, either."

Whatever he was, Dene's mind sent him a vulgar directive

for intruding at that point. But since he had intruded, she thought it might be worthwhile to find out what branch of the police department employed him. She said, "Every New York policeman I've seen seems to have sprung full-grown in his uniform from the womb of a busy intersection—his hand frozen into the prescribed position for directing traffic."

Kyrie smiled faintly. "Some of them have a few other little matters to attend to besides directing traffic."

"Of course. Still—I find it hard to imagine any of them with flesh-and-blood mothers—let alone wives like you."

"It wouldn't be hard to imagine if you knew my husband."

"Does he wear a uniform?"

"No—he's progressed beyond that stage."

"He couldn't possibly be one of those plainclothesmen who chew gum on the screen or roll the disgusting tag ends of cigars around their mouths."

"I suppose he could possibly be—but he isn't." Kyrie stubbed out her cigarette and arose. "On second thought, Junie might just choose tonight to wake up and feel strange. Shall I drive you back to the Curtises?"

Dene said, "Have I been offensive and tactless?"

Kyrie walked to Dene's chair. She picked up her dress, which had been flung over its arm. She said, "You've been trying to be offensive and tactless. You don't strike me as the sort of person who could be either without trying." She hung Dene's robe in the closet and stepped into the dress.

"Don't go yet."

Kyrie looked at her. "There's something else you don't strike me as being—and that's the sort of person who gives a hoot whether anyone stays or goes."

"Then you should feel flattered."

"I don't feel flattered," Kyrie said. "I feel puzzled." She added, "I'm usually quite helpful once I know what's expected of me." She zippered the stained dress and rummaged in her evening bag for a lipstick. A fine white handkerchief fluttered to the floor. She let it stay there while she made an automatic pass at her mouth.

Dene indicated the dressing table. "Why don't you sit down to do that? I promise not to make any more stupid remarks about policemen. By the way—just what are your husband's duties?"

Kyrie picked up the handkerchief. She put it on the dressing table with her bag. "He's acting captain of Homicide." She sat down but did not look in the mirrors.

After a moment Dene said, "That sounds important—and dangerous. Is it?"

"Sometimes."

"You've smeared your mouth."

"Have I? I don't really know why I've bothered, since I'm only going to drive through the rain."

"I've found myself putting it on even for a simple excursion to the bathroom. Take a cleansing tissue. You don't want to ruin your—Oh—" She was staring at the handkerchief.

Kyrie echoed her, "Oh," on a small wondering note. "I didn't—"

"You must have been more disturbed than you realized," Dene said. Even slovenly women, she thought, did not use expensive handkerchiefs to blot their lips, at least not since tissues had come into being as one of the few sensible innovations of modern civilization. And Kyrie, if she were to be judged by her underwear, by her general air of fastidiousness, was far from slovenly.

Kyrie had spread the red-streaked square out before her. She was studying it as though it were a chart.

"It is lipstick, isn't it?" Dene said. "You didn't by any chance mop your dress after the wine-spilling?" She paused to congratulate herself for having brought the conversation around again. Then she said with genuine concern, "What's the matter? You look awfully white. Shall I get you a drink?"

"No, thank you—I'm all right."

Dene walked to the dressing table and leaned over her shoulder. She saw that the marks on the handkerchief had not been occasioned by careless usage. They were large, blurred letters, followed by an exclamation point. They spelled out the word, "DON'T!"

She said, "How revolting. But of course it's intended to be a joke. No reason for you to be disturbed by it. If you're in a gambling mood I'll give you double odds on the identity of the culprit."

Kyrie turned to look up at her. She said nothing.

"You witnessed that business of the firecracker, didn't you? Neddy Parks—naturally."

Kyrie said, "But what did he mean—don't what?"

"Who can say? It would be in keeping with his sense of humor to work on the proven premise that even the most innocent of us has some guilty secret or is contemplating some drastic step."

Kyrie's eyes were intent upon her. "But why me?"

It struck Dene strangely that Kyrie wanted to believe it was Neddy Parks. She said, "No deep thought went into it. He might just as well have chosen me." And thinking of the drastic step she was contemplating, she was able to sound convincing. "Neither of us melted to his charm, you know. It might have been his silly means of retaliation. At table he could have noticed that you weren't quite so invulnerable to—well—let's say Paul Debrulet." Somehow she was less eager to pursue the subject of Paul. "Or he may have done it for no reason at all—simply because the opportunity presented itself. You'd set your bag down somewhere within his reach and—"

"The only place I left it for any length of time was in the dining room," Kyrie said. "Later Mrs. Curtis had one of the servants bring it upstairs."

"Well—there you are. Neddy Parks might have left something in the dining room too—and gone back for it—and surrendered to his merry little impulse." That disposed of, she glimpsed another opening, and leaped for it in a now-or-never spirit. "I'm surprised that you forgot only your bag in the dining room. Under the circumstances I'd have forgotten my breeding—although in a way Mr. Debrulet was more to be pitied than you." The opening stretched wider, made her incautious. "I wonder what could have betrayed him into being so clumsy. He's usually—" She broke off as though she had been interrupted. She all but saw the words of the unfinished sentence hanging in mid-air, yet was completely at loss to add to them.

Kyrie said slowly, "I thought you didn't know him."

Dene shrugged. "And I thought I was being so clever. Well—since you've caught me out I might as well admit that I intend to marry him."

"No."

It struck Dene as the most vehement sound she had ever heard. The "I'm sorry" that Kyrie sent limping after it did thing to mitigate its effect upon her.

"Look here," she said coldly, "you *did* recognize him. Moreover you told him so—and he wasn't happy about it. Obviously he prefers—for some reason or other—to keep his past a secret, but now that we've got down to brass tacks you must concede I've a right to whatever knowledge you—"

Kyrie said unnecessarily, "Your telephone's ringing."

"All right—I hear it. It won't be anyone else but Vera wanting to know what's keeping us. I'll tell her the operation was a failure and you've left and I'm prostrated by the fumes."

She stalked over to the headboard and pulled the telephone from its niche. The male voice gave her a momentary twinge. But it was Vera's butler speaking. She went through her excuses rapidly, watering down to a sick headache the portion that applied to her.

The butler too seemed to be under stress. He said, "Then that's all right, madam," and stumbled over himself to repair his tactlessness. "I beg your pardon—I wasn't referring to your headache. I'm sorry, madam. Shall I send someone over with—er—aspirin?"

"No, thank you. I have everything I need."

"Very well, madam. I'll tell Mrs. Curtis when she gets back—"

"Gets back? Has she gone out?"

"Yes, madam. I was to ring you up to inform you that all the guests had left as well, so that you would be spared an unnecessary trip in the rain. Good night, madam."

"Wait a minute. It's not eleven o'clock. Isn't that rather early for a party to break up?"

"Well—you see—Mrs. Curtis doesn't want you to be worried—they don't know for certain—the message was not quite clear and we're all hoping there's been a mistake."

"You're not being very clear either."

He braced his voice, managing to achieve some of the authority of his calling. "I was following Mrs. Curtis's instructions not to alarm you. As you may know, Bridie has been with the family for years—"

She looked over her shoulder and saw that Kyrie had left the room. She said impatiently, "Oh, for heaven's sake—what's Bridie to do with it?"

"The person who telephoned the message believes that she's been in an accident in Quintogue, madam. So I'm sure you will understand why my employers found it necessary to go there to verify the information."

She had not heard the front door open or close, but she was vaguely aware of a car's motor throbbing outside the house. She said bleakly, "Yes—of course I understand. Do you know what kind of accident it was?"

"No, madam."

"Will you please call me as soon as you hear anything more?"

"If you wish."

She stood with the receiver in her hand. Then, since he was waiting for her to break the connection, she did so.

The house was very still. She walked out of the room to the entrance hall. She opened the door and the hard rain blew in upon her. The car was gone.

She thought, That's a dirty trick, and could not have said whether she meant Kyrie's departure or Bridie's accident.

IX

Kyrie Nelson left the gatehouse before the butler parted with the bit of information concerning the accident. But she had digested enough of Dene's portion of the conversation to learn that the Curtises' party was over. A glance at a small traveling clock on the dressing table had set the time as a quarter to eleven, and as she made her somewhat stealthy exit she was not dwelling upon the fact that it seemed peculiarly early for the guests to have departed. She was merely grateful that Louise and Charles Cotter would be at home when she arrived. She could talk to them. With them she could examine, if not unload, the contents of the burden which had so unexpectedly settled upon her shoulders. Louise and Charles were mature, intelligent people. Their counsel would be wise. Not so wise as the counsel of Grid. But then Grid was not there to give counsel.

She thought of telephoning him. It would be after eleven when she reached the Cotters' house, and close to midnight by the time she had looked in upon Junie and put the call through. Grid would awaken in the darkened bedroom ... She had started the car and was rolling down the narrow country road that led to the highway. Over the rain, over the rhythmic click of the windshield wipers, the steady whir of the tires, she could almost hear the sound of the bell ringing through the New York apartment. She could almost feel the stir of Grid's long, hard body, its sudden tautening as he waked completely and sat up and reached for the receiver. She could almost hear his deep cautious, "Hello," which would be flooded with pleasure when he recognized her voice....

Her forlorn, "No," bore no kinship to the syllable that had been torn from her by Dene Cameron's announcement. She would not call Grid. He needed his sleep, if he was asleep. And if not he needed no new problem to take to bed with him.

She concentrated upon her driving. Fortunately her sense of

direction was good, and she had automatically recorded the turns taken by Charles on the way to the party. Once she reached the main road it would be easy going in spite of the darkness and the rain. She hoped for no more than a reasonable amount of traffic. It was a holiday night, but perhaps the weather would keep revelers indoors. There was certainly nothing to worry about on this preliminary stretch. Not a car in—

Was that a truck? Yes. It had come out of nowhere to speed down the center of the road. Only one of its headlights was working. The other nearly blinded her. In the moment before she steered clear, she had the terrible sensation that a crash had actually occurred, that some ruthless monster was climbing over the mangled remains of her car in pursuit of further prey.

Shaken, she pulled over to the side of the road and braked. She turned in her seat, but there was not even a distant misty taillight to tell of the truck's swift passage. Indignation steadied her more than the period of self-imposed rest. Lunatic, to drive like that on such a narrow road. She opened her bag for a cigarette. Closed it firmly. She had smoked more that evening than was habitual to her in a full day. She had, she told herself severely, very nearly panicked more than once, behaved in a manner that was not consistent with a policeman's wife.

As she started the car again, she wondered what Dene Cameron had made of her almost demented, "No." She felt like a coward for sneaking away. But if she had stayed she might have blurted out the truth about Debrulet, or at least that she believed was the truth. And she had based her belief on nothing but a few pictures in a magazine. The world was big, and surely in it there could be more than one man with that distinctive assemblage of features set arrogantly above distinctive, dinner-jacketed shoulders.

She forced herself to drive slowly and carefully until she reached the main road. There the discipline came from an outer source. Fourth of July revelers, it seemed, were undeterred by the rain. The traffic was considerable. She inched along wishing that she had absorbed more of Grid's patience, hoping that Louise and Charles would not worry about her, that Junie slept undisturbed in his bed. It was with profound relief that she took the turn leading to the Cotters' house, and entered the wide central gap in the high box hedge that fronted it.

The house was a converted stable of poured concrete. It had been built in palmier days by a millionaire who loved his horses better than his fellow man. It rose to two stories, the upper originally intended for a battalion of grooms, and stretched out gracefully to many times its height. The Cotters had bought it because of its lines and its sturdiness, and because the metal-conscious Charles, who came from a renowned family of silversmiths, had fallen in love with its handsome hardware.

Kyrie got out of the car and slid back the doors of the garage. The rain fell upon her soft, fair hair, her borrowed waterproof. She must, she thought fleetingly, remember to send the coat back with the car. But Mrs. Curtis, who had spoken as though she had cars and coats to spare, would be unlikely to need either before morning.

In the garage she sighed with disappointment because the house, with its generous blaze of lights, had not prepared her for the absence of Charles's Lincoln. Well, Louise and he would probably get in by the time she had seen Junie and changed her loathsome dress for something clean and comfortable.

She ran up to the front door, unfastened the great metal hasp, and gave a tentative push. She was not pleased when the door swung inward upon its oiled hinges. She had grown away from the countryman's faith in his neighbors. Mr. and Mrs. Babcock, the couple who served the Cotters, had their own small cottage some distance from the house, and she did not like the thought of Junie and his young cousins protected only by a nurse from whoever might see fit to walk in out of the rain. She did not like her uneasiness, either. It was far from characteristic and she tried to banish it.

Before she went upstairs she stood in the doorway of the huge living room. Its attractive furnishings seemed full of peace and welcome. Very much like Louise and Charles, she thought. She wondered where they were and supposed they had stopped somewhere along the route for a private celebration. Their life together was a scarcely interrupted series of quiet private celebrations, and for participants they needed only themselves and their two young children. Everyone else, she suspected, was extraneous. But they made such a generous business of giving and sharing that few people were aware of not being indispensable to their happiness.

She considered briefly the endless variations of the basic human pattern. Herself and Grid, loving each other and their son, and yet different from Louise and Charles in that Charles could have taken in stride the loss of his work so long as his family unit remained intact. Whereas Grid could never receive full compensation from anyone for the loss of his chosen occupation. From the outset she had accepted this with a little pain, a passionate pride, and a deep sense of inevitability, as an integral part of her acceptance of Grid.

Her thoughts went on to touch upon Dene Cameron. Mrs. Curtis, more by way of a boast than in censure, had spoken of two marriages in that beautiful woman's past, and confided that she hoped to be instrumental in bringing about a third. For choice, the eligible Neddy Parks. Kyrie frowned. But at that he would be preferable to— She shook her head and went upstairs.

The nursery was a suite of three cheerful connecting rooms. One of these Junie shared with his four-year-old cousin, Chad. The central one was occupied by Nurse, who greeted her softly, and returned to the book she was reading. The third room belonged to Lou-Ann Cotter, aged six.

Chad lay in untroubled slumber. Junie slept with a determined scowl on his face. She bent and touched her lips to his forehead. The scowl disappeared and he gave a small grunt of contentment. She wondered, as she straightened his curled body and tucked him in, to what awesome far-off place a little boy's dreams might lead him. She was glad she had the magic to erase the scowl. She prayed there would never be a time when the magic would fail her, and ached to know there would be countless times.

He had gone to bed with two of his current favorites, a battered cardboard kaleidoscope which he frequently peered through from the wrong end—Grid said this surely meant he would be a cop—and one of the crime magazines he had rescued from the incinerator. He had wanted to transport the lot until Sammy intervened, sacrificing her dignity to a pretense at weeping. What was she going to do, she said mournfully, without those old magazines to keep her company while he splashed around in the sea water? He had not been fooled by the weeping, but he had been diverted enough to compromise.

Magazine and kaleidoscope had fallen to the floor. Kyrie picked them up. She searched the magazine from cover to cover before she placed it on a low play table. It had been too much to expect that this one out of all the others would contain what she sought. If Grid found time to call her from his office in the morning she could ask him to look through the rest, provided that Sammy had not disposed of them. But even if she described Debrulet and gave a precis of the accompanying story, she would have to wait until Grid went home and hunted for it and sent it on to her. And then what? Should the shock she had received be founded on fact, was she to wade in singlehanded to make a capture? But of course Grid would not send the magazine to her at all. He would take steps, but they would be steps that placed her beyond involvement. Quite probably he would lay the matter before the local police, bidding them, if they decided that Debrulet *was* a wanted criminal, to act as they saw fit. She shuddered and hugged herself. Her bare arms were the strange, chill arms of an informer.

She crossed to the central room and forced herself to exchange a few words with the competent, middle-aged nurse. Nurse's authoritative eyes, tactfully avoiding her stained dress, made her want to fidget. She was on the verge of wailing childishly, I didn't do it, he did, when Lou, all pigtails and blue pajamas, tiptoed out of her room.

"I thought you were Mummy," Lou said cheerfully. She flung herself upon Kyrie, and, clinging, said, "You smell all nice and rainy."

Nurse said, "Mrs. Nelson, your hair and your shoes are quite wet. You'd better change. We don't want any sneezes around here." She turned her attention to Lou. Kyrie, anticipating the command on her lips, picked the child up and carried her back to bed.

Lou showed no inclination to close her large gray eyes or her small, impish mouth. She said in a social voice, "I heard you talking to Nurse, but it didn't bother me. I was awake anyway."

"Well—let's not wake the others."

"We won't. Chad didn't even wake when Junie yelled in his sleep."

Kyrie said casually, "Was it a very big yell?"

"Not very big because Junie's a very little boy. It was about like this—"

"Shhh."

Lou used a conspirator's voice. "Nurse went in to him and I got up and went too. We turned him on his side and smoothed his bedclothes and he didn't even know. Your dress is dirty. Did you spill your dinner on it? Chad spills his sometimes. I don't. I don't yell in my sleep, either."

Kyrie asked her to prove that she did not yell in her sleep. So Lou lay back and closed her eyes. Kyrie said she would count to twenty slowly, the idea being that if Lou had not yelled by that time the game was hers. When Kyrie had counted to sixteen, each number sounding like a note in a lullaby; she was able to make her exit.

Nurse, whose indulgent attitude seemed to question the fact that parents were people, permitted her to take another look at Junie. He breathed regularly, and his little face was serene. She went to her room and undressed. She stepped under the shower for a few minutes, rubbed her body dry, and put on a soft green housecoat. Junie's supper had probably disagreed with him, she told herself, or perhaps he had managed to swallow some contraband during the day, or perhaps he was troubled by the absence of Sammy, who had been his almost constant companion since birth. It could not be that the actual texts of those magazines, transformed to light, gay nonsense for his innocent ears, had somehow penetrated his subconscious. Her nerves were betraying her into idiocy, she thought. Now was there anything to breed nightmares in the pictures he studied so tirelessly. Just pictures of men and women one met on the streets or—

Louise and Charles came in while she was still on the stairs. She looked down at the slight sandy-haired Charles, at Louise, whose abundant proportions could have served as concept of the earth goddess.

Louise looked up. "Hi, Kyrie. Glad you're home safe. Kids all right?"

"Sound asleep." Kyrie took the last few steps.

"That's good. We'll be with you in a little bit. We're soaked. Go along to the kitchen and see if Mrs. Babcock left a tray for us."

Charles added, "And if there's a thermos of coffee throw it out and make some fresh. There's a kind lady. Thermos stuff always tastes corky."

"I thought you might have stopped off somewhere for refreshments."

"No—we—" Louise looked at Charles. He took her arm and urged her to the stairs.

Kyrie went to the kitchen. Both of them, she thought, had sounded dispirited in spite of their light words. But undoubtedly, feeling the way she did, she would see her own mood reflected wherever she turned. She found coffee and a large drip pot. The brew was ready when Louise and Charles joined her.

They sat at the kitchen table and drank. No one seemed interested in the tray of sandwiches that Mrs. Babcock had prepared.

Louise said, "You haven't had much of an evening, have you, Kyrie?"

"Worse than you think."

"Well—be thankful you weren't in at the—"

Charles silenced her with a shake of his head. Kyrie had not even heard the interrupted sentence. She was seeking a beginning for the tale she had to tell.

Charles said, "Why worse than we think? Did the Cameron enchantress prove too much for you?"

"No...."

"Vera Curtis told us you'd gone back with her to see what could be done about your dress," Louise said. "That was awfully nice of her. She didn't strike me as a woman who'd leave a party where there were men—just to come to the aid of a sister in distress."

Kyrie said, "There's something I want to tell you." She started with Junie's acquisition of the magazines, rushed on to explain that she and Sammy had pretended to read from them often enough to be on familiar terms with the actual contents, and got as far as her recognition of Paul Debrulet. Then she gave a brief summary of the crime in which he was involved. "Only in the magazines his name wasn't Debrulet. It was a Scots or Irish name. All I can remember is that it started with M-c or M-a-c."

Charles's thin, sensitive face was doubting. Louise regarded her younger cousin with affectionate disbelief. "Your mind's played you a trick."

"I don't think so."

Charles said, "Pictures cheaply reproduced in a cheap magazine? How can you go by that?"

"But I've told you—it isn't as though I looked only once. For some reason or other Junie always stopped me from turning the page when I came to that particular face, and in the process of transforming it into a harmless, whimsical character both it and the text that went with it took root—"

"It couldn't have been very firm root, if something as important as his name escapes you." Louise reached for Kyrie's hand. "What you did, my girl, was to conceive an immediate dislike for that handsome, scornful man—whereupon you promptly connected him with something horrible." Kyrie's hand was cold. She rubbed it gently between her own. "I don't mean to joke about it. I can see you've had what the English call 'a bit of a turn.' But what would a murderer be doing at Vera's party—especially a murderer who ran all the way from California to escape the law? Surely he wouldn't chance an unnecessary social appearance."

Charles gave his wife an approving nod. "There's logic, Kyrie."

Kyrie withdrew her hand from the comforting warmth. She said doggedly, "I don't know what he was doing at the party. I do know that I read an account of a successful sculptor who killed his wife in California five months ago and disappeared, leaving no trace—and that the only difference between Debrulet and the magazine pictures is that he wore his hair longer—so unless he had an identical twin—" She gave up. "Look—I've had a certain amount of training...."

Louise and Charles looked. They looked back to the year of her marriage to Grid, when she had done a stint for the FBI. That was the year in which their own marriage had been threatened, and she and Grid had helped to remove the threat.

Charles cleared his throat. "How many pictures of him were there in the magazine?"

"Two. One of his head and shoulders—and one standing beside another man. It showed his height. You saw how he dwarfed everyone in the room." She turned her cup in its saucer. She said, "I've been giving myself the same arguments you used, but it's no good. I'm sorry I bothered you with it. I'll call Grid in the morning."

"Sorry I bothered you indeed!" Louise said. "Call Grid by all means. It's the only sensible thing to do—but don't get stiff about it."

Kyrie smiled reluctantly. "Well, I *am* sorry I bothered you. Both of you think I'm making mountains out of molehills. I didn't take a dislike to Debrulet on sight. What woman would? We were getting along very well at table. That was when my mind played me a trick if you like. I hadn't made the association yet—or not consciously—and then—suddenly—it popped into my head to ask him if he was a sculptor." She paused. "That was when he spilled the wine. He went white and the glass slipped from his fingers. No—I know what you're going to say, but he went white before he spilled the wine—not after."

Charles said, "You say the murder took place five months ago? Let's see—Sam Curtis did mention that Debrulet was a newcomer to Sandy Crest. Five months ago—that would be February." He tried to sound reassuring. "It will be easy enough to find out when he arrived. And here's hoping it was somewhere back in a wintry December."

Kyrie said unhappily, "Whenever it was he hasn't wasted a bit of time." She was thinking of the progress he had made with Dene Cameron.

"What do you mean he hasn't wasted time?"

"I'm not sure what I mean." Dene Cameron's disclosure of her intentions had been private. Nothing would be served by revealing it to Louise or Charles. "But all things being equal—I'm sure he realizes that I'm a potential menace to him." Quickly she told them about the lipsticked "DON'T" on her handkerchief. "Dene Cameron insisted it was a practical joke—something the Parks man might have busied himself with in an idle moment—but—"

Charles said, "She could be right. It seems a pretty silly precaution to take against possible exposure for murder. The man didn't give me the impression of being silly."

"Did you tell Miss Cameron what your own suspicions were?" Louise asked.

"No. I was with her when I discovered the handkerchief, but naturally I didn't tell her."

"Poor baby—you kept it all bottled up until you could tell us, and we haven't helped you a single bit." Louise hesitated. Then, she said, "I don't like to think of you being a menace to a—" She could not finish it.

"To a murderer? Then you do believe I'm not just hysterical. That helps."

"Kyrie Martens Nelson—no one on earth would ever accuse you of being hysterical, even if you do need slapping this minute. Be ashamed of yourself."

"I am. And you really have helped by letting me get it off my chest." She tried to conceal the heaviness that still invaded her. "What a rotten ending for your festive evening. This should teach you not to invite relatives to stay. The party ended early, didn't it?" She saw Louise and Charles exchange glances again. "What happened?" The heaviness rose to her throat. "It wasn't—it had nothing to do with what I—"

"Now you *are* getting hysterical," Charles said. "Something did happen, but it had no connection with Debrulet—and there's very little point in dumping it on you." His smile was a failure. "What makes you think the party ended so early? We didn't get home until twelve." He glanced at his watch. "It's almost one now—and long past country bedtime."

"Never mind that. The butler phoned Dene Cameron while I

was with her—to say the guests had left. What did happen?"

Louise said, "Charles is right. There's no point in adding to your troubles, but now I suppose we've got to tell you. One of the maids who'd been with the Curtises for years was knocked down by a truck. When the news came, Vera and Sam were too upset to even think of carrying on as usual, so the guests left by common consent. Charles and I went along to Quintogue, where the accident had taken place, to see if we could be of service. But the poor woman had been taken to the hospital—and by the time we got there she was dead."

Kyrie said, "Oh." Then she said, "How dreadful. Was she young?"

"In the early sixties—happy—enjoying her life. Sam Curtis was even more upset than Vera. I never thought him an emotional man, but he broke down and cried." Her own eyes filled. "She looked so little and so—so—" She took a handkerchief from the pocket of her robe. She blew her nose.

Charles said heavily, "It's happened—it's over—and there's nothing anyone can do about it. If we tortured ourselves with every newspaper account we read of a stranger's death our mechanisms couldn't stand the strain—and this death comes under the same heading, except that we just happened to see the victim." His misinterpreted the expression on Kyrie's face. "Come out of it. Under the circumstances it's natural for Louise to take it big, but you weren't even there." He got up and seized the coffeepot. "I'll heat this. If we're not for bed we might as well be thoroughly awake."

Kyrie reddened, and was glad his back was to her. She had not been grieving for the unfortunate maid. Since she bad known her neither alive nor dead, her imagination had taken refuge in the protective shell that nature provided against onslaught by tragedies beyond the personal realm. The shell vibrated, but that was all. Almost before the uneasy tremors subsided, she had gone back to Debrulet. His tragedy she could encompass, merely because she had met him, heard his voice. Guilt for her shortcomings forced her to say, "Was anyone responsible for the accident? What about the driver? He must be—"

Louise said hotly, "He should be damned forever. He hit and ran." She added, "The police chief said there was glass where she lay—a broken windshield or something. Maybe they can trace him from that."

"Did they get a description—or license number?"

Charles brought the coffeepot back to the table, filled their cups. "What's the use in talking about it?"

Out of their separate urgencies they ignored him. "No description or license number or anything," Louise said. "It was teeming rain—and it happened too suddenly. Bridie, the maid, was crossing the street to the bus stop. After the show she and her friend had gone into the drugstore for ice cream and the friend was waiting on the curb to give her a good night wave—and then this monster came racing out of nowhere—"

"Monster," Kyrie echoed. She thought of the truck she had met on the road. Now you are getting hysterical, she thought. She closed her eyes.

Once more Charles misinterpreted. "Here—this won't do, Drink your—"

"I'm all right, Charles." She opened her eyes. She thrust back her chair.

"Where are you going?"

"To call Grid. I—I don't think it's too late...."

X

Dene was seized by a violent reaction to the emptiness of the precise little house. Disconsolately she took off her evening dress, put on a robe, and sat down to brush her hair. She hoped that the message had been a mistake, or that at least Bridie's injuries were negligible. She wished that Kyrie had stayed. Whatever lay behind her vehement "No" was the key to all that puzzled Dene. And no one, she thought resentfully, had the right to withhold that key.

Unconscious that her mind had so directed, she found herself back at the telephone. She asked information to give her Paul's number. It would be listed under Tate or Debrulet, she said.

The operator told her that it was listed under Tate, and asked her to record it. She did. For a long time the series of buzzes that followed brought no response. She hung on because it was something to do.

Tim Masters's voice sounding breathless was no reward for patience. She gritted her teeth. She said, "I want to speak to Paul."

His surprise was too elaborate. "This *is* Miss Cameron, isn't it?"

"Yes."

"Do you want him for something urgent, Miss Cameron?"

"Call him, please."

"But he's retired for the night, and I don't wonder. You'd never believe what time he's been getting in these last mornings." His tone was knowing. "It would be as much as my life is worth to wake him."

"Then wake him by all means." Her fingers tightened on the receiver.

"Now that's hardly a friendly way to speak—especially since I got out of my own bed to take the phone."

She did not answer. She heard his footsteps receding. She waited, her pride consoled with the thought that the effect of the Curtis liquor was still upon him, unconsoled because Paul could sleep.

Tim Masters's voice was at her ear again. "The sly devil—there's no predicting what he'll do from one moment to the next. He's not asleep—but he refused outright to talk to anyone. Are you sure I won't serve your purpose? You'll find me willing and able—"

She dropped the receiver as though it were a toad. She sat down on the bed feeling soiled and sick. She was unaware of how much or how little time had passed before the knocking came. She went to open the door. And Paul was there.

He wore a waterproof that he had neglected to button. Under it his white shirt front was pasted wetly to his chest, and when he stepped into the hall his shoes made squishing noises.

There was, in his slumped shoulders, his lowered head, not even a lingering trace of arrogance. She saw this clearly and painfully, while on a more superficial level her mind was casting about to supply the immediate need, dry clothes for his sodden ones, a hot drink.

She swallowed. She said coldly, "I called your house. Tim Masters told me you'd retired for the night."

His voice was hoarse. "He's there?"

"He's there, all right. He said you refused to come to the phone."

"I wasn't—"

"I know—I didn't believe him. Let's not stand here."

He grasped the doorknob. "I'm going. I just stopped in to—"

"Paul—don't be silly. You're not going anywhere for a bit—and you know it."

He looked down at his shoes. "I've muddied everything up." He enunciated as though his lips were numb.

She tugged at the waterproof, and mechanically he shed it.

She took his arm and urged him toward the bedroom. He crossed its threshold and dropped to the nearest chair. She left him to get a bottle of scotch and a glass. When he had swallowed the drink she brought a towel from the bathroom and knelt to remove his shoes and socks. It seemed natural enough to her to perform these services although throughout her life she had smugly played the role of recipient.

He leaned forward suddenly and pulled the towel from her hand. He shook his head.

She arose. "Then dry them yourself. And take off your wet clothes. I'll give you a blanket to wrap around you." She walked over to the bed.

"I can't stay."

"All right." She turned and smiled at him. "I won't hold you against your will. Would you like another drink?"

He stared at her. After a moment he said gravely, "Thank you, Dene."

"For the offer of a drink—or for not trying to hold you?"

"For playing the ministering angel."

"I'm not playing—and I think you're being sarcastic, but if it means you're feeling better I don't mind." She sat down on the edge of the bed. "When you came in you looked much too miserable to be one of those romantic souls who walk in the rain for pleasure. What made you choose a night like this to leave your car at home?"

"Don't—"

"Don't what?"

"Don't ask questions." He got up and padded toward her.

The gesture of warding him off was implicit in her attitude. "Of course you realize that I must ask questions—and that you must answer them."

He had halted before her. He said, "I see."

"Don't say it that way—not as though I'm proposing to barter my beautiful white body for your secrets."

His smile was feeble. "You're way ahead of me. I hadn't a thought beyond kissing you."

"Then I'm thinking for both of us. If you made love to me I'd either forget what I need to ask—or you'd forget what you think you need to conceal."

"I'll risk that."

"I won't. Perhaps I'm less sure of myself than you. Sit down, Paul."

He went back to the chair. He busied himself with the

discarded socks and shoes.

She watched his hands. "You're not so sure of yourself after all," she said. "If you go it will be the second time tonight I've failed in my search for information."

He was bending forward, struggling to thrust his feet into the wet shoes. Lines branched on his forehead. "Where else did you search for information?"

"I asked Kyrie Nelson under what circumstances she'd met you before."

"She hadn't."

"That's what she said—and she clung to it even after I told her I had a right to know because I intended to marry you."

"No." He groaned it.

"How odd. That was her word exactly—no more—no less."

"No more?"

"She fled into the storm the moment my back was turned. I can't altogether blame her. The warning on the handkerchief must have been a shock. I told her it was only a practical joke, but she seemed to feel she had reason to be afraid."

"I don't know what you're talking about."

"I didn't really think you would—not so far as the handkerchief is concerned."

"Dene ..."

Embarrassed, she turned her head away. It was strange that such a big man could make such a hungry, lonely sound. "Well?"

"I want—I want to—"

She held herself down so that her own want would not betray her.

"I want—to say goodbye."

Startled, she met his eyes. "Goodbye?"

He nodded. "I want to say it with my arms around you."

She spoke with exaggerated patience. "You're not going anywhere without me. You couldn't have been listening when I declared myself."

"I can't marry you. It's impossible."

"Some men," she said, "shy away from marriage because they've had an unhappy experience. I doubt if you're that sort of man—any more than I'm that sort of woman. I've had two unhappy tries, but they haven't made me shy away. Rather the reverse. Without them I could not have been so sure that I've come home at last—"

"Dene—it's no use—"

"And you've come home too. I'm not such a fool as to expect that you haven't been sidetracked along the way, but that part of your past doesn't interest me in the least because it's done with."

"No—"

"Paul—it is done with—or are you trying to say there's another woman?"

"There is another woman—"

"Don't be absurd. There isn't. I couldn't be fooled about a thing like that. I don't care how many wives or mistresses you've had—or even if you murdered them in their beds." She went on, heedless of his suffering face. "It's now I care about." She might have been a surgeon performing a necessary operation the results of which would justify the patient's ordeal. "Now—and whatever it is that reduces you to clumsiness at a chance meeting—and whatever it is that makes you give house room to a man like Tim Masters—and whatever's responsible for your receiving letters like the one I found and read—and—"

He had left his chair again. He was limping toward her, one foot still half out of its wet and shrunken shoe. The way he raised his arms was a threat. She arose, almost completing a motion to shield her face. But the arms closed around her and his mouth was the instrument of silence.

It was he who broke the one-sided embrace. The effort to remain passive in his arms had drained her. She walked away from him. She found a cigarette and lit it with an unsteady hand.

He said bitterly, "So if I made love to you you'd forget what you needed to ask. I could feel you forgetting. You might have been standing in a railroad station waiting for your train to come along."

She turned to face him. "I suppose that's rather funny. I suppose I should give it at least a courtesy laugh." Her voice rose passionately. "Paul—how can I make you understand? I'm willing to swear that black is white for you, but don't you see—I've got to know what it is I'm lying about...."

"Fine words. Wrap them up in cotton wool and put them away—and sometime take them out and examine them and note their fragility and be glad you never had to put them to the test." He moved to one of the windows. "Someone's driven up," he said, and the furtiveness of his retreat into the room hurt her as no physical blow could.

"It's probably your watch dog, Tim—"

"It's not."

"Well, then—stay here and I'll see." Suppression iced the words. She wanted to say, Stay here, darling. I won't let anyone hurt you. She hurried to the entrance hall.

She called, "Who's there?"

Vera Curtis answered, "We saw the lights, Dene, and knew you must be awake."

She opened the door. Vera and Sam stepped in. They dropped their raincoats over Paul's and followed her to the living room. Bridie's fire had gone out long ago. The air carried the smell of dead ashes. Sam walked over to the fireplace, leaving erratic, wet tracks behind him. He poked at the ashes and threw some kindling upon them. But no spark remained to catch and flare. He sighed. Echoing the sigh, Vera sank into a chair.

The bulk of Dene's thoughts shifted to make way for what lay behind this visit. She said in shame, "I'm sorry—the butler told me of the accident. Is Bridie very—"

Vera burst into tears. "That's why we came—she won't be here in the morning—she—"

Sam left the fireplace, and Dene saw that his eyes were red. Awkwardly he patted his wife's shoulder. He said, "She had a good life—she was like one of the family. It happened too quickly for her to suffer...."

Dene could think of nothing to say. For a moment it seemed as though Bridie's face was clearly projected before her, a blunt, forthright face, aging but vigorous, and shrewd and very likable. She sat down. She looked at Vera, at Sam, and neither they nor the surroundings nor the tidings they had brought had any reality. She thought foolishly, Of course Bridie's not dead. Why should she be? She's a strong, sensible woman. She'll come shouting in the morning, irritating, amusing, and most astonishingly engaging.... Then she became aware of something intangible in the room that did seem real. A ribbon of hostility that flowed from Sam to coil itself around her. He had not looked at her or addressed her when he talked of Bridie's death. It was as though they were not on speaking terms and he had found it necessary to communicate through a third party.

He was not looking at her now. He was muttering to Vera, "Well—that's that. Let's be on our way. It's late—and there are the arrangements to be made tomorrow."

Dene said, "Would you like a drink—or coffee?" She ought that she had done little that night but offer refreshments to reluctant guests.

Vera was sniffling, dabbing at her eyes. She said, "Thanks, Dene. A hot drink might help if you're sure you aren't too tired—"

"Come along," Sam said. "Warm milk is what you need—and bed."

"I guess you're right but—" Vera made no move to rise. "Oh dear—I can hardly believe it happened. Poor Bridie—so unnecessary—those hit-and-run drivers ... She was awfully difficult at times, but you couldn't be really angry with her. It's worse for Sam—he's known her since he was a kid. As for Patsy—Patsy just adored her. Would you write to her, Dene, if you were us? It will spoil her vacation but— Then there's your vacation, too—we'll have to arrange for another maid. If only Sam hadn't got those tickets. Not that you're to feel in any way responsible, Sam, dear. You couldn't have known—"

Sam's face had purpled. "Will you stop talking, Vera, and come home. I'm sure your guest couldn't be less interested. She for one won't let anything spoil her vacation. *She's* having a good time—you can bet on that."

"Sam—Sam Curtis—you're the one who needs bed! How could Dene be having a good time when everything's gone wrong since the beginning?" She appealed to Dene. "Please don't mind him—it's nerves—and that back of his—and he told me that he cut Bridie short the other day when she wanted to talk to him, because he was tired of her complaints about the cook—and that makes him feel—"

Sam yelled, "For Pete's sake!"

Dene, anxious as she was to see them out the door, could not let his outburst pass. "Sam, you've been strange toward me since this morning. May I know why?"

Sam ignored her. "Vera—are you coming or not?"

Vera pulled herself out of the chair. She gave her husband a bewildered stare. "I want to know why, too. I can understand how bad you feel about Bridie, but that's no excuse for letting it out on Dene. I won't leave this room until you've apologized to her."

"I don't want an apology," Dene said. "Just a reason—if there is one."

He was beside himself. "You don't want an apology because it might take too long. You came here at our invitation, but you don't want to spend a minute longer with us than you have to." He looked at her robe, her loosened hair. "We disturbed you, didn't we? You weren't asleep, but neither were you waiting up to hear news of Bridie. That was his raincoat I saw in the hall. I'm not so stupid as you think—"

Vera's eyes bulged. "Whose raincoat?"

Dene said softly, "Be patient, Vera. Let him finish. You've more to say, haven't you, Sam?"

"Yes—I've more to say. I saw him early this morning—leaving this house—my house—"

"Who?" Vera cried distractedly. "Who? Will somebody please tell me what this is all about?"

"And while people are in my house it's my business to see that they conform to decent standards of behavior."

Dene said, "You should have stated that in your invitation—because quite obviously our standards of decent behavior are different." Part of her mind was wondering miserably why the sound of Sam's anger had not flushed Paul from cover. But there was no misery in her low, contained voice. "For example, no circumstances exist in which I could insult a guest in my house."

"You've insulted yourself—and me—and my wife. You've known Debrulet hardly more than a week and you—you—"

Vera squealed.

"You can't say it, can you? Your notion of being a gentleman forbade you to mention it to your wife in cold blood—and now it prevents you from sullying her ears by accusing me outright of—"

"You don't deny it?"

"Why should I? Your notion of being a gentleman doesn't forbid you to think the worst—although there might be a number of innocent explanations for what you saw. There aren't—but there might be." She eyed him steadily. "Which is neither here nor there. You're delivering an ultimatum, aren't you? You're saying, in your subtle way, that I conform or else. Well—do I shoulder my little bundle of shame and disappear into the night—or will you relent in your righteous wrath and permit me to wait until morning?"

Vera had recovered control her open mouth. She interposed herself between them. She said loudly and strongly, "I've never heard such nonsense in my whole life."

Sam turned upon her. "Nonsense is it—that a so-called friend of yours has put us in such a position—"

"She hasn't put me in any position—nor you either."

"What?" Incredulousness settled thickly over his rage. "You

condone—"

"Who's asking anybody to condone anything? I'm surprised at you—behaving like some old provincial fuddy-duddy. It isn't as if you'd never been anywhere or seen anything. What's the good of that European trip we took if you didn't pick up some worldly knowledge along the way? I certainly hope that I for one am sophisticated enough to live and let live."

At the smug pride in her voice, at Sam's round, ordinary face trying to cope with a surplus of emotions, Dene wanted to throw back her head and roar with laughter. She stood, clenching her hands, the nervous impulse souring in her throat.

"Dene's beautiful and free and it's only natural that she should be attracted to a man like Paul Debrulet. You with your small-town notions! Everyone can't be happily married—and just because you're lucky doesn't mean you should set yourself up as a—judge of other people's morals—"

"While those other people are in my house—"

"Oh, be quiet. It's not your house. You gave it to me—and Dene knows there were no strings attached to my invitation."

"Suppose Patsy were here? A fine example—"

"Patsy's not here—besides—she takes after me. She's not going to be a narrow-minded ..."

Dene thought hysterically, He's looking at the wife of his bosom as though she's suddenly turned into a viper. She choked on the soured laughter, struggled to produce her voice. "Please—don't quarrel over me. I'll leave tomorrow—"

"We never quarrel—and you'll do no such thing." Vera sounded almost gay. Dene had the fleeting impression that she was enjoying herself, regarding the moment as one of the few high points in the level, sheltered stretch of her years. "Now, Dene, you're to go on acting exactly as you choose—and we won't keep you a moment longer. Pay no attention at all to poor old Sam. He'll feel better in the morning—Sam—Sam—you wait for me." She rushed after him.

Dene followed them into the hall. Sam halted there and looked balefully in the direction of the bedroom. He squared his shoulders, and Dene had a vision of Paul towering above his prone stocky form. But Vera threw his raincoat at him, and demanded help with her own, and spattered him with words until he was safely out the door, which she closed behind her after flinging Dene a conspiratorial look.

Dene drew long, spasmodic breath. Paul had been wise not to show himself, she thought without conviction. It would have made matters worse—if they could be worse. Again it struck her painfully that she knew nothing at all about her lover—nothing beyond the exchange of their bodies. Was he quick to violence? Would he have rounded upon Sam? Slowly she walked to the bedroom. Was it wisdom or apathy that had kept him from making an appearance—or simply that he did not care enough? Surely he must have heard. Could he even have smiled cynically at Sam's little homemade melodrama, and asked himself what all the fuss was about? Was it possible that she meant no more to him than— Where would she go tomorrow? Where he went, of course, but where? She came to a dead stop.

She stood like a statue inside the door of the room. One of the long panes in the wall of windows was open wide, and a ragged circle of rain glimmered on the floor beneath.

She moved. She tried the bathroom door. It opened upon a blank vista of tile and chrome.

He can't be gone, she thought stupidly. His coat is in the hall. The kitchen? But the open window mocked her hope. She made of her beautiful lips a set, ungiving line. He came to say goodbye. He did not say it according to plan, but apparently he had been willing to cut his losses. Then let him go.

She shook her head. No—never. Her lips softened to fullness. She was at the closet, pulling a dress from its hanger, shoes from their rack. She was shedding her robe, clothing herself against the night outside.

XI

Kyrie opened her eyes the next morning, heard a hesitant little sound, and turned toward it. Junie sat in a patch of sunlight on the floor near her bed. He said, "Shhh, Mummy sleeping," and barred his lips with a finger. Then he smiled widely.

"Now there's a fine view to wake up to," she said.

He cocked his towhead. "Vee-u," he said carefully. "Vee-u," and ran to her outstretched arms.

"You're an escape artist," she said, hugging him. "How did you manage to find your way here from the nursery?"

He wriggled out of the embrace. His eyes accused her. "I washed and dressed." He patted his stomach. "Juice all gone—egg all gone—milk all gone."

"That's right—always set your lazy mummy a good example."

"Up, Mummy. Up. Fifteen."

"You're exaggerating." She glanced at the clock on the night table. "It's just struck nine." She sat up suddenly. "Junie—do you know what? Your daddy's coming."

"What daddy?"

"Junie—it's only a few days. You can't have forgotten!"

Nurse stuck her head through the half-open door. "Oh," she said. "Good morning. I couldn't imagine where he'd got to. For his age he's very quick on his feet. Come along, Junie. You want to go to the beach with your cousins, don't you?"

"No," said Junie. He pushed out his rounded little jaw.

"That's my fault," Nurse said cheerfully. "I ought to know better than to ask a question that can be answered by n-o. They all go through the same stage."

"Daddy," Junie said.

Kyrie cried, "He does remember. He had me frightened a moment." She explained to Nurse. "He wants to stay because his father's driving up."

"How nice, Mrs. Nelson. What time is he coming?"

"I'm not sure. It depends on his schedule—not before noon—perhaps much later."

"I see. Then …?"

Kyrie nodded.

Nurse said firmly, "Well—I'll just leave Junie here."

Junie said, "No," and reached for her hand. He waved other at Kyrie. "By-by."

"Goodbye, my fickle son. Be good."

"I very good," he said virtuously. He freed his hand and made a sweeping gesture to show the width and breadth of goodness. Then he darted from the room.

"Quick as a flash," Nurse said. "I'd better go after him before he gets into mischief. Have a nice morning."

Kyrie thought as she bathed and dressed that she could not help having a nice morning. The sun shone, and the breeze that blew in through the windows was fresh and sweet. And Grid was on the way. Of course he might not arrive until afternoon—even late afternoon. But he would arrive. He had been definite about that on the phone.

"But, Grid—truly I didn't mean you were to drop everything and come. I only wanted you to check with—"

"Do you grudge me my first vacation in years? I was planning to surprise you. I'd made all the arrangements. Now I've got to go somewhere or I'll look an awful fool. Of course if you're busy I can take a fast plane to Paris or—"

"Stop—I don't believe a word of it. I think—"

"You're not to think. You're to go right to sleep. And when you wake you're not to think either. You're to do nothing but wait for me—and maybe see that Junie shaves with extra care in honor of his old man. He is shaving by this time, isn't he? It's been that long since I set eyes on him."

She said yes—it had been that long, and suggested a pink carnation for his buttonhole to ensure recognition on her part. She talked further nonsense just to hold to the comfort of his deep, pleasant voice.

And soon she would see him. She went downstairs, looking very much like Junie when he approved of something.

Louise, who had breakfasted earlier, joined her for an extra cup of coffee. She said that Charles had driven the Curtis car back, complete with raincoat.

"But that was my job."

Louise waved it aside. "Charles thought it only decent to check on how the Curtises were feeling, and since I'm driving over to a farm near Sandy Crest to pick up some supplies, I can call for him."

"Supplies? You're not to make any extra preparations for Grid."

"Is that so? I dare anyone to deprive me of the pleasure. Grid was a favorite of mine when you were nothing but a nuisance in bibs—and I'm not sure I won't write that man, Debrulet, a thank you note for bringing him here."

Kyrie could laugh. Last night seemed very far away.

Louise said, "Could I persuade you to come along for the ride? I'd love company, and the whole business shouldn't take more than an hour and a half."

Kyrie calculated. "That means we'd be back at about a quarter to twelve. Grid couldn't possibly make it before then, not if he stops at headquarters first—and he's sure to."

"Swell. I didn't really expect you to leave the premises. How soon will you be ready?"

"Five minutes." Kyrie hesitated. "Will I be likely to run into Dene Cameron. It isn't that I don't like her. I do—but—"

"You needn't run into anybody. You can sit in the car while I fetch Charles."

So Kyrie tied back her hair with a black velvet bow to keep it from blowing and went along for the ride. On the way Louise helped her to enforce Grid's command not to think until he arrived. Louise remarked on the sparkling, clean day, and said that Long Island summer weather was apt to run in threes, three hot muggy days such as they had just experienced, then a division of rain, then three days like this one, and *da capo*.

Kyrie said she hoped there would be three days like this one. She wanted everything to be perfect for Grid. It was funny, she said, that although Grid had carried off a swimming trophy when he was a boy, she had never, since their marriage, gone swimming with him, and was looking forward to the experience if—if there was time. She sighed and Louise said quickly that this was the first summer young Chad had consented to do more than lave his big toe. Lou had been timid at first too, although now she was an absolute fish. But Junie showed no fear of the water—or of anything else for that matter. He had splashed right in as though it were his natural element. And what with the three of them, Grid would be treated to some distracting "look at me" capers the moment he appeared on the beach. If she knew Grid, however, he'd take it in stride—as he took everything else.

Kyrie said gratefully, "Yes, he does, doesn't he?" and Louise said, "Of course—so stop brooding."

When they stopped at the farm, Louise went into the house to negotiate for poultry, and Kyrie wandered about in the sun. She wished that Junie had come along to inhale the good, pungent mixture of fertile earth and barnyard and stable, to be introduced to the brand-new calf, and to meet the clucking producers of his breakfast eggs.

She voiced this wish to Louise as they loaded the luggage compartment with fresh produce, and Louise said that Junie could come next time, that it was always fun to witness the first impressions of children, and sometimes a letdown because you never knew how they would react. Lou, for example, had been unimpressed by her first visit to the zoo, complaining that the animals were much too big and not half so pretty as the ones in her picture books.

They made a few more stops. Louise said that she enjoyed shopping, and besides, it relieved Mrs. Babcock, the housekeeper, who had enough to do. Then she said that the shops in Sandy Crest weren't too well supplied, and since it was still early would Kyrie mind if they drove back to the town of Quintogue before they fetched Charles, because he disliked shopping and there were still a few things she had to get.

Going through the town of Quintogue, Kyrie noticed the

summer theater and said that Louise and Charles must be her guests there one night. Louise started to reply, but interrupted herself to ask if that wasn't Mrs. Nesselrode on the corner. Kyrie said she could not venture an opinion because she had never met Mrs. Nesselrode, although the name sounded familiar, and Louise said that the pudding made it familiar and that the children were having it for dessert at lunch. Which was why, but she did not say so, that it had happened to pop into her head when she needed a change of subject. For she had been on the verge of reminding Kyrie that a visit to the summer theater had led to the death of the Curtises' maid. And there was nothing to be gained by introducing that grim note into their light chatter.

They were on the dirt road to the Curtises' house when Kyrie said, "Does this turn off to some highway before it reaches the bay?"

"No—the bay brings it to a stop. Why?"

"Just curiosity. Are there many houses after the Curtises?"

"Not one, but people have the right of way because there's a public beach where the road terminates."

"Oh. Who lives here?" They were passing the Tate place.

"I don't know. If you don't want to visit with Miss Cameron I'd better step on the gas when we reach the gatehouse—though I hardly think she's the type to rise before noon. Beauty like hers needs considerable upkeep."

She seemed to be right. The gatehouse showed no signs of activity.

Charles must have been watching for the car. Before it came to a stop he was out the Curtises' front door. "Hi," he said when he reached them. "I don't think there's any need for either of you to go in—unless you specially want to. They seem awfully low, and I doubt if they feel like entertaining."

"Nothing we can do?" Louise said.

"No—I asked. Sam was up betimes taking care of everything. The funeral's on Monday." He got in beside Kyrie on the wide front seat. He said belatedly, "Want me to drive, Louise?"

Louise shook her head. She started the car. "Was Miss Cameron with them by any chance?"

"No, she wasn't."

"Didn't I tell you she wouldn't be a morning girl?" Louise said to Kyrie.

"You haven't proved it." For no fathomable reason Kyrie felt impelled to defend Dene. "She may just think, as Charles does, that the Curtises don't want to be bothered with guests."

Charles shrugged. "On the other hand maybe Sam thought she should be there giving them aid and comfort—because when Vera said something about her he looked ready to explode."

"I know one thing"—Louise was only making conversation—"I wouldn't tempt my husband with a dish like that—and don't be insulted, Kyrie. You don't come under the 'dish' listing. You're only my little cousin."

Charles said, "And it's been bruited about that I prefer brunettes anyway." He looked affectionately at his dark-haired wife. "Or, to be precise, brunette, singular."

Kyrie asked if the clock on the dashboard was right, and Louise laughed and said, "My little cousin feels out of it. She's in a hurry to get home to the gentleman who prefers blonde, singular."

"Do you think he could be there waiting, Louise?" Kyrie gave the speedometer a glance of disapproval, and, obligingly, Louise accelerated.

But Grid's car was not in evidence when they rolled in through the opening in the hedge. Neither were the children, although it was nearly time for their lunch.

The housekeeper and her husband came out to help with the supplies. Kyrie lent a band too, and when boxes and bundles had been transferred to the kitchen, she sat in a deck chair on the lawn to sun herself and wait. In a few minutes the housekeeper hurried to her side.

"Oh, Mrs. Nelson, I forgot to tell you. A gentleman was here—just before you came back. I told him you'd gone with Mrs. Cotter to do some extra shopping because your husband was expected and that you'd be home soon, but he said he couldn't wait." For a moment Kyrie had the absurd thought that Grid had arrived and departed. She said, impatient with herself, "Who was he?"

"I asked his name, ma'am, but he didn't seem to hear. He just thanked me and walked away."

"Walked? Was he someone from around here?"

"Well—he wasn't anyone who'd ever called on Mr. and Mrs. Cotter—and when I say 'walked,' I don't mean he didn't have a car, because he did. I happened to step out a few minutes later and I saw him again, driving by. I guess when he came he overshot the house and parked down the road a piece." She added helpfully, "But from his tan and the way he was dressed I'd say he hadn't come from the city. He was a very big man—with close dark hair. Very big," she repeated, "and handsome, too."

Kyrie said, "Thank you, Mrs. Babcock." Unseeingly her eyes followed the woman's progress back to the house.

She did not hear Louise coming across the lawn. She jumped at the sound of her voice.

"Kyrie—I didn't mean to scare you. Next time I'll bell myself." Louise pulled a chair over and sat down. "You're not developing a case of nerves because Grid hasn't turned up? You said you didn't expect him at any special time."

Kyrie told her about the caller. "He couldn't be anyone but Debrulet, could he?"

"There isn't anyone else around here who answers that description."

"I don't even know anyone in the city who does."

"Well—there's no need to stew about it. His reason for coming seems quite obvious. He probably figured he could wheedle you into keeping mum. He's got a lot of wheedling equipment."

"Then why didn't he wait? Mrs. Babcock said I'd be back soon."

"She also said you were expecting your husband, and thanks to Neddy Parks everyone at the party learned that Grid's a police officer. Debrulet turned tail because he realized he was too late—that you'd already passed the word along."

The thought occurred to both of them at the same time. Kyrie uttered it. "If that's true he's not going to sit around and wait for Grid or the local authorities to investigate him." She tried to negate the relief in her voice by adding, "Oh, why couldn't I have kept a poker face last night?"

"Because you only half recognized him at first—and the fat was in the fire before you knew there was anything to keep a poker face about. Shouldn't we phone the local police and ask them to stop him from leaving town?"

Kyrie looked miserable.

"Well, I will—or Charles will. We're on friendly terms with Chief Comerford, who's practically the entire force. We could suggest that he take—well—tactful precautions, in case it's all a mistake." She did not look happy herself. At Kyrie's reluctant nod she got up and went into the house.

When she returned Kyrie was sitting stiffly on the chair's footrest, her eyes fixed on the hedge gap.

Louise said cheerfully, "It's out of our hands—thanks to

Grid. He phoned Chief Comerford early this morning. The chief's busy with that hit-and-run affair, so he didn't have a man to put on Debrulet, but he's notified the state troopers to watch the roads and the railroad station. Will you please quit looking like an orphan?"

"I feel more like a louse than an orphan. Now I know what Grid goes through when he's forced to make an arrest that goes against the grain. I wish Junie had never brought those wretched magazines into the apartment—"

"Nonsense. You should be feeling very pleased that your husband has enough faith in you to consider your suspicion important enough for immediate action." She tried to divert her. "Speaking of Junie—want to walk down to the beach and see what's keeping our young? Funny—when we bought this house Charles and I were disappointed that it had no beach of its own, but the public one turned out better for Lou and Chad. What with all the other little hellions to play with they don't get in each other's hair—and Nurse has company too. Well—what about it?"

"If you don't mind I think I'll stay here."

"All right." Louise walked off.

Presently Charles came out. He sat in the grass beside Kyrie's chair. He looked at her quizzically. "It's awfully quiet around here." When she did not break the quiet, he said, "What you want is a tower with one of those widow's walks that the fishermen's wives used to have. Then you could pace back and forth with your eyes out to sea."

"Sorry, Charles. What did you say?"

"Too much of a mouthful to repeat. Which reminds me—it's past the kids' lunchtime. Nurse usually brings them back ravening on the stroke of noon."

"Louise went down to the beach to call them."

"Here she comes now—and alone. Maybe it's one of Chad's difficult days—or Lou might be holding out for a picnic." He got up and went to meet Louise. Kyrie saw them converge at the lawn's end. The breeze ruffled Charles's sandy hair and he raised a hand to smooth it back. They stood talking, their words indistinguishable. Kyrie thought fleetingly, If he keeps worrying his hair like that he won't have any left. Then they parted, Louise hurrying toward the kitchen door, Charles walking swiftly in the direction of the beach.

When Louise reappeared, Will Babcock was with her, carrying a basket. Kyrie called, "What's going on?"

"It's such perfect weather we didn't have the heart to bring them up for lunch. So we're taking it down to them. No—sit still. You might miss Grid."

"What's happened to your voice?"

"Frog in my throat. See you."

Kyrie left her chair and went to the other side of the hedge so that she could see the road. The vehicles that passed while she stood there were widely spaced. She saw a baker's van, a Mercury, a battered old Chevrolet with fenders like cauliflower ears, a Ford sedan with "Suffolk County Police" printed on its door, two bicycles pedaled by boys in swimming trunks, a telephone installation truck.

This is stupid, she told herself drearily. He may not come until evening. Another Ford, a limousine this time, and following it a Buick ...

The Buick was driven by a man with curly white hair and a pointed, olive-skinned face. He braked as she started running down the road.

XII

Long before noon Dene Cameron half waked from what had been no beauty sleep. Her head ached and she was hot and terribly thirsty. Opening her eyes was an effort, but she knew that she must, because the alternative was drifting back into a feverish darkness torn painfully by fragments of broken dreams. So she forced her lids apart only to be greeted by a bewildering green dimness. And when she tried to move she could not. And when she tried to cry out, what issued from her gagged mouth was the ugly, muffled voice of nightmare.

She thought she was still asleep, still dreaming, had imagined the act of opening her eyes. I must really pull myself out of it, she thought. Because if I don't, Bridie will wake me—and my head hurts too much to endure her shouting. Why does my head hurt? Engaged with that puzzle, she drifted off again, treading her way through the piled-up shards of dreams.

An ash-blond Neddy Parks threatening her with an exploding lipstick—the disembodied voice of the butler announcing that accidents were being served, madam. Rain and a tangle of wet shrubbery. A massive silhouette on wheels. More rain and the frustrated melancholy of the rejected, and a patch of light on grass melting into a livid bruise that spread over the face of the earth as she fell. And wanting to answer the beloved voice that called her name, but she was a suckling pig with an apple....

Three times she tried to struggle back to full consciousness, and on the third achieved it. Her clothes were damp with sweat, or was it rain? Her hands and feet were tied, and a piece of cloth had been stuffed into her mouth. And the most important thing in life was to free her hands so that she could remove the cloth and drink—and drink. That done, there would be time enough to find out how it had come about that she lay bound and gagged on the sofa in Patsy's hideaway.

Extreme physical discomfort became unbearable torture. Robbed of blood by the tight cords, her hands, pressing into her back, were like lumps of ice. She managed to turn on her side to relieve the pressure, and strained to locate the knots. But the numbed long fingers had lost all suppleness and would not curve palmward. Tears rolled down her cheeks, tears that she could not brush away or even discipline away by biting her stretched lips. Easy, she warned herself. Easy. You'll do it. You've got to do it. No one is here to help and no one will come to help unless Sam takes it into his head ... She envisioned Sam's closed, censuring face. Sam, the Puritan, the avenger, descending upon her in crusading wrath, punishing her for daring to lapse from virtue within the gates of his kingdom. You're running a fever, she told herself. Someone hit you on the head and you're running a fever. You know it wasn't Sam. He's a family man. Narrow, but not cruel. Who was it? Easy. The skin will be burned away. Scars—deep scars on the smooth white wrists. Don't— Is it possible to run a fever and sweat at the same time? Not Sam. Who? The day I was here with Sam I noticed a knife on Patsy's desk—a knife with a rusting blade. If I could reach the knife ... Stop thinking. Blank your mind to what you're doing and sometimes it does itself. Is the cord loosening? Don't think of it. Long-sleeved dresses from now on to hide the seared flesh. Will it ever heal? Will I ever ...?

When Vera and Sam left I went back to the bedroom. I went back to Paul, but he was gone. If he'd stayed or if I—I couldn't let it end that way. I had to go to him, make everything clear between us. So I dressed. I put on the first dress I could reach—this damp crumpled thing—and a coat for the rain. If it could rain now—rain down through this roof—seep through the gag into my dry throat. Where is the coat I wore? I had a flashlight, too. I rummaged for it in a kitchen drawer. Bridie will set the drawer to rights—

Bridie is dead. That's what they came to tell me. Dead—killed by a truck. I saw a truck. Where? Will I die—here in Patsy's hideaway? I came to Sandy Crest in a dirty train to die—to meet Paul and to die of thirst. I could laugh. Perhaps I am laughing. Internal hemorrhage of laughter ... Easy ... easy ...

I walked through the rain to Paul's house. I felt so brave—so sure—a woman who would fight for what she had. I walked fast and when I got there no light was showing. But I used the flashlight. The path to the dark house was narrowed by overgrown shrubbery. I could hardly keep to it. My stockings were soaked and torn before I made the front door and knocked. I pounded. I didn't care who heard—Tim Masters or anyone. But no one came. Then I thought, Perhaps they don't use this door—perhaps they don't use the front of the house at all and can't hear me....

Is the cord slackening? If I squeezed my fingers together would it slide? No—don't—it hurts—how it hurts. My head feels very strange. Is the skin broken? Does that taut sensation mean clotted blood on my scalp—my hair? In my hurry I pinned it up any old way. It's loose now—the pins fallen out—hag loose.

I walked around to the back of the house. There too the windows were dark. I couldn't understand it. Paul had come to me on foot to say goodbye. But even if he had planned to run away in the night he would surely have to return for his possessions, his car. Then why wasn't there light to show he had returned? He couldn't have packed and made off so fast, not even if he left my bedroom the moment Vera and Sam came. They didn't stay so long. It seemed long, but it wasn't.

The rain fell in almost opaque sheets. My flashlight wasn't much help. I must have wandered afield, because I couldn't find the back door. Something brought me up short. I banged my knee and my shoulder against it. A shed? Not a shed. It was hard and I think I swore with the pain. At any rate I stood quite still to get my bearings. And I couldn't. And I thought, To hell with Tim Masters. And I shouted like an angry child, Paul, I'm here. Come and find me.

If I could shout now. If I could drink—or just let the saliva flow—and swallow. The cloth of the gag must have been too big for my mouth. I can feel a piece of it against my chin. Could I get a purchase on it without using my hands—roll on my face and wedge it between cushion and couch—and pull? But what if I roll and cannot roll again? I'll smother—and my last breath will be the dust of Patsy's cretonne cushion. End of a scarlet woman. Patsy can change the name to Horror House and charge admission. Don't let me lose control—don't let my mind give way—don't let me smother.

Adults don't smother so easily. I'm adult. Soon someone will find me. Sam spoke of remodeling as a surprise for Patsy. Maybe he— No he'll be busy making arrangements for the funeral—Bridie's funeral—my funeral.

She heaved herself around, and the couch seemed to heave. Almost she let her eyelids droop to shut out the swirling green dimness. It's because I need water, she thought. Maybe food, too. Nothing since the party. How long ago was that?

It took precious strength to keep the eyelids raised, to inch herself into position, to wedge the end of the gag under the cushion, to secure the cushion with her shoulders, to arch her neck. But the cushion was too soft to act as a vise. The cloth slipped from under it, dangled mockingly. And all was as before, and nothing gained, and something lost as the cushion slid over the back of the couch to the floor. All was— All was not lost. A nail. A thin bent nail sticking out of the wooden frame. For want of a nail ... She relaxed her arched neck, declined her head. A black tangle of silky hair obscured vision. She had to shake it back to start again after the room stopped heaving. The nail was sharp. It made a vicious scratch on her chin. Let it hook the cloth, she prayed. Let it—please ...

When it happened she could not believe it, she was afraid to put it to the test. But it held, did not tear the material as she twisted and squirmed toward the foot of the couch until she felt the wad move in her mouth, become smaller, small enough for her to expel with breath and tongue the last clinging piece.

She squirmed upward again, seeing as she moved what was impaled on the hooked nail. A man's square green neckerchief, limp and revolting. She fought and mastered the rising nausea, and, panting, was content to rest her cheek on the hard cushionless upholstery, to moisten her lips, to swallow the gathering saliva.

I had shouted, "Come and get me." And I waited, certain that Paul would emerge from the dark house. And I thought I heard a door opening, and I moved toward the sound. And I found the door. But it was closed when I reached it, closed and locked. And there was nothing for me to do but find my way back to the gatehouse.

The walk back seemed endless. My knee hurt where it had

banged against the—the truck. Why was a truck parked behind Paul's house so late at night? Had he been lurking all that while at some window, watching me, waiting for me to go so that he could make his departure bag and baggage? And then, did he follow my limping retreat to make sure that I would trouble him no more? Paul? Never Paul.

I can't get it straight. I'm muddled still. Is there water here in this cabin? Water would clear my head. But Sam said something about installing electricity. And no electricity means no running water. When we walked that day did I imagine seeing a well at the back? How can I get to that well? With hobbled feet how can I even limp? Not that my knee hurts now—it's better.

Limping along the road like a stoned dog. If anyone followed me back to the gatehouse the footsteps were covered by rain and rustling leaves. Finally I saw the lights I'd left. They looked sane and reassuring. Suddenly I was no longer defeated. Light is important to me, I thought. If artificial light has this effect, tomorrow's sun will help me even more. Now I'll have a warm bath, and I'll get into my beautiful, comfortable bed and sleep. And in tomorrow's sun I'll make sane reassuring plans. I'm Dene Cameron. Paul can't leave me just like that. No reason exists with power enough to keep him away from me.

But I never reached the gatehouse. I got no further than the trees at the lawn's edge. I felt the blow and I felt the wet grass on my face. And very far away I heard Paul's voice. I tried to answer. I couldn't have answered even without the hand that clamped over my mouth. Not the hand that went with the faraway voice. The small, hard hand of the leprechaun. Green neckerchief of the leprechaun. Yellow eyes of a goat. I saw them. I'm not imagining. I did see them. And then I saw nothing.

He had warned me against Paul. I thought he wanted me himself. Did he take ...! Put that thought away. Conscious or unconscious, awake or dreaming, you'd know. You'd know.

Was he strong enough to carry me here—me a dead weight? He must have been. Anyone else is out of the question. That day on the beach I was surprised to see his steely, compact build, the tight muscular arms ...

Why? Mad? Greedy because they had some sort of money deal on? Frightened that I would spoil their plans? Was it his intention to escape with Paul before Mrs. Nelson had time to reveal whatever it was she knew. Homicide. Her husband works for Homicide. No—that doesn't mean— It couldn't. No one's been killed. Nothing like that. Money—something to do with money. Masters is that sort. And I'm here trussed like a pig because he was afraid I'd spoil his game—prevail upon Paul to stay and face the music.

Well—the pig is at least rid of the apple. The pig can squeal to attract attention should anyone pass by—and that's a miracle.

Once more she began to struggle with her bonds. It was sweet to be able to moan, and she gave way to moaning between endeavors, her mind detached and busy at its own laboring.

Where was Paul when I heard him call my name? Had he returned to the gatehouse to tell me he could not leave after all? And was he, too, defeated by the belief that I lurked inside and would not answer? Where is he now? At the wheel of his car, lengthening the distance between us? Does Tim Masters sit beside him, smiling falsely, knowing what he knows, secure in what he knows and in what Paul does not know? But he is not secure unless he took steps to silence Mrs. Nelson. I saw by her face that she did not intend to let the matter rest. What a fool he was to imagine that a lipsticked warning on a handkerchief would stay her. And my apologies to Neddy Parks. If Neddy Parks walked in now I would clasp his hand—after he freed mine.

She did not discover at once that the second miracle had occurred, was only vaguely conscious of a different sensation in the region of her fingers, a tingling that had not been there before. She worked experimentally, holding her breath for fear of disappointment. But it was true. Somehow in her striving, the constricting circlet of cords had enlarged enough for one hand to wriggle through. She eased her arms to her sides and lay flat for a few moments in exhausted pain-laced triumph. Then she began to flex her fingers. She even addressed them in a low hoarse voice. "You'll be all right. You'll be part of me as soon as I can send the blood back into you."

She spread them out from the palms and slid them gently up and down her sides. They warmed a little, and the tingling lessened. She thought that presently she could sit up and give them a real massage and untie her ankles—and find that well—and drink.

When she did sit up she had to avert her eyes from the lacerated wrists. They will heal, she promised herself. I have good blood. If there's anything to worry about it's my head. She was able now to touch the clotted hair at the back of her scalp. The area beneath it was sensitive. She withdrew her hand, deciding that for the moment it might be better not to know the extent of the injury.

Knees drawn almost to her chin, and with thirst as a goad, she persevered with the rest of the program. There were interludes when she had to stop and grit her teeth. And finally, when the task was done and she stood upright, it seemed a dangerous mile to the door of Patsy's hideaway. And when she had achieved that mile, the door was padlocked on the outside.

Fury revitalized her. She forgot her wounds. She picked up a book and flung it through the window. Bits of shattered glass flew into the room, but she did not think to step aside. Sanity did not return until she was just about to force her head and body past the jagged opening. Then she shuddered and drew back. She, Dene Cameron, for whom a broken fingernail or the sting of an insect had once been tragedy, saw herself cut to ribbons by her own willful offices. And there was the flimsy window catch to be released at a touch. She raised the window as far as it would go, studied the sill for treacherous bits of glass, and somehow, somehow climbed through.

She scarcely felt the petty scratches inflicted by the shrubbery outside. But she blinked at the sun as one who had undergone years of imprisonment in a dark cell. Steadying her shaking body against the boards of the cabin, she propelled herself around to the back.

The well was there, a roped bucket beside it. The well's cover was half off, and it seemed to her that she could see water glistening very near the top. She dropped to her knees, and then pitched forward.

XIII

"To the rescue on horseback," Kyrie said breathlessly, because of the way that Gridley Nelson swooped her into the car was reminiscent of a knight hoisting his lady to a pillion. She flung her arms around him.

When they separated they looked at each other and each sighed with satisfaction. Then they both grinned.

Nelson said, "So you've been drumming up trade for me."

"It drummed itself up." Her face clouded. "Grid—the housekeeper said he came to talk to me a little before twelve this morning—only I was out with Louise. Grid—if I hadn't gone to that party—"

"The 'ifs' started much further back than the party—and none of them are your doing."

"I've been telling myself that. But it's much more comforting when you say it. Did you bring the magazines with you?"

"I brought the one you think is significant. And up to the moment I left the office, I've been checking into the life and times of Brian MacKenzie."

"Poor Grid. I bet you got there at the crack of dawn this morning." Then she repeated, "Brian MacKenzie," and nodded. "I knew it began with M-c or M-a-c. It's much more like him that Paul Debrulet."

"Well—they'll both keep until I get my bearings. Now then—how long is the last lap of the journey?"

She indicated the Cotter hedge, not more than a few yards away, and could not help laughing at his expression.

He approved the laugh. "And me thinking you must be footsore and weary from trudging over hill and dale to greet your lawful husband." He started the car. "Has Junie put a candle in the window?"

"Junie's picnicking on the beach with Lou and Chad and Nurse. It was sort of a last-minute decision—and of course we couldn't be sure when you'd arrive."

He turned in through the hedge, spotted the garage, and headed for it.

"Don't bother to put the car away, Grid. You might need—I mean it will be a nuisance to take it out every time."

So he parked, got out, and did the habitual little jig step to flex his long legs. The sun shone on his curly white hair. "Pretty near perfect," he said, seeming to take in everything at once.

"It is now." She thought that no matter where he was he always added something to the background. It was not so much that he stood out, as that he belonged.

He held out a hand to her. "If you sit in that car mooning much longer, Louise and Charles will accuse me of having a soppy wife."

"I don't think they've come back from the beach." She took his hand and got out. "I am soppy. You haven't had lunch—you must be starving."

"Not exactly. Sammy fixed me an outsized breakfast and seasoned it with messages for you and Junie." He slung his bag out of the car, laid an arm across Kyrie's shoulder, and they walked up to the house.

Mrs. Babcock was crossing the front hall as they entered. She gave Nelson a startled look and turned quickly toward the kitchen.

Kyrie called her back. "Mrs. Babcock, this is my husband."

Nelson smiled at her, extending his hand.

She accepted it gingerly. Her "pleased to meet you" was completely lacking in pleasure. She said, "Excuse me—I—I must see to lunch," and retreated.

"What's the matter with her?" Nelson asked. "You wrote that she was such a cheerful, friendly woman."

"She is. Perhaps she's upset because Louise and Charles are delaying lunch. Come on—I'll show you our quarters." Upstairs he dropped his bag, included her in his survey of the room, and said, "Who could ask for more? Where does Junie hang his hat?"

"Far away—around the bend in the corridor. But this morning he found his way here all by himself. He'll be back for his nap soon, and while he's getting set for it you can talk shop to him."

"Don't worry. I have all day tomorrow too—and a slice of Monday."

"Darling—how wonderful—or it would be if—"

"It will be. Don't I hear a phone ringing somewhere?"

"Yes—Mrs. Babcock will take it."

"It might be Chief Comerford. I stopped at his office on the way, but he was out so I left word for him to get in touch with me."

"Oh." Kyrie listened to the ringing. "Then maybe I'd better answer. There's an extension in Louise's room. Don't go 'way."

Chief Comerford was not on the telephone. Vera Curtis was. She said, "Mrs. Babcock? I've been ringing and ringing. Is Mrs. Nelson there? She's the one I'd like to speak to...."

Kyrie identified herself. She thanked Vera Curtis for the party, and for the use of the car, expressed sympathy for the death of the maid, and waited.

"You're very kind, but I'm afraid it wasn't a successful evening for anyone," Vera said. "I do wish you'd send me the bill for that beautiful dress. However—that isn't why I called. You spent some time alone with Dene, and I know how it is when women get together, so I wondered if she'd mentioned anything about her plans?"

Kyrie said slowly, "We talked, but—"

Vera interrupted her. "I don't mean to pry, but did you talk about anything in particular?" She floundered. "That is, did she happen to say— No—I guess I'm just wasting your time. Dene doesn't make a habit of confiding in—in people—and of course you were with her before Sam delivered his little—which is neither here nor there." She drew breath. "It's just that I'm a bit worried. This morning I phoned the gatehouse to tell her not to get her own breakfast—I'd send a maid over. You see—poor Bridie was assigned to look after her and— Well—anyway Dene didn't answer the phone. I didn't want to keep ringing and wake her so I decided to try later on, only the morning went so quickly I didn't get around to it until a few minutes ago. And then I thought I might as well drive over because there were so many things I wanted to discuss with her. But the funny thing is she's not there. When she didn't come to the door I let myself in. After all, it's almost one o'clock and I knew she wouldn't be asleep. Well—the lights were on in the entrance hall and in the living room and in her bedroom, and her bed was made up, which certainly means she couldn't have slept there, doesn't it?" She did not wait for confirmation. "Even if she did make the bed when she got up, the lights put a different complexion on it, don't they? She wouldn't have slept with them on, and she wouldn't have turned them on in the morning because on a day like today that room is fairly flooded with sun. I don't want to go to Sam with it—I know what he'll say —so I just called you on the chance that she—"

Kyrie, who had been listening hard, managed to break in. "Are her clothes gone?"

"No—the closets are full, and her luggage is there. Really, I don't know what to think."

Neither did Kyrie.

"She has such good manners. I can't believe— No matter what happened I can't believe she'd disappear without even leaving a note, but women do such rash things when—when— I haven't a doubt Dene can take care of herself under any circumstances, but with those lights on and all I—"

Kyrie said, "Mrs. Curtis, I think you should tell your husband. The lights aren't so unusual—people often turn them on absent-mindedly in broad daylight—but she might have gone out for a walk and turned her ankle or—"

"Oh dear—I never thought of that. Would she have gone without breakfast? The kitchen's absolutely spick and span. Well—all right. I will tell Sam. He knows the grounds better than I do. As a matter of fact he took Dene over them while I was away—my aunt, you know, but he'll probably scoff at the whole thing and start off on the same old track again. Excuse me, Mrs. Nelson—Kyrie—I'm sure you haven't the faintest notion of what I'm talking about."

Kyrie had a faint notion. She hesitated. "By the way—one of your guests called here this morning while I was out—Mr. Debrulet."

"He did!" The exclamation was ripe with relief. "Then Dene can't be with—I suppose he wanted to apologize for spoiling your dress, which proves he's a gentleman no matter what Sam— Well—speaking of husbands, Charles said you were expecting yours."

"He's just arrived."

"Why didn't you tell me—I wouldn't have kept you. I do hope he'll stay long enough for us to have a get-together. I'm dying to meet him."

Kyrie murmured a politeness, and added, "Will you please let me know as soon as you find out about Dene?"

"I will, but I'm sure it's all a tempest in a teapot, only, after last night my nerves are edgy. But your theory about the lights in the gatehouse is very reassuring—I've done it myself, not in all the rooms, though—just a lamp when I wasn't thinking. Anyway I will tell Sam—although I hate to. Goodbye for now—and thank you."

Kyrie said goodbye and hung up.

Nelson had unpacked and neatly disposed of his belongings. A few large manila envelopes, the magazine, and some interesting packages lay on the bed.

"I take it that wasn't Chief Comerford," Nelson said, "unless he's more long-winded than he was when I spoke to him." He indicated the packages. "Gifts for you and Junie and the Cotters."

"Thank you, darling. Which one is mine?" In spite of herself she sounded halfhearted, and her eyes glossed over the packages and clung to the magazine.

"Never mind. We'll have a grand opening later." He picked up the magazine. "Here—I've marked the page. Study the pictures carefully. Take your time."

She took her time. Finally she said forlornly, "There isn't a doubt in my mind."

His deep-set brown eyes regarded her gravely. "But there *is* a doubt that he's guilty until he's been tried and convicted—in spite of all the evidence against him. Hold on to that thought." He took her hand. "Who was on the phone?"

She told him in less words than Vera had used, including in her brief recital Dene's self-confessed involvement with Debrulet-MacKenzie. She ended by getting the handkerchief with the spindly red "DON'T" printed on it.

He examined it without much interest. "We're looking for a murderer—a murderer who is by no means a half-wit."

"Then you don't …?"

"It certainly doesn't seem consistent."

"Do you think Dene Cameron's disappearance ties in?"

"I don't know if it is a disappearance. I'm so new and cold to the whole case that what I don't know far overbalances the little I've managed to dig up." His expressive mouth looked rueful.

She said loyally, "If you hadn't come to it cold—if you'd been on the scene—he'd never have got a chance to skip, but this way it's as though it happened in another country."

"And besides, the wench is dead."

She shuddered. *But that happened in another country—and besides, the wench is dead.* Neither she nor Grid was sure of the quotation's accuracy or of its source, although Grid held out for Marlowe. But it had become a shared habit to repeat it as scoffing comment upon conversational irrelevance. She hoped with all her heart that the disappearance of Dene Cameron was irrelevant to the death of a California wife.

He said, "Kyrie—if you're worried about the Cameron girl I'll take a run over to the Curtises and—"

"No—then you'd miss the police chief's call. I wish he *would* call."

"He's probably out chasing down that hit-and-run driver of last night. When I talked with him on the phone I gathered that he's never had so much happen at once in the whole tenure of his office."

"It was the hit-and-run thing that really decided me about calling you."

He knit his brow.

She told him about her encounter with the truck. She said, "But thinking it over it can't have anything to do with the California murder—or with Dene not being home. She's certainly not with Debrulet—I mean MacKenzie. Tim Masters's presence in his house would make that sort of situation impossible."

"Who's Tim Masters?"

"Haven't I mentioned him? He's MacKenzie's guest. He was at the party too—not very—" She searched for words. "Vulgar.

Not that I mind a certain type of vulgarity, but—well—I just didn't like him. MacKenzie and he didn't seem to have much in common either."

"Is he from around here?"

"I don't know. I don't suppose so, or he wouldn't be a house guest." She went back to Dene. "If Dene were with MacKenzie she'd have too much sense to let him come to see me this morning. She'd realize it wouldn't do any good."

"But she doesn't know he's a murder suspect—or does she?"

"She does know there's something in the wind. I've a feeling she knew it even before I did my best to spill the beans last night. But she's so definitely on his side that even if she is with him it's unlikely he'd do her harm. According to the magazine story, it's not as though he's a psychopath who kills for the sake of killing—unless the checking you did revealed ...?"

He shook his head. "Up to the time his wife was found dead he'd led an exemplary life. He had an excellent war record, and is considered to be an outstanding sculptor. He and his wife lived alone in a large house in Belvedere. Their only child died when he was about three and—"

"Oh—how ...?"

"An accident." Nelson hurried on. "They entertained occasionally and they had house guests—usually males. It appears that his wife had more than a mild predilection for males."

"What about him?" Kyrie asked, thinking of Dene again. "Did you discover that he had more than a mild predilection for females?"

"No—there's nothing to indicate it. His work seemed to be the beginning and end of his existence, especially after the child died. I got all this from conversations with the California police who had done a job of interviewing his friends and acquaintances. Just before his wife's murder he had won a competition participated in by various leading American sculptors to do a statue for the garden of a children's hospital in Santa Monica. The prize money, ten thousand dollars, was presumably what he used to make a getaway. At any rate he had cashed the check at his bank a few days earlier, and the California authorities believe that this points to premeditation. The money was awarded on the merits of the sketches and models he submitted—with the understanding that it would give the winner freedom from possible economic strain while he completed the work. And naturally it follows that the sponsors of the competition are very much interested in finding him. But I have a theory that—" He broke off. Someone was running up the stairs. Because he was facing the door he saw Charles first. Before Kyrie turned he was shaking hands with him.

Charles said in a curiously flat voice, "Swell you could come, Grid. Can you use a drink before lunch?"

Nelson inspected him briefly. "I can."

"Then let's go down."

"Stag party?" Kyrie said.

"Well—Louise is coming up in a moment to discuss private domestic business with you."

Nelson called over his shoulder, "You and Louise might investigate those packages while you're about it."

"A brush-off," Kyrie said. But she addressed the empty doorway.

Neither of the men spoke until they reached the foot of the stairs. There Nelson halted and said, "What's wrong, Charles?"

"Junie's lost."

"What?" Nelson gripped his arm.

Charles got it out fast. "The kids were playing in the sand and Junie threw a handful at Chad. It blew into his eyes and he ran up to complain to Nurse. She was attending to him and she thought that Junie was safe with Lou—and when she looked up again he'd gone. Lou hadn't seen him wander off either."

Nelson said, "The water …?"

"Take it easy. Not a chance. The tide in the bay is way out—even a baby like Junie would have to walk pretty far to have it come past his knees. Anyway, a couple of women said they caught a glimpse of him in the lane behind the beach. There were a few cars parked there and they thought he belonged in one of them."

Nelson unclamped his fingers. "How long ago did it happen?" he said quietly.

"On toward twelve—just as Nurse was thinking of returning to the house for lunch. She couldn't believe Junie had strayed very far, because she hadn't stopped watching him for more than a few minutes. There were about ten other people on the beach, which isn't large, and they all joined in the search. They covered the private beaches on either side which belong to the waterfront houses, although it's unlikely he could have climbed over the stone boundaries, and they looked in the cars in the lane in case he'd crawled into one and fallen asleep."

"Where does the lane—"

"It's short. It angles onto the road. But when we're walking we don't bother with the road. We cut across the level field at the side of our house and it takes us right to where the beach starts."

Louise came into the hall. Her voice was unsteady. "Junie will be found, Grid. We called Chief Comerford. He's down there now asking questions and he's sent out an alarm. The people around here are all good and helpful—they'll be on the lookout."

Nelson tried to smile at her. "Go up to Kyrie and be as natural as you can—and keep her as long as you can."

She nodded, and started up the stairs. Charles said, "Grid, do you want to talk to Nurse? I can—"

"No—I expect she's told you all she knows. Where does MacKenzie live?"

"MacKenzie?"

"Debrulet. He was here at about that time, wasn't he?"

"Good lord!"

"Where does he live?"

Charles pulled himself together. "Curtis said he'd rented the Tate place, but—"

"Come on, then." Nelson was at the door. "You'll have to show me where it is." He ran out of the house and was at the wheel of his car, pressing the starter before Charles slid in beside him. "Kyrie told me not to put the car in the garage," he said expressionlessly. "Which way?"

"The way you came. Listen, Grid, according to Kyrie, the fellow is in enough trouble. A stunt like that would only buy him more."

Nelson did not answer, and Charles let some of the scenery rush by before he spoke again, nervously, as though he could not help it. "I don't know what to think. We looked under the tarpaulins in the few boats that were beached; we looked behind every tree, almost beneath every blade of grass in the field, and in every structure on the road along the way. A small crowd joined in—maybe two dozen people—and every one of them used their eyes and their wits. Nurse had started the search before Louise went down to see what was keeping her. She wasn't too worried at first. Junie had a habit of wandering off. Nurse is a sane, conscientious woman—she—"

"No one's to blame, Charles."

Charles cleared his throat. "What makes you so sure that Debrulet—"

"I'm not sure of anything. The timing may be pure

coincidence. I'm looking into it because it's the first thing that jumped into my mind. From what you say there's no point in going over the area of your search again, and I've got to do something. Junie's a very little boy. He's quick on his legs, but the distance he can cover by himself is limited. So it stands to reason that some car picked him up. And it stands to reason that anyone but MacKenzie would have taken him to the nearest police station. If he said he was Junie Nelson it wouldn't be a name that even a resident could place—and I doubt if Cotter has registered with him."

Charles said mechanically, "Take the next turn." Then he said, "You are sure MacKenzie and Debrulet are the same man?"

"Kyrie is sure." Distress tugged at Nelson's mouth. "I'm glad Louise is with her. She'll manage to keep her occupied?"

"You can count on Louise. And Kyrie won't ask questions, because she thinks Junie is with the other children." He groaned. "I hope to God she never has to know."

"Was Junie wearing only bathing trunks?"

"No—Nurse makes them wrap up after they've got wet. He had on a red terry-cloth robe. Kyrie told us she'd bought a red one so that she could spot him easily. He was—he's such a little eel." He forced a heartiness. "That robe will be easy for anyone to spot, and at least we needn't worry about a traffic accident, because, as you say, he couldn't have reached the main road by himself and the traffic on the side road is practically nonexistent."

"How much further is it to the Tate place?"

"See where that line of trees ends? ... it's there. Grid—do you carry a gun?"

"I won't need a gun—and you'll wait outside."

"The hell I will. He's a big powerful guy, and if he turns nasty you might need me."

Nelson looked sideways at his slight figure. "I might. Do you know anything about the man who's staying with him?"

"The man who came to the party, Masters? No—I'd never seen him before last night. Sam Curtis said he only turned up in Sandy Crest a week ago. I remember thinking that he and Debrulet were a Mutt and Jeff combination." His smile was self-deprecating. "Well—if he's around and wants to play at least I can take him on. This is it. Do we drive right up to the door or—"

"I'll leave the car here," Nelson said. He braked and got out.

The overgrown path to the house was not wide enough for the two of them. They walked single-file, Charles close on Nelson's heels. A breeze moved the unpruned branches of trees on either side, releasing drops of last night's rain. Neglect of the grounds was in evidence everywhere. The grass grew coarse and high, and weeds all but obscured the signs of former landscaping.

The house was a large sturdy affair built in the days when men were proud of their labor and of the materials they used. Nelson tried the knob of the door with one hand, and knocked with the other. The door did not give, and no one answered the knock though he repeated it several times.

Charles said, "I've been thinking. If he did make off with Junie is it likely he'd bring him here?"

"We'll try the back door," Nelson said.

An attempt had been made to order the grounds at the back. The grass was cut, and a patch of soil had been turned over and fenced off with cords and stakes. Within its limits green sprouts promised a kitchen garden. But the promise would not be fulfilled, because the fencing job looked unfinished. It left great gaps for rabbits and other small vandals.

Charles said unnecessarily, "There's a car here, but it might belong to Masters." He walked over to a huge barn and peered in. "I guess this is what he uses as a garage when— Well, what do you know? He's planning a getaway all right."

Nelson gave the barn no more than a brief, abstracted glance. His attention was focused upon the house.

A lean-to had been attached to the parent structure. It was not a recent addition. Its shingles were as weathered as the rest. But its entrance was boarded up with new lumber.

Charles turned away from the barn. He lowered his voice, "Grid—he's got a truck in there."

Nelson walked to the door in the house proper. He tried it and met with no opposition. He had reached the center of the old-fashioned kitchen before Charles caught up with him. Then he wheeled and almost seemed to point at the door on the lean-to side.

Charles whispered, "He's—he's talking to somebody—" Nelson gestured him to silence.

They heard a male voice say, "Look here, old boy, you've got to cooperate. You mustn't think for a moment that I want to get rid of you, but that's the way it is, so—"

Then came the anguished wail of a child.

XIV

Nelson knew the voice of his son. He knew every note of its considerable range. Yet it was Charles who took action, shoving past him to burst into the room.

Once the room had been a summer kitchen. Now it was a working studio dominated by a block of pink Georgia marble on a low wooden platform. Near the platform a bench held a variety of implements; short-handled iron hammers, chisels, and texturing tools. The floor was littered with orthographic drawings on newsprint paper, the wall shelves crowded with clay figurines.

Opposite the block the man who called himself Debrulet sat on a tall stool with the red-robed Junie in his arms. He was addressing the child earnestly, desperately. "Don't cry, old boy. Be a sport. Listen—if you come with me I'll give you a big lump of the stuff—much bigger than the piece you've got—and you can—"

Charles, weaving his way around obstacles, shouted, "Put him down!" He planted himself before the stool.

Junie stopped wailing. He regarded Charles with mild interest and said, "No." The lump of plasticine in his hand was roughly modeled to the shape of a dog. It flattened in his clutch as he threw his arms around Debrulet's neck.

Debrulet said, "Hey—don't strangle me," and Junie laughed and released his hold. He waved the plasticine with dangerous abandon. "Poor dog sick—fix him all better."

"Put him down," Charles repeated lamely.

"Easier said than done. Want to try to take him?"

Before Charles could interpret the remark as a challenge, Nelson stepped into view. He said easily, "Do I see Mr. Junie Nelson?"

Junie started at the familiar voice. His eyes widened. He said, "Daddy," uncertainly, and wiggled in Debrulet's arms. "Down—that's my daddy—down."

"Stop squirming. You'll fall." Debrulet got off the stool and set him on his sturdy legs.

Nelson swooped. He swung the child to the level of his cheek, trying not to hold him too tightly. He sat down suddenly on the vacated stool. His throat was dry. "Charles, you'd better telephone Louise."

"You'll find the phone in the hall to the right of the kitchen,"

Debrulet said.

Charles looked doubtful, nodded stiffly, and went off.

Junie pressed contentedly against Nelson's shoulder. "We stay here. Make more dogs—tenteen big big dogs."

"That's the way it's been going," Debrulet said.

Nelson looked at him. "How has it been going?"

"Your son is like the man who came to dinner. I take it he is your son—and that you're the New York police officer—"

"And you're Brian MacKenzie." Nelson did not need corroboration. Even without the magazine's testimony it was there on the handsome, defeated face.

"How did you get that far?" Debrulet said tonelessly. "Until last night I never saw your wife. How did she ...?"

Nelson told him. Then he said, "How far did you hope to get with this last move?"

"You're off your beat."

"Am I?" Nelson glanced at the top of Junie's silky head. The child was quiet, engrossed with the plasticine.

"Yes—if you share Cotter's belief that I planned to hurt the boy," Debrulet said. "He was crying because—"

"You needn't explain his cries to me. I recognize the variations. The one I heard when I came in wasn't pain—it was, 'I'm going to have my own way and see if I don't.'"

Debrulet gave him a speculative glance. He almost smiled.

"Suppose you tell me how he happens to be here," Nelson said.

"I went to see your wife this morning—and I overshot the house. So I got out of my car and walked back to it. I hoped to beg a little time from her—that was all. But she was out. When I got back to the car I didn't know I'd taken on a passenger. He'd climbed into the back and he must have slept for the length of the ride home. He woke when I hit a bump in the driveway and said he was hungry, so I took him into the house to give him some milk before the ride back. I wasn't sure who he was—he didn't feel like supplying his name—but I had a suspicion because he resembles his mother—you more, though, now that I—" He broke off to address Charles, who had reentered the room. "Find the telephone?"

"Yes—and if your story's true why didn't it occur to you to use it? You must have realized that his mother would be—"

Junie looked up and said, "Mummy?" as though he had made a rather frightening discovery.

Debrulet said, "I'd lost my urge to speak to his mother." He added bleakly, "No—it didn't occur to me that she'd be worried, since she'd allowed him to wander off on his own. It was my intention to drive him back and deposit him behind your hedge—and go about my business as though the whole incident had never happened, but he had other ideas. He slipped in here the minute my back was turned and refused to be coaxed out again—and it didn't suit me to be caught in public with a screaming, struggling child."

"That I can understand," Charles said belligerently.

Junie dropped the plasticine. It landed on the floor with a soft plop. He said, "Down. Find Mummy."

"Uncle Charles is going to find her right away," Nelson said. He set Junie down and waited.

Junie picked up the plasticine. "Big Uncle fix dog?"

"Big Uncle's sick," Nelson said.

Debrulet nodded. "Sicker than any dog, Junie."

Junie's lips formed a mock-mournful, "Oh." He patted Debrulet's legs with the sticky lump. Debrulet made a gesture toward him, then thrust both his hands into his pockets.

Nelson risked all, using the authoritative voice of his profession. "You go with Uncle Charles and find Mummy."

Surprisingly it worked. Junie said a loud clear, "Yes," and tugged at Charles's slacks.

"But you'll need the car, Grid," Charles said.

"I'll manage."

"Well—" Charles caught the signal and closed his mouth. He squatted and said, "Pickaback?"

Junie was willing. He climbed on and thumped Charles's sides with his bare feet. At the door Charles turned and said loudly, "I told Louise to get in touch with Chief Comerford, Grid. He should be here any minute."

Debrulet's mouth twisted. "That ought to relieve you, Nelson. It means you're quite safe."

Nelson took a package of cigarettes from his pocket and offered it. Debrulet said, "Thanks," and produced matches. Outside the kitchen door slammed. Nelson went to stand before the marble block. Enough of it had been chipped away to release the stone's inner life, and the form the sculpture would take was emerging as a massive unit suggesting a group of small human bodies.

"Art critic, too," Debrulet said nastily.

"Is this what you wanted to beg time for?"

"What else is there?"

"I see."

Again Debrulet gave him a speculative look. He shook his head. "Loose talk. You couldn't possibly see."

"There's nothing very subtle involved," Nelson said. "I managed to unearth some information about you before I left town this morning. This simply confirms a theory I'd been toying with—that life no longer holds anything for you equaling the importance of your work."

"Except for a short while it never did hold anything of equal importance. I only thought it did."

Nelson wondered if "a short while" referred to the brief existence of the man's son. He said with less condemnation than seemed warranted, "So naturally you couldn't let a murder investigation obstruct the current project."

Debrulet dropped his cigarette and ground it out with his heel. "Funny thing—I've often imagined what it would be like when the police caught up with me, but I never imagined a conversation like this. The dialogue ran more to the 'Come quietly, I've got you covered' routine."

"I'm afraid it amounts to the same thing."

"Afraid? What's the matter—don't you like your job? Is that what's turned you white so young?"

Nelson observed the insolence on his face. He also observed that he was hard put to keep it there. He said, "You don't have to answer—but did you kill your wife?"

"In the interests of originality I'm almost tempted to say yes."

"Is 'yes' the truth?"

"No—and I'm sure you believe me."

"I know too little about the case to have arrived at any conclusion. Your guilt or innocence is a matter for the California courts to—"

"And of course you intend to see that I get back to California to stand trial." Debrulet's voice choked. "Why in God's name did you and your wife have to horn in? Isn't there enough crime in New York to keep you busy?" He turned away abruptly. His hand went out as though to caress the marble. It was like the half-completed gesture he had made toward Junie. He said, "What are we waiting for—or does etiquette demand that Big Chief What's-his-name get into the act?"

"What were *you* waiting for?" Nelson said. He recalled Charles's mention of a truck in the barn. "You have a truck standing ready. Why didn't you leave last night—or early this morning?"

"You've figured everything else out unassisted. Carry on."

"I'll take a guess or two. First, that strong as you are you can't load that statue onto the truck unaided ..."

"You don't need the second guess."

"What about the friend who's visiting you? Couldn't the two of you—"

"Look—your social sense is getting the better of you. You don't have to entertain me with polite conversation until the reserves arrive." His eyes were glued to the marble. "If you really want to be helpful see that my—that the stone is shipped to California—and use what influence you have to get me a cell big enough to work in."

"You said you didn't kill your wife."

"What difference does that make? Since you're so open-minded here's another tidbit for you to chew on. My wife was a bitch. Her death left no gap. You couldn't mention any woman living who has made smaller contribution to society." With no warning he picked up a short-handled hammer from the workbench. Its weighty iron head looked murderous. Nelson's body tensed. But Debrulet mated the hammer with a tooth chisel, and attacked the stone in one of the untouched areas that bore directive markings.

He used deft sure strokes. It seemed to Nelson, out of his limited knowledge of the art, that as he watched, the planes in the area clarified. It also seemed that he himself had completely faded out of the sculptor's consciousness.

Then Debrulet, stepping back, collided with him, and said, "Hell—hell—hell," and relinquished his tools. His hands, which had been steady, trembled, and he clenched them. "What shall I do?" he said. "Why couldn't they have let me finish it? After that I wouldn't care." He began to pace the room, kicking obstacles out of his way. "Damn Mothy—he —" He wheeled, and for a moment it appeared that Nelson was another obstacle to be kicked out of his path. Instead he walked around him, sat down, and dropped his head to his hands.

Nelson said, "Is Mothy the Tim Masters who's staying with you?"

Debrulet did not answer.

"Did he come here from California?"

Debrulet looked up. "Is that your business too?"

"It might be. If he does come from California he's aware that you're wanted for murder, which makes him guilty of withholding knowledge of your whereabouts from the authorities—or worse, of complicity, because obviously he's gone off somewhere to get something you need for your second escape. That's why you've been delayed."

"He comes from Timbuctoo. He's a bum and I never saw him before he turned up here at the back door to beg a handout. I took him in because I'm a very kind murderer."

"You're doing him a disservice by announcing that he needs to be shielded."

Debrulet yelled, "Go shield your—" He lowered his voice. "No—don't. Let's by all means keep this on its genteel level."

"Let's." Nelson glanced at his watch. It was after three, and among other things he was hungry. If Charles had not sent word to Chief Comerford when he delivered his exit line, surely he must have done so by this time. What was keeping the man?

His casual, "Does Masters have a car?" caught Debrulet off guard.

"He rented—" He stopped himself. "He doesn't need a car. He flies. His real name's Peter Pan."

Nelson said, "I don't wonder that Junie found you entertaining. And your success isn't limited to children. You've made another conquest."

"You? Dear fellow—shall we dance?"

"We'll sit this one out," Nelson said patiently.

"We wouldn't if I had a choice."

"Neither of us has a choice—nor did the conquest I referred to have one, although she appeared to think so. She isn't upstairs, is she?"

After a moment Debrulet said, "Who?"

"Miss Cameron."

There was a longer pause. Nelson said, "Her hostess is worried about her. Is she with you, or has she gone to some meeting place where you're to—"

Debrulet spoke with ominous control. "No one has to worry about Miss Cameron. She's not with me—and she's not a conquest. She's not—I'm not anything to her." His face was unreadable.

"But she's become something to you, in spite of your wholehearted devotion to your work."

Debrulet's control broke. "You had me fooled—the façade had me fooled. You do like your job. It gives you an excuse to root around in the stinking remains of what were once private lives. All right—have fun. Miss Cameron might have meant something to me, but I said goodbye to her last night. Later the goodbye didn't seem—it seemed too casual, so I had an argument with myself and my noble half won out and I went back to supply the explanation I thought was owing. I hammered on the door, I called out, but she wasn't having any. There's conquest for you."

"Perhaps she wasn't there."

"Oh, sure—with the lights all on and the rain beating down outside. She was there all right—snug and cozy—and probably pleased no end to have me come crawling back. To have me crawl could have been exactly what she wanted from the start. It's a goal for all of them. Only I thought—" He looked lost. He said, "Let me alone. Let her alone. If it's complicity you're after she had no idea of the charge against me."

Nelson said, "The lights are still on in the gatehouse—and it's broad daylight—and Miss Cameron is out."

Debrulet stared at him. "I don't know how your mind works. I don't know what you hope to haul in with that bit of bait, but I do know I'm sick of your voice. Try it on the telephone for a change. For the sake of respite I don't mind telling you it's been ringing its head off."

Nelson had heard the bell, yet he hesitated to leave Debrulet to his own resources while he answered it. He did not think that the man would run away, not without the unfinished marble, which seemed to be his primary concern. But he could not be sure. He said, "This is your house. It might be Masters calling to explain his delay."

Debrulet shrugged. Nelson was at his side as he strode out of the studio, through the kitchen, and into the hall where the telephone pealed on its table. He lifted the receiver and aimed a surly, "Well?" at the mouthpiece. A woman's voice answered.

At Nelson's whispered, "Miss Cameron?" he muttered, "How wrong can you get?" Contemptuously, as though he were gratifying an unpardonable curiosity, he held the receiver well away from his ear. Then he said politely enough, "Sorry, I was speaking to someone else ... No ... I ... She isn't ... What?"

Out of the receiver a torrent of sound poured without cease. Nelson could make nothing of it. Debrulet, it seemed, could and did. His second, "What!" was shocked rather than inquiring. A moment later he slammed the receiver down, pivoted, and raced through the hall to the kitchen. Nelson called after him, but he did not halt. The kitchen door opened and closed, and when Nelson reached it and flung it wide, Debrulet's car was junketing down the drive.

Nelson paused only to see which direction it took. He ran to the barn, thrust its doors apart, and climbed into the truck.

The car was still in sight as he hit the road. He anticipated no difficulty in keeping it in sight, nor even in overtaking it if necessary, since the truck's motor had a smooth, obedient sound. He wondered if Debrulet realized he was being pursued, and if he cared. The truck was gaining more than seemed advisable, so Nelson slowed, and a moment later came to a dead stop. From where he sat he could glimpse the turn that led to a low modern structure quite near the road. Debrulet had braked before the turn, hurled himself to the ground, and was continuing to his destination on foot.

Nelson started the truck again, circumvented the car, and parked in front of a well-kept lawn. He watched Debrulet run up to the door of the little house, push it inward, and enter. He got out of the truck and did not follow. While he waited he noted idly that the body of the truck had seen more wear than its excellent motor. Then, not so idly, he noted the headlights. He got back into the truck.

Debrulet catapulted across the lawn, apparently too distraught to do anything but take Nelson's presence for granted. "That way," he said, gesturing frantically, and jumped to the seat beside him.

Nelson nodded, and took the direction indicated. He said, "Were you out in this truck last night?"

"Me? Oh, sure. I always drive a truck in my dinner jacket." He dismissed the question with no curiosity as to what had prompted it. "Hurry, will you?"

Nelson wanted to ask a great deal more, but none of it was pertinent to Debrulet's frenzied exodus from the studio, and it was plain that there would be no answers. So he was silent until Debrulet shouted, "Pull up."

The butler answered the door. He looked inquiringly at Nelson, and doubtfully at Debrulet. In response to Debrulet's unadorned query, he said that he would see if Mrs. Curtis was at home.

He did not have to see. He backed away as she came galloping into the hall. She reared like a startled horse when she saw Debrulet, and cried, "You're here! I didn't know what to think when you hung up so rudely. Please—are you sure you don't know where Dene is? Believe me I'm far from—I'm not unsympathetic toward you, but I'm so worried. I sent Sam out to look for her in case she fell or something, but that was quite a while ago and he hasn't come back, so he couldn't have found her. You'll admit it's strange for her to disappear without a word, and you and she—well—" Her eyes veered suddenly to Nelson. She said, "Oh—you must excuse me. I didn't realize that Mr. Debrulet had brought—"

Nelson wondered if the logorrhea was chronic or merely due to her disturbed state. He said, "My name is Nelson, Mrs. Curtis. You've met my wife."

"Yes—yes, of course." Vera made a weak stab at the amenities. "She's charming—she's told me so much about you. You're a lieutenant, aren't you—only more than a lieutenant, really, because you're the head of the detective—"

Debrulet grabbed his shoulder "Detect, then, for God's sake—this is your chance—this is really important."

Nelson disengaged himself. "May I use your phone, Mrs. Curtis?"

"Yes—certainly—there's an extension near the stairs."

"Thank you." He called the Cotter house and spoke briefly. As he hung up he heard Vera scream.

Sam Curtis stumbled into the hall. He was panting and his round face was a sick gray. "I couldn't manage alone," he said. "My back is still— Someone will have to give me a hand." Nelson and Debrulet might have been members of his household for the way he accepted their presence. "Don't stand there—get a doctor."

The butler, who had been a detached observer, came forward. "Sir—may I ask—"

"Not now—get to that phone—call Freystadt." Sam winced as Debrulet gripped his arm.

"You found Dene. Where is she?"

"Patsy's hideaway—in the back—there's a well—I don't know how long she's been lying there. First I unlocked the door and went inside. The window was broken and—Wait! You don't know where it is—you're not supposed to move them when— She was lying on her face. I only turned her on her side so that she could breathe. She is breathing but—"

He was not talking to anybody. Except for the butler, the hall had emptied.

Surprisingly Vera was in the lead, her thin legs flying over flower beds and grass and stone. Then Debrulet passed her. Nelson was forced to run third because he did not know the way.

It seemed a long mile to the edge of Sam's property. There, Debrulet's head lowered and he looked quite ready to batter his way through the weathered boards of the cabin. But Vera skirted it, calling breathlessly, "The well—Sam said the well."

Nelson sprinted and finished first after all. He was kneeling seeking the girl's pulse, when the others cast their shadows over him.

Debrulet looked down and made a strange, supplicating motion. His lips worked but he seemed past utterance. Even Vera Curtis was having difficulty with words. She got as far as "Is she—"

"She's alive," Nelson said. The girl was lying with her cheek to the wet grass. He saw the clotted patch at the back of her skull. He lifted the dark hair away and gently probed for the injury.

"Don't—don't," Debrulet said painfully.

"I won't hurt her." Deftly he eased her around, keeping her head clear of the grass. For a moment he stared at the sweep of lashes, the beautiful mouth, the line of cheek and chin. Vera's voice returned in a sobbing rush. "Those scratches on her poor face—how could it have happened? No—you shouldn't move her. Sam will be here with the doctor."

Nelson said, "It's all right. We can't leave her lying here in the wet grass. I've had some experience." He glanced up at Debrulet's face, and felt compelled to weigh that experience against Debrulet's obvious need. "We should really carry her in a blanket, but perhaps you ...?"

"Yes—no—I can do it alone."

He did it alone, and Dene had never taken a smoother journey. He lifted her with infinite care and walked to the cabin as though he carried no weight at all. Once, on the way, she moaned, and he stopped and whispered comfort, his lips to her flowing hair. In the cabin it seemed he could not bear to put her down. And when he had lowered her to the couch, he did not know what to do with his arms. They hung loosely, accessories that had outlived their use. As though to test them he picked up a cushion from the floor. His eyes protested as Nelson took it from him and placed it under her legs, and turned her head a little so that the wound did not touch the upholstery of the couch.

Nelson said, "It's better for her to lie that way until—" He stopped because Debrulet's attention had wandered. Debrulet was gazing at the crumpled neckerchief caught on the couch's frame. A redness was creeping toward Debrulet's hairline.

Nelson did not betray his interest. He walked to the broken window, stooping once to pick up a rumpled coat and lay it across a chair, twice to pick up lengths of cord and thrust them into his pocket, his object seeming no more important than a feeling for tidiness. He returned to the couch as Dene Cameron stirred. "She'll be thirsty when she comes to," he said. "That's probably why we found her at the well."

Without a word Debrulet started to search.

"There's a pitcher and a glass on the bookshelves."

Debrulet took pitcher and glass and went out. It did not occur to Nelson that he was allowing a murder suspect unusual leeway.

Vera Curtis had been mulling something over. She voiced it. "What in the world made her leave the gatehouse to come here—without breakfast or anything? Of course Sam did insult her, but this is his property too and if she was being proud ..."

Nelson said the obvious, unable to believe that it was necessary. "She didn't come here of her own accord." He said it with less than his customary patience. He was anxious to be off, to check the facts he had been gathering while a check was still possible. Silently he cursed the minus quantity of the law enforcement facilities in Quintogue and its environs and wondered what, if anything, engaged Chief Comerford.

"Not of her own accord?" Vera said. "Now that's silly." She spoke in the tone of an adult accusing a child of applying comic book precepts to everyday life. "You can't be suggesting that someone brought her here. This isn't New York City, you know. It's Sandy Crest and there are no gangsters." Then she said, "Dene—my dear ..."

Dene had opened her eyes, deep, deep blue and only for a moment blank. She looked at Vera and then at Nelson. Her voice came huskily. "Am I supposed to know you?"

He smiled down at her. "Not yet."

She seemed to accept that.

"How do you feel?"

"Not bad—I thought I'd gone to the well. I think most of the way I feel is due to thirst. If I had water—"

"It's coming."

It was there. Debrulet was advancing with it.

She saw him. Her lips curved. She said contentedly, "Then that's all right," and closed her eyes again.

Debrulet knelt beside her. He took her hand and for the first time noticed the ugly markings at the wrist. He groaned and the sound reached her. Her eyes opened and settled upon his face.

She said, "Nice friends you have."

"Dene ...?"

"Are you going to give me a drink?"

He brought the water glass to her lips.

Vera said, "Just sip it, dear. What in the world happened to—"

Debrulet gave her a fierce signal and she subsided. The sound of motors sent her to join Nelson outside the door. Three cars rolled up. Sam Curtis got out of the first one. The second erupted a long slat of a man whom Vera welcomed as Dr. Freystadt. The man in the third car stayed behind the wheel.

Vera said, "Sam—what's Chief Comerford's car doing here?" She did not give him time to answer. "Doctor, I'm so glad Sam was able to get hold of you. It isn't as bad as we thought it was at first, though. We moved her inside. Sam didn't want us to, but Lieutenant Nelson has had a great deal of experience, and anyway she's conscious."

Sam looked immeasurably relieved. The long, thin doctor looked annoyed. He said to Nelson, "Have you had medical training?"

"I've encountered quite a few casualties."

"Well—we'll see." He gripped his bag and marched purposefully into the cabin, denying Vera's intention to accompany him with a "I'll call you if I need you."

Vera drew Sam aside. Nelson, as he walked toward the third car, heard her say severely, "Next time maybe you'll think twice before— What?" Her voice ascended, "Sam Curtis—that's impossible—I don't believe it—" Sam hushed her, and what further conversation they had was low-pitched.

The man in the third car was far past middle age. He had a ruddy, good-natured face, and what Nelson could see of his torso looked vigorous. Nelson said, "Chief Comerford?"

"That's right—and you're the high muck-a-muck from the big city." They shook hands. "Glad you got your little boy home safely. I had a hard time tracking you down. If it wasn't for you phoning the Cotters from Sam's house I'd have thought you'd met with foul play too. Nothing would surprise me right now. Well—soon as I could I hopped over to Sam's and found him high-tailing it for here."

The doctor had evidently shooed Debrulet out of the cabin.

He was standing alone, staring at nothing, oblivious of the fact that Vera, clinging to Sam's arm, kept sending him furtive, fearful glances.

Comerford whispered, "I brought the cuffs with me."

"I don't think you'll need them."

"Maybe not, but he don't look like an easy customer." He gave Nelson no opportunity to say what was foremost in his thoughts. "I got the other fellow—didn't know if I was supposed to, but it's always best to be on the safe side. After all, he came out of nowhere to team up with our friend"—he nodded in Debrulet's direction—"so it seems likely he knows more than he wants to say about the business in California. Anyway, when I drove over to the Tate place looking for you, he was throwing things into a car. It stuck out a mile he was in a sweat to get somewhere else quick and it seemed only natural to nab him."

"Where is he now?"

"I took him back to Quintogue and put him in custody. Then I called Mr. Cotter and came right along to Sam's."

Nelson said warmly, "Congratulations. You couldn't have done better."

"That so?" Modestly he changed the subject. "That lady visiting Sam—her accident's got nothing to do with—"

"I'm pretty sure it has," Nelson said. Quickly he gave his version of Dene's accident. As Exhibit A he took from his pocket the cords he had picked up in the cabin. He offered a guess as to the use to which they had been put prior to serving as bonds for Dene Cameron.

"You don't say! Might be that, unbeknownst, I killed two birds with one stone."

"Perhaps more than two. You'll find a truck parked outside the Curtis house. Was there broken glass at the scene of the hit-and-run fatality?"

"There sure was. A piece of it had lodged in the clothes of poor Bridie Mulvey."

"Well—that might have been what delayed Masters. He might have been trying to replace it today in case you'd sent out a warning to watch for a shattered headlight."

It took a few moments for that to sink in. Chief Comerford said grimly, "Looks like someone's clean out of his head. I noticed that truck standing there, but didn't give it a thought except that Sam was having stuff delivered." He gripped the steering wheel with heavily veined hands, and shot another look at Debrulet "Do you figure cahoots?"

"Not where Miss Cameron is concerned. For the rest, I agree with you that it's best to be on the safe side."

"Hmmm. Well—now that you've given me chores to do I guess we better attend to him right away so I can get busy." He started to get out of the car.

Nelson said, "This end of it is pretty much under control, but that truck left out in the open bothers me."

Chief Comerford's eyes judged him and arrived at a verdict. "Whatever you say. Shouldn't wonder you know what you're doing."

Nelson hoped he knew. He noted that the car's loud, rickety departure did not penetrate Debrulet's consciousness, and was sure of nothing, except that neither the joint efforts of himself and Comerford plus handcuffs and wild horses could have budged the man from his vigil before the cabin.

Nelson walked over to him and said experimentally, "Your friend Masters has been arrested."

Debrulet jerked his head toward him and then turned to face the cabin. At the same moment Vera and Sam came out of their huddle and the cabin door was besieged.

XV

Dene appeared, supported by the doctor. Debrulet took a step toward her, but she gave him a cool, impersonal look and he backed away. She gave Vera and Sam no look at all, averting her eyes as though by that act she could render her beautiful, grimy, scratched face invisible.

Vera reached for and somehow missed her hand. "My poor sweet! Doctor, did you have to cut the hair away under that patch? Never mind—we'll have our patient right in no time at all, won't we?"

The doctor did not spare her a glance. He said tenderly, "Just lean on me, Miss Cameron. I'll drive you back to the gatehouse, myself, to make sure you aren't jolted. Easy now." He might have been a proud father assisting his cherished offspring with her first steps. He helped her into the car, settled her, and went around to the other side.

Vera cried words of protest. "Not the gatehouse, Doctor. Our house. We've better facilities there for taking care of her. Sam insists, don't you, Sam?"

If Sam insisted, his voice was diluted by the sound of the starting car. It took off before Nelson could prevent Debrulet's sudden leap to the back seat.

Too quickly Vera recovered the power of speech. "Well! I do think that was extremely officious of—"

"Maybe she wanted to go to the gatehouse," Sam muttered. "Her things are there, but as for—"

"Of course she wanted to, and I don't wonder—not after the way you carried on."

Unceremoniously Nelson herded them both toward the Cadillac. Out of habit he slid behind the wheel, received Sam's nod of permission, and cursed the time it took for Vera to rattle off unnecessary directions, and cursed the moments that were lost while she decided whether to sit behind him or beside him.

They sat beside him, Vera in the middle. She went on talking. He, not listening, hoped that he only imagined the need for hurry. Across Vera he glimpsed her husband's face, and took it as a minor mercy that Sam Curtis refrained from translating his obvious bewilderment to questions.

He saw, as he turned down the Curtis driveway, that the truck no longer stood before the main house, and thought grimly that at least Chief Comerford had been attending to business. He lost a little more time maneuvering past an undertaker's van that was hogging the center of the drive.

"Camp chairs for Bridie," Vera explained brightly. "We're not burying her from the funeral parlors. She always said ..."

He was not to know what Bridie always said. He noted as he pulled up before the gatehouse lawn, the absence of the doctor's car.

The doctor himself was waiting in the living room. "Ah—here you are. I've left Miss Cameron in her bedroom. I want to satisfy myself by giving her a more extensive examination."

Nelson interrupted him. "Is Debrulet with her?"

"Of course not. She's undressing." The doctor sounded as though Nelson were casting a slur upon all of womankind. Then he said, "You mean the big fellow who rode up with us? He didn't even come into the house."

"What's the license number of your car, Doctor?"

The doctor reeled it off automatically before he asked the inevitable, "Why?"

"A hobby of mine." Nelson's eyes searched for and discovered the telephone in the dining section of the room. He commandeered it, thankful that a fresh monologue from Vera redirected the focus of attention. He was thankful for nothing else, except that it proved unnecessary to draw a diagram for the man who answered the phone in Comerford's office.

When he cradled the receiver, he was under a direct attack from Sam. "I understand from Ray Comerford that you're a police officer—and that Debrulet is wanted in California. If that's the case, why—"

Vera said, "There—I didn't believe it for a moment. Sam, you must have misunderstood. Lieutenant Nelson is a police officer, all right, but he's come to Long Island simply because he's the husband of that lovely blonde. You know—the girl who came to our party last night. I telephoned her when I found that Dene wasn't here, and I suppose she thought the lieutenant might help. But that part about Mr. Debrulet is ridiculous. Otherwise Chief Comerford wouldn't have gone away and left him. Doctor, did Dene explain how the accident happened?"

"Accident indeed! My dear lady, I respect your intention, but I assure you that an occasional hoodlum in the vicinity of Sandy Crest won't damage its good name." He addressed Nelson, "If you're a police officer you'll realize that I must make out a report. Any facts that you can supply ..."

Nelson said, "Didn't Miss Cameron supply them?"

"No. She seems to recall only that she went for a walk in the rain last night and tripped over something and struck her head. She can't account for the condition of her wrists and ankles. She seemed amazed when I told her she'd been knocked out and tied up."

Vera's eyes, nostrils, and mouth were stretched to capacity.

The doctor continued, "It's natural that she should be muddled. But from the superficial examination I gave her I predict it won't last." A smile redesigned his nutcracker face. "A very healthy young woman. Very healthy." He glanced at his watch. "Mrs. Curtis, will you see if she needs a hand? She insisted it wasn't necessary but—"

Vera said, "Hoodlums—muddled! Let me tell you I couldn't be more muddled if I had tripped and fallen. Yes, of course—I should have gone in to Dene long ago—what am I thinking of?"

A few minutes later she came rushing back. "Doctor, you can't imagine what that headstrong girl has been doing. She's been taking a bath—bandaged wrists and all. And now she says that all she wants is a square meal."

Again Nelson became aware of his own hunger. A square meal was not all he wanted, but it might help him to think. Removal from his familiar setting, he told himself, had made him singularly dull, and humbly he wondered if too much dependence upon the gigantic involved machine he commanded in New York was responsible for his recent inefficiency. He was not particularly worried about Debrulet's departure. What did worry him was his own lack of alertness. He said, "Doctor, as soon as you've finished with Miss Cameron, I'd like to question her, provided, of course, that she's well enough."

"I'll decide that after I've seen her." The doctor picked up his black bag. Vera followed him out of the room.

That left Sam, sitting gingerly on the edge of a chair. Sam was not to be denied. He glared at Nelson and said bluntly, "Has Debrulet anything to do with this?"

"Not directly."

"What kind of an answer is that? You're not talking to a child—or a woman. I knew from the start there was something wrong with him, and I was sure of it the day I sent the maid over to help him out."

Nelson's interest was captured. "The maid—Bridie?"

Sam shook his head. "Bridie was more than a maid. If I could get my hands on that hit-and-run skunk—but they'll never find him. He was probably just passing through Quintogue."

"What about the maid you sent to clean?"

"Well—he'd done me a favor and I didn't want to be under obligation, so that was my way of reciprocating. But I suppose a man like him would suspect even an act of plain neighborliness. He sent the girl flying in short order—only not short enough to prevent his nasty little pal from making a pass at her. I was so mad I took a special trip to town to give old Morton Peters a piece of my mind. Those real estate fellows will rent to anybody. Debrulet drove up to his office in a taxi, and, instead of references, he plunked down a year's rent in advance and moved in as soon as the bargain was sealed. He didn't even wait for the gas and electricity to be turned on. That was five months ago—which by itself was phony. Sandy Crest's a summer resort. Only natives who can't help themselves stay here in the dead of winter. But would you believe it—Peters hasn't been in touch with him since, or checked on him. His excuse is that the minute a tenant sees him coming he hands him a list of things that need to be done, and he says he's got too much sense to go out of his way looking for trouble. Sense! He looked me straight in the eye and swore that Debrulet is a solid citizen who likes his own stuff around him—and he bases this on the fact that even though the Tate house is fully furnished one of the village shopkeepers who'd gone around to drum up some trade on the afternoon he settled in mentioned a mover's truck parked in the backyard. Seems the moving men had gone off for a bite of lunch, so in the interests of good will the tradesman and his boy helped Debrulet to unload the last piece on to a hand truck. He said it was as heavy as a boulder, too, and expensive, from the way it was tied up in blankets. I ask you! Could have been a lump of Fort Knox—but was anybody concerned?"

Nelson looked appropriately shocked. He said, "What about the others in your household? Bridie—for example. You mentioned that she was more than a maid. What was her opinion of Debrulet?"

Sam said morosely, "I don't know that she had an opinion of him, although she did about everything else." He looked ashamed. "Got so every time she wanted to talk to me I expected complaints about the cook or the laundress or what not, so the other day when she said she wanted a few words I cut her short. I wish I hadn't, but that's the way it goes." He had forgotten Debrulet.

"Then you never discussed Debrulet with her?"

Sam shook his head. Again the rancor welled up in him. "Another thing—the man didn't know how to drive a car when he got here. He bought a secondhand one and took lessons from a fellow at the garage and passed his license test in Riverhead. If I'd guessed that I certainly wouldn't have trusted him at the wheel on the day I had to meet Dene at the station. Not that I had much choice. My chauffeur was away and I'd hurt my back." He added grudgingly, "He did handle the car like an expert. I'll give him that."

Nelson, who had witnessed a demonstration of Debrulet's driving, knew that he was an expert. Expert at covering his tracks, too. Bringing the truck all the way from California with its precious load. Salting it away in the barn, and under his assumed identity starting from scratch to procure a car. Sam's spate had clarified a few details, but it had yielded nothing pertinent to the case as it now stood. It was no news that the sculptor, Brian MacKenzie, had achieved a successful, if temporary, metamorphosis into the rather disreputable character known as Paul Debrulet. Yet Nelson listened to Sam, partly because he had nothing better to do until he received word of the next development, and partly because he felt that a man with a wife like Vera deserved every opportunity to exercise his vocal chords. He said encouragingly, "So it was at the station that he met Miss Cameron."

"Yes—damn it, and—" Sam shut his lips upon the rest of it. But his outburst seemed to have provided relief for his outraged sensibilities. He sat further back in his chair, and for the first time his horn-rimmed eyes really admitted Nelson to the realm of his consciousness. "So police work is your line, is it?"

"I've always thought so."

"You mean you're not so good at it? Well—that doesn't surprise me." He continued to take stock. "Could be you're fitted for something a cut above. Must be a lot of opportunities for a man of your appearance. Ever tried selling?"

"I might look into it," Nelson said meekly. "If you distrusted Debrulet, what made you invite him to your house last night?"

"That was my wife's doing. She's got the best heart in the world, but just between the two of us she's inclined to be a little taken in by—" He jumped as her voice was projected into the room. "I think you're wanted in there."

Nelson went to the archway, turned, and said, "I expect the doctor will be leaving. Have you a car to lend him until his own is returned?"

"What?" Then Sam produced what was undoubtedly his first smile that day. "You mean Debrulet had the nerve to run off in his car? Now that strikes me fully—I can't help it. Freystadt's one of those know-it-alls who has the idea nothing can ever surprise him. I can't wait to see his face. Sure, I'll let him use the Cadillac if he's in any frame of mind to listen to the offer. I can walk home, soon as I hear how Dene is."

Vera and the doctor met Nelson at the bedroom door. The doctor said, "All things considered, Miss Cameron is in remarkable shape. What puzzles me is that memory gap. The scalp wound's superficial, and her mind's so clear otherwise that concussion seems ruled out. I think her long period of unconsciousness was due to lack of circulation, or perhaps it was nature's escape from the discomfort of being bound and gagged. I'll look in again tonight. You may ask her questions, but I'll rely upon you not to be too insistent or to tire her. Good day."

Vera said, "I'm off to get her a tray. I'm sure he won't tire her, Doctor. When I told her he was Kyrie Nelson's husband she asked to see him of her own accord."

Kyrie Nelson's husband hoped there would be an extra cup of coffee on the tray. He went into the bedroom.

With so much composure did Dene Cameron regard him that

she might have been seated behind a desk. Her beauty made light of the scratches on her face. The long sleeves of a rose-colored bed jacket partially concealed her wrists. Her hands were tranquil on the sheet's wide cuff.

She smiled up at him. "Apparently I'm not gruesome enough to make you avert your eyes. Please sit down."

"To quote the doctor, 'You'll do.'" He took a chair near the bed. "Shouldn't you be lying flat?"

"Not unless I want to choke when I eat, which will be soon I hope." Still regarding him, Dene said reflectively, "Do you know? ... I felt a bit sorry for your wife when she said she was married to a policeman."

"At times I feel sorry for her too."

"Quite unnecessary. But you want to talk about Paul Debrulet, don't you? Has he come back yet?"

"Did he tell you he was coming back?"

"He didn't have to—he'll come. But you do have to tell me whatever it was your wife kept secret last night. I know he's in trouble—so it won't come as a complete shock—yet, knowing him, I doubt that it's really serious." She qualified that. "Not, at any rate, his share in it."

"From all reports his is the lion's share—provided, of course, that he's guilty."

Dene did not stir, but her eyes seemed to darken. "Has he committed a federal offense?" She corrected herself. "I mean is he supposed to have committed one?"

"You say you know him—and that his being in trouble doesn't come as a shock. Yet he hasn't confided the nature of that trouble?"

"He hasn't confided anything. He lost a letter which I deliberately sacrificed my principles to read." She smiled faintly. "You see—from the beginning I was much too interested in him to worry about playing fair."

"And the beginning was your meeting at the railroad station?"

"Of course. If we'd met before, this situation would never have existed." The reason for his question penetrated. "Are you entertaining some sort of wild notion that I'm a—what's the phrase—a gangster's moll?" She looked like royalty outraged. "You can disabuse yourself quite easily. I've been out of the country for years and can produce my passport to prove it, together with a list of names to refer to—names well known in diplomatic circles abroad."

Nelson's lips twitched. He said, "I had to ask. Tell me about the letter you sacrificed your principles to read."

Her laugh was unexpected. "I did lay it on a bit, didn't I? But you took me by surprise. The letter? Well—it didn't make very attractive reading matter. It was signed by a semi-literate individual named Mothy—and I have a feeling that if you're seeking the perpetrator of this nameless crime Mothy is your man."

"You have no idea of Mothy's identity?"

"Surely we're not going back to that again. How could I have? I've met none of Paul's friends or associates except Tim Masters." She raised her hand and touched the scratch on her chin.

"Mothy is Masters."

"He can't be. Masters was here—and the letter was postmarked California."

"Air mail?"

"I don't think so—no—not air mail. Oh—you're intimating that he posted the letter before he decided to put in an appearance, and then arrived ahead of it. That would explain his frantic interest in its recovery. How stupid of me. Tim—Timothy—blast him."

"Masters struck you and tied you up?"

She said slowly, "Yes, I wanted to keep that to myself until Paul had weakened sufficiently to make a clean breast of everything. I didn't want Masters arrested before I learned the full extent of Paul's involvement."

"He has been arrested."

"He has? How did you—"

"Let's get a few other matters out of the way first."

"Very well. There's no point in concealing what little I know from you—especially since you intend to be equally honest with me. You do, don't you?"

"Yes—I do."

Without wasting words she described the events that had led to her captivity in the cabin, including her telephone call to the Tate house, her talk with Masters, Paul's visit to her, his exit, and her going after him. She ended with a puzzled, "The only conclusion I've come to is that Masters must be playing for high stakes, and that after your wife's brainwave he needed to spirit Paul out of Sandy Crest at once and was afraid I might influence him to stay. So he decided to remove me until he'd got Paul away." She made a grimace of disgust. "He wasn't clever about covering his tracks. I'd seen that loathsome neckerchief the day he joined me on the beach. I'd have recognized it anywhere, but he probably thought he'd be light years away by the time I recovered consciousness, and that I wouldn't complain for fear of hurting Paul." At Nelson's nod of agreement, she said, "But why didn't he get away? Did Paul refuse—"

"He didn't really want to leave." He saw that she was satisfied with that, and went on. "You still haven't told me what was in the letter."

"Nothing very enlightening. Masters called Paul 'Mac,' and acknowledged some contribution he'd sent, and congratulated him on the way things had turned out—and said that 'You know who' had given up the hunt, and that Mac was guaranteed privacy to complete the job on hand. I can't remember much else. There was something about missing the good old days. But it all had a kind of furtive quality, so I assumed that 'You know who' meant the police—and that Paul was engaged in shady activities."

"But that didn't make you forswear him."

"I forswore him resolutely several times, but wasn't strong enough to hold to the resolution."

Nelson let that pass. "When you were alone with him for those few moments in the cabin was Masters's name mentioned?"

"It didn't have to be mentioned. It infected the air. We didn't speak at all after I told him there'd be no further conversation between us until he saw fit to give me his full confidence." Then Dene said, "But when he rode only as far as the gatehouse with me and didn't come in, I hoped he'd gone to find Masters and punish him suitably and send him packing once and for all. Only, if Masters has been arrested ...?"

"I gave him that information, but he was so concerned with the state of your health that perhaps it didn't register." Nelson felt a little better because what she had said confirmed his own opinion of her lover's sudden departure. He asked his next question abruptly. "Did Bridie read the letter too?"

"Bridie? I gave it to her to take back to Paul but—" Dene's composure ebbed away. "Oh no—you're not suggesting—she was knocked down by a truck—"

He said, "You've asked me to be honest with you. Yes—Bridie was run down by a truck—and on the way home last night Kyrie had an encounter with a speeding truck on the road that goes past the Tate house and leads to a dead end after it passes the Curtis property. Today I saw a truck parked in the Tate barn—beyond doubt the one that brought Debrulet to Long Island and the one that was being made ready for his getaway. Would you put all that down to coincidence?"

"I'd like to." Her beautiful voice was almost brittle. He felt that it would shatter if she permitted any seepage of emotion to enter it. "Would you pour me some water, please—I—I just can't drink enough. Thank you." She drank. She said stonily, "I was fond of Bridie. I think she was growing fond of me. I don't go in for self-recrimination, but it's hell to think I might have been responsible for her death. Masters must be raving mad."

Masters, Nelson thought. Masters without hesitation. Never Paul Debrulet. He said, "I don't believe that rather vague letter was responsible for Bridie's death. She must have stumbled upon something more incriminating."

"That doesn't help. If she did she stumbled on it when she returned the letter. She did say she heard Masters quarreling with Debrulet, but she didn't hear what was said, because she walked over to the barn and—"

"And saw the truck?"

"I don't— Yes—she did say she'd seen a truck, but still—"

"Perhaps they thought she'd overheard something, too—"

"They!" Dene said scornfully. "Not they—Masters. Bridie didn't like him and I imagine she didn't bother to hide it yet—"

"Did she like Debrulet?"

"She hardly knew him. He never came during her working hours. She went back to the main house to sleep. She'd seen him about in the village, I expect, and heard him spoken of, but I think the very first time she spoke to him was the day I arrived and he brought my luggage in." Dene's eyes looked somewhat less haunted. The corners of her mouth lifted a little. "She insisted he reminded her of a Mr. Jock Fraser she'd met in her younger days."

Nelson said, "He might well have done. He has Scots blood. His real name is Brian MacKenzie—which accounts for the 'Mac' in the letter."

"Brian? Brian ..." Dene made music of it. Immediately, and just a shade self-consciously, she returned to the moment. "You can't really believe he had anything to do with Bridie's death?"

Nelson said nothing.

"You haven't even put a name to the other business—or am I to guess? Larceny—forgery? Whatever it was I'm certain that

Masters blackmailed him into it. Nothing but blackmail would explain his connection with a type like Masters."

"Does Brian MacKenzie—or Debrulet if you like—appear to be a man who'd submit to blackmail?"

"No—unless he's protecting someone else." She could not seem to take his connection with crime seriously. "Tell me—what does Brian MacKenzie do—aside from his illegal activities? Is he a painter?"

"A sculptor—a successful one. What made you guess the arts?"

She told him about the sketch and about its disappearance from the cabin. She said, "I expect it was as good as his signature to those who were acquainted with his work—and that's why Masters made off with it. Masters has been a busy man—"

Vera entered the bedroom, wheeling the outsized tea cart. Dene's eyes lighted. She glanced apologetically at Nelson. "It seems heartless to have an appetite after what you've just told me, but I can't help it—I'm famished."

So was he. He got up and helped Vera with the cart. The smell of the coffee almost unmanned him.

Vera said, "Scrambled eggs and bacon and toast—it's really your breakfast, Dene, so you mustn't overdo. I—" Her manner showed that she had been thoroughly coached either by the doctor or Sam. She was quite plainly clamping the lid upon her curiosity. "I hope it will be all right. I haven't tried my hand at cooking for quite a while."

"It will be wonderful, Vera—and thank you. I'm sorry to be a nuisance."

"Not at all—there isn't a thing Sam and I won't do to make up for this dreadful ordeal you've been through. I still don't —Well—Sam said I was just to leave the food and not interrupt anything. He's gone back to the house, but he'll be in to see you later. Let me fix your pillows. Lieutenant—please hand me that tray on the lower rung—it has legs. We'll set it up in front of her and— That's it. Now if you'll pass me that covered dish.... I've brought an extra cup and some sandwiches for you because after all it's five o'clock and I'm sure you can do with a snack."

Nelson added his thanks to Dene's, and had the grace not to pounce upon the food until Vera had made her reluctant exit. Dene imposed no such restriction upon herself. They ate in companionable silence. Dene's sole remark was that he must excuse her if she did not talk, because there were times when manners became too much of an effort, and this was one of them. He said he understood. He was removing her tray when the telephone rang. It was hushed before he got to it. Then Vera came to the door to announce that Chief Comerford wished to speak to him. She indicated the extension in the headboard, but said rather wistfully that perhaps he preferred privacy. Fortified against everything, including the reproach in Dene's eyes, he made for the living room. When he picked up the receiver he heard a distinct click and knew where it originated.

Chief Comerford said robustly, "I've got 'em both now. Debrulet walked right into the Quintogue station house and demanded to see his sidekick."

"Have you questioned him?"

"Ever tried questioning a volcano? Same thing. I got no place and I don't know as I have to. That's California's job—after the extradition business has been attended to." Nelson admired the older man's rational attitude and wished that he could emulate it. With the two men in custody the case, he told himself, was even less his concern than it was Comerford's. Yet he was so constituted that he knew he could not rest until all of its loose ends had been joined. "Meanwhile," Comerford said, "I'll have 'em both shifted to the jail in Riverhead. Quintogue's not fitted for big-time criminals. Mac-Debrulet has got his nerve all right. First he steals Doc Freystadt's car to get here—and from the nasty look in his eye when he asks for his pal there's something else on his mind than giving himself up—then when Cliff Perry and me convince him there's nothing doing he tries to bargain. Says he'll tell all if we let him have one last visit with Miss Cameron ..."

Nelson heard breathing that was not Comerford's, and realized that he would have done better to take the call in the bedroom.

Comerford went on. "But like I said, over and above being glad to lend a helping hand where it's needed, I got no further interest in a murder that happened all those miles away from my own little corner. Masters is another matter. You were right about him and I'm much obliged. That cord you gave me matched the gaps in the cord used to fence off the kitchen garden at the Tate place—and I was lucky enough to find a piece of glass on the spot to match that broken headlight. Fellow at the garage also told me he tried to buy a new pair, but they didn't have any in stock. Well—thought you'd like to know. Guess I've earned my supper tonight."

Incredible as it seemed, Comerford seemed willing to let it go at that. Nelson said carefully, "California will want Masters too—at least as an accessory. I'm afraid you'll need even tighter evidence than you have to hold him here for trial." He waited. He could almost hear Comerford chewing on it.

"Tighter evidence? It seems clinched to my way of thinking. You mean like a confession ...?"

"Yes—but you'll probably be able to extract it."

"Well, I don't know. Tell you the truth, I'm kind of rusty when it comes to that third-degree stuff." He hesitated. "Say—you wouldn't want to try your hand? Anyone can show you the way to the Quintogue station house. I'd be much obliged. Don't need to be tonight, of course. Guess you want to get home to your supper too."

Nelson said, "I'll be right over," and hung up.

In the bedroom Vera avoided his eyes. She looked shocked. "Dene's in there," she said, nodding toward the closed bathroom door.

"Did the telephone conversation upset her?"

"Oh—how did you— But you mustn't blame her too much for listening. She isn't herself."

"Mrs. Curtis, I have to go to Quintogue. Is there a taxi service?"

"Yes—but it's never there when you need it. Let's see—Sam lent the Cadillac to the doctor. I'll ask him to send the chauffeur over with the Buick." She went to the telephone.

Nelson waited in the entrance hall. Exactly seven minutes later the car was at the door, and Dene, fully dressed save for a hat, had materialized at his side. Behind her, Vera cried, "See if you can reason with her, Lieutenant—"

Nelson said dryly, "So you've sacrificed your principles again, Miss Cameron."

"Not unduly. He wants me and I'm going to him."

"How do you feel?"

"Much better than I'd feel if I didn't go."

He offered her his arm.

XVI

The chauffeur, not too successfully masking his curiosity, said that he knew the way to the Quintogue station house. Nelson let him drive to save time, and sat in the back with Dene.

The scratches stood out sharply on her face, but except for her extreme pallor she showed no manifestation of strain. He thought that she was quite a woman, and noted that in spite of the wounds on scalp and wrists, she had managed to pin up her hair in a coronet.

Once she bit her lip as the car went over a rut. He put his arm around her to steady her, and she leaned against him with no display of coyness. He said, "Does your head ache?"

"My head? No."

"I'm sorry you had to hear it that way."

"It doesn't matter. I had to hear it some way. Who is he supposed to have murdered?"

"His wife."

"His—his wife?" Then she said, "I don't know why I'm so surprised. I've been married too. But somehow I'd got the feeling he had fought shy of—of ties." Her voice became preemptory. "Tell me about it."

"I think he'll tell you."

"He will, but I want to be prepared—I want to have this little time before I see him to formulate my arguments against any noble renunciation he'll think his circumstances indicate. All right—he's a sculptor and he comes from California. Go on from there."

"He had a good war record—"

"Never mind. It doesn't make the slightest difference to me whether you build him up or attempt to tear him down. I just want to know how he managed to get himself into this jam."

Nelson said mildly, "I'm leading up to it. He married before he went into the Army and his child was born while he was overseas—"

"Child! Paul has a—Brian"—she swallowed—"I *do* need preparation. Boy or girl?"

"A boy. About two years old when MacKenzie returned. The wife, it seemed, wasn't at all maternal. She neglected the boy, and, according to reports, MacKenzie was with him constantly, trying to atone for the mother's shortcomings. Then, one day, when he had to go to San Francisco, the child fell off a jetty into the water. Some man who was staying at the house jumped in after him and was able to pull him out and apply artificial respiration. But the child had been suffering from a cold which developed into pneumonia—and a few days later he died. After that the marriage—never a good one—deteriorated steadily. Friends of MacKenzie's say that his wife was often heard insulting him in public and that there were increasing rumors of her promiscuity." He paused and nodded at Dene's rude comment. "Exactly. After the police discovered her dead body in his studio, the consensus was that she had asked for it. Layman's opinion, of course—although there were some who believed that, following the child's death, he became too wrapped up in his work to be aware of her insults, promiscuity, or even of the fact of her existence. However, one of his mallets had been used to inflict the fatal blow, and he was seen leaving the house after the murder had occurred. That was taken to be doubly damning because he had not been living there for over a week. He had been staying with a friend in San Francisco who knew what his home life was like and who tactfully accepted his explanation that he had business to transact in San Francisco, and that it would be more convenient for him to be on the spot until it was concluded. But the friend admitted reluctantly that on the morning of the murder he overheard him in an angry telephone conversation with his wife. Furthermore, it was found that during the week he spent in town, MacKenzie had cashed a check for ten thousand dollars." Nelson told her the significance of the ten thousand dollars before he went on. "And he'd purchased a secondhand truck and made other obvious preparations to do a skip. The description of the truck was broadcast, but he'd changed its license plates and its color." He paused. "Policemen all over are a realistic force. The facts as they totaled them added to unmistakable guilt."

Dene said hotly, "Then they ought to stop being realistic and use some imagination. He could have got a divorce—or he could have done just what he did do—escape to where he'd have peace and quiet to get on with his work. For all his size—and for all his cynical manner—which by the way is entirely put on—he's not a violent man. I know. Why don't they accuse the one who says he saw him leave the house? What was *he* doing there? Probably an ex-lover who'd been turfed out and didn't like it."

"Each of her acquaintances was questioned. This particular man—barring a taste for philandering—is a reputable bachelor with an unbreakable alibi for the time of her death as established by the medical examiner—even if more than the usual margin for error is allowed on either side of the clock. And she hadn't turfed him out. He was still, according to people who'd seen her with him from time to time, an accepted suitor who had no motive for wanting her out of the way."

Dene said irrelevantly, "How did Kyrie recognize

Paul—Brian? I must get used to calling him Brian."

Nelson hoped she would have a chance to get used to it. He admired her unshakable faith. "Kyrie saw his picture in one of the true crime magazines. He was wearing a dinner jacket in the picture too—but his hair wasn't cropped—and perhaps if he had been dressed as he was today she might not have made the association. I take it the somewhat picturesque costume he affects here is intended as a disguise. He's known as one of the best-dressed men in art circles."

"Poor, ridiculous Brian MacKenzie. He's had it." Then she said passionately, "But I'll make it up to him."

Nelson thought that, given the opportunity, she could undoubtedly fulfill the promise. In view of that thought her next words were a disappointment.

"Aside from the ten-thousand-dollar check that he cashed—which must be well bitten into by this time—what's his financial standing?"

"I haven't any details as to investments, but he inherited money and there are substantial sums in his savings and checking accounts."

"That's good. I have some money too. When we get to California the first thing to do will be to find the best lawyer going. How does Tim Masters come into it?"

"I'm not sure. The facts I've given you were gleaned from the magazine story, from the newspaper morgue, and from a telephone talk this morning with the San Francisco chief of detectives. So many unfamiliar names were reeled off that I can't be certain Masters was among them. I've a hazy recollection that it was, though—and for the past few hours I've been trying to fit it into its proper place—without success. For all I know, the terrible zeal Masters has been employing to keep MacKenzie's identity a secret may be due to nothing but the sheer loyalty men sometimes have for each other."

Dene scoffed at that. "You haven't met the little horror."

"No ..."

She shifted her position to look at him. She gave a slight nod. "You're no hundred-per-cent realist. You've got imagination. When I listened in on the bedroom extension, I heard you practically extracting an invitation to go on from where that provincial police officer left off. He seemed entirely willing to rest on his laurels. But you weren't. Why did you all but beg to—"

He pretended to misunderstand her. "A matter of courtesy.

I'm an outsider. Under the circumstances it would be natural for Chief Comerford to resent it if I sat in without invitation."

"But you wouldn't want to unless you were interested. You've seen Brian MacKenzie—talked to him—in spite of the evidence you—"

"Don't ask me to speculate. Wait until we know a little more."

The Quintogue Police Station was an ugly frame building on the edge of town, and Chief Comerford's office did nothing to dispel the impression of gloom left by the façade.

When Nelson introduced Dene, Chief Comerford said severely, "This is no place for you, young lady. The way I heard it you've had about enough of that pair."

"They're not a pair." Nelson held a chair for her and she sat down.

Nelson said, "Miss Cameron wanted to come—and I don't think her presence will be a drawback."

"Hmmm—but the size of it is you're giving in to that nervy fellow's demands to see her. Well—if that's the way they do things in the big city I guess it will have to be all right with me. Want 'em brought in here or—"

"Here, please," Dene said. "It might inhibit Brian MacKenzie to talk through bars."

Comerford turned his seamed, weathered face full upon her. "Young lady, I guess you don't understand. Talking through bars is the only kind of talking that fellow's likely to do from now on. You got your whole life before you and you look much too smart to me to figure on wasting it—"

Nelson said, "If you think it's too much of a risk to let them out we'll go to the cells."

"I'm not worried about the risk. I got young Cliff Perry armed and standing guard, and my own gun's handy in the desk drawer. But it just goes against my grain to encourage foolish notions." He strode out of the office.

Nelson looked down at Dene. "Are you sure you feel equal to this?"

She looked around the dingy office. "I'll try to be—although nothing in my experience has qualified me for it." She pinned a decoration on him. "Your presence helps."

The sculptor with two identities entered the office first, followed by a small compact edition of a man. Comerford and a squarely built policeman in uniform pushed in after them.

The small man leaned against the desk with a show of

nonchalance that was not quite successful.

Dene barely glanced at him. Nelson saw dismay in her eyes as she took in her lover's shackled wrists. Indignantly she turned to Comerford. "That's not fair. Why isn't Masters handcuffed?"

"We only got one pair is why—and we can handle Masters." He cleared his throat and addressed the prisoners. "Sit down if you've a mind to—but no tricks." He pushed straight backed chairs toward them.

Tim Masters sat down. Brian MacKenzie ignored the invitation. The uniformed policeman went over to the window and locked it.

Comerford said to him, "It's kind of crowded in here, Cliff. You wait outside the door in case the little fellow tries to squeeze through the keyhole or something—and remember to aim for his legs."

When the door had closed, Dene said in her throaty voice, "Sit down, Brian."

Startled, he sat down. "So you know ...?"

She said, "Lieutenant Nelson's told me most of it. You've only to fill in the gaps."

"Gaps?" Their eyes held only each other. "Dene—it was good of you to come—even if—even if nothing good can come of it. But I shouldn't have asked for you. It's over—and this is no place for us—for it to end."

She said calmly, "This is not where it ends. I'm coming to California with you to—"

"Dene—no. They couldn't have told you. I'm wanted for murder—it's a rotten mess."

Tim Masters spoke. "A rotten mess is right, Mac. And she's made it worse—" He seemed to shrivel under MacKenzie's glare. He said plaintively, "I'm your friend, Mac. Haven't I proved it over and over again?"

Chief Comerford, seated behind the desk, scratched his head. He looked bored and a little embarrassed.

Nelson said casually, "How did you prove your friendship, Masters?"

Masters achieved a return to nonchalance. "The big city cop, huh? Well—I'm not the man to boast. Mac knows how I've proved it. That's good enough for me."

"He's not the only one who knows." It passed through Nelson's mind that he sounded like "The Shadow."

But his pronouncement caused no more than a flicker in

Masters's yellow eyes. "Oh, sure—cops always know everything. They're kept so busy knowing everything that their wives have to get their kicks by prying into other people's affairs."

Nelson subjected him to a prolonged scrutiny and was slightly rewarded.

Masters began to fidget. He said childishly, "See much?"

Nelson sat down on the side of the desk. He said to MacKenzie, "Where did you meet him?"

"What diff—"

Masters said quickly, "That's right, Mac. Don't give him any answers. Wait till you get a lawyer. I'll stick by you. Not even a hick judge is going to hold me long when I tell him I was only trying to help a pal. They've got nothing on me except that I knew where you were—and as soon as I'm loose I'll head for California to testify for you. It looks like they've got you, Mac, and you'll have to stand trial, but no jury is going to give you the full works when they hear what I have to say in court—"

Dene shouted, "You call yourself a friend—and you believe him guilty of murder! Paul—Brian—you're to tell Lieutenant Nelson whatever he wants to know. He's on your side."

MacKenzie said dully, "All right. I met him in the Army."

"Make something out of that," Masters said. "Hang us for defending our country while slobs like you—"

Comerford pounded the desk with his fist. "Be civil or I'll make up for the lickings your poor misguided mother spared you."

Nelson sighed inwardly, wishing that he were in a position to command the floor. With constant interruption the line he was using would catch nothing. Silently he tried to convey this to both Dene and Comerford.

He said, "And when the war ended, Masters was at a loose end—so you invited him to stay at your house in Belvedere?"

MacKenzie nodded.

"Was he staying there at the time of the murder?"

"No—he'd left a month or so before."

Masters was registering sorrow. Registering it hard. Nobody noticed him. They were intent on MacKenzie, who stared down at his cuffed wrists.

Dene appealed to Comerford. "Take those manacles off. It hurts me to look at them. Can't you see he's done with running away. How do you expect him to talk freely when he's made to feel like a slave?"

Comerford shrugged and glanced at Nelson. He produced a

key and unlocked the cuffs.

Nelson said, "Where did Masters go when he left your house?"

Absently MacKenzie rubbed his wrists. "He rented an apartment in San Francisco."

"He has an income then?"

"He—I helped him out."

Masters said, "Sure—it was give and take all the way."

Nelson ignored him. "MacKenzie, you yourself moved out of the house before the murder was committed. Will you explain that?"

"It had got so I couldn't work at home—and I had important work to do—for a children's hospital." His bleak voice warmed. "Even before the contest results were announced I'd decided to do that group—no matter where it ended up. I'd already completed two of the three pieces of which it was to consist. You saw the third. I planned to wait until it was finished to get a divorce from my wife ..." The chill was there again. "But there was no time to go through the complicated proceedings. The group was the only thing on my mind. So I moved out and stayed in Masters's apartment while I made arrangements to lose myself—to go East—find a place to work—and finish what I'd started to do. I took the name of Paul Debrulet because it was so different from my own. It belonged to a man I'd met once in Paris—a lucky man." His mouth twisted. "On the morning of my wife's death I telephoned to tell her I was calling at the house that evening to pick up a few things—clothes—one or two tools. That's how I happened to be there."

"Why was it necessary to call her? Didn't you have a key?"

"I didn't want her to think I was spying—I don't know. Maybe I didn't want to walk in on an awkward— Hell—what I wanted was not to see her. I thought if I called and set a time she might have the decency to be out."

"And you quarreled with her on the phone?"

"It would have been news if I hadn't. She said she'd be there all right and was looking forward to a cozy get-together. I said no—and it ended in the usual way."

"But in spite of that you went to the house—knowing there was bound to be a scene."

MacKenzie, the sculptor, said simply, "The tools I wanted to pick up were favorites. I felt I'd work better if I had them."

"And ...?"

"I let myself into the house and went straight to the studio. I heard nothing and I thought she'd gone out after all. But there was that hot metallic smell in the studio—the blood smell—and she was lying on the floor with one of my heavy hammers beside her." No emotion colored his voice. "She was dead—her skull caved in—and when I had made sure that no doctor could do anything for her I left. I didn't touch the hammer. I knew it pointed to me, but I had the futile hope that the police would find fingerprints on it to fix the guilt where it belonged. I got the truck, which I'd left ready—the stone had been loaded on earlier—and I started to drive East that night."

Dene breathed sharply. He gave her a pleading look. "I know the way it sounds—callous—inhuman—but I couldn't have done any good by staying to fight it out. And I could do good by getting on with my work. At least that's how I saw it. To me she'd become less than the meaning of an echo. There may have been several men she could have provoked to violence, but not me—not even after my son—" He stumbled over it. "I'd been drained—emptied. Try to understand. Her death to me was no more important than her life had been—except as it interfered with what I considered to be my sole justification for being on earth. I was even sure that I could never again want any woman until—until you—"

Once more they were the sole inhabitants of their own little planet. Nelson turned his attention to Masters, who was now registering a blend of sorrow and skepticism.

Nelson said, "Obviously, in spite of his story, you are convinced that he did murder her."

"Well—it looks bad for him. And it isn't what I believe—it's what the jury will believe."

"Yes—that's true. During the time you were in the Army with him you undoubtedly saved his life."

Masters looked surprised. Then he smirked. "Did he tell you that? I'd forgotten it myself. It wasn't much. I only tripped him so that he fell flat on his face and the sniper's bullet whizzed right through the spot where his chest had been a split second before. Remember how mad you were, Mac? You thought I was just horsing around."

Nelson said, "How long did you stay with MacKenzie after the war?"

"Huh? What do you think you're getting at?"

Comerford's face repeated the question. Nelson hoped he would keep it to himself. He said, "You offered to testify for MacKenzie—and by that I assume you mean you would reveal conditions in his home life that had led to the murder. The court will probably want to know if you were around long enough to get your information at first hand."

Masters said, "I was living there long enough to see how the land lay."

"Long enough to know his wife very well?"

Dene made a sudden return to the world, her eyes vivid with interest.

There was a pause. Masters said, "Sure—not that I couldn't size her up the minute I saw her."

"And you moved out more than a month before the murder. Did MacKenzie ask you to leave?"

"He did not. Did you, Mac?"

MacKenzie moved restlessly.

"Why would he? He wanted me to stay. We were buddies. We'd been through a lot together. Maybe he's mad at me now because he's hypnotized by that—I don't know why I'm putting up with this crap. You've got nothing worth mentioning on me—and you haven't got his interests at heart either. I'm the one who's been looking out for him from start to finish—"

"Do you consider it not worth mentioning that you made an attempt on Miss Cameron's life?"

"Who says?"

"The gag you used says—and your fingerprints all over the cabin—"

"You think I'm a dope? I wore—"

"Yes?"

"I fell for that old one, didn't I? Well—sue me. It was a practical joke. You can see for yourself I didn't hurt her or she wouldn't be here. I only did it for Mac's sake—so she wouldn't be around to work on him and make him stay and be pulled in. If you want to start blaming anybody blame that big-mouthed blond broad of yours for sticking her nose where it doesn't belong."

Nelson used angler's tactics, paying out more line to lull the fish. "Was the lipsticked 'DON'T' on my wife's handkerchief another practical joke of yours?"

No one had ever accorded more welcome to a change of subject. "Mine—that kid stuff? I saw the jerk named Parks do that with my own eyes. He put it on the redhead's handkerchief too. The only reason he stopped there was he couldn't get hold of any other pocketbooks. He said dames were always up to something and he thought it would be funny to give them a scare. So if that's all you've got on your mind—"

Nelson said softly, "One more thing. Did you wear gloves too when you drove the truck last night and killed an innocent woman who'd been unfortunate enough to cross your path?"

MacKenzie's chair scraped. Chief Comerford, who had been like an unwilling eavesdropper waiting to go about his own business, sat up and looked alert.

Masters said, "I never beard of an innocent woman—and I don't own a truck."

"Naturally you wouldn't permit not owning a truck to stand in your way. You used the one belonging to your valued friend."

"And you found my fingerprints all over it—the same as in the cabin."

"No—I found glass missing from its headlight—and Chief Comerford found matching glass at the spot where the woman was killed. He also found the imprint of the truck's distinctive tire treads on her legs."

Chief Comerford gulped and quickly switched to a cough. He drew a pad and pencil from the desk and began to scribble.

"Who's interested?" Masters said. "Anybody at the party will tell you I was drunk." He pointed at Dene. "Even her. What would I want to go driving in a truck for? All I wanted was to sleep it off—and I shocked my horse-faced hostess by using her library as a boudoir. Ask her."

"I've asked. Mrs. Curtis went to the library long before the party was over to see if you'd awakened. She discovered that you'd left without troubling to say goodbye."

"So what? I'd left. I went home to bed."

"When did you go to bed?"

"How do I know? I don't punch a time clock and I was still under the influence."

"You weren't under the influence when Miss Cameron telephoned. She says that the telephone rang for an unusually long time before you answered. Then—when you did answer—it was neither drunkenly nor sleepily—but breathlessly—as though you'd just come in."

"Prove it." He looked sideways at MacKenzie. "Mac—next thing they'll be pinning that old biddy's death on you—just because it's your truck and you were out at the time."

MacKenzie said nothing, but he stiffened and raised his head.

"Yes," Nelson said, "that's a fair sample of the way you've helped your friend from start to finish. Fortunately he has an alibi for this murder. After the party he found it necessary to walk for miles in the rain. He had several reasons. One was that he thought you were drunk and wanted to find you. Probably he had learned from past experience that you were apt to be unpredictable in your cups. He also realized that his identity was in danger of being revealed, and he was trying to decide upon a course of action." Nelson warmed to his improvisation. "He stopped for coffee along the way at a certain all-night lunch wagon. The owner is prepared to swear to his presence there at the exact moment the truck performed its fatal hit-and-run maneuver in Quintogue."

Chief Comerford said guilelessly, "That would be old man Jelke's beanery just outside of Sandy Crest."

MacKenzie opened his mouth. He closed it as Dene dug her fingers into his knee.

Nelson said, "MacKenzie didn't find you but he came to the conclusion that he must quit Sandy Crest—and he walked back to the gatehouse to take leave of Miss Cameron. So you see—he couldn't have been driving that truck."

"I didn't say he was. Are you trying to make trouble between us? I only said—"

"You only said what you thought would divert attention from yourself. It's been your consistent line throughout. No sacrifice too great to protect the skin of one Tim Masters. You came to Sandy Crest because you'd run out of money and it made you uneasy to be so far from its source—"

"I didn't—I wanted to see how Mac was doing—I—"

"You were driving that truck."

"Prove it." This time the words limped.

"I intend to—and there's a certain amount of poetic justice involved in the proof. You mentioned my wife freely during this session. But you have more reason to dislike her than you know. She saw you at the wheel of the truck last night when you were returning from Quintogue. In fact she barely avoided a collision with you. Perhaps if you think hard you can recall the incident."

A dirty white had seeped through Masters's tan. It was plain that he recalled the incident. He licked his lips.

Chief Comerford flexed his fingers. "That's it—that's it for sure—"

"It's lies—nothing but lies."

Reluctantly, Nelson, who loved truth, dealt it another blow. "The woman's companion also gave a description of you—"

Masters shouted, "She couldn't—she was standing on the

other side of—" Cornered, he made a horrible squeal of his voice. "I had a skinful—I didn't mean to kill her—break her leg or something—put her out of the running till we were too far away for it to matter. It was an accident."

Comerford sighed and started to scribble again.

"It was murder with a motive," Nelson said, "even a side motive. You knew that she went to the gatehouse early each morning to work for Miss Cameron and it would be to your advantage not to have her discover Miss Cameron's absence until you and MacKenzie were well on your way. In spite of the early start you planned—which, due to one thing and another, didn't work out—you couldn't have covered much distance before she gave the alarm. Your main motive, however, was that she had called at the Tate house one day to return an incriminating letter which you suspected her of having read. Additionally you thought she was spying on you and had heard a conversation between you and MacKenzie which, if repeated, could have put MacKenzie behind bars." Masters seemed to be aging before his eyes. He looked like a crafty little old man. Like a ...? Nelson said involuntarily, "MacKenzie behind bars would have meant that you'd have to search for another pot of gold." He gathered his wandering thoughts. "Your opportunity to silence Bridie didn't come until the night of the party when you learned she'd gone to the theater in Quintogue. The weather, which would keep possible witnesses indoors, was with you. You parked the truck at the deserted end of the street and waited. Luck as well as the weather seemed to be with you. When the theater emptied, she went into the drugstore to have ice cream with her friend. They sat talking until the crowd had dispersed. Then they came out and parted—and you got Bridie as she was crossing the street."

"I didn't—it was an accident." Wildly he appealed to MacKenzie. "They're trying to frame me, Mac, like they framed you—"

Nelson said, "Then you do believe in MacKenzie's innocence?"

"Mac!" He was frantic. "I always believed in you. Do something. Didn't I jump into the water after your kid? I'm your pal—Anita wouldn't move—she just stood there—but I—"

Nelson's words were cold and very distinct. "What were you and Anita doing when the child fell off the jetty?"

Now it was MacKenzie who turned to the little man, his eyes blazing.

"It was Anita who insisted upon your leaving the Belvedere house," Nelson said. "She'd tired of you."

"She was a bitch. Mac—quit looking at me—you know what she was—a pushover—I never meant—she flung herself at me. Mac—it wasn't as though I was the only—"

Nelson said, "Did you kill her because she was tired of you or because she threatened to tell MacKenzie?"

In spite of his frenzied state a cunning entered Masters's eyes. "I was sick in bed that day—I had a virus. Mac was there when the doctor told me not to go out."

"And you were there when he telephoned his wife—a bit of information which you relayed to the police after you had made certain she wouldn't tell MacKenzie a few home truths about the friend he was staying with. And the evidence against him seemed so conclusive that the police didn't find it necessary to probe into your affairs beyond a routine check with your doctor and with the landlord to see if you paid your rent. It was understandable that they didn't go further, since money played no obvious role—"

MacKenzie was on his feet, grasping the little man's collar, heaving him out of his chair, shaking him. "You—my friend! When the Army dispensed with your services after that fit of nerves you threw, I felt sorry for you—I took you in the way I'd take a sick cat—"

"Mac—let go—I am sick. I did you a favor—she won't bother you anymore—I got rid of her for you. Mac—you'll kill me!"

MacKenzie dropped him suddenly. He turned and walked to the window. He stood there, his back to the room. Masters, his eyes screwed shut, crouched on the floor, ludicrous, and somehow pathetic. Nelson too turned away from him. The hand he raised to his forehead came away wet.

Comerford cleared his throat but attracted no one's attention. He came forward and put the cuffs on Masters's unresisting hands. He said, "So you got rid of her—eh? And Bridie Mulvey, too. I've put the gist of it on paper and as soon as it's sorted out you'll sign it—or else. What can you lose? The evidence we have on Bridie's death cooks you, so it's only a question of who gets first licks." He bellowed, "Hey, Cliff—come in here."

Together he and the uniformed policeman carried the shriveled leprechaun out of the office.

Dene was at Nelson's side. She took his hand, speaking low. "If I weren't afraid of you I'd raise this to my lips."

He did not feel like smiling, but he smiled.

She glanced at MacKenzie's immobile back. "Will he have to return to California anyway?"

"I think so. I'll call and put the facts before them." He thought it was not improbable that he himself would be summoned.

Dene whispered, "You should have been a lawyer. How did you know?"

Nelson did not look proud of his achievement. "Everything Masters had done since coming here pointed to a man playing for his life."

"If it weren't for Bridie I—I'd be inclined to— Never mind. Are you going to stay over until Monday?"

"Yes." It cheered him slightly. Kyrie—Junie—the warmth of the Cotters. If he did make a flying trip to California he'd take Kyrie and Junie—

"Good. We'll come and thank you properly."

He watched her walk to the window. He saw MacKenzie's arms close around her. It occurred to him that there was no longer any need for his presence.

As he started for the door he heard MacKenzie say, "Dene—are you sure? Men with work like mine make poor husbands. It won't be any bed of roses...."

"So long as it's our bed," Dene said confidently.

THE END

MISCAST FOR MURDER

RUTH FENISONG

Chapter One

Bess picked a manuscript from her desk and began to read. The dreamy contentment of her face was not due to the manuscript's quality. Conversely, she did not owe her less than profound concentration to its shortcomings, nor to the open window through which came the unseasonably warm advances of the October day. Mother's recent letters were responsible. They had not so much as touched upon the usual theme of the dangers that threatened a young girl in a big city. They had contained neither advice, reproaches, nor hints as to Aunt Alma's inadequacy in the role of guardian. They had been full of Mother's new husband, her new surroundings.

Bess crossed her fingers. Her world had at last assumed a pleasant and durable pattern. Employed by the agency to assist the head of the fiction department, she had a little office all to herself, along with the services of a secretary. And while she was not yet entrusted with the work of really important writers, she regarded every manuscript that came to her as a potential discovery, an approach which made her job not only satisfactory but exciting. Just yesterday the owner of the agency had praised one of her reports and hinted at future promotion.

But far more important than her own success was Mother's well-being. Mother had settled down under the protection of James Haskell, a man so dull that by law of compensation it was only logical to suppose him good. The qualities in him that had charmed Mother were obscure to Bess, and no matter. What did matter was that he was steady and solvent, and that his large racing stables in Massachusetts seemed to provide sufficient outlet for Mother's excessive vitality. It mattered so much that at odd moments Bess uttered devout little prayers for continuance. Freed of her burden, she was for the first time conscious of its weight.

It seemed to Bess that almost as soon as she could talk she had felt older than Mother. Mother, who had little more judgment than a strong-willed child, was unaware of this. She went through the motions imposed by her adult status, firmly convinced that Bess was fortunate indeed to command the loving guidance of one so wise as herself. Bess subscribed, too loyal to admit that most of the guidance backfired, whether it dealt with a broken doll, a school dress, or the decorum to be observed on her first date. But somewhere below the surface she hid her knowledge of the relationship's true shape, never resorting to it on her own behalf, assuming control only when Mother seemed about to injure herself. As a very small girl she had thought seriously that it was too bad she had not been on scene to prevent Mother's marriage to Father.

Father had walked out before her third birthday. Raised on a one-sided account of his defection, she had believed that the fault lay entirely with him. Any doubts that arose from time to time she quashed.

Now such doubts need be dealt with no more. Everything had resolved happily for Mother, and everything was beginning for Bess. In spite of Mother's pleas and the obedient echoes of her chosen mate, Bess had found the strength to bypass the new nest. She was twenty-two. She was on her own, because sharing Aunt Alma's apartment was almost as good as being on her own. She was free.

And she was hungry. She set the manuscript aside, determined to do it justice after lunch. With pleasure she confirmed the blankness of the desk calendar. There were no minor writers to be soothed, spurred, or entertained. She could lunch alone, indulge in the treat of furthering her acquaintance with the new Bess. She would go to the restaurant on the corner. It was not very grand, but the food was good.

She stood up, a large well-made girl with fair hair and a clean honey-smooth skin. She was enjoying a thorough stretch when the door of the office opened.

A stocky red-haired man stood on the threshold. His eyes found hers and some of the fighting cock quality went from his stance. "Where am I?" he said.

She lowered her arms. She smiled her best business smile. So far she had been unable to do anything about her naturally hearty voice. "I'm afraid you're in the wrong office, Mr. Basset."

"Maybe not." His light gray eyes were unexpected under the uncompromising red hair. His nose was roughly cut, and his mouth was either crooked or he wore it that way on purpose. "You know me?"

"I've seen you here before—and I used to watch your television program."

"You must be older than you look."

She ignored that. "If the receptionist steered you in here she's made a mistake—"

"Then she's a kindred spirit."

Bess tried not to show that she understood. There were many who believed that Link Basset had overspent his quota of mistakes. His sense of the ridiculous, untempered by discipline, had become the tenor of sponsors. Few remained who were hardy enough to brave his handling of commercials. Fortunately for him he had talents other than showmanship. Lately he had been much in demand as a scriptwriter.

He said, "It wasn't the receptionist," and added, "She asked me to wait and I'm not the waiting type—so I struck out on my own."

Bess wished he would strike out for somewhere else. She said, "Did you have an appointment with anyone?"

"Yes—Art West—"

"You'll find him down the hall. The door says 'Radio and Television.'" She took her coat from the rack.

"Not so fast. Before I left for California I spotted you here and made up my mind to have a closer look when I returned."

Bess did not believe it. She said, "You'll miss your appointment."

"It will keep. I've lost the Mr. Art West mood. Where are you going?"

"To lunch."

"I'll walk a piece with you. What's your name?"

"Bess Rohan—fiction department." She tacked that on because she suddenly needed the reassurance of her position.

He considered her. "Against this background you do have a fictional air. There should be tinkling cowbells and the scent of hay."

She was not flattered. She knew she looked "small town" in spite of her efforts to acquire the urbanity that seemed the heritage of the youngest office boy. But she thought that to accuse her of looking bucolic was carrying it too far. She said, "Excuse me—I'm going to the ladies' room."

She lingered deliberately, and when she returned, Link Basset had quit the office. But he was in the reception room talking to the girl at the desk. She heard him say, "Tell West I've changed my mind. I'm too busy to take on anything else." Then he saw her, and his "Trying to wriggle out of it, are you?" was delivered as a stern reproach. He took her arm and steered her toward the corridor.

On the sunny street, Bess said, "I'm only going as far as the corner—"

"Are you ashamed to be seen walking with me?"

"No—of course not—"

"Would you be ashamed to be seen eating with me?"

"No—"

"I choose not to hear the note of hesitation in your voice. Come along."

The agency had inured her to some outstandingly odd behavior. She walked beside him, normalizing the situation with a comment about the fine day.

He said, "I'll discuss it with you after breakfast."

"Breakfast?"

"Haven't you heard? The great Basset is now a disk jockey." He gave her a sidewise glance. "No—you haven't heard. If your complexion wasn't won crouching over a desk you certainly didn't get it staying up nights listening to platterpusses. I broadcast from eleven to two in the morning. Then I streak for my lonely couch. Breakfast is whenever I have strength enough to face it."

"Have you been doing it long?"

"A few months—interrupted by my trip to the Coast."

She said lamely, "What network are you on?"

"No network. An independent station emanating from a restaurant called the Bull and Bean—in the Village."

"Oh."

"Don't make it sound so mournful. It's not such a comedown as all that. It might wear thin after a while, but for the time being I enjoy it. Most people are asleep or drunk or otherwise employed at that time of night, so I can say and do pretty much as I choose without let or hindrance—and let's face it—I'm a man who likes to be heard and who doesn't like let or hindrance. Well—here's the corner—is this your eatery?"

"Yes—but if you don't—"

"I don't. We'll go across the street to Gilly's. Why not?"

"Wait—the lights haven't changed."

He did not wait. He grasped her arm again and, dodging traffic, maneuvered her to the opposite curb.

She hated unnecessary risks, and several cars had barely missed her. She opened her mouth for rebuke. But he was staring at Gilly's sign as though it might be an enemy. And that, she thought, was understandable. The restaurant was frequented by the radio and television crowd. Becoming an all-night disk jockey after an unusually successful start as an entertainer was, she thought, a demotion that few would care to flaunt. She wondered why a man like Link Basset should insist upon flaunting it, and supposed vaguely that he was urged by the same principle that made a man remount a horse from which he had been thrown.

She offered him a chance to change his mind. "I hope you won't be offended, but I really did plan to eat alone. I've things to work out in my mind and—"

"I won't interrupt your thinking. I can chew real quiet when I want to." He marched her through the door.

Bess was relieved that their entrance caused no stir. Then she thought that to a man like Link Basset this must be an added blow. A man like Link Basset? A silly phrase, since she knew nothing at all about him beyond the dubious tidbits featured in his publicity.

A few tepid greetings marked his passage across the room. The groups at the bar and at the tables seemed engrossed in conversation. They were, of course, talking shop. That was a safe guess even without the corroboration of stray technical terms that struck the ear. But in spite of the general atmosphere of preoccupation, Bess caught, or thought she caught, several glances directed at her. Amused, she gave them leave to make what they could of her unspectacular appearance. Link Basset was rumored to have a way with women. Not a good way—there were those who took liberties with the last syllable of his name—and not with women like herself. When lunch with a client was scheduled she took more care to be smart. She wished that she had taken more care today. But it was only a fleeting wish. She was sensible. Mother's sensible girl. Mother spent hours at her toilet. But Mother said to her, "You haven't a natural flair, dear. We must be realistic about it. So long as you're clean and neat—"

A waiter seated them at an empty table. Link Basset did not consult the menu. He ordered a pot of coffee, scrambled eggs, and toast, and left Bess to shift for herself. She settled for a sandwich and coffee. It was less than her appetite demanded, but she assumed that Link Basset would pay, and she was uncertain of how much or how little a disk jockey earned. She did not credit his assertion that he liked the job. She thought that the grapevine might have exaggerated his success as a scriptwriter.

He drank coffee with a desert thirst. He did not speak, and Bess wondered why he had made such an issue of accompanying her. He could have been quite as happy gnawing his bone in solitude. Her polite essay at small talk died unwatered. Her sandwich eaten, she sat at a loss, hearing with something like envy the easy rise and fall of the room's voice.

The waiter shoved the menu at her again, and without thinking she ordered an expensive dessert.

Link Basset chose that moment to exercise his voice. "Finished working things out in your mind?"

"Oh—is that why you were so silent?"

"Why else? Know what? You won't keep your looks long."

"My looks?"

"Starchy sandwiches—fattening desserts. You should have had a steak and a salad. You're the type who puts on weight fast." He added darkly, "I've seen it happen."

I might have ordered steak if you hadn't horned in, she thought. But she was too interested to be annoyed. Rarely had her vanity been fostered by compliments because the strong shadow of Mother's personality had all but obscured her. And now this unexpected companion hinted that she had looks to keep. Naïvely she asked for more. "Do you think I'm too fat?"

He seemed entertained. "Not for me."

"I didn't mean—"

His crooked mouth held a cigarette. He said without bothering to remove it, "But then—I'm tired of bed slats masquerading as women. Only don't overdo it."

The waiter brought a large serving of pastry bogged down in heavy cream. She consumed every bit of it.

Link Basset said, "You burn easily."

She fumbled in her handbag. She shook her head as he pushed the cigarette package across the table.

"You *are* burned—and that's quick work even for me. It often takes as long as three or four dates."

She said, "I'm hunting for my purse."

"You intend to pick up the check?"

"Yes. It isn't as though this is a real date. It—it's just an accident."

"Not fatal, I hope. Well—it couldn't have happened to a sweeter kid—meaning me. Anyway—it wasn't an accident. I've called on Art West enough to know where his office is. How long have you been in New York?"

"I don't see—well—about four months."

"I thought so. How old are you?"

"Older than you seem to think—old enough to enjoy intelligent conversation."

"All right. You launch it."

She could think of nothing to say. Her duties at the agency had laid on a thin coating of worldliness untried by outside contacts. Now, at first test, it cracked open, leaving her exposed. She felt gauche and lumpy.

Suddenly he was kind, a schoolmaster encouraging a backward pupil. "So you work in the fiction department. Are you a literary agent by calling or couldn't you find honest work?"

She said stiffly, "I've always read a great deal." It sounded stupid. The annoyance she directed at herself helped to mend the cracked veneer. "One of my professors at college knew Mrs. Purdy, who runs the agency. He recommended me to her."

"A college girl," he said. "What college?"

"I doubt if you've heard of it." She had attended a small institution within commuting distance of Salisbury, Connecticut, her home town. She had longed to go further afield, but Mother could not spare her.

"You have the advantage of me," Link Basset said. "I didn't even finish high school."

At least he had stopped being kind. He was lighting another cigarette, staring moodily at the burnt match in his hand. There's nothing frightening about him, she thought. He's only a conceited young man who makes a cult of bad manners.

She said, "I'll have to be getting back to the office."

"Wait until I've finished my cigarette. Smoking in the street is too feminine."

She smiled at that. One of the first things she had observed in New York was the number of women who found it necessary to smoke outdoors. But the charming transformation of her face was lost to Link Basset. He was glowering at a couple heading for the next table. The girl, a small dark beauty, seemed barely twenty. So, Mother might have looked and held herself at that same age, except that Mother's face had never worn that moody withdrawn expression. The man was tall and straight. He walked young, but his face bore a record of more than sixty years. Bess watched him preempt a table, watched him make a ceremony of holding the girl's chair, kept watching until Link Basset called her back to him.

Link Basset said loudly, "Didn't your fine college education teach you that it was rude to stare?"

Agonized, she whispered, "Shhh—they'll hear you."

"Not a chance." He did not lower his voice. "One of them's mislaid her wits—the other's left his ear trumpet at home."

"Please—"

He stood up. He muttered something that might have been

an excuse, and when she dared follow him with her eyes he was standing over the table of the latecomers. The girl looked up at him with obvious distaste. Then her escort spoke and Link Basset's face grew ugly.

Bess waited for no more. She picked up her purse and made blindly for the open air. She almost ran the distance to her office. Link Basset caught up with her as she reached the entrance.

"Talk about bats out of hell," he said. "Do you have to punch a time clock? You haven't been gone a full hour—and any time I want to reach an agent he's out to lunch from dawn till dusk."

Her words were ragged. "Did you—did you hit him?"

"Hit who? Oh, him? A good idea. Too bad you didn't submit it sooner. If a man his age acts my age why shouldn't I take full advantage?" He stared at her curiously. "What's the matter with you? Are you president of the anti-violence league or something? You couldn't be a fan. Kevin Culhane was long before your time."

She released her bitten lower lip. "I don't like scenes."

His astonishment was real. "Do you call what happened in Gilly's a scene?"

She said desperately, "I'm sure it wasn't up to your usual standard."

"You've been taking my press notices too seriously. I see my work's cut out for me. I'm going to have a king-size job undoing—"

"If you'll excuse me—"

He blocked her way. "Is there a bar in the building?"

"I don't— Yes—yes, there is. Will you please let me pass?"

He stepped aside. But when she reached the lobby he was with her. He said, "If you really don't like scenes you'll come quietly. I'm going to buy you a drink."

"No—"

"Yes."

"Why are you pretending an interest in me?"

"I'm not pretending. You're riddle enough to interest anyone—a girl who conjures up everything wholesome—"

"Stop—"

"—and who's so neurotic inside that she trembles and goes white around the gills because her escort turns out to be no gentleman. Listen—at first acquaintance I may not be the most lovable little character in the world, but grant me some kind of a conscience. If I've brought on that strange pallor I want to make amends."

"You didn't bring anything on," she said. "I just feel a little—a little funny."

"Sickish? Maybe that dessert—"

"No. But thank you for trying to help." She felt as unreal as the prim words. She looked around her at the people scurrying toward the elevators. She fancied that they looked back with avid searching eyes. She thought that they could see through her wholesome exterior, had free access to the tumult within. She wanted to hide, and all because a chance encounter had shaken her beyond reason. She heard herself saying in a small voice, "This is ridiculous—"

"Agreed. Nevertheless, I'm sticking to it that you need a drink. I forgot to offer you one at lunch. But you forgot your promise to pick up the check, so maybe we're even." He stopped her instinctive play with the catch of her handbag.

"A public money transaction might be witnessed and misinterpreted by one of the agency's spies."

She went with him. If she looked the way he said she looked it would be wise to pull herself together before she returned to the office. She welcomed the dimness of the quiet bar, the close safe confines of the booth to which he led her.

He ordered two double brandies. "To the end of it," he said, and marked her faint grimace as she sipped. "In case there's any doubt, I don't mean to the end of us. I mean the end of whatever's eating you."

She had not even heard the toast. She said, "Oh."

"That's informative. Well—one thing they don't accuse Basset of is prying—maybe because he goes about it so subtly. Why are you making faces? Me or the brandy?"

Through her preoccupation she thought that now it was he who must assume the burden of small talk. She made an effort to cooperate. "If I'm making faces I suppose it's the brandy. It's rather strong, isn't it? I don't know much about liquor."

"I thought that was one of the first requirements in your racket. How do you manage when you entertain the clients?"

"I'm only an assistant so I don't entertain much. When I do I ask what they want and I take the same."

"Making believe it's your favorite tipple?" He approved her smile. "Then make believe I'm a client—and have another."

Surprised, she glanced at her empty glass. She shook her head. The drink had dispelled her feeling of unreality, or perhaps emphasized it to the point where it no longer troubled her. "I'm much better," she said, meaning it.

"You look better. The stuff has an insidious effect when it's sipped. More so than if you gulp it down."

"It seems as though it should be the other way around."

"It isn't. I know because I work that way on people too. Witness the way you've been seeing me for the last minute or so—through a glow that almost persuades you I'm human."

"You're much nicer than I expected you to be."

"Sure. Me and brandy. Fool you every time. By the way—do you know Selene Rolfe?"

It was not by the way. His slight change of tone made that clear. Gravely she considered the question. "Selene Rolfe? No. Is she a celebrity?"

"Not yet—but she will be if her old lady has any say in the matter." He shrugged his square shoulders. "Maybe I've been jumping to conclusions again. Why should I be modest about it? No man living can compete with me in the field of jumping to conclusions. Well—if you don't know her why the hell were you staring in the restaurant?"

She said uncertainly, "Is Selene Rolle your girl?"

"That poor chick is nobody's girl unless Kevin Culhane—Kevin Culhane! A euphonious handle—and I do mean phony. He's managed to keep it dark, but his real name is probably something that would stink in lights—not that he's been in lights for many a year. Did you say something?"

She had been trying not to say something, but it pushed through her lips with irresistible force. "Kevin Culhane is his real name."

Link Basset said caustically, "An interesting assumption—strongly based, I'm sure."

"You needn't go back to being rude. Kevin Culhane is my father."

"Your what?"

He was so patently embarrassed that she forgot her own mixed emotions. "It's all right," she said comfortingly, "we've never really tried to make a secret of it."

He swallowed. "We?"

"My mother and I. It was just that I didn't realize he was in New York. Running into him like that upset me a little—"

He muttered something. His voice came back full volume. "And until lunch I had him pegged as a decent old party. I think I'll go right around to the Gretna and finish the round."

"The Gretna?"

"The fleabag that shelters him when he's in town. He says he goes back there out of superstition because that's where he lived when he got his first professional engagement. I'll fix his luck. One good poke should—"

"But why?"

"He's begging for it is why. He had me fooled—not even the decency to recognize his own daughter."

"How could he recognize me? He hasn't seen me since I was a baby. I wouldn't have known him either—except that Aunt Alma kept some pictures of him—"

"Aunt Alma?"

"I'm living with her. She's my mother's sister."

"Is your mother alive?"

"Oh yes—she's just married again and—"

"Married? Again?"

"Yes—I told you—" Bess reddened. "Oh—I see. I guess you thought—" She could not help laughing at his expression. "I'm sorry. It was nice of you to want to avenge a—a wrong, but—"

He said coldly, "It is to laugh. You did tell me your name was Rohan."

"It's Mother's maiden name. She—we preferred to use it."

"So I haven't even an illegitimate excuse to clobber the guy," he said.

Chapter Two

Bess Rohan's Aunt Alma was a widow who had been left with a more than adequate income. She lived in the Washington Square area on a side street off Fifth Avenue. The brownstone house was a reconverted private dwelling. It contained four separate apartments and Aunt Alma had leased its spacious first floor for years. She had come to love that section of the city, and she experienced a sense of loss each time a group of its small old buildings gave ground to a teeming warren of modern design. Once Bess had heard her threaten to stage a sit-down strike should her own quarters be sold from under her.

Bess did not take the threat seriously. Aunt Alma showed none of the qualities that stamp a fighter of causes. Always she seemed to accept what came to her, and if it had been necessary to cut or compress her desires drastically in order to fit them into the uncomplicated form of her existence, the effect was unnoticeable. She had the face of a philosophical gypsy, and the city's tensions had drawn few lines upon it. Nor had the fact of widowhood after a brief early marriage left perceptible scars. She looked a slim modish woman aging with comfort and grace. Bess hoped to meet the years with equal poise. Bess had often been troubled by the sense of outrage with which Mother greeted oncoming birthdays. But of course Mother, a real beauty, had so much more to lose. And, too, she was without the insulation of solid financial circumstances, or had been until James Haskell took over. Her struggle to make a decent home for herself and her child, eased only by sporadic alimony and by gifts from Aunt Alma, would naturally have affected her outlook, Bess thought. In making comparisons between Mother and Aunt Alma, Bess was conscious of no disloyalty. Mother would always come first with her, but Aunt Alma would not come second or third or fourth. Aunt Alma, with no apparent effort, had made her own place in Bess's heart.

Aunt Alma had taken the advent of her niece with habitual composure. She maintained a hands-off attitude, treating the girl as she would have treated any respected guest, presuming in no way upon blood kinship or superior age. An outsider might have supposed her attitude to spring from lack of proper interest. But Bess, rather than feeling slighted, drew from it peace and privacy.

Bess came home a little early that evening. The bulky manuscript she carried was by way of penance for the restlessness that had driven her from the office, the bunches of daffodils an impulse purchase from a street vendor. So laden, she managed to fit her key to the apartment's lock. When the door slammed behind her she called out apologetically, "It's Bess, Aunt Alma. Sorry I made such a racket."

She dropped the manuscript on the hall table beside the telephone and took the flowers to the kitchen. She stood on the threshold for a moment to sniff a tantalizing oven fragrance. Then she went to the cabinet where spare vases were kept. She found one with a wide mouth, filled it, and dropped the flowers in. She bore them to the living room, calling, "Happy Indian Summer." Under the high archway she stood foolishly, contemplating the empty room.

A small table near the idle brick fireplace was set for one. The folded sheet of paper propped between salt and pepper shakers caught her eyes. She placed the vase on a bookshelf and crossed the thick-piled rug.

"Dear Bess," she read. "I thought you would like to eat in here for a change. The dining table might seem lonely without company and I've been invited out to dinner. The casserole is almost done. Just turn on the light in the oven for about fifteen minutes. I've washed the salad greens and mixed the dressing, and there's plenty of fruit. Good appetite. Aunt Alma."

Obediently Bess went to turn on the oven light, came back, and sat down on a soft couch. She glanced absently at the silver-gray walls made interesting by bright prints, at the books, the pleasant easy furnishings. She sighed because the apartment seemed empty without Aunt Alma, and because she was bursting with an account of her day.

She had become so accustomed to the older woman's companionship each evening that for a moment she experienced a pang of resentment at the break in the pattern. I'm spoiled, she told herself. I've been taking things too much for granted. Probably Aunt Alma went out a great deal when she was alone. I must be careful not to grow dependent upon her. She has her own life to live.

Still, she could not help wishing that Aunt Alma had chosen another night to live her own life, especially since under her roof the subject of Kevin Culhane was not taboo.

Bess had discovered a folder of his photographs in a desk given over to her use, and Aunt Alma had said casually that they must have been taken on one of his tours. Now Bess wondered how they had come to be in her possession. She had asked no questions at the time because somehow it seemed unfair to Mother to show curiosity. Curiosity was not exactly the right word, but then, what emotion should she be expected to feel for a man who had never evidenced the slightest affection for her? None, she told herself. And she felt none. Or had felt none until today. And whatever it was she felt today was due to the surprise element in seeing Kevin Culhane in the flesh.

She had managed a good look at the pictures before Aunt Alma put them somewhere else or, for all she knew, disposed of them entirely. Clear prints, unyellowed, the edges not even curled, the likeness strong enough to make today's instant recognition possible. But they had been in a flat folder, protected from exposure to light, and the heavy theatrical makeup made it impossible to judge the age of the sitter. Anyway, if Aunt Alma had kept in touch with him after the divorce, she would have said so.

Funny that this morning she had not mentioned a dinner engagement. Perhaps an unexpected friend had arrived from out of town. Or maybe she was with a neighbor in distress. She was always performing neighborly services, from babysitting in the Square to running up a small party dress on her sewing machine. Still, at this hour it was unusual for her to— Mind your own business, Bess. And you've business to mind. Get dinner over with and settle down to that manuscript.

The casserole was delicious. Aunt Alma's cooking tasted of the pleasure that went into it. She kept the kitchen as her own province, employing only a daily maid to clean the large apartment. Too bad, Bess thought, ambushing the last mushroom on her plate, that she had not remarried and borne children. She would have made a perfect wife and mother. She loved children. Bess did too. Someday she hoped to have a large family; lusty little boys and girls, happy in each other's warmth, secure, never lonely—

Suppose, she thought, that someone other than Link Basset had walked into her office. Say an ordinary everyday young man, not too clever, not too handsome. Just nice. And suppose she had lunched with him and liked him very much. And he had liked her too. And they shared interests that made further meetings a mutual need. Dreamily she eyed a lettuce leaf. And suppose—

A street sound pierced the adolescent fantasy. With a deprecatory shrug she rose to clear the table. Link Basset was the one she had lunched with, and he was neither everyday nor nice, even though for a while there in the bar she had—well—liked him. But the only interest she shared with him was the one she would have preferred to keep from him, and he had undoubtedly thrust her from his mind as soon as they separated. Not that she cared.

She stood in the kitchen to drink coffee so that she would not be tempted to idle away more time. She disposed of the dishes, fetched the manuscript from the hall table, and sat down at the desk in her bedroom. She sharpened a pencil to a fine point. She placed a stack of yellow paper at her elbow so that she could make notes. She got up for a drink of water and, coming back, stood on the threshold to admire the way that Aunt Alma had furnished the room. The desk, set back in a small alcove, was quite detached from the very feminine sleeping and dressing quarters. My own private place, she thought with satisfaction, and wondered if she could ever thank Aunt Alma enough for all she had done.

She attacked the manuscript, reading a whole chapter, but using her pencil only to correct unimportant typographical errors. Either the writer was unusually obscure or she was unusually stupid. She wriggled. She looked at her watch. How had it got to be past nine?

She decided weakly that a bit of exercise might work off her restlessness. Besides, there was no real hurry. It was Friday and she had a whole free weekend before her. Ample time to tackle the job in the way that it should be tackled. She put on her coat and went out.

She walked up a well-peopled Fifth Avenue. The air had cooled and was as fresh as New York air could be. Without the sun's emphasis, its perversely stimulating blend of coal dust and gasoline and refuse and human smells was weaker, yet still heady. Her stride, acquired on country roads, devoured the city blocks. She had almost reached Thirtieth Street before it occurred to her to turn back.

For variety on the homeward stretch she cut across to Sixth Avenue. She was nearing it when her attention was arrested. She had probably passed the dirty gray building several times without noticing it. Now, not fully conscious of why she did so, she halted her steps. The legend on the tattered green canopy claimed her eyes. Hotel Gretna, it said. And she recalled a voice amending it with, *"The fleabag that shelters him when he's in town."*

Standing there, she could classify at least one of the emotions aroused by her father. It was pity for an aging man who had lingered on miserably after the death of his success. How did he live? Putting up a prosperous front was the be-all and end-all of unemployed show people, she knew. But when he was not putting up a front at places like Gilly's, did he eat enough? Did he need money?

Her move toward the entrance was involuntary. The lobby, seen through a glass door, looked no more shabby than that of the hotel in her home town. But its meager dimensions had never been intended for the jostling crowd it contained. In the act of entering she stepped back as two nondescript men emerged.

The smaller, less prepossessing of them glanced at her and said, "Live here, sister?"

"No—"

He put his hand on her arm. "Then how about postponing your visit?"

Indignant, a little frightened, she pushed his hand away. In the dim light under the canopy she saw him grin at his companion. It seemed an evil grin. He said, "Excuse it. I didn't mean to scare—"

But she was in flight for the second time that day. For the second time she was all but racing over the pavements toward shelter.

It took a while before she could command her pace to slow, before her imagination stopped vesting every tread behind her with sinister intent. Able to think with more or less calm, she was grateful that her impulse had been thwarted. What had possessed her? How could she have dreamed of doing such a ridiculous thing? To walk in uninvited upon a strange man—strange, for all that he had fathered her—was worse than ridiculous. It was lunatic. Would she have followed through by asking him bluntly if he needed money? Or would she have simpered sweetly, "Daddy darling, I am your long-lost daughter, Bess. I have come to lift you out of your sordid environment. Embrace me and let bygones be bygones."

There on the dark street she dealt furiously with herself, demanding in bitterness if she would ever achieve the barest margin of sophistication, just enough to keep her from playing the fool. He had found money to take a young girl to lunch. He had looked well-dressed from where she sat. And no matter what his straits, how unlikely that he would receive a full-grown offspring with anything approaching welcome. She shuddered at the embarrassment so narrowly escaped.

Someone touched her shoulder as she was about to climb the brownstone steps of home. She turned angrily, sure in her overwrought state that she would confront the wolf of the Gretna Hotel.

"Don't strike me," Link Basset said, pretending to duck. He was hatless. The shadows turned his red hair to black. It needed a comb.

"Where—where did you come from?"

"Baby dear."

"What?"

"It's 'Where did you come from, Baby dear?' And I answer, 'Out of everywhere into here.' End of quote." He sounded like a man trying and failing to sound flippant. "Do you ask me in?"

She glanced at the living room windows. She had left the lights on. They shone palely through the drawn curtains. She said, "I don't know if Aunt Alma's home."

"I'll try not to miss her. Keys, please."

She handed them over because she did not know how to

refuse. "The larger one is for the house door."

The apartment was still empty. She was glad of that. She hoped that Aunt Alma would stay out until Link Basset had left, because she was in no mood to offer even the token explanation that might be required to bridge a social gap. She had also lost her desire to mention or hear mentioned the name of her father. If Link Basset had sought her for that reason it was too bad. But perhaps his being here was no more than coincidence. He worked in the Village. Could he just have been passing the house when—?

He stood in the archway of the living room. She became conscious of her duties as hostess. "Won't you sit down?"

He said, "Charming place. If Aunt Alma's responsible for it maybe I do miss her." He passed under the archway, and when she seated herself he took a facing chair.

She thought that he did not look at ease, but supposed that he might be reflecting her own sense of awkwardness. She said, "How did you get my address? It isn't listed under Rohan."

"The night operator at the agency gave it to me. I said I was Ernest Hemingway. I'm not, of course. Still—you never know. One of these days I might become a client of yours."

"I thought you were a client."

"Of Art West's. I mean I might become a fiction department client."

"I keep forgetting that you write too."

"Thanks for the 'too.' Writing was my first love. Someday maybe I'll do a book."

"Really?" Her attention strayed. She looked down at her wristwatch. She wondered if Aunt Alma had telephoned while she was out. Not that there was any reason for her to telephone. It was only a little after ten. Not late, but—

Link Basset said, "They call her Bess, the elusive—as hard to nail down as a blown leaf—"

She drifted back to him. "I'm sorry."

"You should be. I was about to elaborate wittily upon my future ambitions when you up and vanished."

"Well—you see—I brought home some work to do—"

"You've the whole weekend to do it in. Live at first hand for a change."

She said on a note of resignation, "Shall I make coffee—or a drink?"

"Later."

"Oh. What time did you say your broadcast started?"

"At eleven. But tonight some political outfit bought time on the station, so I don't go on until twelve." He laughed at her shocked expression.

After a moment she joined in, and the air between them cleared a little. He clouded it again with, "Aren't you going to ask me why you're being honored with this visit?"

She heard herself say a firm "No."

"Well—I'll tell you anyway."

"Please don't. If it's more about Kevin Culhane I've said everything there is to say."

It was his turn to look shocked, but he recovered before she could decide whether or not he had been acting. "Is the girl completely devoid of vanity?" he said. "I came here under strong compulsion. The truth is that since we parted you've been growing on me until you assumed such mammoth proportions that—"

She cut in dryly, "You do make me sound attractive." Then she said, "Why *are* you here?"

"Haven't you been listening—or don't you recognize an honest declaration of passion when you hear it?"

She did her best to enter into the game, feeling hopelessly ignorant of its rules. "I recognize that it would be sensible of you to go home and rest before your broadcast."

"I am resting. Restfulness is part of your allure."

She lost patience. "You must be pretty hard up if this sort of thing amuses you. It doesn't me."

"I'd be insulted if it did. What, by the way, *is* your reaction to Basset? You may speak frankly."

"Very well. Frankly—I'm bored."

"That's a lie. Basset is never boring. If you'll come with me to the Bull and Bean, I'll prove it by the way I hold the worst lushes in the palm of my hand. What's more—you've never been bored in your life. You see things with a child's clear wondering eyes—as though they were happening for the first time."

"I know this line of yours isn't happening for the first time."

"Not bad. Under the proper tutelage you—"

"Oh, for heaven's sake!"

Unaccountably she was not altogether relieved to see him rise. But instead of heading for the door he began to roam the room.

He said, "I had an idea that innocent country girls who come to New York to make their fortunes surround themselves with photographs of the folks they left behind. You don't even have a picture of your mother."

"Of course I have—"

"Well—why isn't it out in the open? Or do you hesitate to clutter Aunt Alma's living room with her sister's pan? What's the pitch? Don't they get along?"

"Really," she said. "Really—!"

"Now, now—don't burn. It only spurs me on to further effort." His voice became pacific. "I would like to see your mother's picture. A man whose intentions are honorable can't help wanting to know the worst."

"The worst? My mother's beautiful—far more beautiful than your Selene Rolfe. If I looked like my mother I—I wouldn't have to put up with— I'd know how to deal with a man like you."

"Then why are you making a song and dance of such a reasonable request?"

"What possible pleasure do you get from goading me? I didn't invite—" Unable to complete the rudeness, unable to stand firm against the goad, she stalked from the room and came back carrying a silver frame.

Link Basset took it from her and held it under a lamp. She could make nothing of his expression.

Chapter Three

A few blocks from the Hotel Gretna was a steak and chophouse so long established that it had become a landmark. As prices went, the items it offered were reasonable, and from six o'clock onward it had been crowded. At a little before nine, most of the tables were empty, and on the uniform mask of the staff individuality began to reassert itself.

One young waiter would have frowned if he dared. His mind had speeded before him to the locker room where he would shed the garments of his trade in preparation for the real business of living. He had nothing against his two remaining clients except that they held him back. He gave the slim well-groomed woman full counts for not trying to look like a chicken. She had been up to no tricks with her graying brown hair, but her eyes had stayed young, and so had her figure. Earlier he had thought that she looked like a stage version of a gypsy. Something to do with her high cheekbones and fine features and the remains of a summer tan. Or maybe it was just the way she carried her head.

The old gent would not have been out of place behind the

footlights either. Two to one he had walked the boards in the past. But if you were to go by the suit he wore, someone had upstaged him plenty.

The waiter needed new clothes, himself. And he had a date with a girl who never listened to excuses. And he would be late, which meant that the tips he had been able to save were as good as spent for appeasement. Suppressed profanity pushed against his teeth. If he was any judge, this couple would add nil to the right side of the ledger, unless the lady picked up the check. He doubted that she would, because whoever spouted that stuff about the woman paying and paying was nothing but hard up for material. And anyway, the old gent looked proud.

The boss had given the old gent a big greeting, but that did not mean money. The boss was sentimental, barring his treatment of the hired help. Sardonically the waiter reviewed a few of the boss's rules. "When not serving, fade out. Always be near enough to catch their signals, but not near enough to listen to their conversation."

In this case there was nothing to listen to. They had talked sixteen to the dozen at first, the lady encouraging the old gent, while he put on the usual act about an expected contract. But for the last few minutes they had been acting like mutes. Were they married? He thought not. The lady had arrived first, and when the old gent appeared it was more of a reunion than a routine setup. Lovers? He shook his head. Men of that age on the loose generally ran to cute little bundles like—well—like his date for tonight. Reminded of her, his sense of urgency was renewed. He thrust his uncooperative jaw as far forward as it would go and stepped out of prescribed obscurity to tilt the silvered pot over Alma Elliot's cup.

He let the few remaining drops trickle down and said, "Do you wish fresh coffee, madame?" his tone challenging Madame to wish for anything so unreasonable. And at the same time his sharp eyes raked the top of the old gent's bowed head. To hell with the rules.

Alma Elliot saw Kevin Culhane stir uneasily. She saw the inadequately fleshed structure that was his hand rise to touch his soft thinning hair. She looked up at the waiter, forcing him to meet her gaze. He stood his ground. But he expelled a breath of relief when she turned to the old gent.

She said, "I'm afraid we've outstayed our welcome, Kevin," and could almost follow his journey back from leagues away. Then she stifled an exclamation because in lowering his hand he struck and overturned his coffee cup and some of the liquid spattered his white shirt.

He said, "Sorry," brushing aside the waiter's halfhearted attempt to mop up. "I—I was thinking. Shall we go, Alma? I'll ask for the check."

The waiter had it ready. He reached without ceremony for the bills that bled out of the old gent's remarkably thin wallet, and made a record run from table to cash register and back. The tip exceeded his expectations. Yet, watching the couple leave the restaurant, he felt as though he had betrayed a kinship. As soon as the pooled tips were divided he would be off to spend his and the old gent's hard-earned share on a—? Life was one horse laugh after another. Still, there were compensations. He cleared the table and made a frenzied dash for the locker room.

Outside, Alma Elliot and Kevin Culhane started walking. She said, "That was an excellent dinner. Thank you—but are you sure—?"

"Your company is worth more than a million dinners. Next time there'll be champagne. At least there will be if—"

"Stop worrying, Kevin."

"I shouldn't have dumped my troubles on you."

"They're troubles that won't materialize."

"I've learned to count on nothing."

"Then unlearn. You're off to a new start."

"Not quite."

"You will be—as soon as the contract's signed."

"It isn't signed yet."

"Kevin—you haven't told me everything. Is it Lisa?"

He hesitated. Then he said, "I've told you too much for your peace of mind."

"Very well—but if your present mood has anything to do with Lisa—"

"It's just that she—if she— At any breath of scandal television folk shy like frightened horses."

"I'll handle Lisa."

He halted and turned toward her. "Alma—do you think you can?"

"Yes," she said firmly, and changed the subject. "I suppose we'll be in for a spell of bad weather any minute now—but it's nice tonight—isn't it? I wouldn't mind walking home if it was a bit earlier, but—"

"You've been a good friend, Alma."

Her voice went dry. "Someone must uphold the honor of the

family."

"Is that why you've always gone out of your way to—?"

She took his arm. "I had no right to say that. We're good friends to each other because we're fond of each other. It's quite simple."

"It might have been simple once," he said. "We'd have been happy together if only I'd seen straight—"

Again her voice dried. "Let's be realistic. I was never attractive to you in that way, Kevin."

"Your husband was a fine man. You were engaged to him when Lisa brought me home. I—"

She laughed as though she were genuinely amused. And after a moment he said, "Yes—I suppose it is a ridiculous conversation—all things considered. Do you want a cab now?"

"I suppose so. Bess will be wondering what's happened to me."

"It was kind of you to take her in."

"Kind? She's my niece."

"I know—and it's sheer effrontery for me to thank you—or to express any interest in her."

"It's unlike you to be so touchy, Kevin. Besides, neither the fact that she's my sister's child nor yours has much to do with it. If Bess were a complete stranger I'd love her. She's that kind of girl."

"Has she mentioned me—told you how she feels about me?"

Alma Elliot fished desperately for something to assuage the hunger in his voice. "She came across a folder of your pictures and was extremely interested."

"She was?" Two empty cabs rolled by, one after the other. Kevin Culhane did nothing to arrest them.

Alma Elliot said, "Look—why don't you come back to the house with me and see your daughter?"

"If the contract were signed—if I didn't have to present myself as a beaten—"

"Don't talk that way. You're not beaten. And if you were it wouldn't influence Bess in the slightest."

"You're right," he said heavily. "My financial status is minor as weighed against everything else. It's Lisa's influence I dread—and in the face of that, what sort of reception can I expect?"

"Come and find out. You want to—don't you?"

"Yes—I want to—I've always wanted to." Suddenly he seemed to grow a little taller. He said with touching eagerness,

"I want to and I will—but not in a coffee-spotted shirt. Alma, come to the hotel and wait for me. It will be the quickest change I've made in years."

As soon as she accepted the impulsive invitation, Alma Elliot began to doubt its wisdom. But she could not bring herself to lower his lift of mood. She walked to the hotel with him and waited in the so-called writing room that was no more than a musty box off the lobby. Waiting, she worried.

Bess, open in all else, had never spoken his name until the photographs were discovered. Even then she had revealed nothing. And now her aunt bemoaned the tactlessness that had engineered a situation for which no groundwork had been laid. She wanted neither Bess nor Kevin to be hurt, yet realized that Bess could not be blamed whatever her reaction. The one-sided diet she had been fed from childhood would not make for straight thinking any more than a diet of sugar and starch would make for straight bones. It was miracle enough that she had weathered her upbringing so well. Poor Bess. Poor Kevin.

Very poor Kevin. Either he could not find a clean shirt or he had lost his touch at making a "quick change." She prayed with all her heart that he would be granted the opportunity for a new start, that at least some part of his life would prosper. How unfair it was to be deprived of his own flesh and blood. How unfair it had always been. If only Bess responded in the hoped-for way. Was there time left to warn her? She might refuse to see him, leave the apartment before he arrived. But that would be better than a cold unprofitable meeting. If that happened, Kevin would never know that he had driven her away. He could be allowed to think that she was just out, as was consistent with pretty young girls. There must be a telephone somewhere about.

Alma Elliot left the dusty box and braved the few seedy loiterers in the lobby. In passing she glanced at the clock above the desk, and what it told her made her forget her objective. It had been ten minutes to nine when they left the restaurant, and the walk had taken less than ten minutes. Was it possible that she had been sitting in that wretched hole for half an hour? What could have happened to Kevin?

The desk clerk seemed blended of boredom and oiled hair. He nodded when she asked if the clock was right, but did not trouble to look at her.

She said, "Will you ring Kevin Culhane's room, please."

At that he gave her a grudging glance, making it plain that

he saw nothing to hold his interest. Then he unhitched the telephone and said into its mouthpiece, "Gimme seven-eighteen." To the brooch at her throat he said, "You wanna speak to him?"

"If you please."

"No dice. He's out."

"He can't be out. I've been waiting for him—he—"

"I gave him plenty of time to answer, lady." He replaced the receiver. "You heard me ring his number—"

She walked away from the desk. Kevin had not answered because he was on the way down, and she had better not telephone Bess or she would miss him. The hotel was equipped with two elevators. She took up a stand near the one that was working, and waited for five more minutes. During that time two trips were made to accommodate a total of seven passengers. None of the passengers was Kevin.

Her uneasiness increased. On the elevator's third trip upward she was a passenger. She got off at the seventh floor and made her way down a long narrow hall, harshly illuminated, as though the management had determined to prevent any questionable activities from overflowing the rooms.

Seven-eighteen was near the hall's end. She knocked several times, unwilling to accept the answering silence. Behind other doors life spoke in the high-pitched voice of a woman, in loud male laughter.

I couldn't have missed him, she thought. He must be there. Her heart grew heavier. Perhaps he took a drink for courage—and then another— But he told me he had finally learned to handle liquor—and he proved it by not even finishing the one cocktail he ordered at dinner.

"Kevin," she called softly, "are you all right?" and grasped and turned the doorknob.

He was not anywhere in the cheerless room. Someone else was. Someone else lay face downward on the single bed, perilously close to its edge. A bulbless fixture depended from the ceiling. The only light came from a standard lamp turned toward the bureau. The bed was almost in darkness, but she could see the feminine contours of the sleeper.

Her span of relief was short. So that's it. The clerk rang the wrong room. She started to back out quietly for fear of disturbing the woman. It must have been the vibration of loose boards under the worn dun carpeting that caused a limp arm to slide off the bed. The arm swung like a tired pendulum and then was still.

Alma Elliot went the few short steps to the bed. She looked down once and her trembling hands reached out to touch. Then she fell upon her knees. She could not touch nor even look again. But she had seen enough. In the next few minutes all her efforts were bent at self-command. I must not scream. I must not scream. Inside her head she repeated it over and over, clapping a hand to her mouth, keeping it there to ensure obedience. I must not scream. It is Kevin's room and I must not scream.

She regained her feet, swayed, and sat down in the room's chair. She sat rigidly, her will invoking the return of strength and clarity. The tears that burned her cheeks were unbidden and unnoticed.

Presently she could stand again. She saw the black coat on the floor and used it to cover the dead body. That was sane and right and compassionate. She turned to the telephone and turned away. To notify the police would be sane and right, but not compassionate. She could not do it, not though conflicting loyalties were to make her a battleground forever after. The police would find Kevin soon enough—Kevin who had panicked and bolted.

There was a mirror above the rickety bureau. In it she chanced to see her numb and ravaged face, a face that would interest even the bored desk clerk. No luxury of bath adjoined the room, no washstand added to its ugliness. Mechanically she worked with the tools she carried, handkerchief, lipstick, powder. Then she performed an action of sheer reflex, an action that would neither help nor harm Kevin. She plucked a small framed photograph from the bureau and dropped it into her bag. The picture might have been that of any proud father holding any attractive six-month-old baby. But the baby was Bess, and she could not bear to leave Bess alone with death.

She found her way back to the lobby. She had almost gained the exit when the desk clerk shouted, "Hey, lady!"

She would have continued on and out, but a loiterer barred her passage, his intention kindly. "Lady—he means you."

She retraced her course, her feet moving in slow precise rhythm. The clerk's sleek and oily head seemed twice its normal size. "Yes?" she said.

"He called up. He said he got detained and couldn't get back in time to see you."

"Who called up?" she said coldly.

"Mr. Culhane. He asked to speak to the lady who was waiting, but I guess you must have gone to the john because I couldn't spot you no place—so he left a message." His boredom made way for uncertainty. He squinted at her expressionless face. "Say—weren't you the one who got me to ring his room?"

"No—I was not."

"I could've sworn—"

She made her escape, aware that it was only temporary, aware of her denial's futility. Two careful blocks from the hotel she watched for a taxi, warming herself on the thin flame of Kevin's message, on the fact that the thought of her fruitless wait had cut through his panic. Where was he now? She must find him, talk to him. She tried to recall some of the places he frequented when he was in New York. A taxi halted and, stepping into it, she was able to give the driver the first of several addresses.

Chapter Four

Link Basset seemed to be examining Mother's picture with concentration worthy of a scientist. What irritated Bess was that his face wore neither approval nor disapproval. What irritated her more was her own eager anticipation of the compliments that he so perversely withheld. As if his opinion mattered. Mother's curling dark hair, her regular features, the vivacity that lit them had been acclaimed by those who really knew beauty when they saw it.

She said, "Of course the picture doesn't really do her justice. It gives you no idea of—" Then she said, not knowing whether to be relieved or regretful, "Wasn't that someone at the door? I guess Aunt Alma's come home." With a malice foreign to her she was pleased to note that Link Basset looked self-conscious. He might have been counting the approaching footsteps.

A moment later Aunt Alma was in the room. Bess went to her and kissed her cheek, surprised at its heat against her lips. "I hope you haven't been rushing because you thought I—" She broke off. Her aunt's appearance was out of character. She never used rouge, yet there were ragged unnatural patches of red upon her cheekbones, and her eyes were bloodshot.

Link Basset came forward, still holding the silver frame, and Bess introduced him. She stumbled over his name, not in gaucherie, but in concern for the way Aunt Alma looked.

He bowed quite civilly. "How do you do, Mrs. Elliot."

Whatever distressed her did not color the sweet clear tones with which she acknowledged his presence. "Has Bess been entertaining you properly, Mr. Basset?"

"Yes—even to trotting out the family album." He held up Mother's picture. He cried, "Hey!"

Bess tried to catch the falling woman, calling her name on a note of disbelief. She sat upon the floor. She lifted the limp hands and rubbed them strongly between her own. She spoke to Link Basset, her blue eyes dark with worry. "Please—will you call the doctor? You'll find his number in the little book on the hall table. Dr. Giraud—"

He did not move. "A doctor won't do any good."

"What do you mean? She's not—she's only fainted—can't you see—?"

"Sure—I can see she's breathing. Call the doctor tomorrow if you like—when the hangover sets in. Meanwhile, if I were you I'd let her sleep it off."

"Sleep it off?" Her voice trembled with anger. "Aunt Alma doesn't drink more than a glass of wine—or a cocktail now and then. If you won't help, stay with her while I—"

He squatted, bending close to the quiet unlined face. He said, "I'm wrong. No fumes. I guess I move in the wrong circles—but she did look a bit—well—overheated. Does she have fainting spells often?"

"Never that I know of. Do something."

He did something. He put his arm under Aunt Alma's back and lifted her to sitting posture. He kept forcing her forward until her head hung over her legs.

Bess said, "Are you sure that's the right—?"

Aunt Alma whimpered. Her hands came up to her head, straining to raise it, succeeding. They saw her eyelids flutter open.

Bess pushed Link Basset away and encircled her protectively. "It's all right. Don't try to talk. I'll get you to bed—"

"I fell," Aunt Alma said just above a whisper. "I—"

"You were tired—that's all. Maybe you did too much today—"

"Is there any brandy in the house?" Link Basset said.

The forced blood drained from Aunt Alma's cheeks. "I'm sorry, Mr.—Mr. Basset. This isn't a very good way to receive guests. If you don't mind, I'll retire so that you and Bess can get on with your visit."

She permitted them to help her to her feet, but refused further support. Bess followed her out of the room. A little while later she returned to find Link Basset standing at the window. He said, without moving, "How is the patient?"

"I got her to take a little brandy, but she won't have the doctor. She won't even let me help her undress. She says she's all right."

"She ought to know."

"But fainting is surely some sort of danger signal—isn't it?—especially since she's never done it before. Mother always said Aunt Alma's constitution was so strong that she couldn't even imagine what it was to have a simple headache."

He came over to her. "Well—you can't expect a state like that to last forever." His tone was negligent. "People do get on."

Bess said indignantly, "Aunt Alma's not old—just a few years older than Mother."

"And how old is Mother?"

"She—" Bess did not know. "You saw her picture. She hasn't changed a bit since it was taken."

He did an odd thing. He took her by the shoulders and kissed her forehead. "I'd like to have you on my side," he said, and his mouth was not crooked at all.

Self-consciously she moved away from him. "Do you—would you like a drink now?"

He shook his head. "I'm on my way. I'm a guy who demands undivided attention—and your mind's on your aunt."

"Well—I suppose I'm not being a very good hostess—but I can't help worrying—"

"Do you have any other relatives in New York—aside from Cul—your aunt?"

She said hastily, "No. Why?"

"I just wondered. Friends?"

"Aunt Alma has lots of them—but my job's kept me so busy I haven't had time to make any outside the office."

"Got a fellow pining away for you in your hometown?"

The question provided fleeting diversion. In the space of seconds she tracked back to the boys who had singled her out for attention before they went down under Mother's fascination or equally devastating criticism. "Not a one," she said, trying to make it light.

"Well—I might do in a pinch." He qualified it. "Either as friend or beau. If you get that desperate I'm in the phone book—or you can reach me late at the Bull and Bean."

She said, "Thank you," in the manner of one acknowledging an empty courtesy.

At the outer door of the apartment he hesitated, then he said very earnestly, "Happy weekend—good night," and strode away.

She went back to Aunt Alma's room. Aunt Alma had made no effort to undress. She sat upright in a chair beside the bed, her hands a rigid knot in her lap.

Bess tried to sound cheerful. "If you aren't in bed by the time I count to twenty I'm going to call the doctor. That's a threat."

Aunt Alma did not look at her. "Is your friend gone?"

"Yes—but I wouldn't exactly call him my—" She decided against refuting or claiming Link Basset. "I'll tell you all about him when you're feeling better."

"Sit down, Bess. There's something I must tell *you*."

The tone of her voice was disturbing. So were the lowered eyes and the slim pretty hands showing patches of white as they tightened around each other. Bess pulled a chair from the dressing table and sat upon its edge. "Won't it keep until tomorrow—whatever it is you want to tell me?"

"I don't want to tell you. I don't even know how to begin. It—it's about your father—I—" Her mouth struggled with it.

Bess said in a warm rush of words, "Never mind—I know he's in town. I saw him—at lunch. Not to speak to. He wouldn't have recognized me—" As she thought of the experience, sympathy for her aunt's distress ebbed away. "Naturally I didn't identify myself—he—"

Aunt Alma was not listening. Aunt Alma was talking over her, and what she said held no element of surprise.

"I had dinner with your father. He's been in town for about a week—but quite busy. This is the first evening he's been free—" She had lifted her eyes to the girl's legible face. "Yes—we've kept in touch through the years. We were always friends—"

Bess could not hold it back. "After the way he treated Mother?"

"My dear—I hadn't mentioned it because I didn't know what your attitude would be—although I might have guessed—"

Bess said passionately, "Yes—you might have guessed—and, if anything, my attitude's worse than it ever was. I hate him. He was with a young girl—he—"

"You must not sit in judgment—"

"I don't want to—I don't even want to talk about him."

She saw her aunt's shoulders sag, saw with dismay that her eyes were brimming over. She said, "Aunt Alma—I'm sorry, but—”

“Bess—listen to me—in your mother’s last letter did she—did she say that—?” Then Alma Elliot gave way to it. Her interlocked hands broke free. She covered her face and wept.

Bess left her chair. At loss, she touched the soft curly hair, stroked it timidly. She felt her throat constrict. Her aunt, her calm sane aunt to faint, and now to cry. At what? Could she have been in love with Kevin Culhane—lost him to Mother? No—for if that were true Mother would have known and made no secret of it. Mother was frank. Sometimes too frank. She had withheld little, even when Bess was supposedly too young to understand her sweeping confidences.

“What is it?” Bess said. “What’s happened? Don’t cry. No matter what it is I’ll do all I can to—” She jumped at the sound of the doorbell.

Aunt Alma took her hands from her eyes. Blindly she gestured toward the bureau. Bess got a handkerchief for her. Bess said, not because she believed it but because it was a commonplace to be seized upon in the bleak atmosphere of the room, “Perhaps Link Basset forgot something—”

Aunt Alma’s voice was waterlogged. “I can’t—I don’t want—”

“Of course not.” The bell rang again. “I’ll just—”

“Stay here—”

“But whoever it is has seen the light from the street windows and knows we’re home. I’ll say you’ve gone to bed.”

“No—”

The third peal had a sharp and urgent sound. “It will keep on ringing and ringing,” Bess said. “I’ll be right back.” She left the room and hurried down the hall.

It was late for visitors, especially for the visitors Aunt Alma entertained. As a precautionary measure Bess called out, “Who is it?”

“Alma—let me in.”

Surprise stayed her hand upon the knob.

“Alma—”

She opened the door a few inches. The tall thin figure thrust it wide with such force that it hurtled against her shoulder. Without glancing at her he made for the front of the apartment.

She followed. In the living room he turned to face her. Mechanically she rubbed the bruised place on her shoulder, not conscious of pain, conscious only of the almost audible whir of his mind as it recorded her.

The quality of his speaking voice had not been thinned by

the years. He said, "I'm sorry. I didn't mean to hurt you," and it was a declaration that covered a lifetime's span.

"You haven't hurt me."

"Shall I—is it necessary for me to introduce myself?"

"No—it's not necessary."

"Elizabeth—" he said. "Bess—"

She had to steel herself. She said tonelessly, "Aunt Alma's gone to bed."

But Aunt Alma was coming into the room. Bess saw glances exchanged that shut her out. She saw the man who was her father open his mouth, but it was Aunt Alma who spoke first. "We'll talk later, Kevin. Sit down. I'll bring you something to drink."

Something to drink, Bess thought. By all means. Something strong to drink. Forget poor Mother, who had laid the brunt of her troubles to his taste for liquor, his recourse to it whenever he wished to evade responsibility.

"I'll get it," Bess said out of her longing to escape.

Aunt Alma nodded. "If you will."

She took her time. Ice and soda from the refrigerator. Scotch from the fire-mahogany buffet in the dining room. When the tray was arranged she stood staring at it, dreading her role as an extraneous third.

They stopped talking as she reentered the room. Kevin Culhane accepted the glass with a hand that shook. He is an old man, she thought. Much older than he seemed at Gilly's restaurant. But at Gilly's he had been in stimulating company. Here, in the presence of an unwanted daughter, he need be at no pains to conceal his age. An unbeautiful lump of a daughter—a beautiful old man—skin-deep beauty and a grown daughter who thought in clichés.

Delicately, absently, he sipped the drink. Not like a drunkard. *"Insidious when it's sipped. More so than if you gulp it down."* From a dissertation on brandy by Link Basset. His eyes were the faded blue of sailcloth. They were intent upon the face of his unwanted daughter, and his dry lips were shaping for speech. He could talk his way out of anything, Mother had said. If you listened you were lost.

Bess did not intend to listen. "Excuse me," she said. "I've brought home work to do. Good night."

"No, Bess, stay," her aunt said, and her father added something, but she managed to quit the room, plodding steadfastly through the unexpected protests. Polite protests, she thought.

She went to her bedroom, shut herself in, undressed feverishly, and got into bed to read. But the heavy quiet was more distracting to her than the sound of drums would have been.

What were they talking about in their desired privacy? Their voices were too well modulated to penetrate her closed door. Certainly she played no part in their conversation. They had forgotten her existence the moment she left them. Why should they need to talk at all? Tonight they had dined together, and dinner must have provided ample time to exhaust such topics as linked them. Aunt Alma had got home late enough—

Clear in the room's silence she heard the far-off echo of a teasing voice. *"My baby's nose is out of joint."* She closed her mind to it, but it was truer than it had been when Mother accused the thoughtful child, Bess, of sulking. Mother! Link Basset had left Mother's picture face downward on one of the bookshelves. She wished it back in its customary place on her night table. It seemed profane that it should bear witness to—

The doorknob turned and Aunt Alma entered the room. She looked long at the girl in the bed. "Your father is leaving. He wants to talk to you."

Bess said stonily, "I'm undressed."

"It doesn't matter."

Bess pretended to misunderstand. "No—I don't think he has anything important to say."

"Bess—"

"Are you feeling better?"

"I wish—"

Bess armed herself against persuasion. The armor must have looked impregnable because her aunt did not persist. She made a weary little motion of capitulation and said, "Perhaps it's just as well. Try to have a good night, my dear."

Alone once more, Bess tested the words. Try to have a good night? Was that meant as a reproach? Did it mean have a good night, conscience permitting?

She wondered how it was that suddenly she had become so cruel to someone who had never been anything but kind. Would it have hurt her, since Aunt Alma wanted it, to behave in a civilized manner to—to Aunt Alma's guest?

In the act of rising from her bed she steeled herself again and took a firmer grip upon the manuscript. She was tired of always trying to please others. She was an entity to be

considered. She had a right to draw the line. She would get to
work—

Why had he sought Aunt Alma out so soon after the recent
parting? Why the desperation with which he had all but forced
an entrance? He wore a stained shirt, and the sleeves of his coat
were a little frayed at the edges. She had noticed the sleeves
when he took the glass from the tray; had noticed how the glass
almost slipped from his weak grasp; had been reminded of the
pity experienced earlier when impulse carried her to the door of
his hotel.

Once he had been a great success. Talent, fame, wealth, love
had been his, and he had thrown them all away. Not recklessly,
but, according to Mother, deliberately. He had been late to
professional appointments or, worse, failed to keep them. He
had spent money as though in covenant with himself never to
let it linger long enough to soil his pockets. He had risked his
singing voice in drinking bouts. And of his home he had made a
minor battlefield. That was the story of Kevin Culhane. He had
rushed to the top of the ladder and then crawled down, rung by
painstaking rung, until, at least so far as his family was
concerned, he had disappeared into a self-dug pit. And when he
reappeared, an old man with worn sleeves, beautiful, delicate—

Her eyelids drooped. The typescript blurred, fusing into
amorphous inky clots. I should get up and bathe and cream my
face, she thought. And as she thought it, gave way.

Light from the bed lamp showered her eyelids with sticky
warmth. It made an uneasy affair of sleep until she sheltered
from it by turning and burrowing into her pillow.

Hours later she awakened to discover that another light had
entered the room. Dazed, she sat up and sought the clock and
saw that it was nearly eight-thirty of a cool still morning.

A still morning? Within the apartment she heard what
seemed to be more than customary activity: a loud knocking,
footsteps going down the hall, a door opening. Voices.

Aunt Alma's up, she thought drowsily. She's letting in the
maid—?

Recollection flowed toward her on a stream of guilt. I'm a
fine one—shutting myself in. Aunt Alma might have needed me
during the night. She should be resting in bed. Anyway, Hazel
has keys. Did she lose them? But it's Saturday. She doesn't
come on Saturday morning—

She got up and put on a robe. She went to the bathroom and
brushed her teeth. She washed hurriedly and made swift order

of her tossed hair. Her mirrored face was alien to her, puzzled and strained.

Aunt Alma had not opened the door to Hazel. Those were male voices. They came from the living room now, crude, threatening. Or was it the early hour that made them sound that way? Reasonless prickles of fear stung her flesh. Tradesmen, she thought impatiently. But she tightened her robe, straightened her back, and marched forth, prepared to do battle if battle were indicated.

Two hats had been dropped on the hall table, black and brown fedoras that revealed nothing except complaint of hard usage. Their owners sat at ease in chairs that flanked a stiffly poised Aunt Alma. They looked up as Bess walked under the archway. But Bess's attention was all for Aunt Alma. Aunt Alma was fully dressed in the clothes she had worn last night.

Aunt Alma did not introduce the men. She said, "Good morning," so impersonally that she might have been a landlady greeting a transient roomer. She even found it necessary to explain the ways of the household to that roomer. "Would you mind getting your own breakfast? My maid doesn't come today and I'm afraid I'm too busy to—"

Bess refused to accept the cue, refused to recognize that for some reason or other Aunt Alma wished their relationship to be hidden from the visitors. She said, "Aunt Alma—?"

Immediately one of the men rose and addressed her. "Who might you be?"

She answered mechanically, "I'm Bess Rohan." Then she drew herself up. "Who might *you* be?"

He answered with matter-of-fact acceptance of her right to know. "My name's Judd." He indicated his companion. "This is Sergeant Clevis. We're police officers." He was a thickset freckled man. He did not look threatening, but he had moved so close to her that his undistinguished face became a menace.

She stepped back. "Why are you here?"

"Do you mean why are we here so early? Well—we explained to Mrs. Elliot. We would have hung around outside awhile—but we saw her pass the window so we knew she was up and about—"

"I meant why are you here at all?"

That question he ignored, giving her a long weighty stare. He said, "Rohan—eh?" and bobbed his head at Clevis. "That ring any bell?"

Clevis, a smaller, thinner figure whose clothes hung upon

him scarecrow-fashion, had drawn a folded paper from his pocket. He studied the chicken scrawls upon it and nodded.

Aunt Alma said, "Miss Rohan is my niece. Rohan's my family name."

The thickset man turned to her reproachfully. "You didn't say you had a niece living with you. You said a guest."

"She *is* my guest."

"Your brother's daughter?"

"No."

Clevis, the scarecrow, was shoving the paper into a bulky pocket. "We don't need to go the long way around," he said. "Rohan's the name of the family Culhane married into. I got that from the chief last night. There were only two daughters. Mrs. Elliot is one—his ex-wife's the other. Mrs. Elliot's childless and his ex had one—so it stands to reason where this girl fits in. Maybe she wants to call herself Rohan, but her born name's Culhane. Also, she shouldn't be news to us. We saw her last night when we were leaving the 'scene of.' She was acting real nervous."

Aunt Alma said, "You're mistaken—"

Judd was weighing Bess again. "Yeah—could be." He added, "But she wasn't going—she was coming."

"They've been known to return," Clevis said.

Chapter Five

Lieutenant Gridley Nelson, acting captain of Homicide West, was being Mr. Private Citizen. He let himself into the little house that he and Kyrie had bought several months ago, cautiously ascended the stairs, and ducked into his dressing room. He shed his suit, collected a robe, clean underwear, and spare shaving kit, and tiptoed down the hall. His objective was the bathroom in his son's domain. Except for rare occasions, Grid Junior's sleep was deep and sound, but Kyrie had been known to awaken at the drop of her husband's hat, and like any private citizen, he wished to keep from her the fact that he had been out all night. There were times when he experienced slight nostalgia for the old walk-up apartment on Lexington Avenue, but this was not one of those times. To begin with, he was almost too tired to have faced the four steep flights of stairs. And having faced them, it would have been impossible not to arouse the household.

His excuse was fairly legitimate. Friday's working hours had been extended to nearly 6 A.M. on Saturday. But even wives as reasonable as Kyrie could ask embarrassing questions such as: "Grid, was it really necessary? Couldn't you have delegated the work to some member of that large impressive staff of yours?" And the truth was that he could have delegated the work. The truth was that anyone could have done the preliminary research on the latest murder to reach the acting captain's desk. But his interest had been captured, and he had mislaid his sense of time. He had spent most of the small hours in the morgue of a leading daily newspaper, searching for background material on a miscellaneous collection of items laid away in the storehouse of his mind. Detective Sergeant Clevis had accompanied him, but Clevis had been no help because he considered the search a waste. Clevis said that the case was a "meatball," which in the jargon of the department meant there was no doubt at all as to the guilty party.

Nelson looked into Grid Junior's room as he passed. The little boy was curled like a hedgehog and did not stir. Through Sammy's open door came the sound of peaceful breathing. So far so good. A shower was noisier than a bath. It might upset the status quo. He would run the water slowly and softly into the tub, and then he would lie long in the relaxing warmth, and his tired muscles would uncoil, and his torpid brain would revive, and he would think. "Meatball" or not, here was a dish with all the ingredients to hand. He had only to measure and mix to obtain the required result.

Sammy opened her heavy-lidded eyes as he passed her room, and her mind supplied such details of his familiar form as were omitted by the young morning's light. A few moments later she heard the running of the bath water.

Sammy was friend, cook, and housekeeper to the Nelson family. At the advent of Grid Junior, she had forsworn her home in Harlem to become nursemaid as well.

Once Sammy would have scorned the notion of working for a policeman. She had entertained no high opinion of "New York's Finest" until Mr. Grid-dely crossed her path en route to the solution of a problem in which she was innocently involved. But of course Mr. Grid-dely was no store-bought policeman. Full of education from that Princeton College, he was, and with horse sense besides. A real gone man who could have done anything or been anybody if he set his heart and mind to it. Of that she was sure.

She reached out a long-fingered hand for the clock and

depressed the button that controlled the alarm. No more than a few minutes past six. Not worth while dropping off to sleep again. Didn't seem fair, anyway, for folks to sleep so much when, if she knew the signs, Mr. Grid-dely hadn't been to bed at all. Least she could do was see to it he got a breakfast guaranteed to stick to his ribs before he went back to that job of his. She had taken her own all-over bath last night. She would just give herself a lick and a promise and go downstairs. Junie was good for another hour or so, she thought with satisfaction. And if he waked he knew where to find her. No ivy grew on that three-year-old. He was almost as sharp as his father.

She arose, a very tall woman, supple of back and limb, her skin a shade deeper than golden apricots. Moving with dignity and precision, she carried out the first part of her program.

When Nelson emerged, shaven and robed, he followed his incredulous nose downstairs to the kitchen. Sammy was breaking eggs into the frying pan to companion sizzling ham. Strong coffee and toasting bread added to the hearty smell of a man-sized breakfast. On a shelf near a shining rack of pots and pans, a portable radio played softly.

Over the barely distinguishable words of the news commentator Nelson said, "Good morning, Sammy. And it is—thanks to you."

Sammy gave him a preoccupied glance and indicated the place set at the kitchen table. She said in her rich dark voice, "Start your grapefruit—'less you want me to serve you inside."

"You know I like breakfast here." He sat down, as always noting with pleasure that wherever Sammy was, order and cleanliness came into being. "Have you eaten?"

"I took me a drink of coffee. I don't fancy no more right now."

He smiled at her. "What made your timing so perfect?"

"I hear you tracking for Junie's bath. I got ears."

She had ears, well-shaped and flat to her handsome head. But for once they were not tuned to her employer. They were intent upon the radio. She switched it off almost angrily as the broadcast ended.

"I did try to be quiet," Nelson said. "Was Miss Kyrie playing possum too?" Something is a bit out of kilter, he thought, and wondered if he thought it merely because he was accustomed to Sammy's full attention.

"Miss Kyrie's sure enough awake," she said. "She call out as I start downstairs."

"I'm sorry."

Sammy came out of her abstraction. "It ain't no big matter. Miss Kyrie going to wait to talk to you till after you fed. I coax her to stay in bed—and she willing if you promise to visit with her before you go."

"That's an easy promise. She didn't try to wait up for me—did she?"

"Not after you telephone. But she stay up late anyway. Them neighbors drop in—the Blakes from the next house—and they forget they don't live here."

"Oh." He was glad that Kyrie had not been entirely alone, even though the rather tiresome Blakes were not the best of company.

Sammy poured coffee for him. As usual, she had managed to keep every ounce of its flavor intact. She filled his plate. He ate with appetite, the virtue of the food completing the revitalization process of the bath. Soon he began to feel as though he had spent hours between smooth sheets.

Sammy brought him more toast. As he buttered a piece, she stood looking at him, her wide brow shined.

He said, "Yes, Sammy?"

"What keep you from your bed all night, Mr. Grid-dely?"

"The same thing that generally keeps me from being a nine-to-fiver."

"I ain't talking about no 'generally.' I talking special."

He regarded her, his deep-set brown eyes grave under the premature white of his curly hair. "Has something in the news troubled you?"

"I troubled sure enough. It ain't none of my business, but I troubled just the same. You been studying about this Mr. Kevin Culhane?"

His pointed olive-skinned face showed no surprise. He nodded and reached into the pocket of his robe for cigarettes. His hand came out empty and he looked at it unseeingly. He said, "Do you know Mr. Kevin Culhane?"

Sammy did not answer. She left the kitchen and returned with a cigarette box and a lighter. She waited until he inhaled smoke. Then she said, "You remember the time I working for Miss Catherine—before her husband—Mr. Bede Mortimer—come back from being war correspondent?"

"Yes." He remembered well. Catherine Verney and Bede Mortimer had figured in one of his earliest cases. Moreover, that was how he had met Sammy.

"Mr. Kevin Culhane—he come calling at her place," Sammy

said. "And sometimes he sing for her. I still got me some records he make long ago. They out of the market now—and they scratchy—but scratchy and all, any time I listen I feel real good. He sing the way no white man sing. He got him a throat like a songbird." She paused.

Nelson waited.

"He sing in Harlem too—at a benefit they give for orphan babies. He sing his heart away—" She moved her shoulders helplessly. She said, "So how come he mix himself up in killing?"

"Even songbirds have been known to behave like people."

"Maybe so—when some no-gooder start messing with they nest or they mate or they young. But this poor Mr. Culhane, he ain't got no nest nor no young. He nothing but lonesome—leastways he was when I see him."

"He had a mate once," Nelson said, "and a child."

"That right?" Then Sammy said indignantly, "What they think they at—turning him out?"

"Perhaps he broke out."

"If he do he got reasons."

"He made quite an impression on you, Sammy."

"I know a fine gentleman when I meet him."

Nelson stood up and did a little jig step to flex his long legs. He was just six feet, and he had width in all the right places: to his shoulders, to his brow, to his expressive lips, and to his outlook. He saw that Sammy, who rarely showed indication of inner turmoil, was really disturbed. It startled him into sententiousness. "It's always a kind of betrayal when anyone we know is even slightly connected with an unsavory news item."

"Mr. Grid-dely—it sound to me everybody ready to swear Mr. Culhane worse than slightly connected. Happen you know more about it than what the man say on the radio?"

"Just what did he say?"

"Only that Mr. Kevin Culhane ain't around no place—and he talk real fancy about the hotel and how the room look with that cold body in it." Sammy did not move, but the shiver seemed contained in her strong motionless frame. "He don't put a name to nothing. He step real soft—but he can't help showing plain what he think. You fixing to go to work on it personal, Mr. Grid-dely?"

"As much as I can." He thought of the hundreds of cases that reached his desk and wished he could go to work "personal" on all of them.

Some of the anxiety left Sammy's face. She began to clear the table. "I glad," she said. "If Mr. Culhane know you, he glad too."

He doubted it. He went upstairs to the room he shared with Kyrie and glanced at the empty bed. The door of the bath was shut, but it opened as though his entrance were a cue, and Kyrie came out wearing a robe and the delicate aura of soap and flowers. Kyrie was lovely from head to foot, a slim ash blonde whose deceptively fragile appearance was cored with strong intelligence. She said, "I'll kiss you first and fight later." And then she said, "Grid—no fair. There'll be no fight left in me."

When they separated, she gave him level scrutiny. "A man who's been up all night should have the courtesy not to look and act so vital."

"A bath and Sammy's breakfast were excellent substitutes for sleep. By the way—I thought you promised her to stay in bed."

"Very well—take the offensive—but don't think I'm fooled. Bed failed to hold me. Quite a while ago it stopped being merely a matter of sheets and blankets and pillows."

Nelson grinned. "'Stone walls do not a prison make,' et cetera. In reverse. Anyway—I appreciate and share your sentiment." He looked at the clock. "Will you keep me company while I put some clothes on?" He went into his dressing room and she followed.

He said, "I'll bring you coffee before I go."

"Sammy did."

"Poor Sammy." He took a suit from the clothespress.

Kyrie opened a drawer and brought out a clean shirt. She said, "Just so you won't think I'm trying to detain you."

He turned. His outstretched arms ignored the shirt.

"Careful—or you won't be able to wear it." She touched his forehead with her lips and drew away. "I was trying to detain you."

"You never have to try."

"I know. But I wanted confirmation. Now I can afford to be magnanimous and bid you Godspeed with whatever it is that sent me to my lonely rest last night."

With what appeared to be one deft continuous motion he buttoned on the shirt and added a tie. "Did Sammy give you any hint of what it was?"

"No. Does she have a hint?"

"One of her past heroes plays a leading role. Kevin Culhane."

Kyrie thought back. "Wasn't he a singer?"

"He is a singer."

"Oh—you said past hero—and you said he played a leading role—"

"No—he's alive."

"But then he must be quite old. Surely he hasn't committed murder?"

"He's not old as age is rated these days. He's sixtyish—and it's highly probable that he's committed murder."

"Grid—as long as you don't demand privacy, there's more space for you to move around in the bedroom. It's lighter too—and I like a good clear view of your face."

In the bedroom she said, "Does Sammy really know Kevin Culhane?"

He repeated what Sammy had told him. He added, "It seemed to matter a great deal to her."

Kyrie said warmly, "Too bad." Then she said, "Sammy's a good judge of character."

He nodded. "But with sufficient provocation the best of characters have turned sour."

"Did he have sufficient provocation?"

"I don't know—yet." He sat down to fasten his shoes, and again she had no clear view of his face. But she thought from the somber tone of his voice that he did not wish to discuss the matter further.

Deliberately she launched into inconsequence. "When I told you Sammy'd brought me coffee and you said, 'Poor Sammy,' I was sure you meant I was imposing upon her. There's a tremendous amount of work to do in this house—notwithstanding the daily cleaning woman—but every time I suggest more help she changes the subject. Heaven knows we can afford a full domestic staff—"

"Sammy considers herself a full domestic staff," he said absently.

"And with justification—only it doesn't seem fair to her. What with the money your mother left—and my inheritance—even after buying this house we're more than solvent."

"Aren't you going to tack my salary onto our larger assets?"

"Darling—did I hurt your feelings?"

"I was joking." There were those, but Kyrie was not among them, praise be, who considered the job he held no more than an eccentric hobby indulged in by a man of wealth and background. It was no hobby. It was in the nature of a calling, and he had come to it by a series of eliminations ranging from such diverse fields as little theater work to the laboratory of a famous criminologist. In the laboratory he had discovered that his peculiar talents lay not with theories but with the people who had been responsible for the formation of theories; the warped, the twisted, the undisciplined, the intemperate, the greedy, the jealous, the ego-ridden, who considered it their right to destroy whatever or whoever stood in the path of their set goals. His own path was rarely clear. He had almost empathic identification with humanity at large, the slayer as well as the slain, the parents of each, the issue, the wives or husbands, the lovers, the friends, all those who had been encircled by the elastic radius of crime.

He got up. He strapped on his wristwatch and shrugged into his coat.

Kyrie looked at him questioningly. "Grid—I wasn't belittling your hard-earned salary. I was only talking nonsense anyway—to give you a graceful out. I didn't even think you were listening."

"I always listen to you."

"One of your minds does. Sometimes I wish you had two heads instead of multiple minds."

He laughed. "My other minds aren't productively employed, I'm afraid. This business of Kevin Culhane—"

"Hush. He's what I was giving you a graceful out from."

Nelson scowled at her. "What manner of unnatural wife is it who refuses to listen to her husband's explanation of why he stayed out all night?"

"I suppose I am unnatural. I'd forgotten that part of it. But if you're in a hurry, save it until I can work up a little decent annoyance again."

"That's what I'm trying to avoid. And it's still a bit too early for the call I want to make."

He sat on the edge of the bed. She joined him and he told her why he had not been with her last night. He said that to start with he had attended a policy meeting in the Commissioner's office on Centre Street, and that when he returned to his own desk uptown the call had come in from the Hotel Gretna. "The Gretna," he said, "is not one of the worst hotels in the city. On the other hand, it's far from the best. It's filled with all sorts of people whose common denominator is lack of cash and a need to be sparing of the little they have." He went on to explain unnecessarily that Homicide was short-staffed and that he had decided to accompany the lab boys. If the case proved to be an involved one, he said, his being on the scene at the beginning might save time.

At Kyrie's skeptical expression he looked as nearly sheepish as was possible for him to look. "Well—all right. No matter how short-handed we are I know I can't go out on every call that comes in—and this one did sound more or less routine. But the Commissioner's conference was long—and action of some kind seemed imperative."

"Your trouble is," Kyrie said severely, "that you'll never have the proper attitude for a desk man."

He admitted it. Refusing to take advantage of pull, he had risen by force of his own attributes from rookie cop to his present position. Sometimes he longed for that middle satisfying period as detective sergeant, when no one had expected him to sit back and relinquish the greater part of the leg work, which was, of course, the real work.

"You were setting out for the Hotel Gretna," Kyrie said.

Briefly he told her of what had awaited in Kevin Culhane's room, glossing over the corpse on the narrow bed. Bleak thoughts made background for his words. He had seen prison cells more attractive than that room with its ugly blistered walls, its one small window on an air shaft, its dun carpet, and its furnishings that time and use had brushed with the tinge of dun.

"Kevin Culhane had checked in at the Gretna a week ago," he said. "He'd stopped there before, and the manager, who knew him, said he was much as usual, except that he smiled more. According to the manager, he was not a man who overindulged in smiling. According to Sammy, he had little cause to smile. He has less now. He was seen leaving the room just before the body was discovered. Incidentally, it was discovered by a maintenance man. Culhane had phoned down that morning to ask that a burnt-out bulb be replaced, and the maintenance man had just got around to doing it—at five after ten that night."

"Was it he who saw Culhane leave?"

"No—that was one of the guests. We questioned everyone on the floor, of course."

"So you spent the rest of the night hunting for him? Did you find him?"

"No twice. I spent the rest of the night being a desk man. Not at my own desk though. After I'd sent out a general alarm and made what observations I could I went to a newspaper morgue to see if I could dig up any helpful information. He'd been given quite a bit of space in the early days of his career. I searched through mountains of stuff."

"And found it so interesting it stopped your watch."

"Yes. Are you seriously angry?"

"If I were angry at things like that I wouldn't have a minute left for anything else."

"You're my love. My entirely satisfactory love."

Kyrie said with intentional smugness, "You could have fared worse." Then she said, "It does seem cut and dried."

"My apology?"

"No—the murder."

"It won't be cut and dried until we've found Culhane. Perhaps not then. So far we have no proven motive—only guesses as to why she was killed."

Kyrie looked at him. Infrequently he brought his problems home, but only at some turning point where the sound of his own voice or a chance comment from her might lead to clarification. Now she was bursting with questions, but she repressed them because she did not feel he had reached the stage where he needed or wanted to talk.

He sensed her restraint. "There isn't much more to tell. I'll let you know when there is."

Fresh air in the guise of Junie entered the room. Junie wore pajamas, and a coonskin cap was clamped over his tow hair. He was Daniel Boone, and the room became his Alamo. He made Nelson prisoner, and at least ten minutes of rough-and-tumble took place before the prisoner could escape to his own private jungle.

Chapter Six

Nelson drove to headquarters first, made a few phone calls, and went over the material on his desk. Then he drove downtown to the Village.

He rang the bell of the Elliot apartment and presented his credentials to the fair-haired girl in the blue bathrobe. She would be an attractive creature, he thought, if she stopped looking as though she shouldered the world's ills.

"Are you Miss Rohan?" he asked.

She nodded. When after a moment she spoke he realized that she was close to tears. "Do they have to send the whole police force?"

He gave her time to gulp and swallow. "Was another officer here?"

"Officers," she said, making the word a bitter insult. "They're still here—asking and asking questions. What if—?" She gulped again. "It's nothing to do with us. I tell you, wherever he is—whatever's happened—it's nothing to do with us. Why should it have?" Clearly she did not expect an answer. She pushed moist tendrils back from a brow whose recent smoothness had been grooved by fear. Nelson's eyes met and held hers. Presently she looked away. "You might as well come in," she said, her voice less ragged. "You can't make matters worse."

He followed her to the living room. What he observed there made him think that he might be able to improve matters at least fractionally. Experience warned him that the slim dark woman who sat frozen in her chair would dissolve if the heat to which she had been exposed was increased by so much as a point. He knew by long association the two men who were the source of that heat, and so he swallowed his anger at the obvious botch they had fashioned of a job to which neither of them had been assigned. The record of each was excellent, and in taking on the extra duty each was acting upon that vaunted and in this instance overrated asset called initiative.

Judd and Clevis had bounded from their chairs. They stood at ready like good little soldiers. Judd might have posed as the pride of his company, Clevis the butt. Yet Judd was commonplace, an unimaginative plodder who usually achieved his objective by force of perseverance, while Clevis, whose height had barely met police specifications, not only concealed beneath his baggy clothes a tight, well-coordinated body, but had been known to produce inspirational rabbits from his deceptively slack mouth.

Satisfied that he commanded Nelson's attention, Clevis assumed his village idiot's expression, detracted from only by the bright little buttons that were his eyes. He hunched his shoulders, dropped his jaw, and spread his hands in a gesture that conveyed total lack of success.

Nelson, judging by the condition of the woman and by the distraught girl, thought grimly that Clevis was understating. He turned his flat triangular back upon him and addressed the woman. "Mrs. Elliot—have you had breakfast?"

At the sound of his pleasant voice she stirred, but otherwise showed no reaction to the presence of yet a third invader to her home. Her voice was numb. "I'm sorry—I'm afraid I didn't hear—"

Detective Sergeant Judd opened his mouth, read Nelson's face studiously, and closed it. The girl said, "No—my aunt hasn't had breakfast. How could she? They didn't give us a chance—"

"You haven't eaten either?"

"Of course not—I haven't even had time to dress—"

He looked at the woman's rather rumpled appearance. The girl said, "She was—she happened to be ready when they came."

He nodded gravely. He ignored her motion of protest as he moved toward her aunt. He assisted her to rise from her chair. Then he murmured something which seemed to penetrate, because he received an answering nod.

He said to the girl, "This will keep until you've both had a decent meal. Take your time."

Wordlessly she put her arm around the woman and turned her toward the archway. Nelson waited until he was alone with his subordinates. Then he said, "Well?"

Clevis shuffled his feet. "We didn't expect you, Lieutenant."

Nelson said, "Which means we're all surprised."

"It's this way. You skimming some of the family history off the clips last night—plus what that punk behind the desk said about a lady showing up who didn't seem to fit the Gretna scenery—gave me the notion we might save you time by making this our first port of call."

But they had not saved him time, Nelson thought. Owing to their zeal, it might take hours before the woman and the girl were restored to a state where they would cooperate. He said, "Evidently your notion didn't pay off."

"Nah—it didn't. After the first five minutes this Mrs. Elliot must've plugged her ears or something. All she kept saying was, 'I'm sorry—I'm afraid I didn't hear.'" He had switched to an unlikely falsetto.

Nelson said, "Perhaps you should have left after the first five minutes."

Clevis looked uncertain. "You sore, Lieutenant? We didn't pull no rough stuff, if that's what's eating you."

"Thanks for not breaking their bones," Nelson said. He knew he was being unfair.

Clevis blinked at him. "Listen—is it our fault one of them goes dumb and the other decides to go deaf? You notice she heard good enough to catch your whisper about breakfast. We figured you'd be busy with bigger fish—"

Judd came to the aid of his partner. "We didn't figure it for anything but routine until we laid eyes on Bess."

"Bess?"

"What the aunt calls her—an alias," Judd explained earnestly. "Elizabeth Culhane, alias Bess Rohan."

Clevis recovered his aplomb. He grinned largely, and Nelson suddenly found it work to keep his expressive mouth set. Clevis said, "Well—maybe it ain't exactly an alias, but she's the old man's daughter all right—even if Auntie tried to deny it by making out she was a boarder. Seems Mama took back her maiden name after the old man blew or was booted into the cold." He punched his head with his fist. "Get me—passing you back the same info you dished out. Something new I can give you though—only a theory, because the case is still a 'meatball' on my menu. Culhane could just be innocent. Auntie just could have been in love with him all these years and suddenly got sick of the competition. So why don't we take her and Bess to the morgue—?"

"The corpse has been officially identified," Nelson said. "I've just come from headquarters. Her—"

Clevis interrupted, "I didn't mean for identification. I mean watch their reactions when we give them a long look-see. Because I got a hunch the murder ain't news to them."

Nelson's brief amusement had passed. He said evenly, "With your permission I'd like to give them time to digest their breakfast—and then say a few weeks to recover from your visit."

Clevis said, "Huh?"

Nelson said, "When you interrupted yourself weren't you about to tell me something significant that concerned Culhane's daughter?"

Judd took over. It had dawned upon him that neither he nor Clevis was being awarded good-conduct medals. At Nelson's question he brightened. "Sure, Lieutenant. Last night while you were in a huddle with the lab boys we went downstairs for a few minutes—not to be in the way. We was just about to catch some air when we saw this Culhane-Rohan girl right outside the entrance. We didn't question her because we didn't guess who she was—but Clevis said something real nice and polite about she should postpone her visit—meaning that with the excitement going on it's no place for a young lady—and before we knew it she turned and ran like caught in the act. What do you make of that?"

"It occurs to me that she might be allergic to the advances of strange men—or of what she took to be advances."

"But, Lieutenant—Clevis says—"

Clevis said it for himself, making it plain that his superior officer had no corner on sarcasm. "So we pulled a boner coming here. So we should leave the polished higher-ups to deal with delicate ladies on account of coarse types like us make them allergic. Maybe the poor thing did break out in a rash last night when I opened my trap. It was dark—and I ain't no maiden's dream. Also, I ain't ready to broadcast I'm present as part of a murder investigation—being I don't want to collect a street crowd. But in broad daylight I don't scare ladies worth a damn—hand them a laugh is all. So how do you account for the way she's acting this morning, when the only advances I make is to show my credentials? Except she don't run away, she gives me exactly the same treatment. She shivers in her boots—clams up—and won't even crawl out to say she was paying an innocent call on her old man—let alone admit she was anywhere in that neighborhood at that time. She won't even admit she's seen him to spit at since she was a babe in arms. And what makes it smell is neither Judd nor me spill that Culhane's wanted for murder. We dish out the usual rigamarole we're seeking his whereabouts so's he can help us clear up a matter that's come to our attention—but we could save our wind. If we told the two of them we watched him kill the dame with our own eyes they couldn't be more cagey. Why? Because they know all about it is why. They don't need to be told a thing. It stands out a yard."

Nelson said mildly, "All right, Clevis."

Clevis seemed to appraise his tone and find it pure gold. The ghost of his grin returned. "We shouldn't have spent so much time at the newspaper office. I guess you didn't get much sleep."

"I guess not." He was reviewing what Clevis had said, trying to give it true place in the picture. Even people of good conscience were prone to be disturbed if police officers sought them out. It was all part of the universal guilt which everyone, no matter how upright, shared. But there were degrees of disturbance, he thought. And this girl and her aunt had surely gone beyond the normal allowance made in such cases. It was therefore quite possible that the aunt at least was suffering from delayed shock and not from brutal police tactics, especially since the nature of the inquiry had not been revealed. He took himself to task for maligning Clevis and Judd and made what amends he could at the moment.

He said, "There's quite a bit to be done—and offhand I can't think of two better men to do it. But weren't you both supposed to be off duty as of 8 A.M.?"

Clevis said, "What's a little overtime? My wife's away and Judd's got a houseful of visiting in-laws."

"Then he can go home with you and get some sleep—or you can use the rest room in the precinct."

"Translation—take a powder," Clevis said. "Well—as long as we're out of the doghouse."

"It was a doghouse built on sand. See you tonight." He escorted them both to the door. On his way back he heard what might have been a dish escaping from a nerveless grasp to shatter upon the floor. He frowned.

He walked about the living room, noting in spite of his preoccupation its comfort and good taste. He wished that the theory of judging people by the backgrounds they chose were infallible. If so, he could give the inhabitants of this apartment a clean bill of health. But he had known hardened criminals possessed of a deep instinct for beauty, and strictly moral characters who set great store by hideous surroundings. Bookshelves could be misleading too. Rogues were often addicted to poetry, and he had encountered many a high-minded citizen partial to distinctly purple prose.

He paused at a low bookcase where a silver frame had fallen or been dropped upon its face. He picked it up and adjusted the easel device at the back. When he returned the frame to the case he glanced absently into the wide retouched eyes of the picture it contained. The eyes seemed to be obeying a stern command to "look at the birdie." His own became as fixed.

He lifted the frame again and examined its support. A notch held it firmly in place, indicating that the position in which he had found it was not casual. Someone had dropped it hurriedly. He wondered who, and told himself that while it might not be important it could be interesting to know. Thoughtfully he placed it as he had found it.

He was at the opposite side of the room when the younger of his unwilling hostesses entered.

Bess Rohan looked at him accusingly. She said, "I heard the

door close. I was sure you'd left."

"The other two officers left. I'll follow as soon as I can." Her disappointment was so open that he could not help smiling.

An answering flicker touched her lips. She banished it as though it were shameful. She no longer wore her robe, but she had dressed too hastily for care. One of her stockings was twisted, and several buttons had been skipped on her simple coat dress. Somehow it added to her air of vulnerability.

She said, "All right—get it over with. You're about to say something like, 'When did you last see your father?'—aren't you? Or is that a quote from a story? Isn't there one about a little boy in the time of the Civil War—confronted by a group of uniformed inquisitors? Only I'm not a little boy—"

He could have taken the short cut she indicated and said, "When did you last see your father?" but he proceeded upon the premise that there was often noteworthy scenery to be observed in the byways. He waited for the nervous spate to subside before he said, "Does Mrs. Elliot think I've left too?"

"She's taking a shower. She couldn't have heard the door."

He thought that if a shower would restore Alma Elliot she was welcome to the extra time it consumed.

Bess Rohan said, "She—she isn't well. Must you bother her?"

"I'm afraid I must."

She accepted that as final. "Then she'd rather see you alone—without me. I don't know why. I—I don't know anything." She sat down. She held to the arms of the chair as though she were bracing herself for a dentist's drill.

His next words were equivalent to "Open wide." "You do know something, Miss Rohan, or it wouldn't be necessary for you to lie in order to cover it up."

"I didn't lie."

"You led the other detectives to believe that you hadn't gone to the Hotel Gretna last night."

"I didn't exactly go there—but it didn't seem any use to explain that to them." She searched his face and evidently concluded that it might be of some use to explain it to him. "I went for a walk—and I found myself passing the hotel—and I had a sudden impulse—but I didn't follow it. That's all there is to it."

"You had a sudden impulse to visit your father after not seeing him since you were a baby?"

"Yes—no—I saw him yesterday—by accident—in a restaurant. I didn't speak to him. He was lunching with—with someone." She expected comment. When none came she added defiantly, "It's true. I'm not making it up. He was with a girl named Selene Rolfe."

Nelson repeated, "Selene Rolfe," slowly, neither his face nor his voice expressing particular interest. "Is she a friend of yours?"

"No—I don't know her."

"But you know her by sight. You must if you know her name."

"Link Basset told me. He's the man I was with." She might have been responding to the slight lift of his eyebrow. "I don't really know Link Basset either—at least I didn't until last—I mean—I work in the fiction department of the Jessup-Purdy Agency—and he happened to come into my office as I was going out to lunch—so he came along and we went to Gilly's. A lot of radio and television people go there." Her own words created a visible atmospheric shift on the legible chart of her face. New clouds darkened it. She said lamely, "I don't usually talk as much as this. I'm only mentioning names and places because you seem to doubt me. I hope you won't think you have to check by asking Link Basset about it. He—there's no reason why he should be dragged in."

Nelson wished he could determine the direction from which the fresh clouds had come. "Did I understand you to say that you got to know Link Basset better last night?"

"I don't know how you— Well—he works in the neighborhood at a place called the Bull and Bean. He dropped in after I came back from my walk. I guess he just wanted to kill time until his broadcast."

"What time is that?"

"At eleven—but last night for some reason or other it didn't start until midnight, so he had more than an hour to spare. He got here at about twenty minutes of eleven."

"He's acquainted with your father, of course, since he pointed him out to you in the restaurant."

She made a poor job of hedging. "I—I suppose most people in show business have heard of my—of Kevin Culhane. But he didn't point him out. I'd seen pictures of him."

"They would have been rather old pictures. Your father hasn't been in the public eye lately and a man changes quite a bit in twenty years or so."

She said doggedly, "I recognized him."

"But you didn't speak to him."

"No—I didn't."

"It must have been a bit of a shock for you. Did you and Link Basset discuss him?"

Again she hedged. "Link Basset didn't even know he was—of the relationship until—" She bogged down.

"Until you told him in the restaurant?"

"I didn't tell him in the restaurant." She seemed outraged by the compulsion that forced her to respond to Nelson's look of patient waiting. "It was after I—after we left. If you must know, I guess I *was* a little shocked—and Link Basset noticed it and insisted upon buying me a drink of brandy—and I told him. Why not? I've nothing to be ashamed of. It's not my fault I've a father like— I didn't choose him."

A faint pattern had emerged from her answers. Nelson attempted to clarify it. "You used the pronoun 'I' when you spoke of leaving the restaurant."

Bess Rohan stared at him helplessly.

"Did Basset stay behind to talk to your father or to Selene Rolfe?"

"He—I told you we had a drink together—" It was patent that she searched for wording to say no more than she wanted to say.

"Go on, please."

"I went out first because I was in a hurry. I don't like to take more than an hour for lunch. He caught up with me in the street. I didn't want to stop for a drink, but he was being kind—and there's a bar right in my office building—so it seemed silly to make a fuss."

"And then?" Nelson said.

"I went back to the agency. That's all. I came home a little early because I—I took a manuscript home to read. Sometimes I can work better away from the office."

"But you didn't work last night. You took a walk."

"I needed exercise. Besides—I had the whole weekend to work in—" She tacked on a resentful tail, "Or I thought I did."

"Was your aunt at home?"

"You seem to know everything, so I suppose you know she wasn't. Anyway, there's no reason to lie about it. She had dinner with Kevin Culhane. They—they've kept in touch. Aunt Alma's nice to everybody."

"But you didn't know she was dining with him when you had your impulse to visit him at his hotel."

She tried too hard for a tone of airy sophistication. "My aunt and I aren't accountable to each other for dates and things. We lead our own lives."

"I see. And after you got back from your walk Link Basset dropped in."

"He was there—I ran into him outside the house. What difference does it make? Why are you so interested? I don't believe that nonsense about all this being routine. If it was, you wouldn't be taking so much trouble with it."

"You're right," Nelson said. "It's something more than routine."

The quiet statement hung over her like a sword and then descended. She had been expecting it. That much was certain. But judging by her intent face, she had not known where it would strike. It seemed to Nelson as though she were trying to probe the exact place and nature of her wound. She said in a small tight voice, "He hasn't—my father hasn't been hurt? He couldn't have been. I—" Her lips met in a wavering line. She tried to hold them firm. The effect was that of a heavy padlock nailed to a flimsy door.

In view of her recent coldness, Nelson found that anxious "My father hasn't been hurt?" provocative. He said quickly, "Did anyone threaten him?"

The padlock held to its weak support.

She did see him last night, Nelson thought. That's why she's able to dismiss the fear that he's been hurt. To pry the padlock loose he used a purely conversational tone. "I expect Link Basset dropped in to make sure you'd recovered from yesterday's unexpected shock."

It worked. She said, "We didn't even mention it. We just—just talked."

Basset's reputation made it difficult to believe that he would seek out a girl like this girl just to make idle chatter. But Nelson appeared to believe it. "Was he here when your aunt came home?"

"Yes—he was. I introduced them and he left soon after."

"Did she come home alone?"

"Yes—yes, she did—she came home alone."

In the same conversational tone Nelson said, "Where is your father now?"

"I don't know. If I did, what—why should I keep it secret? I can't even guess what you want him for. Look for him at his hotel, why don't you? And if he's not there he'll be with some woman or in some bar—" The indifference and the cynicism were as synthetic as the topping of whipped-up anger. "If that's all you're after why didn't you say so in the first place? These silly aimless questions!"

Aimless or not, they had gathered a bit of fruit, he thought.

"You won't get me to answer another one," Bess Rohan said, "until you tell me why it's so important to find him."

If she did not know—and Nelson inclined toward acceptance of her ignorance—there had been too much feeling behind her overprotested coldness toward her father to leave the telling to such instruments as newspaper or radio. He said tentatively, "Hasn't your aunt given you some hint?"

"She won't or can't. Whatever she knows about it—if she knows anything—it may be that she wants to spare my feelings—but that's ridiculous—and anyway, it can't be why *you're* holding back."

Can't it? Nelson thought. He turned toward the archway. The girl turned too, making an instinctive gesture of protectiveness.

Alma Elliot had shed her wrinkled suit for a dress of unrelieved black. Her high-boned Romany face was haggard, but her eyes, searching the room perhaps for Clevis and Judd, seemed clear.

Nelson got up and drew a chair for her. Evidently she had heard enough to realize that her niece was still in darkness, and as evidently, the basic acts of eating and bathing had replenished in her a measure of courage. It was in the look she gave him, and something else was there too.

She expressed it with a "Thank you," and he took it to mean either that she was grateful for being rid of the others or that she knew the reason for his presence and thanked him for waiting until she could break it to the girl. She was welcome to the privilege, he thought, and the sooner she exercised it, the better.

She said, "Bess, I should have made you listen to me last night, but things seemed so distorted—even to me—that I couldn't find the right way to tell you. I couldn't while we were having breakfast either. It—I thought I'd wait. But now I see it's impossible to wait longer. First of all, no matter how it seems or sounds to you, remember this—it's a mistake. It's not true. You must promise to keep that in mind. Bess—the police are looking for you father because they believe he has committed a murder—" She put out a restraining hand as the girl pressed back in her chair. "Bess—darling—that isn't the worst of it—"

Bess Rohan's voice was an icy little trickle. "Not the worst of it—he's wanted for murder and that's not the worst of it?"

"Child—I can't—I still can't find the words—" She had been holding the girl with her eyes, holding and covering her with a compassion that seemed completely selfless. Only for a moment did she abandon her, and that was when she sent a swift involuntary glance elsewhere. Nelson followed its course to the picture that lay face downward upon the bookshelves. Something jabbed crazily at the back of his head. The dimly lit hotel bedroom—the mourning dress.

He said, "There's no need to go on, Mrs. Elliot. I'd like to speak to you alone—and since Miss Rohan understands now why it's necessary to find her father—"

"Yes, I understand," the girl said. "I understand all I have to understand."

She left the room, moving stiffly and carefully inside her clumsy, ill-fitting armor.

Chapter Seven

Alma Elliot stared at Nelson's good listening face as though she were drawing sustenance from it. She said, "You sent the other men away?"

He nodded.

"I'm glad."

He thought that here the short cut was advisable and directed her to it. "Mrs. Elliot, it's been established that you were in the Hotel Gretna last night. What happened while you were there?"

Her silence was not denial or resistance. She was trying to wrap her unwieldly thoughts into a transferable package. The laboring was reflected upon her features. Haggard as she was, there seemed a hint of lawlessness about those features, something that contradicted the habit of gentle voice and submissive attitude.

She said, "I didn't expect to hide the fact that I was there. I hoped only for a little breathing space. Kevin called me a few days ago and we made a dinner engagement for last night."

"At the hotel?" Nelson remembered the down-at-heels coffee shop that bore the hotel's name. It seemed an unlikely place for her to dine.

"No—I was to meet him at Bennet's a few blocks away. It's

been one of his favorites since the days when—when he was more prosperous."

Nelson was sorry he had interrupted. It seemed to have sent her off the road. He waited to see if she could set herself right without help.

"Kevin usually called as soon as he reached New York," she said. "But this time he waited because he wanted to bring me good news. He'd been on the Coast and he'd had some luck there—a bit part singing in a picture that's soon to be released. A television producer, urged by an acquaintance of Kevin's, attended what they call a 'sneak preview.'" She paused to study Nelson's face for a sign that he was following. He gave her the sign and she went on. "Perhaps you think that none of this is important. But it is. The television producer was impressed by Kevin's performance—so impressed that he offered to build a program around him. The contract has been drawn up." Again she paused.

"Yes?" Nelson said.

She shook her head. "You don't see, do you? I thought you might. You seemed as though you might." She spoke reproachfully, as though he had betrayed her into a false estimate of his intelligence. "It's all so clear. Anyone should be able to see it. A new career is opening for Kevin after years of—well, whatever you like—heartbreak—frustration—failure—" Her eyes were quite lucid now. They blazed with conviction. "He'd do nothing to jeopardize it—nothing."

Nelson said the words as gently as he could. "It might work the other way. It might be that neither would he *allow* anything to jeopardize it—even if it proved necessary for him to remove the obstacle."

"Remove the obstacle? You mean by committing murder? No—not Kevin. I know Kevin."

The doorbell of the apartment rang loudly. Nelson heard it, but she seemed to be registering nothing but the echo of her own words.

Her expression changed. Her voice became listless. "Your mind is made up. I'm a fool to try to alter it. Yes—I'm aware of how this seems to you. You'll class me with the mother who swears there's been a mistake—that her boy couldn't kill because he's always been a good boy—or perhaps you'll think I'm in the same category as the poor deluded young wife who cries her husband's innocence from the housetops because he brought home his wages regularly and never laid a hand upon her in anger. But I'm not a mother and I'm not a wife. I'm Kevin's friend—the only one he has—"

Not the only one, Nelson thought, harking back to Sammy's earnest plea. Another part of his mind was aware of voices, the voice of Bess Rohan and of the visitor. Somewhere in the apartment he heard a door close.

"And precious good I am to him," Alma Elliot said, "no matter which way it goes. He's doomed. The contract will never be signed. The story will be in all the papers, of course. And that will be enough to finish him. From now on wherever Kevin Culhane is mentioned people will associate it with murder. It's always the initial connection they remember—never the outcome—and there isn't a producer living who'll dare to risk employing him."

Nelson said, "Again it could work the other way. People often show sporting tendencies. If he's innocent they might contribute to his success by rallying—"

"*If* he's innocent," she said scornfully. But hope hid behind the scorn. It peered out as though to determine whether the mind to be stormed was open or shut.

"What happened after your dinner?" he said.

She shuddered. "I've been skirting the real issue, haven't I? It isn't callousness. It's that I can't force myself to believe what I saw." She closed her eyes.

He led her as one leads a cripple. "What did you see? Take it slowly—step by step."

She raised her eyelids, but no light showed, as though the room within was pitch black. "Kevin and I talked at dinner—about the contract—and about Bess. He's never stopped loving his child. Separation from her was perhaps the worst blow he suffered. The injury sapped his will. It took him years to find his way again." She groped in her own dark. "In the restaurant he spilled coffee on his shirt. If not for that, we wouldn't have gone back to the hotel. He wanted to change because I'd asked him why he didn't come home with me to see Bess. I wouldn't have asked him without preparing her—but I wanted to take his mind off the contract, which was to be signed this morning. He was so nervous—so sure something would go wrong—"

"Something specific?" The interruption struck a brief light.

Alma Elliot's voice was too vehement. "Nothing specific—just overwrought imagination—or was it—could it have been second sight?" The light flickered out. "Whatever it was—he imagined true."

"You went back to the hotel with him—and?"

"I waited downstairs. I could understand how he felt—unsure of the reception he'd get from Bess—keyed to the point where he thought a soiled shirt would influence her. As if Bess—"

"When did you reach the hotel?"

"A little after nine. It isn't very far from the restaurant. I sat in the room off the lobby—and then after I'd been there a while I got up and went to telephone Bess to tell her we were coming. But I didn't phone her. I looked at the clock and realized he was taking an unusually long time. He was accustomed to making quick changes—it was part of his—"

She was talking to stave off the evil moment, not deliberately, but at the dictation of an insistent inner voice.

Nelson said, "What time was it then?"

"Twenty after nine."

"You asked the desk clerk to ring his room. There was no answer. And—?"

"I thought he must be on the way down. I watched the elevators."

"But you didn't see him?"

"No—" Suddenly her face aged. "What have I done? Instead of helping him I've betrayed him—given him into your hands. I should have lied. All night I sat up trying to find a way out for him—and yet the simplest way eluded me. Why didn't I think of it? I shouldn't even have mentioned the dinner. I should have said I went to visit him and he was out. The desk clerk would have backed me up—because he phoned the desk clerk from—from somewhere else to give me a message—that he'd remembered another appointment and couldn't see me. If I'd lied it would have given him an alibi. Then you couldn't have proved he was there when— Dear heaven—why didn't it occur to one of us to lie!"

She swayed dizzily on the gaping rim of hysteria. Nelson cried out strongly, "Listen to me," roping her with the words, pulling her back. "The man in the room opposite to Kevin Culhane's saw him come out at ten past nine and make for the service stairs. He is ready to swear to that on the witness stand. He even furnished a description of the clothes Culhane wore. You haven't betrayed him. You can betray him only by lying, because lies will prove that you—his friend—believe him guilty.”

“I don’t—I don’t.”

“Then stop trying to give him the cover you protest he doesn’t need. You watched the elevators and you didn’t see him.” Nelson’s eyes were upon her twisting hands. “Can you go on from there?”

“I went upstairs,” she said. “The door of his room was open and I walked in. The light in the corridor was harsh—the room dim—just a kind of bridge lamp near the bureau. The bed was in shadow.” She spoke fast. Obviously each sentence she uttered was a hurdle to be taken without weighing consequences, or not at all. “I couldn’t see very well—” There she stumbled. “But I could see it wasn’t Kevin lying on the bed. At first I thought I was in the wrong room. I started to leave—and then—and then she moved.”

The stiffening of Nelson’s limbs was reflex. He managed to control his voice. “She was alive?”

“No. Perhaps the vibration of my steps—I don’t know—but her arm slid off the bed and it moved—the way *things* move—lifeless things. So you see—I knew even before I was aware of knowing—before I went to look. Her black hair—so vain she was of that hair—so sweet she was sometimes—so like a child—” The fine features seemed to shrivel, as though Alma Elliot had rushed forward to meet the years that yet remained her. She said brokenly, “Where is she now? Where have they taken her?”

The cure for shock, Nelson knew, was sometimes as dangerous as the shock itself. He said, “Think back, Mrs. Elliot. The room was dimly lit—the body lay face downward. You saw a mass of hair and little else—”

“It was enough—”

“You didn’t move the body?”

“No—I—I touched her hair and it was matted where blood had dried—and her wrist—I touched her wrist, trying to find a pulse. And I knelt and laid my head to her back—and I listened—but there was nothing. So I—I sat down. Afterward I covered her with her coat. It would have done no good to move her—but that wasn’t why I couldn’t. The blood on her head made me afraid of what might have been done to her face. I was a coward—I didn’t want to see—”

He thought of how much she could have been spared had she looked. He leaned forward and laid a hand over the cold intertwining of her fingers. It was an action that no one had thought to include in any manual for a police officer, but Alma Elliot did not find it strange. Nor did she draw away.

He said, "Undoubtedly your sister was very much on your mind. Perhaps you had discussed her at dinner. And that was why you—"

She did not let him finish. "It's no use—is it? I haven't the wit for lies—and I can't make it any worse for Kevin because it couldn't be worse." She was gazing down at his hand on hers. She might have been committing to memory each detail of the strong lean fingers, the clipped, finely shaped nails. "Yes—we spoke of Lisa. Kevin was worried that she had seen some mention of the contract in the newspapers—and that she would come forward at the last moment to poison the producer and the sponsors of the program against him. But I didn't believe she would. She had remarried. At last she seemed to have what she wanted—money—and a man who worshiped her. She could be spiteful at times—and she had hurt Kevin repeatedly—but I had received letters from her boasting of her new-found happiness. And I reasoned with myself that no happy woman would go out of her way to revive a past that had been anything but happy. So I reassured Kevin—but I was wrong—"

Nelson examined her words. He played with the possibility that they had opened a new road and that she had been wrong only to a point.

"I was wrong," she repeated. "Lisa did come to New York—and she did intend to make trouble. She could have been in Kevin's room for no other reason. But he didn't kill her. He didn't kill her."

Nelson said, "He didn't kill her," and would have elaborated but for the spontaneity of her reaction.

"Thank God," she said, and her hands parted to clasp his.

He had wronged her, he thought unhappily, when he accused her of overprotesting. She *did* believe in Kevin Culhane's innocence. Her "Thank God" had been an affirmation of absolute faith. Her eyes shone with it for a moment and then were somber again.

He started to speak and once more was silenced. She said, "Not yet. Give me a moment to digest what you've just said."

She released his hand. She leaned tiredly against the chair back. "There's so much I want to ask—so much that I don't understand. Was it some stranger—some intruder wandering through that dreadful place who entered the room by chance and found Lisa—? You know who the murderer is. You must know or you couldn't be sure of Kevin's innocence. Yet—if you are sure—why are you here to ask all these questions of me—of Bess? I'm terribly confused. As it is, it will be bad enough for Bess. She will suffer—but now at least she will not suffer the same as she would if her father were accused of such a shameful crime. She loved her mother. Later, perhaps—when she comes to know Kevin—comes to understand—she will love him too—and that will help to ease her grief." She bowed her head. "There's been too much in the way for me to grieve. I can't even seem to accept Lisa's death—let alone sorrow for—"

"Mrs. Elliot—" He filled it with all the authority he could muster.

She broke off at once. She raised her head and eyed him trustingly.

He had seldom, he thought, possessed a piece of information so difficult to impart. He said, "There's no need to sorrow for your sister. She is alive. No—wait!" He could not bear the look of relief upon her face. "You made no mistake there. You found no pulse because there was no pulse. You did see a dead body—the body of a young girl—not your sister. But your mind played you a trick. You had been thinking of your sister—"

"Lisa's hair," she said, "matted. Her black cashmere coat—"

"Look at me," he said. "Try to take in what I'm saying. The dead girl resembled your sister. Her name was Selene Rolfe. I've had a report that her mother identified the body early this morning. The fact that your sister also owned a black cashmere coat must have added to your illusion." Abruptly another thought struck him, but he did not voice it.

Alma Elliot was trying to take it in. Her hands were fists at her temples, pressing it in by force. "My sister is alive," she said, and might have been reciting a lesson not quite grasped. "Lisa is alive. But Kevin—what about Kevin? You said he was inno—"

"You misunderstood me. I did not say he was innocent. I said—"

"He is. Why should he kill that girl?"

Nelson said quickly, "Do you know her?"

"Only by name. He mentioned her when he was telling me about the television show." She was still dazed. She spoke meticulously, as though everything that was at stake hinged upon the clarity of her explanation. "The theme of the show is something to do with the old and the new. She is to represent the new. I think he said they interviewed—no, the word he used was 'auditioned'—they auditioned hundreds of girls and chose her. She is a young singer starting her climb to—"

"She *was* a young singer," Nelson said.

"Was a young singer." Alma repeated it parrotwise.

"So you see—nothing has changed in regard to Kevin Culhane's position—except that from what you say he had no motive for the murder of Selene Rolfe. But by eluding the police he succeeds only in strengthening the case against him." Nelson did not ask the question that needed to be asked. His face expressed it.

"I don't know where he is," she said. "I wouldn't let him tell me. I'm not much good at concealing—"

"Then you did see him after you left the Gretna."

"There," she said hopelessly, "that's what I mean. Yes—I saw him." She told of how imperative it had seemed for her to see him and to hear at firsthand what had taken place. She told of leaving the Gretna, of getting into a cab, of stopping at such haunts of his as she could recall. These had included bars frequented by stage people, and the apartments of acquaintances. But he had not been seen in the bars, and all but one of the acquaintances had moved. "That one," she said, "had not heard from him in years. So I went home and—and—"

"He was here—waiting?"

"No—he came later—almost at midnight. He didn't know I'd gone up to his room. He could have been far away by that time. But he came because he didn't want me to hear the news from anyone else. We talked for a while and he left. If I'd had any doubts, he banished them. He had walked into his room on a simple errand and found—and found disaster. It had been even worse for him than it was for me. He obeyed his only impulse—which was to run. Even afterward, when he was less bewildered, he felt that he had done the right thing. He said there was no hope for him but to get away by himself and think—try to discover who hated him enough to do that to him. He called it a frame—so tight a frame that the police wouldn't bother to look to the right or the left of it unless he gave them sufficient reason. He said he must try to build up some credible defense before he was caught. At first I tried to convince him that he was wrong—that he must go to the police and tell his story—but I wasn't convincing because in my heart I knew they wouldn't believe it." Upon her face the hint of lawlessness became more pronounced. "Under the circumstances I would have done the same myself," she said.

"Did you give him money?"

"He would not take it. He said he had enough."

"Enough for a long journey?"

"I don't know."

"Your niece saw him, of course."

"Poor child. She opened the door to him. But—well—she excused herself and went to bed."

"She told me that she had been entertaining a friend—a Mr. Link Basset."

Alma Elliot said without interest, "Yes—he was here when I came home—someone from her office, I believe—but he didn't stay very long." She moved restively.

He said, "I won't stay much longer either. But there are just a few things not quite clear to me." Inwardly he cringed at the understatement. "Did you remove anything from the room at the Gretna?"

"No—I—wait a moment—yes—"

"Something from the bureau," he said, seeing in his mind the scant but orderly array of toilet articles surrounding a blurred oblong island where dust had been displaced.

"A picture," she said, "of Kevin holding Bess. I didn't like to leave it there. It's hard to explain why—but somehow it seemed important at the time. I think I left my pocketbook in here last night. Yes—there it is—on that little table."

Nelson got it for her. She took the small picture from it and showed it to him.

When he returned it to her he said, "I'm afraid it isn't evidence." And at her crestfallen face he added, "It might be—to Bess. I'd let her see it if I were you." He watched her drop it back into her bag. "There's one more thing. When you talked with Kevin Culhane here it must have been apparent that you thought it was your sister who had been killed. Surely he couldn't have made the same mistake—yet it would seem that he said nothing to correct you."

She was following him with care, her lips moving silently to shape the words on his. She looked bewildered. After a moment she said, "That's true. We neither of us spoke her name. We avoided it. I suppose I took it for granted that we both meant Lisa." She widened her eyes. All at once she was like a woman struggling up out of heavy troubled sleep. "Lisa is alive," she said. "Lisa is with her husband in Massachusetts—"

Nelson got out of his chair. He did the habitual jig step and came to a standstill facing the archway. He accorded the woman standing there a polite nod.

She did not return it. She made straight for Alma Elliot's chair, a purposeful well-girdled figure who would allow no one, he thought, to contest her right of way. And he went on to think that for the second time Alma Elliot had made a mistake. Lisa was not in Massachusetts.

Chapter Eight

Lisa was here, navigating the room full steam ahead, on billows of expensive scent. She dropped anchor at Alma Elliot's chair and blew her whistle.

"Alma Rohan Elliot—I should think you could do something besides gawk at me. I must say, this isn't the sort of welcome I expected—taking that long trip just to see you and my precious baby—and then being left to cool my heels when there's so much shopping to attend to. The things you can't buy in Griswold, Mass., would fill a library. They've never even heard of my favorite skin cream—or anyone else's, for that matter. And while we're on the subject, I do think you might have exercised a little tactful supervision over Bess. Goodness knows you're particular enough about your own appearance. I couldn't help being disappointed when I saw her because I was so sure that if being in New York accomplished nothing else it would at least smooth some of her rough edges. But if anything, she's worse than ever. I had to tell her to pull up her stockings and button her dress—and scarcely a word to say for herself. You'd never dream she hadn't seen me in months. I'm not unreasonable. I shouldn't have minded if after she got over her surprise she'd settled down to a nice heart-to-heart talk—but she's behaving almost as though I'm some stranger she isn't particularly pleased to see. No little secrets to tell me—nothing of any interest whatever except that you had an important engagement and mustn't be disturbed. Really!"

Her voice, Nelson thought, was an instrument worthy of a tune more consequential than the tune she chose to play. But he was pleased to note that Alma Elliot's expression was more alive than any she had worn that morning. There was health in its odd mixture of exasperation and wonder. And as he watched, she arose to clasp her sister in such an embrace as a mother, torn between impulse to hug or smack, gives to a naughty child.

"Lisa," she said. "Oh, Lisa."

Crossly Lisa pulled away. "All right—no need to run me

through a mangle." She rearranged the dab of flower and frill upon her lustrous hair.

Nelson caught the quick glance she flung at him before she dropped into a chair, and knew that she was highly conscious of his presence and that throughout her monologue she had only pretended to ignore him.

He thought that the pretense had gone on long enough. Confronting her, he made deliberate gaffe. "You're Mrs. Culhane?"

"Certainly not." The name might have meant nothing to her. "I'm Mrs. James Haskell." She made various small corrections to her person before she looked full at him. She meant the look to be withering, but her large dark eyes could not sustain the intention. They lingered with unmistakable interest. "Bess didn't see fit to explain the nature of my sister's important engagement," she said. "And it seems that my sister doesn't see fit to introduce us. Alma, if I didn't know you better I'd suspect you of wanting to keep the gentleman to yourself."

"Lieutenant Nelson is from the police department," Alma Elliot said reluctantly. The new flow of color to her cheeks ebbed away.

"Homicide, to be exact," Nelson said.

Lisa produced a cigarette and pointed it his way, as though a match were the only thing on her mind. It was a play for time, he thought, while she altered her reaction into something she wished to exhibit, or it was simply an extremely feminine woman's preempting of any male service available.

Nelson decided that it was a play for time not to be encouraged by providing either a literal or figurative smoke screen. Ignoring the cigarette, he said, "I'm sorry you found your daughter uncommunicative. It would have helped if she'd told you why I'm here."

She said unexpectedly, "I didn't need Bess to tell me—although what this absurd affair of my ex-husband has to do with her or my sister is quite beyond my comprehension." With nonchalance unsuited to the act she took an ash tray from the table near her chair and ground out the unlit cigarette.

"Absurd affair?" Nelson said.

"Of course. I'm more than ready to believe that Kevin had a woman in his room. It wouldn't even surprise me if he kept a harem there. No one is in better position than I to tell you what he's like. But you can take my word for it that violence isn't among his faults." There was a frustrate edge to her tone.

Nelson speculated upon it, wondering if she belonged to that sisterhood who asked for violence as a token of marital love, and if she still nursed resentment because she had never aroused Culhane to the point of delivering a well-earned clout. He said, "Who told you about the murder?"

"Bess sent me a dear little portable radio after she received her first week's salary. I brought it to New York with me. You see, I wasn't sure that the hotel would provide one and I always like to keep abreast of the news. I turned it on as soon as I called room service this morning—"

"What time did you check in at your hotel?"

"Last night." She fluttered her eyelashes at him. They seemed as long as fishhooks. She said with incredible archness, "Probably in ample time to put the present incumbent of Kevin's affections out of her misery," and turned at a strangled sound from Alma Elliot. "For heaven's sake, Alma, the lieutenant has a sense of humor even if you haven't."

Nelson offered no proof of it. Unsmiling, he said, "What time did you arrive?"

"My train reached Grand Central at seven. James had reserved a room at the Waldorf. I went straight there." She raised a meticulously plucked brow. She said indulgently, "You're not actually demanding an alibi, are you? I'm not quite clear as to when the murder took place, but if you like I can offer a satisfactory account of my movements last night."

"Please do," he said.

Years of practice were behind her merry little laugh. "Well, then—let me see. A cab took me to the hotel and a bellboy escorted me to my room. I took a long bath to remove the dust of travel—did a bit of unpacking. At first I thought of having a light meal sent up—but it didn't seem to suit my mood. I'm gregarious—I love having people about me—so I went downstairs to dine. The waiter who served me in the Norse Room was a very intelligent young man. We had quite a talk and he told me his name was Alex, so I'm sure you'll have no trouble checking—because even a place as large as the Waldorf can't have many intelligent waiters named Alex—"

"I'll have no trouble. You said you came to New York expressly to see your daughter?"

"Why, yes. I'm looking forward to having a wonderful time with her. After all—she's my only baby and I can't help missing her—and shopping's not much fun alone. James is a sweet thoughtful husband, but it's not the same thing—is it?"

"No—it's not the same thing. I suppose you were too tired to see her last night?"

"But I did telephone—just as soon as I'd finishing eating and sent a wire to James. I didn't like to call *him* for fear of disturbing him. You see—he's expecting—and you've no idea how edgy he gets—"

Nelson's face cleared as she added, "So of course he was sure to be in the stables. Men who breed horses are a race apart. Horses are too delicate for words—in spite of their size. Breeders usually see to it that they foal in nice balmy months like June or July—but this was carelessness, and the red mare couldn't say no when the stallion broke into her field—" Again she laughed merrily. "Lieutenant, I have a dreadful feeling that I've lost my audience. Are you with me?"

He was too much with her. He said, "You're an actress, Mrs. Haskell?"

"Alas—not anymore. How clever of you to guess. Yes—that's how I happened to meet the great Culhane. Perhaps you're wondering why I never achieved stardom. Well—frankly—my heart wasn't in it. Something inside me kept rebelling against any career outside the hearth and home. All I ever wanted was to be a good wife and mother. That's the function of a true woman, as I keep telling Bess, but she—"

"You said you telephoned her last night."

She assumed an injured expression. "For a full hour. It couldn't have been much after nine when I began—and it was ten before I gave up in despair. I didn't want to call later than that out of consideration for Alma in case she'd gone to bed. Alma and I are so different. She's always slept most of her life away—while I can't bear to waste a minute of it. Of course it wasn't Bess's fault that she was out. I'd planned to surprise her and she had no way of knowing I'd come to town—but still I couldn't help feeling let down and I'm sure the poor operator was worn out with ringing this number—"

"And I'm sure your alibi will be strengthened by the fact that hotels keep a record of *all* the calls made." The slight emphasis he placed upon the word "all" was mildly successful.

Just for a moment her irritating blandness deserted her. But if her narrowed eyes indicated an inward search, the findings were satisfactory. Blandness returned.

"Then that's that, Lieutenant."

"Not quite."

She managed the effect of a blush without the slightest

seepage of red through her pancake makeup. She said roguishly, "You're being very naughty, Lieutenant, if you're hinting that I can produce a witness to my beauty sleep. I assure you that when I lost hope of hearing my baby's voice I went straight to bed. I confess that a handsome escort might have persuaded me to do the town—but there wasn't one on tap—and even if I'd let James come with me, the program would still have been bed. Poor James doesn't vibrate to night life—"

"Did he want to come with you?"

"Naturally. He's so devoted he can hardly bear to have me out of his sight—but it would have been selfish to tear him away from the red mare. Her need was greater than mine."

Nelson could not tell whether it was sheer babble, or babble with some underlying significance. He wrapped it up for future study. He could and would check the statement that she had been on the seven o'clock train from Griswold, Massachusetts, and that she had arrived at the Waldorf at the given time. But it would be difficult to prove that she had or had not left that large busy hotel and found her way to Kevin Culhane's room at the Gretna. The desk clerk there had reported no visitor but Alma Elliot. Even the entrance of the victim had escaped his haphazard notice. Neither could anything conclusive be established by Lisa Haskell's use of the telephone. He doubted that the Gretna would exercise any great care in the matter of taking messages for its guests. The Waldorf would have a record of her completed calls, yet even if she had attempted to reach Culhane the investigation would not profit materially. Ringing an ex-husband was not evidence of intended crime. The black coat in Culhane's room was another matter. Everyone had assumed that it belonged to the dead girl. Alma Elliot had made another assumption. But Alma Elliot had been wrong throughout. He decided to postpone mention of the coat until research upon it had been completed, and so spare Lisa more bland evasions or denials.

Lisa was doing the cigarette routine again. This time he lit it for her, telling himself that he had nothing better to do. Then he took farewell of both ladies. To Alma Elliot he said, "I'll leave my number in case you should wish to get in touch with me."

Lisa used the indulgent tone. "Why should she want to get in touch with you?"

He said, "There's no accounting for taste."

Her laugh rippled gaily. "There—you see—I knew you had a

sense of humor, although I was beginning to doubt it when you asked me all those questions. For a little while you seemed really serious about suspecting me."

"I really was." He thought it a fair exit line and moved to act upon it.

"Wait—that's not fair."

He waited.

Alma Elliot spoke out of mixed anxieties. "The lieutenant is a busy man, Lisa. Don't keep him—"

"I don't see why I shouldn't. If I could spare the time to answer questions with all the things I have to attend to—so can he. He started it. What right has he to suspect me? If he's going around suspecting anybody and everybody, why did the man on the radio start such a hue and cry about Kevin's disappearance? It doesn't make a bit of sense."

"Most murders don't in the last analysis," Nelson said. "Do you happen to know where Kevin is?"

"Me?" This time she barred his way physically, leaving her chair to place an imperious hand upon his arm. "I haven't the faintest notion of where he is—and furthermore, I don't care. That's quite enough of your insinuations. I'll admit there were times when I was tempted to kill him—but he isn't the one who's dead—is he? And believe me—any girl silly enough to get involved with him needs no further punishment as far as I'm concerned. So now that I've provided you with an alibi, the least you can do is provide me with a motive." Her head came only as high as his chest. She thrust it back to look up at him. Her eyes held a peculiar light.

She's stimulated, Nelson thought, but not by anger. She's enjoying herself thoroughly.

"I'm a happily married woman," she said. "I've a beautiful home and the kindest, most thoughtful husband in the world. I've everything I want after years of scraping and penny-pinching. Why should I be fool enough to spoil it?"

He was glad that she had detained him. There were more ways of solving a case than computing the yeses and noes of routine questioning. He stood soaking up the atmosphere of the room. He could almost touch Alma Elliot's aching desire to be alone. From elsewhere in the apartment the restless perambulation of the girl, Bess, reached him. And there was the special atmosphere of Lisa Haskell overprotesting her happy marriage, her fine husband who vibrated to horses rather than to shopping trips and night life, excitements that held high place upon her preferred list.

He said, "You mentioned penny-pinching before your second marriage. Wasn't Culhane required to pay you alimony?"

She tossed her head. "Required!"

"Didn't he fulfill his obligation?"

"Not from my point of view—and anyway, I see no reason to go into it." She went into it. "During our miserable existence together I saw to it that he had more bookings than he could handle. I flatter myself that I served as his inspiration—a spur to his ambition. After we parted I'm sure he realized how well off he'd been, because without me he went steadily downhill and couldn't get any decent engagements. He sent me a pittance—I'll give him credit for that—but it wasn't regular—"

Alma Elliot said sharply, "He neglected to send it only when he was ill and couldn't work."

"Ill? Drunk, you mean. But I bear no grudge. Why should I? Live and let live, I always say. I haven't even kept track of the times he defaulted—still, I can tell you that what he owes me adds up to a pretty penny—"

"He owes you nothing. I took care of—"

Nelson saw Alma Elliot bite her lip and heard her little sister say sweetly, "All right—have it your way, dear. We don't want to wash our dirty linen in public, do we?"

He could imagine the nature of the dirty linen. Lisa had pride of a kind. She did not wish to remember that she had accepted familial help to weather the days of penny-pinching. Nor would her single-track mind allow that one of Alma Elliot's reasons for extending help had been to put paid to Culhane's obligation.

He said dryly, "Since you hold no grudge, Mrs. Haskell, I expect you were pleased to hear of the forthcoming television show."

She hesitated too long. "Television show?" And then with more assurance, "Was Kevin supposed to be on television? I wouldn't put any stock in that if I were you. People in show business are always spreading rumors about big offers. It's their way of staving off creditors."

"But the rumor did reach you?"

She looked vague. "I stopped buying *Variety* long ago. Other interests, you know. Alma dear, perhaps you were right. It's inconsiderate of me to keep the lieutenant when he has his job to do—and I'm afraid he's not making much headway here. Besides—isn't it time to be thinking about lunch? So nice to have met you, Lieutenant." She pivoted away from him on a thin high heel.

Alma Elliot groaned or laughed. Nelson doubted that she, herself, could have classified the sound or the emotion that produced it. Lisa confronted her. "What's the matter—don't you feel well? Let me look at you. I do believe you've aged a bit, though it isn't more than a few months since I saw you last. Listen—I've the most marvelous idea. I simply won't allow you to fix lunch. James has given me heaps of spending money, so I order you and Bess to put on your best bibs and tuckers and we'll all go back to the Waldorf to eat. The change will do you a world of good—"

She went on, making it clearly understood that so far as she was concerned Lieutenant Nelson of Homicide had left. He digested his dismissal with almost guilty amusement, since the basic situation contained few amusing elements. Everything she did and said, he thought, was about as subtle as Junie's maneuvers for an extra stay at bedtime. He hoped, for the sake of all concerned, that her motivation was no more sinister. It was for him to find out.

This time he reached the archway unhindered. The outraged cry that caused him to about-face was not intended for his ears.

"Of all things!"

He saw Lisa reach for the silver frame that lay upon the bookcase. "My picture—the one I had framed especially for Bess. And this is how she prizes it! So much for her promise to keep it near her always so that she'd have something real to turn to the last thing at night and the first thing each morning." She was making a production of it, clasping the picture to her breast, her voice a loud lament. "Her own mother's picture—discarded—turned face downward—not to mention the price of the frame alone! There's only one conclusion I can draw—my child's mind is being poisoned against me—"

Alma Elliot said calmly, "Stop being so silly."

"Silly? Is that what you call it?"

"Bess brought the picture out last night to show to a friend of hers—he—"

"He?" She was at once diverted. She set the picture down with loving care. "How touching—wanting to show me off to him. It's a good likeness—isn't it? I wonder if that photographer is still in business. I believe I'll go back and have a few more poses made. A friend—a male friend? Why didn't she tell me? What's his name, Alma?"

"Basset—I think. Link—"

"You think? I realize it's considered modern to be casual, but surely— Lincoln Basset?" She closed her eyes. "It sounds familiar, but— Is he eligible? How long has she been seeing him?"

The sound of her performance had flushed Bess out. Nelson knew what it was to feel invisible as she walked past him into the room. "Mother—I thought I heard you cry out. What—?"

"Nothing, dear—except that I'm so happy for you. Your aunt has explained everything. To think you never even mentioned him in your letters. I won't say I'm not a little hurt you didn't see fit to confide in me first—but we'll forgive and forget if you'll sit down and start right from the beginning. Then we'll invite this dashing young cavalier to lunch with us and find out what he's really like."

Bess made an involuntary turn toward Nelson, the only reasonable facsimile of a dashing cavalier present. Having become visible again, he bowed out, carrying with him the impress of her dumfounded stare. He also carried the thought that he, rather than Mother, might profit by seeing what Link Basset was really like.

No one offered to see him to the door, and this he took advantage of by making a quick silent tour of every room and closet in the apartment. He searched not because he expected a yield but because it was his nature to be thorough. He felt reasonably sure that if Alma Elliot had hidden her brother-in-law she would have presented no opportunity for search and that nothing short of a warrant would have forced her to permit one.

Chapter Nine

Nelson drove away, humming under his breath, "Don't turn my picture to the wall." At least that bit of trivia was explained, he thought ruefully. Or was it? Certainly it did not seem in character for a man of Link Basset's reputation to be interested in the family album type of entertainment. Nor, as far as first impressions went, did it seem in character for Bess Rohan to exhibit Mother's picture without encouragement. Little games for little hands, he told himself.

And yet? Link Basset had known Selene Rolfe, who had resembled Mother. His mind engaged in a routine that would, he granted, have done credit to any soap opera. Had Link

Basset known that Selene Rolfe was dead when he "dropped in" upon Bess? Why, if not for devious reasons, had he "dropped in"? What was his interest in Bess? Could a pretty but not very exciting country cousin really tempt the conditioned appetite of one whose normal diet was glitter and flash?

Nelson braked less smoothly than was his habit before a drugstore on the Avenue of the Americas and went in to consult a telephone directory. He did not use the telephone. If Basset started work late at night, it was probable that he slept the morning away. And should he have a cloudy conscience, a telephone call might make him sufficiently wakeful to decide against receiving an ambassador of the law.

The listed address was a low number on West Fifty-fourth Street. The car-lined curbs bespoke that mysterious prosperity that somehow withstands the leeches of inflation. Nelson's mental tail-chasing was temporarily halted by the concentration needed to squeeze his comparatively modest Buick into minimum footage.

The small lobby of the recently built apartment house wore its elegance with charm and discretion. The elevator that whisked him to the upper regions had suave efficiency. Directed by an operator who plainly approved the cut of his clothes, he found Link Basset's door and rang the bell.

No one answered his first or his second try, and since he had refrained from announcing himself he felt that the lack of response was legitimate. He was turning away when the door opened.

The elderly woman who stuck her head out was costumed obviously for an obvious role. A cloth bound her hair, an apron her middle. For further identification she clutched a duster.

"Mr. Basset's out," she said. "He always goes out when I clean."

"I'm sorry I bothered you."

"That's all right. Sometimes I answer the door—sometimes I don't. Mr. Basset says to suit myself. No use you coming in to wait. My cleaning stops him from thinking, so he generally makes himself scarce until I've been and gone."

What Nelson could see of the apartment across a small square foyer lived up to its advance notices. The room beyond was a decorator's product, its sleekness marred only by a bridge table supporting a typewriter and a storm of manuscript paper.

The woman, following his eyes, said with defensive pride, "Spoils everything—don't it? It's his Work." She provided the word with a definite capital. "But I'm not allowed to touch it—and he *will* bring it out into the middle of the living room when there's a den fitted up with a real nice desk and everything." She shrugged as one accustomed to the vagaries of mankind and looked at her duster as though she would like to get on with her own work, uncapitalized.

Nelson sympathized with her. He felt a corresponding urge. He could have offered several acceptable excuses for entering the apartment to see if Link Basset's work was even tenuously connected with his. But the suspicions he entertained were too nebulous to warrant such a move, and ethics dictated that Basset be given an opportunity to dispel them. Ethics aside, he doubted that a guilty man would leave clues lying about the house to be seized upon and interpreted by the firstcomer. Murderers, on the whole, were more practical than radio and television and movies led the public to believe, which was why so many of them got away. Or at least he preferred that theory to the current one of laziness and inefficiency on the part of the police.

He smiled down at the woman. Not for a moment would he have admitted that a portion of his scruples consisted of unwillingness to bring down upon her elderly head the wrath of an unpredictable employer. "Can you tell me where Mr. Basset might be?"

"You an actor?"

"No." He wondered if the negation would influence her answer one way or the other.

"You got a real nice smile and my granddaughter collects autographs, so I just thought—"

"I'm afraid your granddaughter wouldn't be interested in my autograph."

Candidly disappointed, she prepared to close the door. "No—I can't tell you where he is—no more than I could tell the lady who telephoned a couple of minutes ago." She added severely, "Between you and me, folks like him never know where they're going until they get there."

"Likewise, I'm sure," he murmured. And when she said, "What?" he thanked her and departed.

"The lady who telephoned a few minutes ago" might possibly have been "Mother" bent upon inviting "daughter's dashing young cavalier" to lunch. Or she might have been some other lady entirely. Nelson acknowledged glumly that this reflection was about par for the morning.

He stopped off for a sandwich lunch. Then he proceeded to headquarters, picking up an armload of afternoon editions on the way. Before he looked at them he went through the late reports on his desk.

Kevin Culhane, he learned, had walked out of Alma Elliot's apartment into a black void. Detectives assigned to the task had made contact with as many of his known friends and acquaintances as could be reached, yet none had come upon the faintest scent or spoor to indicate where he had gone to earth. All of the communications had been utilized to circulate his description. The city's exits had been checked and, so far as was feasible, watch was being kept upon transportation, including trains and planes and cars. But old men in respectable, slightly seedy attire were a dime a dozen, and only the usual cranks had vouchsafed accounts of meeting Culhane here, there, and everywhere, from Connecticut to Kansas. Which covered quite a bit of ground, Nelson thought, and all of it waste. There was a brief report from the plainclothesman who had been sent to question the mother of Selene Rolfe. It proved unenlightening.

The autopsy on the body of Selene Rolfe had not been completed. He called the medical examiner's office for the preliminary findings and acquired little more data than he had received at the scene of the murder. Not that he expected to strike oil. The value of even a completed autopsy lay in its correlation to the rest of the evidence, and he chose to classify what evidence he had as purely circumstantial. And this, notwithstanding the absent Clevis, whom he could almost hear shouting, "Chief—are you nuts! We find her laying in the guy's room—and him skipped to hell and gone. What more do you need to tag it a 'meatball'?"

The medical examiner estimated that Selene Rolfe could have been dead anywhere from one to three hours before the time of police discovery. He refused to be pinned to a closer opinion, basing his stand upon the fact that rigor mortis, attacking the small muscles from the head downward, had been manifest only as far as the stiffened eyelids. But he admitted that the cooling process could have been slowed by a number of factors. Her face was buried in the pillow. She wore a woolen suit. She had been covered by a woolen coat. The day had been warm, and the heat in the Gretna had been turned on full blast. The stomach content was no help. Her lunch had been digested, and according to her mother she had left the house before supper.

Nelson damned him for a cautious scientist and went on asking questions. He took scant comfort from the answers. Yes, she had been a virgin. No, it would be unnecessary to look for the murder weapon. The wound at the back of her skull was superficial. It had not caused death. Death had been caused by strangulation, and the marks of pressure at the front of her throat satisfied the medical examiner that her assailant had stood behind her to do the throttling. The size of the strangler's hands could not be determined. The bruise had spread. There was no clear print to be had from the flesh. Find someone with an outsized temper, he advised, and went on to say that he had never known a manual strangulation to be anything but a rage killing. Nelson was too polite to thank him for nothing. He asked if he could offer a guess as to the blow on the skull, and the medical examiner said huffily that it was not his business to guess. He said that the theory Nelson himself had offered last night held water. The blood he had spotted on that metal projection of the lamp base matched her blood. Her feet had probably tangled with the cord, bringing the whole thing down upon her as she fell. Yes, of course she had been moved to the bed. Her skirt showed particles of that dirty rug. No, there was nothing under her nails in the way of cloth or flesh or blood. She'd had no opportunity to claw or scratch. And now, if Nelson did not mind, he would like to get on with his job.

Nelson hung up. Half idly, half in hope that the busy press might have chanced upon something he had missed, he reached for the newspapers.

Most of the front pages had devoted space to the murder. Two of them featured the pictures of Kevin Culhane and Selene Rolfe, along with an account of the murder and bits of the Culhane biography. A third paper, a tabloid, made hay with a double spread showing Culhane in tights at the peak of his popularity, the murder room with an x marking the spot, Selene Rolfe singing with a band, Selene Rolfe alone, and Selene Rolfe's grieving mother. Owing to either faulty reproduction or to natural causes, the grieving mother had an uncommonly hard mouth.

In yet another tabloid an enterprising gossip columnist headed his story with a cut of the former Mrs. Kevin Culhane and renounced light chitchat to comment upon her startling resemblance to the dead girl. He speculated kindly as to whether this resemblance had caused a poor broken-down old man to "flip his lid" on the eve of a television comeback. There appeared to be strong belief in all of the papers that Kevin Culhane had either "flipped his lid" or committed willful murder, and most of them expressed a pious hope that he would be apprehended before he could do further damage. Lieutenant Gridley Nelson, acting captain of Homicide, was mentioned as being on the job. He was even misquoted as saying that he would not rest until the criminal who had cut off the lovely, promising Selene Rolfe in the flower of her youth was brought to justice.

Nelson groaned at the trite and fulsome license. Given a choice, he would have preferred castigation. They had printed his picture too. He glared at it.

He was about to stuff the papers into the wastebasket when a familiar byline stayed him. He read the story under it and discovered that Bede Mortimer, newspaperman and husband of Sammy's erstwhile employer, Miss Catherine, was the one dissenting voice among those who had convicted Kevin Culhane without benefit of trial.

Bede Mortimer pooh-poohed the concept of Kevin Culhane as murderer. He would not, he said, accept it if the room at the Gretna were strewn with corpses and that gentle singer of songs standing over them, hands bloodied, and packing every lethal weapon known to man. Culhane was frame-prone by nature, he said. He was such a one as had been bullied by fate since earliest infancy. Whereupon in his zeal Bede made out a case for "the gentle singer of songs" that could have done duty as a defense for a proven juvenile delinquent. Or, thought Nelson, reading to the end, served equally well as an obituary.

Born in Ireland, Culhane, at the age of three, had lost both parents to an epidemic of influenza. He had been shunted from stranger to stranger, and finally a fund had been raised to send him to relatives in America. The relatives were too poor to give him material comfort and too mean to give him love. He had been put to work as soon as he was agile enough to dodge the truant officer. The variety of menial jobs he held lent a Dickensian flavor to his boyhood. But where a lesser lad would have sobbed his guts out, Culhane had sung. He sang rag-protected against the winter frost as he fetched and carried for a junk dealer. He sang in an unheated factory loft while his chapped fingers assembled paper boxes. He sang in a bar while he swept the floor and emptied spittoons. And at last someone who recognized quality sent him to someone else who taught him how to use his voice. After long and studious application he got his first professional engagement. He was in.

Had his sordid background embittered him? asked Bede Mortimer. No. Not any more than a period of fabulous success had turned his head. In spite of the trappings of prosperity, the adulation, he remained a modest, sad-eyed fellow bearing always the stamp of the hungry, wanting years. He was unbelievably generous and kind. There were many alive to testify to the soft touch he had been when his pockets were lined. And he never failed to keep a promise. In order to donate his art to a worthy cause he had often braved weather that would have kept an Eskimo in his igloo. He was everyone's friend and no one's enemy.

It was not to be expected, the story went on, that such a man escaped the attention of women. When it came time for Culhane to marry he could have had the pick of the land. But once more fate had hit below the belt. At this point, Bede Mortimer, no doubt with an eye out for libel, had written with restraint of incompatibility, of a disappointed, lonely outcast who in divorce had not only lost his wife and the child he worshiped, but his faith and ambition as well.

There was more. There was a sneer for the fickle public who had permitted an artist of Culhane's stature to sink into obscurity. There was an account of his slow climb back and of the hard-won second chance on television that might have awaited him but for this latest belly-blow from fate. "Make no mistake," Bede Mortimer wrote, "Kevin Culhane's voice is still there. I know because I heard him sing only a short while ago and I was more thrilled than a grown American male cares to admit. In spite of his years and his suffering, his voice is still there. And it is for you to demand that it be heard again." Then he put forth an argument similar to Alma Elliot's. No man, he said, with a new career awaiting him would jeopardize it by an act that must result in gaining nothing and losing all. No sane man. And if Kevin Culhane was not sane, he, Bede Mortimer, would dance on his toes from Brooklyn to the Bronx. Culhane was not a murderer. He had been framed, why or by whom it remained for the police to discover. He closed by adjuring all those who lived by justice not to be fobbed off with a scapegoat, not to rest until the police had found and punished the real criminal.

Nelson's broad brow wrinkled. It was a curious effusion to spring from a hardboiled reporter. He recalled Bede Mortimer as he had first met him, a cynical young man just returned from overseas. Perhaps the patching up of his marriage to Catherine Verney had softened him. Or perhaps the fact that he himself had been a murder suspect accounted for his championship of Culhane. He and Catherine lived in Connecticut now, and according to Sammy, who kept in touch, Catherine was much too happy to long for the days when she had conducted a successful radio program. Sammy, another Culhane champion, was a legacy from the Verney-Mortimer case. Here Nelson went off at a tangent.

Sammy loved the city too well to leave it, and although policemen had never been her best friends, she had consented to make an exception of the quondam detective sergeant Nelson. The trial run she gave him as employer had lengthened into permanence. He did not take all the credit for this wholly-to-be-desired state. Kyrie and Junie had much to do with it, but—

Something happened to his mind to break the chain of reminiscence. "I heard him sing only a short while ago," Bede Mortimer had written.

How long was a short while ago? A night—a week—a month? A short while ago was a loose term, but to the best of Nelson's knowledge Culhane had been in California until six or seven days ago. And Bede Mortimer had been in Connecticut. And since sanity is a transient affair, how could one trained to the business of dealing in spot news attest to Culhane's sanity unless—?

Nelson asked for a Connecticut directory and found that neither Bede Mortimer nor Catherine Verney was listed. He could have called Sammy, who knew the address, but he decided against it. Sammy was quick. It was entirely possible that she would add two and two and be reluctant to supply information that might point to Culhane's whereabouts. The telephone company would have obliged, but that was no time-saving procedure. He called Mortimer's paper instead.

A woman answered and told him to wait a moment. He waited, annoyed because the moment was inordinately long. The next voice he heard was brisk and assertively male.

"Mortimer speaking. What can you do for me?"

He hesitated, realizing from the background noises that the woman had misunderstood his query and connected him with the city room. His rough plan had been a reconnaissance of the Mortimer menage to see if Culhane had found haven there. To speak now would be to give warning. Still, much could be learned from the rise and fall of a voice, and Mortimer's might contain a clue as to whether or not the reconnaissance was necessary.

Mortimer said impatiently, "Isn't it late in the year for April Fool gags? Friend or foe?"

"That depends," Nelson said. He identified himself.

Mortimer showed no surprise. His eager "What's new?" was clearly not small talk.

"I read your story."

"Yes—sure—but you're not calling to talk about my story."

"You did throw out more than a strong hint that the police were barking up the wrong tree."

"So arrest me for subversion."

"I might arrest you for obstructing justice."

"That's a laugh. I'm the index finger of justice."

"On what do you base your claim?"

"Look here, Nelson, I haven't had any sparring practice lately. If you don't know by this time that you've been way off the scent, you're not the guy I took you for and I'm damned sorry I—" His tone changed. "Say—didn't—?" There was an uneasy pause.

"What are you sorry about—and didn't what?"

Mortimer said glibly, "I'm sorry this call doesn't mean a beat for me—new developments—the capture of the right party—and so on. By the way—why *are* you calling?"

"To find out exactly when you awarded Kevin Culhane a diploma for singing and sanity. As I remember, you're not a man who deals out honors lightly."

He heard a distinct groan topped by a round "Hell." Then he heard a match being struck and could visualize the hollowing of Mortimer's lean cheeks as he inhaled smoke. Mortimer said calmly, "Excuse, please—I was lighting a cigarette."

"It often has a soothing effect on the nerves."

Mortimer chuckled falsely. "Not to be outdone in frothy chatter—what do you think of the weather lately? And why didn't you say this was a social call? Catherine will be delighted to have firsthand news of you at long last. She'll be sure to ask did I invite you to dinner sometime. So I will. Westport's only about an hour by train or car. Anyone will direct you to South Compo Road—and we've got a whale of a welcome mat—"

"Thank you. How long ago is a short while ago?"

"You don't have much range as a light conversationalist, do you? Well—it's so simple that it seems to me you could have figured it out for yourself. I do try to write clearly, but if my story was too obscure for you, why not reread it? I didn't say I heard Culhane sing in person. And I thought it too obvious to explain that I heard the recent record of his audition for the television show. As for his sanity, you may not have heard, but television has bred a brand-new species—cautious birds who don't gamble if they can avoid it. And if they were ready to hand Kevin Culhane a contract, he's sane in my book. Do come and see us—any time at all."

"Do you know where Culhane is?" Nelson said.

"I wish I did, boy. I really wish I did."

Nelson could read nothing into that but absolute sincerity.

Chapter Ten

Bess went through all the usual motions. She said, "Yes, Mother," and "No, Mother," and "That will be nice, Mother," so apathetically that Lisa Haskell threw up her hands and asked the heavens why she had been cursed with such a phlegmatic child. "Here I am going out of my way to give you a lovely party at a lovely hotel—and for all the response you show we might as well stay here and eat your aunt's cooking."

Aunt Alma murmured, "A fate worse than—" but Bess did not hear. She was too busy. She was trying to referee a fight between her head and her heart.

She did not know the exact moment the fight had started. She knew that it had been in progress all morning, persisting while the first two detectives were questioning her, and gaining in violence during her session with the attractive white-haired lieutenant.

She had been able to maintain a seeming of detachment until Mother flounced off to the bathroom. Then Aunt Alma showed her a picture.

"Kevin and you," Aunt Alma said. "I thought you might want to keep it."

"No, thank you." But she could not help looking. She could not help seeing the love and tenderness upon his face. It was even expressed in the curve of his arm where the plump child lay secure. "It's nothing but a pose," she said, her eyes straining against the push of tears. "He's an entertainer. He's had practice enough at posing."

Aunt Alma was angry. She opened a drawer in a table. She all but slammed it shut upon the picture. "Elizabeth—I've made my last attempt."

Rejection, Bess thought, of me. And somehow that sounded the bell for the final round, with the decision going to her heart.

Last night he had said in eagerness and sorrow, "Elizabeth—Bess—?" And coldly she had watched the eagerness fade. She said painfully, "He deserted us."

"You deserted him."

"I?"

"You because you couldn't help yourself—your mother because her conception of love had no meeting ground with his."

"He walked out."

"She ordered him out."

"But she said—"

"Whatever she said, she made herself believe—but that doesn't make it true." Aunt Alma spoke with the resigned patience of one whose hopeless task it is to din an obvious fact into a bigot's mind. And then she shrugged and summoned to her lips a coolly social smile. "Your mother will expect us to be ready to go to lunch. Hadn't you better change?"

Bess could not bear it. She blubbered like a hurt child. "Aunt Alma—he didn't—my father isn't a murderer. There must be something we can do—"

Aunt Alma became near and dear again. She said that they would find a way. Integrity shone from the lieutenant, she said. He would never help to convict an innocent man.

"It wasn't only the things Mother accused him of," Bess sobbed. "It was seeing him in the restaurant with that girl that made me feel so hard and mean—"

"I know."

"Not just that she was young—but so—so self-possessed—so everything I want to be and can't. And now— I feel so guilty—"

Aunt Alma comforted her.

Lisa returned as Bess sniffed her last sniffle. "What's the matter?" she said, as though very little had been the matter before. "If you're catching a cold don't come near me. I'm extremely susceptible." She eyed Bess keenly, her assumption of shrewdness broad enough to appear farcical. "I do believe you've been crying. Has it anything to do with love's young dream, dear? Don't worry—Mother's here. Mother's going to telephone your beau this minute and ask him to join us at the Waldorf—and then we'll see. What's his number?"

Bess clung to the tail of her escaping wits. "Mother—wait—"

"We may not get a table unless we hurry. Never mind the

number. I'll look it up. A Lincoln Basset shouldn't be hard to find."

"Link is—"

"Is that your pet name for him? How sweet. Run along now like a good girl and titivate—and do find a better bra than the one you're wearing. Heaven knows I'm not a prude, but you should confine yourself a wee bit more. Men like moderation when they're serious—"

"Mother, I'm not wearing any bra—I dressed in a hurry and—anyway, you've got it all wrong. He's only a business acquaintance. He—"

"Then I'll phone his office. Where does he—?"

"He doesn't—that is, not during the day. He—"

"My dear girl, you haven't taken up with a night watchman!"

Bess routed a surprise attack of the giggles. "He's on the radio—he broadcasts from some restaurant—but it doesn't matter because we're not the least bit interested in each other and I don't know where you got the idea that we were."

"Bess, why must you be so secretive? Your aunt's told me that he came calling last night. He'd hardly do that if he wasn't interested. You're not afraid I'll object because he's a performer—are you? After all, the theater is in my blood—and if radio isn't exactly the theater it's the next best thing—aside from television, of course. Lincoln Basset—Link. I'm sure I've heard that name. I'm really quite excited at the thought of meeting him. You must give me more of his background so that I can at least pretend I know of him. A little harmless deception is actually diplomacy in a case like this—and we don't want him to think your mother is a hayseed just because she happens to be buried in the backwoods. Is there a telephone book beside the phone in the hall? No—don't bother —I'll find it—or I can ask Information. By the way, Alma, isn't that black dress a bit depressing? You're not in mourning, you know. Perhaps something gayer might—"

They heard her dialing. Aunt Alma said, "I'm sorry."

"I don't care." Yesterday she would have suffered agonies of embarrassment. Yesterday she had been someone else. She said to reassure Aunt Alma, "Anyway, he's probably out to breakfast."

They looked at each other. Suddenly both succumbed. Their laughter served as ether sprayed upon the areas of pain. They knew it would not last, but while it lasted it was deep relief.

Mother returned, not too disgruntled by her failure to reach

Link Basset. "He's out—but on the whole that's a good sign. I wouldn't approve of a man who lounged about the house all day even if he did work at night. His maid answered the phone. She sounded in need of training—still, just the fact that he has a maid these days means he must be fairly prosperous. I left the Waldorf number. It makes a good impression, don't you think? And I shall leave word at the desk so that they can page me in case he calls before we've finished lunch."

Bess did not think there was any danger of that. She accepted the reprieve, careful to say nothing that would underline Link Basset on Mother's list of things pending. As an offering to peaceful relations she creamed her face, put on an extra dollop of bright lipstick, straightened her stockings, confined her breasts, and wore a simple flattering blouse chosen by Aunt Alma. Mother, coming into the bedroom to hurry her, found her buttoning the jacket of a new sharkskin suit. Beyond remarking that the blouse could stand a frill or two, Mother did not criticize her appearance. And that was flattery.

At lunch Mother was too absorbed by her own food to notice her guests' lack of appetite. Ordering, anticipating, and eating, her expression was almost beatific. Bess, looking from her to Aunt Alma, thought how strange it was that one set of parents could produce two such different beings. As for herself, what qualities were her inheritance? She possessed nothing so definite as Mother's simple greed that transformed gratification of any whim into a high moment. And she had nothing of Aunt Alma's elegance, nor her facility for withdrawal so that even in a public dining room she could sit screened by the foliage of her thoughts. Nor had Father's great gift descended to her, the gift that he had tried to barter for happiness. "Love that asketh love again—finds the barter nought but pain." Who wrote that? No matter. What sort of world was it if love did not breed love? Father had loved Mother. Mother loved Mother—

Mother said, "I can almost hear myself chew—and I must say it's extremely selfish of both of you, considering how I've been looking forward to this visit. Alma—if you insist upon sitting there like a mummy I suppose there's nothing to be done about it—but I've always taught Bess that meals should be a social affair and that not to make conversation is just as rude as eating with a knife."

Bess said the first thing that came into her head. "Do you know who wrote—?"

"Oh dear—must we be intellectual? It's all right in its place, but—" She sighed elaborately. "Very well, my stodgy bluestocking, who wrote what?"

Bess, glad that she had not been permitted to finish, said, "Nothing—a poem I happened to think of."

"Ah—poetry! That's different. And perfectly natural too. My own youth is not so far behind that I can't remember the way I mooned around spouting every verse of every romantic poem imaginable. It was really astonishing how many I'd learned by heart—I always was a quick study. I'm afraid I nearly drove my poor mother mad. With all due respect to her memory, not every girl is fortunate enough to have the sympathy and understanding I've given you—"

Bess thought gratefully that in one way Mother was easy company. All you had to do was wind her up and retire to a safe distance.

Mother was not yet run down. "*The Indian Love Lyrics* were great favorites of mine. I made Kevin sing—" The mechanism faltered. "How silly of me to reminisce when I can see you're bursting to talk about yourself."

But the name she had uttered was like a shot that brought Aunt Alma from cover. She said abruptly, "Lisa—that black cashmere coat that you bought when I went shopping with you before you married James—"

"The one *you* bought. Don't worry—there's no need to remind me of your generosity. I only accepted it because I didn't want to go to James looking like a pauper. Thank heaven that now I'm in a position to reciprocate. What would you like for dessert? Do choose a nice expensive one. You too, Bess. You're not on a diet, are you, dear? No—I didn't think so. Never mind—today we won't let any mean old restrictions interfere—"

"Lisa—about that coat—did you bring it with you?"

"Why on earth do you keep harping on it? No—I didn't bring a warm coat, although James insisted it was going to turn cold. What a fusspot he is—almost like a woman when it comes to putting on rubbers and— Alma—you're not even looking at the menu."

"Just black coffee, please."

Bess, puzzled by the reference to the coat, was about to ask a question. Aunt Alma's ungracious tone stayed her. Even Mother seemed affected by it.

"Black coffee? Alma—of course you're older than I am and I wouldn't presume to give you advice, but you're so thin that it's beginning to show in your disposition. What you need is—"

"What I need is to know how Kevin is faring." Aunt Alma sipped water and set her glass against the cloth with a decisive thump. She sat quite still, probing her sister's bland countenance. "You were close to him once. Surely some residue of affection must have remained. You can't be so completely unconcerned."

Bess saw her mother fidget and then look up to greet the waiter as a long-lost friend, to hold him in almost desperate consultation. If she had lost her form, she recovered it in that interval. When he went off with the order she sat back and surveyed the room.

"Quite crowded, isn't it? Where do all these people get the money and the leisure? They aren't particularly well dressed—but then, I suppose they can afford not to be."

Aunt Alma would not have it. "Don't you care at all that Kevin is in grave trouble?"

"I simply refuse to discuss the matter in front of Bess. I should think you'd have better taste."

Bess said, "It isn't a matter of taste. Aunt Alma and I both feel—"

"Be quiet. Don't make me rue the day I consented to this business of your living in New York—"

"I'm past my majority, Mother. I don't want to be rude, but consent wasn't necessary."

"There! I knew the moment I walked into the apartment that I had made a mistake. The atmosphere told me clearly that I was unwanted—that you and your aunt had banded together to shut me out."

Alma Elliot said calmly, "Why did you really come to New York? It can't be more than two weeks ago that you wrote and said James had to drive to Boston to complete some deal and took you along to replenish your wardrobe."

"Boston," Mother said scathingly. "What's Boston? And what right have you to take me to task for having a sudden longing to see my only child? You can't know how a mother feels—or what it's like to crave the bright lights and do nothing day in and day out but talk and live and breathe the stables. Your own marriage made you independent. You didn't have to—you never had to— Oh, why do I bother? I might as well be talking to a wall—an insulated wall. That's what you've always been—insulated."

She made it sound like a shocking insult. But there was something else in her voice that left a forlorn echo.

Bess was impelled to cry out, "Mother—you're unhappy. Is it James? Because if it is, you needn't—" She searched her mind for the signs she might have missed in the recent letters and realized that although she had ascribed the unusual absence of carping and criticism to contentment and read real interest into the blow-by-blow descriptions of the new life, Mother might have been too deeply engulfed by boredom to spare a thought for anything but its component parts. She saw her new freedom vanish but went on, "I mean we could take a place together in New York. I'll be getting a higher salary soon. We could make it do for the two of us."

"Nonsense. I've no intention of being a burden to you, so let's have no more heroics." Then, as though she repented of her harshness, she took out a lacy handkerchief and dabbed at her dry eyes. She murmured, "I'm just upset because I thought you'd grown away from me—but you do love your mother after all—and you're a sweet child. Ah—here's the waiter at last. Doesn't that look delicious?"

The real or fancied quarrel with her lot did not impair her zest for the complicated sweet the waiter set before her. Fascinated, Bess watched her consume it and tried to cope with her swarming thoughts. Aunt Alma drank coffee and made no further attempt to scrape at her sister's veneer.

"So we've gone into the silence again," Mother said, busily plying her spoon. With a surprising shift of mood she reintroduced the subject she had banned. "Do you know anything about that girl?"

Aunt Alma did not ask what girl. She said, "She was a young singer. She was to have appeared on Kevin's show."

"Was she pretty?"

Aunt Alma looked at her curiously and nodded.

"Well—as I told Bess while you were so busy with your lieutenant—she couldn't have been up to much good—going to his room alone in a hotel like that."

"Do you know the hotel, Lisa?" Aunt Alma's face was still.

Mother said innocently, "It's the Gretna, isn't it? From the description given on the radio, it must be very disreputable."

"It isn't disreputable—merely old and shabby and inexpensive. Kevin can't afford luxury at the moment."

"That's his story—and it's your privilege to believe it. You'll have to pardon me if circumstances have made me somewhat cynical. There were three important sponsors lined up for that show. Even if he wasn't to receive an advance until the contract was signed, you can't tell me he couldn't have raised money on his prospects. It's my opinion that he wants to pose as poor to avoid—"

"Then you did know about the show," Aunt Alma said.

"All right—we subscribe to the Sunday *Times*. I happened to run across mention of it in the theatrical section, but I didn't see any reason to admit that to the lieutenant." Mother laughed. "Not that I've anything to hide—and since you're my sister, I suppose I can trust you not to give me away to him."

Aunt Alma's eyes said, Can I trust *you?* Aloud, she said, "And you came to New York to collect on Kevin's prospects?"

Still plying her spoon, Mother said airily, "It may have been on my mind."

"But why? You don't need money—you—"

"Everybody needs money—and he does owe me quite a sum in spite of the absurd stand you've taken. But perhaps I'm not so material as you think. Perhaps I was thinking of a television role myself, and thought that with his new connections he might be able to discharge his obligation by putting me in the way of something."

Bess, listening horrified, thought that, given more privacy, her aloof aunt would have grasped Mother's shoulders and shaken her. Her aunt's clear voice was clotted with violence. "Did you go to Kevin's room yesterday?"

Mother pursed her lips. "What a shameful notion. I'm not an opportunistic little fly-by-night. I'm a respectable married woman with an extremely conventional husband. If I had any plan at all it was to telephone and ask him to meet me somewhere for a friendly discussion of the situation. Besides—you heard me give an account of myself from the time I arrived—"

"I heard you say several things. I'll say one before we drop the subject. If you did go to Kevin's room—and if you're withholding anything that will help to clear him—we'll never forgive you."

"We?" Spoon held midway between plate and goal, she turned to Bess. "Bess dear, I'm sorry your aunt sees fit to drag you into this. By 'we' I assume she means you. She can't mean to pair herself with my former husband. I wouldn't accuse her of that even though she seems to be accusing me of all sorts of things—"

Bess said, "I'm not being dragged in. I *am* in—" She stopped because of a sudden motion from Aunt Alma.

Aunt Alma said in a detached voice, "Isn't that James?"

Mother lowered the spoon. She said, "Where?" her mouth petulant. Then she said, "Oh."

He came toward them, a short muscular man with a weathered face. He walked with shins curved, the stamp of horseman so plain that Bess almost expected him to hurdle rather than skirt the intervening tables. He saw them and lifted a hand in salute, and when he reached them smiled a stiff shy smile.

"Why, James," Lisa Haskell said. "What a surprise."

"Well—I don't know. I said I'd make it if I could."

"Yes—but I didn't take you seriously. Mother and child doing well?"

"Fine—just fine."

The waiter brought a chair and he sat down.

"Have you eaten?" Lisa said, her voice uncolored by interest.

"I had a bite at the station—but I could stand another cup of coffee." As though he had been mulling it over in his mind, he added with heavy gallantry, "I guess I don't have to ask how this mother and child are doing. Tiptop, by all the signs. Isn't that right, Alma?" With that he appeared to dismiss both his stepdaughter and his sister-in-law from his orbit.

A two-way conversation followed which finally even his wife permitted to die. He said unnecessarily that they had told him at the desk where to find her. And she said, "Really?" and went on to say that as long as he'd come he could see about getting theater tickets. And he said whatever suited her suited him. She asked him if there was any special play he'd like to choose, and he said he wasn't strong on that stuff. And she said no, he wasn't, was he? And after a gap she said they might do a nightclub too. She had one in mind. And he said sure. And after another gap she made resigned inquiry as to how he had left everything in Griswold. But even that did not oil the wheels. He merely nodded absently and repeated, "Fine—just fine." And his wife shrugged and told him to ask for the check.

Yet all the while, Bess saw him stare at Mother with hunger and bafflement and, yes, a flickering of some darker emotion that she could not name. And she was disturbed. And all the while her much-abused loyalty was being forced to take another beating because she could not control the leap of her sympathy toward the second man Mother had married.

Chapter Eleven

If there had been any wheat in Bede Mortimer's conversation, Nelson was not given time to winnow it from the chaff. As soon as he replaced the receiver the phone rang and the desk sergeant informed him that a Mrs. Rolfe insisted upon seeing him and would not be denied. He had no inclination to deny her.

The woman who entered his office was clad in deep black. He had not seen such uncompromising mourning garments since he, as a small rebellious boy, had been commandeered to call upon a widowed great-aunt.

He arose and said a few sympathetic words, breathing the disagreeable odor of musty cloth as he drew a chair beside the desk for her. By the time he was seated again she had lifted her heavy veil to disclose a second masking of stark white powder. Her jaw was strong, he noted, and her mouth every bit as hard as it had looked in the newspaper picture. He tried to estimate her age and settled for the fact that she seemed old to have had the dead girl for a daughter.

It was she who opened the interview. "Sympathy's not enough," she said in a flat dry voice. "I won't rest until that man is strapped to the electric chair."

Nelson could not stem an onrush of distaste, a need to champion the underdog. "If you're speaking of Kevin Culhane, I must remind you that he hasn't been convicted." He drew a pad toward him and seemed to be making idle jottings upon it.

She said harshly, "For the simple reason that he hasn't been caught—and more disgrace to you. You *are* in charge of the investigation? If not, tell me at once who is. I don't intend to waste my time with underlings."

Nelson said shortly, "I'm in charge."

She appraised him, black eyes close-set. Like pincers, he thought, to hold the long sharp nose. "Well," she said, and it might have been her version of an apology, "a detective came to my door this morning—a stupid nobody who asked stupid questions. I gave him short shrift—"

"What questions would you consider intelligent, Mrs. Rolfe?"

"Certainly not who my girl associated with or whether she'd made enemies."

"That line of approach seems pertinent to me."

"Then you're a fool, too. Do you think I permitted her to mingle with riffraff?"

He thought with compassion that it was too likely the poor girl had not been permitted "to mingle" at all; that, faced by such a repulsive duenna, the most well-meaning had been constrained to withhold advances. But because he was innately kind he tried to make allowances for the bereaved woman, to establish some sort of communication with her.

"Was Selene an only child, Mrs. Rolfe?"

She said with no softening, "Yes—I was widowed before her first birthday and I devoted my whole life to her. Everybody—even the most grudging—remarked how pretty she was—and I meant her looks to count for something." She had reached a full stop, but something in his relaxed listening attitude made her continue. "I slaved so that she could have singing and dancing and elocution lessons. I did without to dress her so that she'd be noticed when we went the rounds of the agents. I gave her the best of everything." She spoke aggressively, as though she were unaccustomed to having men hang upon her words, as though she had always to fight for any ears save those of her poor little moppet. "My girl was right on the road to real success when I made my one mistake by taking her to audition for the Culhane show. It looked like her big chance. How was I to know—?" Her voice balked. Her eyes lowered to the black-gloved hands engulfed by a black lap.

"Yes?" said Nelson.

She looked up, flinging it at him. "How was I to know she'd fall in love with him?"

Nelson was seldom surprised. An uncharacteristic "What!" escaped him.

"You may well say 'What!' My girl in love with that sly old goat. Oh yes—I'll admit he seemed safe enough at first—the perfect gentleman—and of course I'd known of him in his heyday and was impressed by the fame he'd had—so maybe that's why I was blind to his tricks—and hers. When she'd widen her eyes and stare at him so sweetly I thought she was showing no more than a daughterly interest. She didn't remember her own father—and just as well—but ever since she could talk she was always asking questions about him and painting some crazy larger-than-life picture in her mind the way children do. Sometimes I'd even catch her making out she was talking to him when she thought I wasn't listening. I ask you!" Her own interpolation broke the spell. "I don't know why I'm telling you all this, mister. It's neither here nor there. Just you go about your business, or if it's the last thing I do I'll make it my business to see you have no fine office to laze in."

Nelson spared no thought for her threat or for his fine office with the abrased linoleum, the scratched filing cabinets, the tired discontinued model of a water cooler, the ancient ugly structure that was his desk. He said, "It's not unusual for a young girl to be obsessed by a father image or to give her affection to someone who seems to fulfill the specifications of that image—nor is Culhane necessarily to blame—"

"Isn't he?" she said. "Isn't he? That's how much you know."

"Are you suggesting that he made improper advances?"

Spite twisted her thin pale lips. "Why else would she act like a common hussy?" His silence spurred her on. "She went to his bedroom—didn't she? And she never thought that up without encouragement."

"In this day and age that hardly indicates an intention of immoral behavior. Her generation doesn't observe quite the same conventions as"—in the interests of diplomacy he stretched a point—"ours. Perhaps something occurred to her in connection with the show that called for immediate discussion."

"Such an excuse might take you in, mister. Not me. I raised her to be decent. I didn't bother to ask myself if decency was in style. A girl goes to a man's bedroom for one reason only, and nothing she said makes me believe different."

A monstrous suspicion kicked Nelson in the pit of his stomach. He swallowed nausea. "Did she give you that excuse?"

The woman looked at him balefully. "Part of it anyway—about going to the hotel—not upstairs—to ask him if he wouldn't have Basset write in some situations she'd thought up."

"Link Basset? He was to do the script?"

"Well—other writers are working on it too—but he's the main one. As I was saying, I found her note when I got back—but it was too late to stop her."

"When you got back from where?"

She spoke with rasping impatience. "I'm human—I couldn't be with her every minute of the day and night. I had a toothache and she seemed safe enough when I left for the dentist—otherwise I would have made her come with me. But she was sitting at the piano going over new songs—and practicing was important, so—"

"Who is your dentist?"

Her response to the unexpected question was automatic. "Dr. Morovski. He's some kind of foreigner, but they say his work is good and he keeps open nights to accommodate business folks."

"What time was your appointment?"

She stared at him. He said, "It might help the investigation to know when your daughter arrived at the hotel."

"Help the investigation? All the help it needs is to catch that murderer you've let slip through your fingers. I didn't have an appointment. I just went. We hadn't eaten supper yet. With her free until the new show started, I took things easy. I guess it must have been around six. I thought he wouldn't be busy then—but the waiting room was full and after sitting around a while I changed my mind and went home and packed the tooth with cotton dipped in oil of cloves—which I could have done in the first place. I wasn't gone much over an hour, but if it's any use to you, I guess she sneaked out the minute my back was turned."

He was chilled at the absence of any emotions but anger and spleen in her reference to her daughter. She might have been discussing a stolen purse. He said, "Did you attend to your tooth before you found the note?"

"Listen—why don't you get down to brass tacks?"

"In view of the watch you kept upon your daughter, I'm wondering why you didn't rush to the hotel after her."

"No call to wonder." She spat out the words. "That's exactly what I did. I didn't even take off my hat and coat. I only stopped to pack the tooth because I knew I could think better if it stopped aching. When I got there I looked in the lobby for them—and in the room off it. I just couldn't bring myself to believe my girl would be so cheap as to go upstairs. But she wasn't around, so I went over to the desk." She seemed quite unaware of Nelson's distrust. She seemed merely intent upon proving her eternal vigilance. "I spoke to some nasty little pipsqueak who won't forget me in a hurry. He was reading a newspaper while I stood there—and when he condescended to look up you can bet I gave him what for. Of course he denied seeing hide nor hair of either of them, which didn't surprise me. He wouldn't have seen a herd of elephants in a bright light."

"Did you ask him to ring Culhane's room?"

"I did—but if you've listened, you heard me say I didn't really believe she'd be there. I just thought he'd been down to talk to her and might have gone back up after she left. If so, I meant to put a bug in his ear about future meetings outside the studio—but he didn't answer."

"And it didn't strike you that he was in and didn't want to

answer for one reason or another?"

"No, it didn't. I turned around and went home, thinking to find her there. You mean that all the while the two of them were—?"

"I didn't mean that. In fact, we knew he had a dinner engagement and had undoubtedly left to keep it before Selene arrived."

"Then she went up to wait for him and when he came back he—"

"You're not being very consistent, Mrs. Rolfe."

"How do you make that out?"

"Earlier you asserted that there was something between Culhane and your daughter. And in the space of the last few minutes you've stated repeatedly that you couldn't get yourself to believe it—and you've borne the statement out by your actions. Now you're back to your original premise, but it doesn't hold water. Because if you had believed it, a woman of your strong character would have skipped the lobby and the desk clerk and gone straight to the room to confront the guilty pair."

Her heavily powdered face darkened. Speech did not come.

"Did you go up to the room, Mrs. Rolfe?"

She shook her head.

"So actually," Nelson said, "your accusations are based upon hindsight. You had no cause to assume wrongful intention on Culhane's part until your daughter was found dead in his room."

Her recovered voice was guttural. "Isn't that enough? What else do you want? She's dead and he'll pay for it. I invested everything I had in her—and now how do you think I'm to get along—?"

His mind supplied, "without a meal ticket." He said because he could not help it, "Are you sure Selene was your own daughter?" and was rewarded by an ugly flush struggling through the powder.

"I'm not the kind to cry and wring my hands," she said. "That won't bring her back."

"Did you save the note she left?"

"Of course not. I tore it up and threw it in the garbage. It wasn't anything to treasure, I can tell you. Listen—I came here to talk sense. I've had enough—"

He shed the fraying cloak of diplomacy. "No, Mrs. Rolfe, you haven't had enough. Evidently you don't realize it, but you've been condemning yourself by the things you've said in this office—and the case against you can be made to look as black as the case against Kevin Culhane. You admitted that you followed Selene to the Gretna, and your manner suggests that you were a stern disciplinarian—not improbably to the extent of inflicting corporal punishment at times." He saw her redden again. "You denied going higher than the hotel lobby, but that remains to be proved—as it remains to be proved that upon discovering your daughter in a man's bedroom your outraged convictions did not carry you further than you intended to go. I've several more questions to ask you. You'll sit there quietly and answer them—and before you leave you'll sign a statement containing the gist of this interview. Is that understood?"

Her small eyes bulged. She sputtered, "What—what are you saying? My girl was everything to me. I—I'd have to be crazy to do—to do what you're hinting."

Nelson felt no better for his outburst. He said, "Culhane had no obvious motive either."

"He did. Maybe my girl was innocent like you said—and he took advantage of her and killed her so she couldn't tell."

Nelson spoke firmly against a second attack of nausea. "We'll go on to the questions. How was it that you permitted her to lunch with him yesterday?"

"There," she said, reverting to her norm. "I read in today's papers that they were seen lunching alone—and that was another of his tricks. The director of the show and one of the studio executives was supposed to go along—so how could I put my foot down even if they didn't have the grace to invite me?"

"What about Link Basset?" he said. "His name has been coupled with Selene's. It seems you had no qualms about that friendship."

"You don't know much about show business. I had to agree to a lot of things that went against the grain. Yes—I let Basset take her around some until I discovered what kind of a reputation he had. It helped her career to be seen at Sardi's and the Pavillon and places like that, and a male escort was part of the act. A couple of times I let him talk me out of chaperoning them because he said it made her look ridiculous to be always tied to her mother's apron strings. I'll say this much for him—he always brought her home early."

She was obviously, Nelson thought, of the school that believed no untoward act could take place before bedtime, which was yet further inconsistency in the face of her testimony against Culhane. A good lawyer, he reflected, could tear her to pieces. Unfortunately she was no more than one small numeral among the awesome red figures in Culhane's ledger. If she could be transferred to the black it would effect a radical change. But could she? Facing facts unemotionally, he doubted that she had destroyed the source of her golden eggs.

She interpreted his slight shrug as further criticism. She said, "Besides—it always pays to be in with scriptwriters."

Her absolute lack of warmth was implausible, Nelson thought. But her story was not. And all things considered, there was little in it either to implement or disarm suspicion, and little possibility of verification or refutation except in minor details. And the yes or no answers to those would carry hardly enough significance to merit the effort. He would, of course, make the effort, and as a start he filed two exiguous items in his mind. One dealt with Dr. Morovski, whose crowded waiting room seemed to warrant a bright receptionist. That Mrs. Rolfe had or had not visited a dentist was unimportant unless she had lied about it. He had known small lies to lead to large disclosures. The second item he filed concerned another session with the Gretna desk clerk.

The unlovable Mrs. Rolfe had been subjecting him to covert scrutiny. She said in almost propitiatory accents, "You didn't mean it about making a case against me? I never behaved in any way but according to my conscience and I've never done a thing to be ashamed of." She hesitated. "I'm going to have trouble to hold up my head as it is—and if such a notion got around it would be enough to smear a saint. People are all too ready to believe the worst."

He nodded gravely. "You're right. People are all too ready to believe the worst."

She missed the irony. "Then you didn't mean it."

"On the contrary—I did and I do. You came here for the purpose of spurring me on to my duty as an officer of the law. I'm sure you wouldn't have me neglect any facet of that duty as I see it. One more question. There's some uncertainty regarding a woman's coat found in Culhane's room—a Peck and Peck black cashmere with a raw-silk lining. It has a gilt bird pinned to the lapel. Did it belong to your daughter?"

Her eyes were vindictive. "My girl had no such coat. You see—he was playing around with others, too. Now will you believe me?"

"And it isn't yours?" He knew it was much too small to fit her.

"Mine? Black cashmere and raw silk? I never spent that kind of money on myself."

"Very well." Nelson lifted the telephone receiver and spoke briefly. He tore the top sheets from his pad and handed them to the stenographer who answered the summons. "You're to take a statement from Mrs. Rolfe. These notes will key you if she omits any of the points she's made." He arose. "Good afternoon, Mrs. Rolfe."

She said angrily, "Just don't think—"

"I must think. I was given a fine office for that purpose." Nothing like a bit of infantile sarcasm to relieve congestion, he told himself.

But he had a bitter taste in his mouth, and for quite a while after she had been ushered out he could do no thinking worth a single tax-paying dollar. Mrs. Rolfe, he conceded sadly, plus the loss of a night's sleep, had drained him of vitality. Especially Mrs. Rolfe.

He went to the window and raised it as high as it would go. The day's temperature had dropped. He stood breathing the freshened air, hoping that it would rouse his sluggish wits. Because he was at such low ebb he grew chilly, and by circuitous process of association began to ponder the matter of the black cashmere coat. His best guess was based on his estimate of Alma Elliot. She did not appear to be a woman given to mistakes. The large one she had made might well have been due in part to the fact that the coat actually was her sister's property. And if Peck and Peck had no record of the sale, there were other ways of determining ownership. Lisa Haskell undoubtedly used distinctive perfumes and powders which would have left traces on collar and lining. Should further proof be necessary, serology tests could be made.

Lisa might have taken an earlier train, visited Culhane, terminated the visit in anger, and flounced off, leaving the coat behind. Nelson could understand her reluctance to claim it. Such reluctance might not stem from guilt but merely from the same instinct that sent chance witnesses scurrying away from a street accident when the police appeared. In most human beings the desire to avoid legal involvement, on whatever side of the law, was basic. He found himself dwelling almost affectionately upon Lisa. In spite of her marked symptoms of arrested adolescence, she profited by comparison with the mother of Selene Rolfe.

He shivered and shook himself and closed the window. He

returned to the desk chair, leaned back, and shut his eyes. He slept for twenty minutes. Then he drank several cups of water. The prescription was effective. His head felt clear.

He called Link Basset's apartment and got no answer. He decided that Basset would make a good detail for Clevis, and dictated a letter to be delivered to the enterprising little detective sergeant when he reported back for duty. He called the ready room and broke up a game of cards by dealing assignments to several of the players. He sent a stalwart personable young plainclothesman on a mission to the Mortimer residence in Westport, object to see if Culhane was or had been there. He selected another to visit Dr. Morovski's office, object a chat with the receptionist. And still another, less personable but very persuasive member of the squad was enjoined to conduct a memory-jogging interview with the Gretna "pipsqueak." Even if nothing was accomplished, he thought ruefully, at least Kyrie would applaud his executive-type delegating of the work.

He was diverted from the case by the entrance of a narcotics man who wished to consult him. They talked for a while about a recent homicide which had a possible tie-in with a current dope racket. It could not be termed a refreshing pause, yet Nelson welcomed it.

As soon as the narcotics man left, more reports on the search for Kevin Culhane were placed upon the desk. He was picking their meatless bones when word came in that a sanitation barge on the East River had spotted a "wet floater," description, male and elderly. "Wet floater" was departmentese for unidentified drowned body.

Nelson sprinted from the office. He was about to fling himself into his car as the desk sergeant rushed out to intercept him. The desk sergeant said that a suicide note had been found and that the superintendent of an East River Drive apartment house had just identified the corpse as that of the building's janitor.

Weak-kneed, and chilled again, Nelson went back to his office. He opened the bottom drawer of his desk, took out a bottle of scotch, and poured a stiff drink. He tasted it and absently threw the rest down the drain of the water cooler. He wished he had not delegated all of the work. He wished he had left some for himself. For example, driving to Westport or even being on a train to Westport would be better than—Train? Lisa's train. Well, it was something to do.

He reached for the telephone and put in a call to Griswold,

Massachusetts. He made it a person-to-person, asking for James Haskell, horse breeder. There were, of course, other avenues of approach to the question of Lisa's train, but it might be interesting to get the answer straight from the horse's mouth. He grinned feebly, thinking of Haskell, the man who was "expecting."

Presently the operator informed him that Mr. James Haskell was not available and asked if he would speak to Mr. Tom Derwenter, assistant. He said, "Yes," and she said, "Go ahead, please."

A nasal voice returned his "Hello" and wanted to know his name.

He said, "Grid Nelson," trying to sound like a friend of the family who is startled at not being recognized.

The man said doubtfully, "What can I do for you?"

"Is this the stables or the house?"

"It's the house. I just got back. I'm eating my supper."

"And Mr. Haskell isn't around?"

"No—he ain't." It was tinged with the flavor of disgust.

"Do you know where I can reach him?"

"No." Tom Derwenter was either an uncommunicative man or he was in an uncommunicative mood.

Or perhaps, Nelson thought, he saved his words for the horses. He said on impulse, "How is the foal?" and heard the voice crackle as though it were giving off sparks.

"Dead—like I expected. The mare ain't doing so good either. You could swear she blames herself. October's no month to foal—too cold—especially in these parts. Damn carelessness to let that stallion at her. I'd like to lay my hands on the responsible party."

Nelson said, "Too bad."

"Ayah—but looks like I'm the only one's taking it to heart. Well—sorry you wasted a long-distance call."

"You might be able to help me. Mrs. Haskell was supposed to come to the city yesterday, but I missed meeting her train. Do you happen to know which one she took?"

"No. Like I said, I was away on business since yesterday morning and just got back. Only person I spoke to so far is one of the hands, who told me about the foal." He added grudgingly, "Ain't but two trains she could have taken—the 8 A.M. and the 2 P.M."

"How long is the trip?"

"Both trains are fast. Do it in about five hours. Not being an early riser, likely she took the 2 P.M." This time the flavor of disgust was stronger, making it seem that the stables had little use for Mrs. Haskell.

Nelson thanked Mr. Tom Derwenter and broke the connection. He looked at his watch and thought that it lied because it said six-five, and time for him had been standing still. Tonight there was nothing to keep him from having dinner at home. Slowly he strolled out of the office. The eagerness that always heralded reunion with Kyrie and Junie was absent. He could not feel that he had earned it.

Chapter Twelve

Nelson unlocked the door of his new house, strode the short entrance hall, cut through to the rear, made a left turn, and paused at the kitchen door to greet Sammy.

Sammy was ironing. She always made a small celebration of his homecomings, but tonight her "Good evening" was stiffly formal. Kyrie made up for it. At the sound of his voice she came out to meet him. She said, "Grid—it's really you—you're home!" and she kissed him and he was.

The new living room sent out a welcome too. Kyrie's special design for comfort and grace was everywhere, and to gild it a small bright fire burned in the large fireplace.

"Junie and I decided to try it out," Kyrie said. "We felt justified because it *is* turning a bit colder."

"Where is my son?" Usually his step alerted Junie, who hid and pounced at what he considered the crucial moment.

"Don't sound so abused. I think he's hunting big game under the stairs. He'll be here as soon as he gets wind of your arrival. Sit down—next to me. The old sofa looks beautiful in front of the fire—doesn't it?" She laid her head on his shoulder. "Oh, Grid—this is lovely. Are you for keeps or will you have to go out again?"

"If I do I'll take you with me." He was not serious, but a moment after he said it he meant it.

She sat up. "Not idle chatter, I trust."

"It needn't be. Do you remember a detective sergeant named Clevis?"

"The shambling one who looks like an empty suit of clothes?"

"That's Clevis. I left him an assignment and he's to get in touch with me if he runs it to earth. If not, I'll visit the Bull and Bean later, and I don't see why I can't combine business with pleasure."

"What sort of place is the Bull and Bean? Somehow it doesn't sound conducive to pleasure."

"It probably isn't. But having you along will be. It's a restaurant and night spot in the Village—quite respectable—and Link Basset does a broadcast there from eleven until two."

"Link Basset? Didn't he have an eight-thirty program not so long ago? If he's the one I mean, his mind is rather original—"

"That's what I'm afraid of," Nelson said.

"Has he anything to do with the Culhane case?"

"In a way. I'd like to ask him a few questions, and a nonofficial approach might yield better results. Most of those late broadcasters play records when they run out of talk—which would give me a chance to tackle him."

"You haven't found Culhane?"

He shook his head. "Will you come with me? I wouldn't suggest it if I expected rough going."

"Of course I'll come with you—to the ends of the earth—even to the Bull and Bean. What with dates being so scarce, a girl can't afford to be choosy."

"You shouldn't have added anything to that 'ends of the earth' recitation. It was perfect as it stood."

"It sounded so sentimental I got self-conscious." Kyrie glanced toward the door of the room. "I wonder what's keeping Sammy with the cocktails. She usually starts them the moment you've crossed the threshold."

"I'm in no hurry. Is Sammy feeling all right?"

"Yes—why?"

"She seemed a bit restrained when I came in."

"You're spoiled. She probably had something on the stove. She showed me your picture in the paper today."

"Oh." He thought that perhaps the false quote about not resting until Culhane was caught accounted for her lack of enthusiasm.

"'Oh' doesn't begin to describe it," Kyrie said. "That picture makes you look like a platinum-blond satyr. If you insist on being so famous, I wish you'd have another taken."

"As soon as I get my hair dyed." He stared at the fire. "What did you think of the words they put in my mouth?"

"They're forever putting words in your mouth. You ought to sue." She looked at him. "No one who knows you would ever believe you could utter such drivel."

"Sammy might—especially since she's so sensitive on the subject of Culhane."

Sammy came in with a tray holding glasses and a frosted cocktail shaker. She set it down on a table beside the sofa. Her face was a wood carving. "Dinner going to be late. When it ready I let you know," she said.

Kyrie's lovely eyes followed her straight-backed exit. Holding the shaker poised over a glass, Nelson said, "Well?"

"Grid, you're right—she didn't look at us—and she's always done special hors d'oeuvres on your early nights. I'll have to insist on extra help. The house is too much for her in spite of what she says."

"I doubt it's the house. I think it's Culhane."

"But she knows you must do your job—and he's really nothing to her."

"He is. Loyalties are oddly enlisted sometimes. If you'd heard her this morning you'd realize that she's deeply concerned."

"She was all right today—at least she was during the little time I saw her."

Nelson tabled the subject. "What sort of day did you have?"

"Let me see." She sipped her daiquiri. "I took Junie to buy some new shoes, which might last all of two weeks if he doesn't increase his activities—then he took me to lunch, and after that we came home. He wanted to get his nap over with because he had a date with his friend Kenneth, who lives down the street. At about three-thirty I went out again—unescorted—to keep an appointment with the dentist." She paused. "Why are you looking so depressed? It was only a checkup. My teeth are in excellent condition."

Nelson had been reminded of Mrs. Rolfe's dentist. He said, "I'm not depressed. Do go on."

"Fascinating—isn't it? It must be my delivery. Well—after the dentist I stopped in at Mrs. Gannon's Saturday afternoon get-together for the purpose of sorting out clothes to be sent to Korean children. I stayed until five-thirty. There—I've put you to sleep."

"No, you haven't." He thought that after dinner he would make his peace with Sammy.

"It wouldn't be such a bad idea at that," Kyrie said.

"What wouldn't?"

"Sleep. No matter what the Bull and Bean holds in store, I hope Clevis makes the trip unnecessary so that you can go to bed at a decent hour."

"I slept this afternoon."

Kyrie looked skeptical. "Where? Or is that an indelicate question?"

He smiled. "In my office."

"For at least ten minutes, no doubt. You and Thomas Edison!" Then she whispered, "Don't move. I think our 'patter of little feet' is sneaking up on us."

Junie whooped and ran from behind the sofa. Nelson jumped the required footage and threw his hands high.

Junie climbed up his legs. He said reassuringly, "Stick 'em down. I'm not Daniel Boone."

Nelson roughed the upended tow hair. "Who are you?"

"I'm the gasman."

"Gasmen don't give war whoops."

Junie assumed a thoughtful expression. "No—they don't," he said finally. "I made a mistake."

"Has the gasman had his supper?"

"Oh yes." He indulged in one of his lesser flights of fancy. "Supper in the cellar. Put me down."

"Right on your two new shoes—or are they?" Nelson glanced at the small scuffed toes.

"Oh yes," Junie said cheerfully. "And a new storybook too."

"I'd like to see that."

"All right. Stay here." He cantered out of the room.

"See what I mean about the shoes?" Kyrie said. "Not to mention the wear and tear on the rest of him. And Sammy was giving him a wash when I came in."

"He does look as though he dined in the cellar."

"Don't say that to Sammy. She scrubs it as clean as the rest of the house."

"Since when has the gasman replaced Boone?"

"It's hard to keep track. Last week he was a space cadet, and I think the only reason he switched to Boone was that the coonskin cap was more comfortable than the space helmet."

"There's a moral somewhere in that, but it doesn't explain why Boone was muscled out."

Kyrie laughed. "Maybe one came to read the meter while I was away—or maybe he was watching television with Kenneth. They have a program called *The Merry Mailman*, so they might have a *Gay Gasman*, too. Not that he's a television fan. Junie prefers the personal touch—being read to or sung to or talked to—"

Junie came back with the book. Skimming through it,

Nelson saw that text and pictures dealt with people city children were likely to encounter in the course of everyday living. He said, "Is this where you met the gasman?"

The question struck Junie as highly amusing. He laughed heartily.

"Come, come! If there was a punch line in that, I missed it."

Junie accepted the "Come, come!" as an invitation. He settled himself on the sofa, leaned against his father, and said, "Read."

Kyrie bowed to the inevitable and went to see if she could help Sammy. Nelson began to read the first picture story. Then it occurred to him that it would aid all concerned if he dumped Junie into a tub and put him to bed. "How about my finishing this when you're tucked in?" he said.

Junie had evidently had a hard day. He was unexpectedly amenable. He mounted Nelson's shoulders and spurred him up the stairs. The job of tubbing and bedding down was accomplished in record time. Junie behaved like a dream child, hardly splashing at all, and squirming into his pajamas with such eager cooperation that Nelson felt his head and was relieved to find it cool.

He settled the suspiciously good little boy between the covers, sat in a chair beside the bed, and took up the reading where he had left off. Junie made only one protest, demanding that he begin at the beginning.

"All right—but don't ask for another."

"Oh no," Junie said virtuously.

He kept his word. But when Nelson had completed the stirring epic of a garbage collector, he begged for a song. "Will you close your eyes?"

"Oh yes."

"Well—what song would you like?"

"'The Rosie Trolley.'"

Nelson puzzled over that, remembered a volume in Junie's library, and wondered if "The Little Red Engine" had been rechristened. He said, "Are you sure that's a song?"

"Oh yes. Like this." Junie illustrated in a voice composed largely of clinkers.

"The lyrics are a bit repetitious," Nelson said, "but the tune evades me."

Junie said, "Repetitious," quite clearly. He liked it well enough to incorporate it into the song.

"I'm afraid you've got me, old boy. Will you settle for

anything else?"

Junie held out for a while, but in the end he fell asleep to a medley of nursery rhymes rendered in the acting captain's soothing baritone. During the concert Kyrie appeared, but backed out silently with an approving nod.

Downstairs, Nelson paid another visit to the kitchen. Pots bubbled on the stove, the oven gave off heat, but Sammy was not there. This was definitely a time to yearn for the walkup on Lexington Avenue. It had been inconvenient and without scope, but undoubtedly it had possessed certain advantages. For example, he thought disconsolately, the members of his household were always where he expected to find them because there was nowhere else for them to be.

The kitchen's blended fragrance taunted him with the reminder that too many hours had passed since his sketchy lunch. He went to the stove, lifted a pot lid, and dropped it as Sammy crossed the threshold. He said, "Now I know what it's like to be caught in the act."

"I going to serve right away. I sorry it so late."

"I'll eat twice as much to make up for it. I've put Junie to sleep."

"Yes, Mr. Grid-dely. Miss Kyrie tell me just now when I go to fetch him." Nelson had never seen her so tensed. "He behave good?"

"Perfectly." Kyrie was right and he was wrong, he thought. The plight of a man met once or twice in the past could not have effected this change in Sammy. Besides, she had been quite serene after their morning talk. He said, "Junie was so angelic that I was afraid he might be coming down with something—and now I'm worried about you."

She tried to smile. "I ain't angelic."

"No—but you're not yourself."

"I fine."

He tried shock tactics, only half believing what he said. "Miss Kyrie thinks this house is too big for you and she worries because you won't let her take on extra help. Perhaps you'd rather work somewhere else and are too kind to tell us."

"No such thing. The cleaning lady come every day and I got a handy man for the odd jobs. What work is left to do?" Briefly she reverted to the old Sammy, the strong, competent woman for whom no task was too great. "You got no call to talk that way. You know good and well how I feel about you and Miss Kyrie and Junie, even if you don't go around like some do—thinking everybody who work for you got to worship the ground you step on. I going to stay put until you say for me to quit.”

“Which will be never. Then what is it, Sammy?”

“Mr. Grid-dely—” She started again, “Mr. Grid-dely—”

“Say it. Is it something to do with Kevin Culhane? Surely you don’t believe—” The telephone rang. He broke off to listen.

“Grid,” Kyrie called. “Where are you? It’s Sergeant Clevis.” He told Sammy that he would be back. He took the call on the extension outside the dining room.

Clevis said, “I got your note. I must’ve hit headquarters the minute you left. Chief—this ain’t my day.”

“You’ve got company.”

“Yeah? Well—far as I’m concerned, we’re suffering in vain, as the fellow says. When we find Culhane we close the case. I’m standing pat on that. Everything else is parsley—including this guy Basset.”

“Have you seen him?”

“I seen him and he seen me—in his apartment. I got a red face to show for it.”

“What happened?”

“I staked out in the lobby. At six forty-five a redhead comes in and the elevator boy says, ‘Good evening, Mr. Basset.’ He goes up and I give him time to settle and I follow. I ring the bell and he opens up—the door, that is—nothing else. He tells me to wait a minute on account of he’s on the phone. So I wait with my ears out and they don’t get filled worth a nickel. There’s a dame on the other end and he’s smoothing her down. It don’t sound like a brush either. If Selene Rolfe was his girl, like you said in the letter, then one girl less is nothing he cries over. Not from the way he was talking. He hangs up after a real sweet goodbye and words to the effect that he’s looking forward to something or other. Then he comes back and asks me what I’m selling. I tell him I’m an officer and start fishing for my bona fides, but he don’t wait. He stares. He says, ‘A likely story,’ adds a push to it, and I’m outside.”

“No foot in the door?”

“Don’t rub it in. Him answering right away with a nothing-to-hide look on his kisser made me lower my guard. And you got to admit the ‘likely story’ routine is a new and different way to shake the law. Maybe I don’t look like a cop, but so far when I’ve owned up to it no one’s doubted my word. Thing is, if I try again it will be a repeat performance or a fist fight—so is it all right with you if I sit on him while I make with the interrogation?"

Nelson knew he was capable of it. More than once he had seen the baggy suit in action. He said, "No fight. If he goes out again, tail him until eleven o'clock—provided he ends up at a restaurant called the Bull and Bean. If not, stick with him. I want a full account of wherever he goes and whoever he sees."

He was glad that Clevis did not ask why. He would have been unable to supply an answer.

Clevis said, "But he knows me."

"Wear a grass skirt or carry a lollipop. Do I have to brief the best tail in the business?"

Clevis sounded aggrieved. "This assignment wouldn't be a substitute for a beat in the wilds of Brooklyn due to this morning's caper?" He answered himself. "No—that ain't your style, Chief." Then he brightened. "You got some lead you're keeping dark—like maybe he'll steer us to Culhane. Okay—don't worry about a thing."

Dinner was on the table. Its main course consisted of chicken and black olives and mushrooms, lifted above the ordinary by one of Sammy's sauces. She had learned her art in New Orleans and she had not permitted her state of mind to mar it. Nelson ate with enjoyment in spite of his preoccupation, and praised everything. The praise had no visible effect. Sammy moved in and out of the room with aloof dignity, and he and Kyrie exchanged troubled glances.

Sammy brought coffee to the living room. They drank it slowly and talked of many things. Nelson had left word at headquarters that he was to be notified if anything broke. Nothing did, but he was summoned to the telephone several times to receive more meatless reports. One of these came from the plainclothesman who had been detailed to jog the memory of the Gretna desk clerk. The clerk had no memory at all, the disgusted plainclothesman said. For that matter, he had no mind capable of dealing with anything above a racing form. He insisted that he had enough to do to keep track of the hotel's paying customers and no time to waste on their visitors. It had been work to make him say anything, since obviously he regarded the police as his natural enemy, but under persuasion he had stated that a woman had inquired about Culhane on the afternoon of the murder. He thought she had headed for the exit instead of the elevators, and could give no description other than that she was dressed in black and looked like "bad news."

He had not set eyes upon the murder victim. She must have had the room number, he said, and gone straight up. He admitted to being sorry that he had missed her. It would have been something to tell his pals. Further persuasion made him recall that later—he could not or would not give a specific time—a man had asked for Culhane's room number. Again no description. The man looked like any other man. He added vaguely that he was carrying stuff. Just stuff. He could have been a salesman or something.

Nelson thanked the plainclothesman with more courtesy than sincerity. He said it might help.

When Sammy came in for the coffee tray she had her coat on. She said, "I going out for a little. They's a few things I need and the corner store keep open all hours."

"We're going out later too, Sammy," Nelson said.

For a moment her warming smile appeared. "You both—you and Miss Kyrie? It been a long while since that happen. What time you leaving?"

"Around ten-thirty."

"I back before then."

Somewhat later she called out to announce her return, and then they heard her step upon the stairs.

Nelson said, "I guess she's going to bed."

Kyrie answered lazily, "Well—you can talk to her in the morning."

Chapter Thirteen

Link Basset said, "Hold on a minute. Someone's at the door." Then he came back and said, "How are you?" as though he really wanted to know.

Bess had hesitated about calling him. But when she did she wondered why she had been so timid. He sounded as friendly and natural as any hometown boy. He even seemed genuinely pleased to hear from her, and once or twice there was an odd note of affection in his voice. Quite matter-of-factly he accepted her explanation.

"You see," she said, "when Aunt Alma happened to mention you, Mother immediately misunderstood and she—well—she jumped to conclusions about our relationship—"

"Don't give it a thought. I'm a conclusion jumper myself. Remember?"

"Yes, but—it's awkward because she—she's determined to

meet you."

"Don't tell me you grudge your old mother a treat. When's the meeting to take place? Now?"

"No—please—this is serious. Not now. I'm home and Mother's at the Waldorf. The thing is, I made the mistake of telling her where you broadcast—so nothing will do but that everybody go there later and—"

"Who's everybody?"

"Mother, of course, and her second husband, who arrived this afternoon—and Aunt Alma—and me."

"For a moment I was afraid they'd planned to leave you home with a sitter. Good—I'll expect a party of four—and carriage trade at that, if the Waldorf is any indication. My stock should go up at the B and B."

"You don't mind?"

"Mind? Sweetheart, I'm looking forward to it. I only wish I'd known in time to buy the ring. I hope Mom won't think I'm a piker. I hold forth in the lounge. Get there early so that I'll be at my freshest."

Bess retorted with, "You always are." Yet she did not feel displeased. She felt somehow that he was a lot kinder underneath than his brittle manner proclaimed, and that he would not let her down. She felt something else, but quickly denied it. Because it simply was not logical to have garnered so much pleasure from a trivial exchange with a stranger.

It was after she hung up that she became aware of a strange omission in the conversation. Neither of them had once referred to the murder. That was understandable on her part. Mother's willful refusal to accept Link Basset as a mere acquaintance had temporarily canceled the circumstances of her initial encounter with him. She had been concerned only with warning him of what was in store. But he? Surely he had read the newspapers. Tact? Delicacy? If so, he possessed more of those qualities than had been credited to him.

Slowly she walked back to the living room. The melancholy that had poisoned her all day worked within her again. She would have given anything to place a comforting hand in the hand of the hunted man.

She herself had read the newspapers, buying them on her way home from the Waldorf, poring over them with Aunt Alma. The varying reports had confused her, but there was no confusion as to where her sympathy lay. She did not stop to assess Kevin Culhane's guilt or innocence. She knew only that the tapestry of Mother's carefully woven propaganda, Mother's lifework, had unraveled, and that the unraveling had begun before Aunt Alma showed her the picture of a father and daughter with love an all but visible emanation between them.

Her mind circled around to Mother and to Mother's letters, which she had taken at face value. If Mother and James Haskell posed for a picture, there would have been no emanation. At least none called love. Face value. Love. All these years she had taken Mother at face value because not to do so would have been to withhold love. Would it? Sudden tragedy had forced adulthood upon her overnight. Tragedy had breathed upon her eyes, compelling her to see Mother as she really was. And yet she loved her still. Love was neither a matter of blindness nor of clear vision. It just was. She saw Link Basset clearly enough—and yet—? She stood stock-still in the hall and tried to pull herself together. Link Basset had nothing to do with anything. How could she even think of love in connection with a man seen only once or twice? If only she did not have to go to the Bull and Bean tonight with Mother and James Haskell.

Must she feel sorrow for everyone in the world and yet be powerless to change what made her sorry? It seemed to her that Mother had no more chosen to be born with a lack that deafened her to all needs save her own than a child would choose to be born with a missing limb. The fruitless pity encompassed James Haskell too. He had been a bachelor until Mother crossed his path. And if his eyes now spoke the truth, he rued the day.

As she entered the living room, Aunt Alma spoke from her chair. "Did you talk to Mr. Basset?"

"Yes—he was quite decent. He didn't seem at all annoyed." Bess sat down. She had an almost irrepressible desire to go on talking about Link Basset. She repressed it. Aunt Alma was clearly in no frame of mind to listen to extrinsic chatter.

Aunt Alma had the radio turned on softly. Someone was playing the piano and dressing whatever it was he played in surplus frills and flounces that made it unrecognizable.

Aunt Alma said apologetically, "He'll finish in a few minutes—and news bulletins will come on."

"Was there anything while I was on the phone?"

"No."

They waited, drawn close by shared anxiety. Aunt Alma's gypsy face brooded. Bess twisted a lock of hair round and round her finger. The pianist stitched on a last silver frill, and the announcer's voice made station identification. Then came five minutes of the latest news. Kevin Culhane's name flashed by. He was still at large, but with Gridley Nelson of Homicide on the job the newscaster predicted that it was merely a matter of time.

"I hate that man," Bess said passionately. "Pretending to be friendly and understanding—and then saying what he did to the reporters."

Aunt Alma switched off the radio. "Reporters have always credited police officers with statements like that—often correctly, I suppose—but not this time. The words just don't fit him."

Bess said, "You like him."

Aunt Alma looked at her accusing face, and her fine lips quirked. "Once you've decided which way to go you go all out—don't you? Yes—I think I do like him. Better than that, I trust him. So much that if Kevin were to get in touch with me I'd try to persuade him to give himself up."

"But—but he wouldn't have a chance."

"He would. The lieutenant has an open mind. I'm certain he's far from convinced in spite of the evidence. If Kevin went to him and told his story it would be far more constructive than what he's doing now—hiding God knows where—miserable—frightened—" At Bess's expression her hand went up to her temples. She said, "My dear—I'm ranting on like an old witch. Perhaps it isn't that way at all. Perhaps he's found friends—"

"Perhaps," Bess said bleakly. "Haven't you any idea of where he might be?"

"No. I tried every place I knew of last night before he came here. He couldn't have stayed hidden long in any of them. He must have managed to leave the city."

"I wish—"

"What time did your mother and James say they'd call for us?"

"About ten-thirty."

"Would you mind if I didn't join the party?"

"Yes—I would mind." She could not bear the thought of her aunt sitting alone in the apartment listening for what surely would not happen. "He won't try to call you," she said. "It's bound to occur to him that the police might be tapping the phone." It occurred to her that if they were they must have enjoyed her talk with Link Basset. Ashamed, she brushed the petty concern aside. "I read somewhere that the evidence gathered by wiretapping isn't admitted in court—but in this case they're not after evidence—they just want to trace him. I wouldn't even be surprised if they were watching the house as well to see if he returned."

"I wish he would," Aunt Alma said, and as though she believed in the power of wishes she added decisively, "Bess, I will stay home."

Bess changed to a dress that she hoped would not disgrace Link Basset, especially since the Haskells, arriving somewhat before the designated time, did not look exactly like carriage trade. Mother would have passed, but James wore an ill-fitting dark suit that rucked below the collar and gave no play to his muscular back.

He waved an envelope at Aunt Alma. "I found this under the door—must be a circular of some kind." Quite obviously he was grateful for anything that would eke out his sparse supply of conversation. "Look at that address—all out of alignment. Makes a bad impression. Seems to me any firm wanting business would invest in a few good typewriters."

His wife said, "I didn't realize you were so observant," and Bess winced at her tone.

Aunt Alma took the envelope without comment. She asked if they would like a drink.

"I am a little thirsty," Lisa Haskell said. "I wouldn't mind a glass of ginger ale. I shall order champagne later and I always think it's such a mistake to mix drinks. But I'm sure James could stand something stronger if you have it. You need to be put in the mood when it comes to urbane entertainment—don't you, James?"

He looked uncomfortable. He rubbed a spread hand over his face. He said he guessed that was about the size of it.

Bess offered to do the honors, and suddenly jumped back into last night when she had made the same offer on her father's behalf, prompted by the same desire to escape. She thought very harsh thoughts about herself.

This time it was Aunt Alma who escaped, saying, "No—let me," and moving swiftly from the room.

Bess found the going heavy. Mother was no less willing to shoulder the burden of talk than usual. But almost every word she uttered was aimed at James.

"Have you noticed, Bess dear, that your stepfather doesn't

care a bit about his appearance? It isn't that he's frugal. He just doesn't give it a thought. Of course the material in that suit he's wearing has held up beautifully, but styles have changed a bit since he bought it. Jodhpurs and breeches and boots are another matter. His closets fairly bulge with them and he keeps buying more every time he goes into Griswold."

Bess fished hard for something to divert her. "What did you do after we left you this afternoon, Mother?"

"Nothing exciting, I assure you. I took pity on James and decided not to bother about the theater. Two big social events in one evening would be more than he could stand. To get back to Griswold—Bess, you can have no idea of what a flourishing town it is. It has all of one drugstore—a large hardware store—two groceries—a man's tailor—a bootery—and an absolutely tremendous hay and feed store. Have I left anything out, James?"

He muttered, "I guess it has all we need, Lisa."

"Salisbury, Connecticut's not so big either," Bess said.

"That's what I used to think."

Bess made another try. "I like your dress. Is it new?"

"I got it in Boston. There—I knew I'd left something out. Griswold has a department store too. They call it the Emporium. I never seem to have much luck shopping at the Emporium, but they do carry the most durable aprons—and as for house dresses, I've never seen a more varied assortment. They don't sell them as house dresses, of course. In fact, the one and only saleswoman seemed quite surprised when I said they were. I'm afraid that I rarely see eye to eye with the natives of Griswold. James gets along swimmingly, though. He has so much in common with everyone there. Ah—here you are, Alma. What on earth took you so long? Oh—I see—you got dressed. I do think you might have been ready when we came. It isn't as though I live around the corner and you can afford to fritter away what little time we have together."

Bess was relieved that Mother had found another target. Her arrows glanced off Aunt Alma, but with James it was plain that every shot scored. Then in bewilderment she stared at her aunt, who was unmistakably carriage trade in a dress that would have passed muster anywhere. Aunt Alma must be coming with them after all, and that was another relief, because in Mother's present mood there was no telling how she would have reacted to a refusal. Even at her sweetest she did not take kindly to the slightest shift in her plans.

Lisa Haskell sipped ginger ale, careful not to smudge her lipstick, and watched her husband down straight scotch. Her eyes said, Not that too! But she made no oral criticism.

James seemed helped by the scotch. He began to talk about horses with an enthusiasm that Bess had not suspected him of possessing. His wife interrupted to say it was time to go and ordered him to commandeer a taxi.

Bess protested. "I looked up the Bull and Bean. It's on Seventh Avenue—near enough to walk."

"I don't intend to walk. It's getting colder every minute, and I had to wear this faille coat because I didn't bring another and it was too late to buy one after you left today." Now she was accusing Bess and Aunt Alma of outstaying their welcome at the Waldorf. And having put this across, she turned to her husband. "If you say I told you so, I'll scream."

He did not say, "I told you so." Nor did he take a bow when she added that at least he was a good weather prophet but should have had the courage of his convictions and insisted that she take a warmer coat. He made an exit, and when they joined him on the sidewalk a taxi was waiting. It covered the short distance in little more time than it took them to pile in and pile out.

Before the canopied entrance Lisa said in disappointment, "I thought all Greenwich Village restaurants were cellars with candlelight and lots and lots of atmosphere." But after a doorman dressed as a cowhand had herded them inside, her disappointment faded. "Why—it could easily be one of those smart places uptown. You should have told me, Bess. An evening dress wouldn't have been at all unsuitable."

Bess said, "You look lovely as you are—and I didn't know. I've never been here." She received a pitying glance.

"Perhaps this young man isn't Mr. Right after all. Perhaps you'd be happier living in the country with someone like James."

Their coats were checked and they walked through a pleasant bar into the lounge of the Bull and Bean. Lisa remarked that the clever indirect lighting made Bess and Aunt Alma look almost handsome. She commented upon the naughty little bulls that romped the walls, but thanked heaven that she was broadminded. And when they had been ushered to a table she settled back on a comfortably padded banquette for a more leisurely survey of her surroundings.

"Not many people," she said, "but I expect we're a bit early."

She grasped Bess's arm. "Don't tell me, dear. Let me guess. He's standing near the piano—the one with the cigarette holder."

Bess glanced at the tall slim man who was definitely not Link Basset. She shook her head. "No, Mother, he—"

"Wait—I'll try again. Isn't this fun? I'm almost afraid to ask, but surely he's not that fat little fellow who just waddled in?"

Aunt Alma ended the game by calmly indicating the platform about fifteen feet from where they sat. It was equipped with a long table, microphones, several chairs, and Link Basset. He was talking to a man in shirt sleeves who had stepped out of a glass enclosure at the platform's right. As they stared he turned toward their inclined heads, and it was obvious to Bess that their arrival had not just dawned upon him. Nevertheless, he gave a realistic start, raised a hand in salute, and jumped down from the platform. A moment later he was threading in their direction.

Lisa said pessimistically, "Of course you can't always judge by appearances. I do hope that red hair doesn't mean a bad temper."

Bess said, "Shhh," and Lisa obeyed, but merely because she was in hurried consultation with her mirror.

Link Basset had reached the table. He paid his respects to Alma Elliot before he turned to Bess. "I must have been a very good boy all day," he said, "to deserve such a charming surprise."

Bess climbed the peak of gaucherie. "It isn't exactly a surprise. Besides—you saw us come in—didn't you?"

Lisa nudged her. "I'm waiting to be introduced."

He switched his attention at once. "I don't think that's necessary. You and Bess aren't alike—yet there is a distinct family resemblance. I wonder why she never mentioned having a kid sister."

Bess thought miserably that he was overdoing it, but Lisa's laugh tinkled merrily.

"I'm Bess's mother," she said, "as if you didn't know. A little bird whispered in my ear that my funny child showed you my picture last night. This is my husband, James Haskell. You, of course, are the famous Lincoln Basset. Do sit down. You aren't due to go on the air yet, are you? I understand your broadcast doesn't start until eleven."

"True. I still have a good twenty minutes' leeway." He sat next to her on the banquette.

"Then you'll have time for a glass or two of champagne." She became all weary sophistication. "Is it drinkable here?"

"No worse than they serve in most joints. In other words, not nearly worthy of you—but what could be?"

"Bess—wherever did you find this wicked flatterer?" All she needed was a fan to tap him with.

Those were the last words she addressed to Bess or to anyone but Link Basset until he left to take his place on the platform. Deftly she balanced her end of what appeared to be a shameless flirtation, blossoming happily for the first time that day.

Bess should have been pleased, because she had expected a barrage of embarrassing questions leading to the extraction of Link Basset's intentions as they concerned herself. But from the fragments she heard, the low intimate conversation was not going that way at all. In fact, it sounded as though Bess Rohan had never existed.

She looked covertly at James to see how he was weathering the tête-à-tête. She caught her breath at his expression and looked elsewhere, anywhere. Then she caught her breath again. An extremely attractive couple was being seated two tables away, and the face of the waiter who ministered to them said that business was picking up. But for Bess it took a downward curve as she recognized the male half of the couple. Coincidence? Business? What sort of business could be transacted at the Bull and Bean by Lieutenant Nelson of Homicide?

Chapter Fourteen

Aunt Alma sat opposite to Bess. It was impossible to judge by her aloof face whether or not she had noted the entrance of the lieutenant and his beautiful ash blonde.

Link Basset's red head stayed close to Lisa Haskell's dark one until he raised it, glanced at his watch, and made his excuses. He was more popular with the clientele of the Bull and Bean than he had been at Gilly's. An exchange of greetings and laughter marked his progress to the microphones, but the Haskell table was an island of silence. Lisa's voice broke over it like a tidal wave.

"I think he's absolutely adorable," she said. "I haven't been so stimulated in years. But I'm afraid he's too mature for you, Bess. One needs to have lived to appreciate his special quality. Now we mustn't talk too loudly once he's begun. He confided in me that there's nothing he hates more than raucous people who presumably come to hear him and who haven't the courtesy to keep their voices down while he's trying to earn a living."

Bess could not have explained the compulsion that forced her to assert herself. "He doesn't have to earn a living this way. He's a highly paid scriptwriter."

"Scriptwriter!" Lisa made it sound like "street cleaner." "You don't know a thing about it. A man of his talents is irresistibly drawn by the lure of a live audience. And no one understands that lure better than I who sacrificed the lights and the music to do my duty as a woman. Quiet—he's beginning, and I don't want to miss a word. The place has filled up nicely—hasn't it? But from Link's point of view Saturday nights are always the worst—"

She missed a spate of words. Link Basset sat relaxed, seemingly unconscious of the microphone in front of him. He was saying something about a funny thing happening to him on the way to this clambake, and the funny thing was that nothing had happened—which left him high and dry for a way to start the program.

A woman at the next table tittered, and Lisa sent her a quelling glance. Bess whispered, "Mother—don't. He wants people to laugh."

"He distinctly told me—"

Link Basset was wondering vocally why people shed comfortable clothes and forsook comfortable houses to fight their way into a smoky unwholesome dive for the dubious pleasure of hearing a loudmouth make with a lot of drivel that would not improve their so-called minds in the slightest. He assumed benignly that his audience did live in houses and not in trees or caves—although it was sometimes hard to believe—and went on to say that since they were here and since he was here and had nothing better to do, he might as well dispose of the few commercials that had been entrusted to his tender care. Whereupon he disposed of them, cautioning everyone to crawl, not rush, to their nearest or—if the family doctor had prescribed a trip—to their furthest stores to buy what he was selling. Reasonably he pointed out that if they were too eager they might break their legs or be killed by traffic, and a fat lot of good that would do him or his sponsors, especially since he didn't happen to be touting any leg-setters or morticians. After he had torn off the commercials he summed up a preview of a three-D picture which he had been unfortunate enough to attend. Then Bess lost track of the broadcast. Lisa was preempting her ears.

"You'll never guess what's going to happen later. I begged Link not to do it, but he simply refused to listen. It seems that he devotes a portion of the program to important out-of-town guests—and I'm to be one of them. Do you hear, James? He'll introduce me as Lisa Rohan—because that was how I appeared professionally—and I suppose he'll mention a few of the highlights in my stage career, since he was so clever about prying them out of me—for example, my role of handmaiden when we took *Helen of Troy* on the road. It was only two sides, but a leading critic said that I played it to the hilt. Then he'll interview me and I'll say I'm visiting New York with my husband, Mr. James Haskell, horse breeder extraordinary, and that we're staying at the Waldorf. I'll be sure to put in a nice plug for the Haskell Stables—"

James Haskell said abruptly, "What's that?"

"Really, James—haven't you been listening to me?"

The waiter had just brought a third bottle of champagne and was twirling it around in the cooler. Haskell said, "Never mind—give it here."

"But, m'sieu—" The waiter clipped his protest short, deciding at a glance that the temperature of the guest needed chilling more than did the wine. He filled Haskell's glass once and, at a peremptory signal, again. Twice Haskell drank as a man cursed by an unquenchable thirst.

"James," his wife said frigidly, "there are other people at the table."

"They're going to stay at the table—and so are you." His eyes cowed the waiter, who retreated. "Interviews be damned. I've had all I can take."

"More than you can take. The lion's share of the second bottle too. Don't think I wasn't watching."

"Don't think *I* wasn't watching."

"What do you mean by that remark? And please lower your voice. Try to remember you're in a civilized place."

"Civilized," he said. "Clowns rubbing elbows with each other—"

"I want to know what's come over you. Am I to understand that you grudge me my little moment in the spotlight?"

"You get my meaning all right. No interview." His groan was like a roar. "Things are bad enough without you making a public spectacle—"

"I like that! Who's making a public spectacle?"

If she was in doubt, no one else within earshot was. Through an agony of embarrassment Bess was aware that Link Basset had stopped talking, whether before or during the quarrel she did not know. She did know and was grateful for the loud band music on the turntable, which swelled above the voices of Mother and her second husband.

Her hushes and pleases were ignored. Haskell said, "I won't have my name bandied about. You don't get up on that platform."

"Put me in chains," Lisa said. "Bury me in Griswold. That's been your aim since the beginning. Well—you won't succeed. I'm a young woman—why shouldn't I be entitled to a little excitement—a little life? And let me tell you that what I've had with you is not my idea of living. From the way you act, there might be as much age discrepancy between us as there was between poor Kevin and m—"

Bess sent an anguished appeal to Aunt Alma, who said, "Lisa—I think Mr. Basset's trying to attract your attention."

That stopped Lisa, but not James Haskell. When she started to rise, either to crane toward or leave for the platform, he gripped her arm. "Damn it—you sit down."

Then Aunt Alma did what seemed like a treacherous thing. She turned sideways in her chair, and her smile covered a distance of two tables away where Lieutenant Nelson sat with his ash blonde. Treacherous or not, the results were effective, and high time, because Mother was trying to free her arm, and James Haskell had obviously reached the stage where he must burst a blood vessel or vent his stress by overt violence.

But suddenly the lieutenant stood there looking down at the group. "I thought I recognized you," he said cordially, and bowed to each of the ladies in turn, calling them by name. Then he spoke to James Haskell. "And you must be Mr. Haskell. My name is Nelson." Somehow he made it sound as though he had heard a great deal about Mr. Haskell, all of it flattering.

Whether or not this subtlety penetrated the flooded areas of Haskell's brain was moot. But he did respond to the outstretched hand, and to do that he had to free Lisa's arm.

He said thickly, "Just a little family argument," and perhaps because it won him a man-to-man smile of complicity, the red mist lifted a little. "You married?"

"Yes—my wife is with me."

Lisa said brightly, "Oh—then you're here for pleasure."

There was no denying her poise, and Bess could not help being proud of her. Bess had mislaid her compassion for James Haskell, who needed the fortification of alcohol in order to oppose his wife. And by what ugly means he had opposed her. Bess could all but see the bruise forming under the tight sleeve. Inexcusable, she thought, no matter how insistently Mother had been asking for it, and no matter how drunk he was.

Haskell was now studying Nelson with glazed eyes. He said suspiciously, "You wouldn't be another actor?"

"Of course he's not an actor," Lisa said, "and now we'll forget all about it. If you don't want me to go on the air, I won't. But I do think it would be nice if we asked the lieutenant and his wife to join us. The more the merrier, I always say."

"What lieutenant?"

"James—don't you think some black coffee would—?"

"I think some straight whiskey—instead of that women's wash you've been ordering."

For once Lisa looked helpless.

Nelson said, "My wife and I would like very much to join you. The people next door seem to be leaving. I'll ask about having the two tables moved together."

He went back to Kyrie, who said, "You seem to have stopped whatever it was."

"I think only temporarily. Would you mind very much if we sat with them? I doubt if the invitation would have been issued unless it was a clear case of damsel in distress."

"Which damsel? The young girl seems even more stricken than the lady with the arm. But the one who signaled to you seems cool enough to handle any number of drunks."

"Maybe I should have said 'damsels.' I don't think any of them have had a happy day."

"Well—don't forget you came here to talk to Link Basset."

"He'll probably head for the microphone as soon as this record is finished—and it seems to be on its last legs now. I'll have to wait until the next go-round."

"I don't see him anywhere," Kyrie said.

"No—but he can't be far away. All right?"

"Of course," she said.

He called the waiter.

Lisa Haskell leaned over and whispered to Bess, "Did you notice where Link went?"

"No. Mother—why did you ask the lieutenant to join us?"

"Really, Bess, for a bright girl you can be awfully stupid. I asked him because I may need help to get James home—and it's obvious that Link can't leave. Besides, maybe he'll tell us what the situation is in regard to—to your father."

"Mother—I didn't think you were inter—"

"Never mind that now. I'm afraid that as soon as the record stops playing Link will go back and announce me. If he does—what with the state James is in, there's sure to be another scene."

"Does he—is he this way often?"

Lisa shook her head. "He takes a drink now and then when he comes in after a day in the open, but I've never seen him under the influence before. You could knock me down with a feather."

"Did he hurt you?"

Lisa brushed that aside. "The thing is, can you manage to get word to Link not to call my name?"

Bess said, "I'll write a note in the ladies' room and ask a waiter to give it to him."

"Hurry, then."

Bess clutched her purse and stood up. She walked away from the table.

"Where's she going?" James Haskell said.

"Don't ask embarrassing questions, dear."

"She's not going there. I saw you whispering. She's going to the platform."

"She isn't—but if she were, why shouldn't she? After all—Link Basset is her boyfriend."

"You'd never know it." He was distracted by a waiter pushing the next table closer. "What the hell's he doing that for?"

Lisa said, "I suppose the lieutenant gave him instructions. Now be nice, James, or he'll think you don't want him. Do you know what? I'm hungry. Let's all have coffee and something to eat. You hardly touched your dinner— Why—here's the lieutenant and his charming wife. I was just saying it would be a good idea to order some food."

"We were thinking along the same lines," Nelson said unblushingly. He presented Kyrie, noting that Lisa's distress did not prevent an automatic appraisal not only of every stitch Kyrie wore but exactly the way she wore it.

Lisa said, "You won't mind if I steal your husband for a while? Sit next to me, Lieutenant."

Some nagging memory of manners had forced Haskell to his

feet, but no further. He said truculently, "No, you don't. You sit next to me. I'm sick to death of women's chitchat."

Lisa shrugged and murmured that her "diamond in the rough" must be humored. Nelson humored him after seating Kyrie and casting a glance at Bess's vacant chair. If he was puzzled that another record had been started and that Link Basset was nowhere in sight, it did not show.

Haskell said, "What branch of the service are you in?"

"I was in the Army."

Haskell said morosely, "Was—eh? I didn't make you as the type who clings to rank after the shooting's stopped." As though he were doing the best he could with a bad bargain, he added, "What are you drinking?"

Nelson looked at his almost full glass which the waiter had transferred from the other table. "Scotch and soda—but when I've had this I'll be ready for some food."

"Well, I won't." Loudly he ordered rye.

Lisa looked at Nelson reproachfully. Then, with an air of having to attend to everything singlehanded, she summoned the waiter. When the rye appeared it was accompanied by a large steak sandwich.

Haskell said, "What's this?" and all but held his nose as he shoved it aside. He drank the rye, muttered, "Rotgut," and rubbed his eyes.

Kyrie, Nelson saw, was making conversation with Alma Elliot and receiving fair cooperation. Lisa had become the silent and abstracted member of the group. Oddly resistant to Kyrie's efforts to include her, she kept shifting her eyes from James to the empty chair. Nelson wondered what was keeping Bess and whether her absence had anything to do with the absence of Link Basset. He wondered why he had been fool enough to subject Kyrie to what was at the least an extremely tiresome situation. He was cheered when Kyrie gave him a reassuring nod. He decided that the best course was to allow Haskell to drink himself beyond belligerence and see that he got home.

He said with no more purpose than to test Haskell's reactions, "Your wife was telling me about the expected foal."

Haskell only grunted, but Lisa roused herself. This time her look was approving. Her eyes seemed to say that if they could get her husband to talk about what interested him the crisis might be avoided. She started the ball rolling. "That was the first question I asked James when he turned up at the Waldorf. I was so relieved to hear that the foal was just fine. Do get him to tell you about horses, Lieutenant. He's absolutely fascinating on the subject. Did you ever realize that they're all called foals when they're born—not colts or fillies—no matter what their sex? I never thought I'd learn so much—"

"You've learned nothing," Haskell said. "You can't even get it into your head that you're no filly." He held up his empty glass. "Hey—"

"James—please—"

"James—please," he mimicked savagely. He drew back his arm and squinted at the target of her face.

Nelson wrested the glass from his fingers and said heartily, "One refill coming up."

James swung his heavy body toward him, almost unseated by his own impetus. He permitted Nelson to right him. He even said, "Thanks," as though he suddenly found himself out of context with whatever had been written upon his mind a moment ago. He made a careful prop of his elbows upon the table, a careful cup of his hands to hold his chin. He said, "Army man, eh? Cavalry myself, once. The filly's dead. No sense to it, but a man gets crazy and can't attend to his work." His lids dropped over his bloodshot eyes.

Lisa cried, "He won't be able to walk. What will they think at the Waldorf when—?"

Nelson said, "I'll take care of it."

Haskell opened his eyes. "You take care of it, fellow. Listen—I don't like this place—too much smoke—blinds me. Never smoke, myself. She does."

"We'll find another place," Nelson said.

"Sure—we don't belong here. Did you drink my drink?"

"The waiter's bringing another."

"'S all right—share and share alike. I'll drink yours." He drew Nelson's glass toward him. He lifted it and gulped thirstily.

Lisa said, "I'm so mortified I—"

Alma Elliot turned to her. "Don't worry, Lisa. In places like this they don't pay much attention when people drink too much. And if the air doesn't make him recover, you needn't brave the staff at the Waldorf. He can sleep it off at my apartment." She spoke quietly.

Nelson remembered the way she had looked that morning. She looked different now. He had no time to weigh the change in her or to speculate as to when it had come about. Other matters were bidding for his attention.

Chapter Fifteen

If they had deliberately set out to choose the table most removed from the ladies' room, Bess thought bitterly, they could not have met with more success. But she found her way at last, and under the benevolent supervision of the attendant tried to write her note.

The attendant was old, with unnaturally brassy hair and a naturally brassy voice. Eying the static pencil in Bess's hand, she said, "Did you have a fight with your boyfriend, dear?"

Bess said, "No," wishing fervently that it was as simple and as normal as that. She was hesitating because she did not know how to salute a hateful man who was not her boyfriend and who had ignored her to give more than polite attention to her mother. My dear Mr. Basset? My dear Link? My dear—? She settled for "Dear Link."

"Dear Link," she wrote. "My mother has changed her mind about being interviewed. Please do not call her to the microphone." It sounded absurdly stilted. It sounded like the sort of note sent to a teacher to excuse an erring child, and it occurred to Bess that she and Mother had reversed roles. Everything within her protested the switch. She was terribly conscious of her inadequacy, of her own present need to draw upon parent strength.

"Well," the attendant said, "you be sure not to write anything he can use against you later. Take my word, it don't pay to eat humble pie."

Bess signed her name, pressing down hard upon the scrap of paper in self-assertion. She tipped the attendant, thanked her, and left. Outside, she walked in the wrong direction and halted to take her bearings. She tried to stop one of the scurrying waiters, but none heeded her signal. And then Link Basset was at her side.

"Alone at last." His words sliced through the thick surrounding din.

She said foolishly, "How did you get here?"

"I was waiting for you. I'd followed your progress from the table. Tact demanded that I give you time to powder your nose."

At once she was sorry that she had not powdered her nose. But of course it did not matter how she looked. And since it did not matter, why must he stare at her? "I was writing you a note," she said coldly, and balled the scrap of paper in her hand.

"Here—that's no way to treat important mail. Let me have it." He took her hand and tried to pry the fingers apart. "No—stop—don't be silly."

"It's mine—isn't it? Surely you can't want to court another public exhibition."

Her face was hot. "You saw what happened at the table?"

"Oh, that. I wasn't thinking of that. I was thinking of a couple of afternoons ago when you told me you hated scenes."

"You were not. You're mean. I'm sorry my stepfather had to pick a place where you work to—to act up—but you're just plain mean to rub it in. Here's your old note. All it says is that my mother doesn't want to be called to the microphone."

"Is that all?" He smoothed the paper out. "Not even a postscript? Not even 'Love from Bess'? Ah well—it seems that strong measures are indicated. Come this way, please."

"I'm going back to my table."

"In good time. But first I want a word with you and I don't want to have to yell it out to the common people—unless you want me to yell."

She went with him, trying not to be conscious of her hand in his, feeling oddly that she was reliving the day when he had insisted upon buying her a drink. He took her into the bar, but he did not buy her a drink. He walked to the far end, opened a door, and pulled her into a small square office furnished with a modern desk and low upholstered chairs. He closed the door and confronted her.

She knew what he would do, and he did it. While she was firmly deciding not to let him, her lips and arms were making a separate decision. Her lips and arms were ready.

He held her very close. The kiss was long. The kiss negated everything she knew of him and of herself.

At last, not wanting to, she tore herself away and was immediately bereft of all she wanted. She sat down because she could not stand up. She was afraid to look at him, afraid to see the twisted smile. And if she could, she would have shut her ears to the slick smart words that seemed inevitable.

But his smile was no wry smile. There was sweetness in it. And the only word he said was neither slick nor smart. It was "Well?" And it was a hesitant, almost humble question.

Bess said wonderingly, "You meant it. You were serious all the time."

"Pretty serious at first. Altogether serious now. And you?"

"Yes," she said. "Oh yes." But still she could not believe it.

He was standing apart from her. It seemed to her that she had imagined the kiss; that by laying dream upon dream she had built a towering moment in which alien lips and limbs conformed to each other as surely as the units of a picture puzzle. It had not really happened. She was alone as she had always been alone.

He came to sit upon the arm of her chair. He touched her hair and she hungered for further confirmation of the miracle. She heard herself say angrily, "It's impossible. People don't fall in love this way."

"How do they fall in love? Tell me. I'm a stranger here myself."

"That's more like it," she said.

"More like what?"

But she could not explain. What she had meant was that the mocking tone and the words were more like her original conception of him and that somehow they restored her sense of balance. She said, "You're not a stranger here if by that you mean you haven't been in love before."

"I haven't been in love before. I thought I was—and that's supposed to be the same thing—but now I know it isn't—not nearly."

"Why should I believe you?"

"Reduced to commonplace terms, it's like this. All these years I've been shopping. I've even taken merchandise home on approval. But if a shopper's lucky, there comes a rare day in his life when 'this is it' and nothing else will do. You're 'it.'" He laughed. "Your lovely face says you don't think much of that as a romantic declaration. But it is. For me it's as romantic as all get out. All right—you needn't believe me. For the moment just believe yourself."

"I don't want to—it isn't fair. Tonight you hardly noticed me. You sat with my mother. You weren't even aware that I was there."

"You're wrong. I was busting with awareness. But I can tell an obstacle when I see one. I realized I had to win your mother first."

"She's not an obstacle. I don't want you to say things like that—"

"Look—you've got to make up your mind what you do want."

"I don't know. I don't know."

He said gently, "Never mind. Everything's settled so far as I'm concerned. I can't expect *you* to be so sure. For one thing, my timing's rotten. You've had an ugly break this last day or so. It's no wonder you're mixed up. I'll wait a bit."

"It—it may not be worthwhile—waiting. There's more than one obstacle in the way—there's my father. He's suspected of murder. You don't want a girl whose father is—"

"Hush." He leaned toward her, but she turned her face away.

She said, "No—it's not right. You make me forget—and I shouldn't. I shouldn't even try to be happy when I don't know where he—when everything's so horrible." She sat up straight. She said abruptly, "Do you believe my father is a murderer?"

He was taken aback. "I—"

"No—wait—don't answer—because if you say yes I—maybe I'll love you but I'll never, never like you—"

"Bess—say that again. Say 'maybe I'll love you.' Even with the 'maybe' it sounds beautiful."

She would not listen. "You were against him before it happened. In Gilly's you were—you almost hit him. You—"

"Don't fight yourself, Bess. Don't feel guilty about love because you think it's had the bad taste to come at an inopportune moment. Listen to me—I'm not against your father. If I was I've changed my mind. I don't believe he killed Selene Rolfe."

"You—you don't? You're not just saying that because—?"

"I'm not just saying it—and I'm not going into it any further now." He pulled her to her feet. "I'm going to take you back to the table."

"Yes—they'll be wondering—" She sighed. She wanted him to kiss her, but he did not. His expression was grave and withdrawn. She took out her compact and used powder and lipstick. When she looked at him again he was the everyday Link Basset, jaunty and slightly belligerent.

He steered her back to the table. As they neared it he said, "Something new's been added."

"Oh—I forgot to tell you. That's Lieutenant Nelson—a police officer—and the lady's his wife. He came to question us this morning—and now he's turned up here. I don't know why."

They had come within earshot of the table, and if Link Basset had a comment, he swallowed it.

Bess slid into the chair he held for her, and Lisa, with an apprehensive eye upon Haskell, asked him to sit down. Haskell did not protest. He seemed to have dropped into a peaceful void.

Lisa rallied. "Lieutenant—Mrs. Nelson—allow me to present Link Basset. But I'm afraid he's a naughty boy to play hooky from the microphone—"

Link Basset said, "Howdy," and it was clear to Nelson that Bess had already explained the additions to the party. "Let 'em eat records."

A medley of Irish songs had been placed upon the turntable. It strove forlornly against the room's steadily increasing din.

"Saturday night's a losing fight," Basset said. "I usually throw in the sponge a little later, but the way things are going, nobody's going to know the difference. Anyway—my best guest reneged."

Incredibly there was a touch of smugness in Lisa's voice. "I'm sorry."

"Don't be." He sat down beside her. "It would have been casting pearls. Just listen to them. At this point nothing but a striptease would go big—and even that would have to be something special—like three of everything—"

Lisa said, "I told you he was naughty." She shirred her lips primly. "Being a professional, I'm broadminded—but still I don't actually like that sort of talk. I hope you're not easily shocked, Mrs. Nelson."

"Not easily," Kyrie said, "but it seems discourteous not to look shocked when I know somebody's making his best effort." Link Basset grinned at her in pleased recognition.

Nelson said, "Have you really quit for the night, Mr. Basset?"

"Maybe not just for the night—maybe for always if the management wakes up to my defection. But I've been outgrowing the Bull and Bean anyway, so it might as well be now as tomorrow or next week. I might change my mind if we drew more customers like your wife. This is a first for you both—isn't it?"

"Yes—we came to hear you."

"Oh my swelling head!" The words had nothing to do with the speculative look. Then he said nonchalantly, "My orchid goes to the inventor of long-playing records. A boon to short-winded disk jockeys. Or hadn't you noticed—my short-windedness, I mean?"

The final note of "The Kerry Dance" had sounded and the record was patiently rolling into "I'll Take You Home Again, Kathleen." Haskell stirred uneasily and muttered, "I thought we were getting out of here."

"The power of suggestion," Link Basset said. He glanced around the crowded room. "Too bad nobody else is influenced." He hummed softly, "Oh, I will take you home, Kathleen," and looked at Bess, who dared not meet his eyes. Haskell was attempting to focus upon him. "Seen you before somewhere," he said.

"I don't doubt it—but can you see me now?" Basset dismissed him and turned again to Nelson. "When I intercepted Bess she told me you'd come riding to the rescue. Do you think you can manage alone?"

"I wouldn't turn down an offer of assistance," Nelson said.

"Consider the offer made." Basset arose. "I'll come back as soon as I've found the manager and warned him of my intentions. It would be mean to deny him the pleasure of firing me."

"No, Link," Lisa said. Again her voice was smug. "I do think it's sweet of you to risk your position here just for me—but I refuse to permit it."

"Why? I'm practically one of the family."

Lisa said, "Oh," without enthusiasm, and watched him move away.

Nelson asked for the check, and Lisa said with more vehemence than seemed warranted that she would not have it. Champagne was expensive, she said, and she was practical enough to realize that a policeman's salary did not run to it. She went on to assure him that she did not for a moment believe all those stories about graft in the department—and by the way—she had been meaning to ask Mrs. Nelson if her dress was an original model.

Bess stared at her hands and wished she were alone on a quiet mountaintop. Alone with Link—Link! As it turned out, the waiter accepted a tip and nothing else. He explained that Mr. Basset had picked up the check. Lisa would not have that either. She said that she intended to settle with Mr. Basset. Bess tried to change the subject and gained no more than Pyrrhic victory.

"Bess—I've something to say to you. You may not be able to see it my way now, but you'll thank me for it later. There's nothing I want more than your happiness, dear, and that's what gives me courage to take the bull by the horns before it's too late. Your ridiculous romance has gone far enough. It isn't only that Link Basset is much too old for you—it's that he's far from suitable for any sheltered, inexperienced girl—and improvident to boot—throwing up a good position just for a whim. I'm sure we could have managed to get poor James home without his aid—and furthermore, talking about stripteasers in your presence proves that he can't have much respect—"

Bess gave up after her third or fourth interpolation. Joy in that Mother was no longer cutting from the whole cloth nearly triumphed over her embarrassment. By the time Link Basset came back she had discovered that she too could perform Aunt Alma's disappearing trick and was giving all her heart and soul to it.

Link Basset said, "No luck. The spiteful man wouldn't fire me. He seemed to think that the ceremony in which I am about to assist is being performed solely for the protection of this establishment's good name. Are we ready?"

Chapter Sixteen

James Haskell was maneuvered to the sidewalk with less than anticipated difficulty. The female contingent walked ahead, looking detached or self-conscious, according to their personalities. Nelson, who had parked his car on the next street, left the doorman to act as a substitute crutch. Kyrie, claiming a need for exercise, went with him to get the car.

The chill dark had an after-midnight aspect. "At least," Kyrie said, matching his stride through it, "you'll have your opportunity to talk to Basset."

"At least," he said absently. Then he said, "Does Junie know any Irish songs?"

"I shouldn't think so. Most of his repertoire comes from Sammy. Was that an idle question?"

"Not exactly."

"What a funny man I'm hitched to."

He said contritely, "You're hitched to an oaf. A fine night out I've given you."

"Grid—I've seen drunks before. You couldn't have expected that development."

When they reached the Buick she got in beside him. "Don't worry—I realize I'll be relegated to the back seat so that you can keep an eye on Mr. Haskell."

He leaned over and kissed her cheek. "A lucky oaf," he said.

"Truly, Grid, it hasn't been too bad."

"It might get worse."

"Then be glad I wasn't raised to be a *Doll's House* type wife."

He had taken an envelope from his pocket. He studied it by the light of the dashboard before he removed the single sheet of paper.

Kyrie said, "Was that what Mrs. Elliot slipped you when we stood up?"

"You've got an eagle eye." He took a flashlight from the dashboard compartment and focused it upon the paper. After a pause he murmured, "I think I'm touched in the head."

"Grid—what is it?"

"Nothing. I should have said I hope I'm touched in the head."

"Vain hope."

He looked at the letter again and returned it to his pocket. He turned the ignition key.

Kyrie, making a supreme effort, asked no questions. She said, "What bothers me is that nice girl and her aunt being left to cope with the sad awakening of M'sieu Haskell—because I'm sure Madame won't be any help. Would you think it a rotten idea if we took him to our place instead? Mrs. Elliot says she lives in the Village. We're nearer to the Waldorf than that. We could dump him downstairs in your little study until he recovers—or should I say Junie's study? He seems to use it more than you do."

Nelson arrested his foot on the starter. This time he kissed her mouth.

"I don't know what I did to earn that—but I ain't turning it down," she said.

"Will you make the suggestion yourself in the most natural way that occurs to you—and are you sure you don't mind my job slopping over into our home?"

"Your job is you—and you're me."

"I wouldn't consider it if I didn't think it was the best possible arrangement under the circumstances and that Haskell and Company could be disposed of before Junie comes down in the morning. I haven't time to explain—"

"You needn't. But there are strings attached. It's after twelve, and something tells me it will be a lot later before we see bed. You must promise to make up for lost sleep tomorrow."

"I'll take the first opportunity I get."

"Hmmm. Do you still want Link Basset?"

"He might be useful."

"All right—get going before they all freeze to death."

Haskell was draped chummily around the doorman. The air had revived him sufficiently to make him renounce any part of Link Basset. Kyrie gave up her place, and Nelson and the doorman eased him into it.

Basset said, "Seems like I'm *de trop*. If my presence is going to inflame him, no reason why I shouldn't take my girl home in a cab."

Lisa said pathetically, "There's plenty of room for everyone in the back—isn't there, Lieutenant? I just can't bear to let my little girl out of my sight for a moment. She's all I have to turn to—"

Bess said, "Of course I'll come. Don't stand there in the cold. Get in."

Basset shrugged with mock resignation. "Mine not to reason why." He held the door for Lisa, Kyrie, and Bess. But Alma Elliot, after a moment of hesitation, walked around to the far side of the car and wedged herself between James Haskell and the door.

Basset said, "I was going to steel myself to do that even though I'd probably get socked for it—but I prefer this." He squeezed in beside Bess.

Alma Elliot and Nelson managed to arrange Haskell's bulk so that it did not list toward the steering wheel. Haskell complained bitterly. He wanted to know what kind of a deal he was getting. He footed the bills, didn't he? This was a taxi, wasn't it? So why the hell should he have to sit with the driver? Then, although his eyes were open, he was seized by a nightmare and he roared something garbled about a plane crashing headlong into the stables. When Alma Elliot made soothing sounds, he lowered his voice to a hoarse mutter. "Sure—you can be sweet enough when you want, but—" He shuddered and fell against her shoulder and snored.

In the back seat, Lisa explained to Kyrie that James was not a habitual drunkard. It was just that he was unused to alcohol, and furthermore, she was sure that third-rate places like the Bull and Bean would as soon poison people as not. The last was directed at Link Basset.

Kyrie did not issue her invitation until the car had crossed the Avenue of the Americas. "I don't like to play the anxious mother," she said, "but I've a small son and I always get uneasy when I'm away from him for too long at a stretch. It's bound to take a bit of time to stop off at Mrs. Elliot's, so I'm wondering why we couldn't all go to my house. It's quite close to the Waldorf, and after Mr. Haskell has had coffee and feels better—"

Lisa interrupted out of habit. "Do you mean to say you've left your child alone? I never left Bess for a moment when she was little."

"No—he's not alone, but—well—it isn't the same thing—is it?" She made silent apologies to Sammy. Then she said shyly, "The truth is, maybe I'm using Junie as an excuse. It's been so pleasant meeting all of you—and my husband and I don't get out very often—and well—you see—I just hate to have the party break up." She addressed a pretty plea to Nelson's back. "Won't you try to persuade them, Grid? After all—it isn't terribly late—"

Nelson responded like any Caspar Milquetoast. "Of course. You'll all be more than welcome." And as though the matter were settled, he continued driving east.

Bess gave a wriggle that was undoubtedly a prelude to protest, but Link Basset's arm encircled her. She murmured to him, not protestingly.

Lisa leaned across Kyrie to peer at her. "Did you say something, Bess?"

"No, Mother, I—"

"Oh—I thought you did." She settled back again. "Mrs. Nelson, I don't want to be a spoilsport. Since you're so set on it, we'll accept your invitation. I can understand how you feel about wanting company. I suppose that in the course of your husband's work he doesn't meet the sort of people he can bring home—but I do hope you won't fuss for us. What with prices as they are, it must be hard enough for wage earners to make ends meet. My husband has his own business, but even so I'm appalled sometimes at the money that goes out for ordinary necessities."

In the front seat, Alma Elliot said softly, "Did you read the letter, Lieutenant Nelson?"

"Yes. Thank you for turning it over."

"Is there any way of tracing it?"

He did not answer. He said, "You have no idea of where he is?"

"Believe me, I'm keeping nothing back. I want you to find him. I'm convinced it's the only way. He's not very strong. I'm worried that he may be hiding in some dreadful place—and even if—" Then she said, "Apparently I trust you more than you trust me."

"Yet it was only by chance that we met tonight."

"I see what you mean—but the letter didn't come until shortly before we left for the restaurant. I couldn't have called you at the time. My telephone is not in a very private place. I fully intended to call you later. In fact I was about to go in search of a phone booth when you came into the Bull and Bean."

"Who delivered the letter?"

"I don't know. It had been pushed under the door." She nodded at the burden on her shoulder. "He handed it to me when he came in with Lisa—a little before ten. Before that I had decided to stay at home in case there was an attempt to reach me—but as soon as I realized there'd be no further communication I went along to please Bess." Haskell's head was slipping down toward her breast. She resettled it, aloof and competent.

Nelson saw the action out of the corner of his eye. He said, "Are you very uncomfortable, Mrs. Elliot?"

"Very—in more ways than one. I—"

"Yes?" The traffic did not permit him to observe her face. He damned the traffic.

"Perhaps I'm putting the wrong interpretation on—on—" He waited for her to complete the sentence. When she did not he said gravely, "Perhaps we both are."

Lisa had been talking at a fairly steady pace. She interrupted herself as Nelson braked before the small house.

"Is this where you live, Mrs. Nelson? How neat and self-respecting it looks. Do you know—I often think it a pity they had to break up these old places into apartments—but of course I realize the need for it."

Kyrie said meekly, "This one isn't broken up," and to prevent thoughts of graft and corruption from running through Lisa's head, she added quickly, "We were able to buy it for a song."

She got out, ran up the steps, and unlocked the door, thinking that the women would follow. But they did not see her beckoning wave, and she hesitated to disturb the street's quiet by calling to them. She stood holding the door, not above hoping that the neighbors were all absorbed in interesting inside jobs. This time James Haskell could not move under his own power, with or without crutches. He had to be carried, Nelson bearing his head and shoulders, Link Basset his feet. And for added funereal effect, his wife, Alma Elliot, and Bess walked behind him like three mourners.

Inside the house the procession split, and Kyrie shepherded her charges to the living room, while Nelson and Basset headed for the study.

"He should have stood at home," Link Basset said after Haskell had been deposited on the couch. "He's the heaviest short guy I ever helped to lift. All muscle." He faced his stooping host, who had loosened Haskell's collar and was engaged in removing his shoes. "And you're the tenderest cop I ever met."

Nelson straightened. "Have you a wide acquaintance?"

"We won't go into that. I read about you in the paper today. You didn't just happen in at the Bull and Bean. What's yours?"

Nelson was direct. "I wanted to talk to you."

"Why?"

"Because you're one of several who knows Kevin Culhane and you're one of a few who knew Selene Rolfe."

"Which makes me?"

"A man to talk to—obviously." Nelson did not sound too interested. "What prompted you to call on Bess Rohan on the night of the murder?"

"I called on her old man first—*after* the body had been discovered, in case you've got ideas. The reporters had arrived and I went up with them to get a squint. Then I thought the news might have reached Bess and that she might need someone to hold her hand."

"Did you share the general belief that Kevin Culhane was the murderer?"

"I did until I paid a condolence call on Mrs. Rolfe. She made me change my mind. No reason except sheer perversity. I just didn't want to be on her side. If you've any more questions, make them fast. I've got to get back to Bess before Mama takes another bite out of her."

"I'll wait until you're in less of a hurry. If you're as serious as you sound, you'll be around a while."

Basset's face darkened. "Anything funny about my being serious?"

"No. Many a jaded man about town has retired to just such a port as Bess Rohan."

Basset looked at him uncertainly. Then he shrugged. "If there's a crack in that, I'm too mixed up to find it—and too polite to slug you in your own house if I did." He turned and left the room.

Alone except for his recumbent guest, Nelson stood motionless for a few moments. Idly he contemplated the strewn surface of the desk in the center of the room. Junie had been using it as a drawing table. Junie had taken his art a step beyond the modern school by adding pied captions as unintelligible as the work itself. Nelson fingered several of the drawings, stacked them mechanically, and laid them aside. Haskell's stertorous breathing thundered in his ears as he left the study, closing the door behind him.

He went upstairs. He looked in on the sleeping Junie.

Treading lightly, he crossed the hall to Sammy's room. Her door was ajar, showing a narrow stripe of light. He knocked. Sammy's "Who there?" was heavy-laden, but not with sleep. He pushed the door inward. She sat in a chair near the bed, some mending in her lap. She raised her magnificent head. "Mr. Grid-dely—?"

"Do you usually sew at this hour, Sammy?"

She moistened her lips. "I got no casuals. Sometime sewing calm my mind."

"Does your mind need calming?"

Her heavy-lidded eyes were resigned. She nodded.

"You delivered that letter to Mrs. Elliot when you went out. If you were plotting against me—and that's what it amounts to—didn't you realize I might connect it with the printing set you gave Junie for Christmas?"

"I didn't think Mrs. Elliot going to show it to you—not after what you said in the newspaper. I thought she his friend."

"I thought you were mine."

She said steadily, "You thought good."

"Where is he, Sammy? In the cellar?"

"Mr. Grid-dely—no matter what—I couldn't do nothing else."

"Nothing else but betray me?" He spoke quietly. "I always thought I could take a joke directed at myself—but now I'm not so sure. The size of this one frightens me. I'm a police officer. I was searching for a wanted man—a search that involves a lot of money—your money and the money of all the city's inhabitants—as well as the brains and the endless tiring physical effort of trained men. And all the while the object of the search was hiding in my own house. My little son knew it—but I who am classified as a detective did not. I'm wondering if I can take that joke against myself. I'm wondering if I can stomach the loud laughter of men whose respect I need in order to earn my salary. But on the other hand, perhaps I won't be asked to take it. Perhaps I'll be asked for my resignation—"

"You stop that, Mr. Grid-dely." Sammy stood up. The small jeans she had been patching slid to the rug. She was Nelson's height, but now she seemed to tower over him. "You stop standing there like a big judge. You going to listen to how it happen. Mr. Kevin Culhane, he come this afternoon when Miss Kyrie away and Junie and little Kenneth up here with the television. They's a ring at the bell and I go see—and he standing outside in his poor old bones—so tired he like to drop. He ask for you and I say you ain't home—and he say can he wait—and I help him in and sit him down and fetch him a cup of strong tea and a little lunch. I think he remember me from Miss Catherine, but he ain't surprised to find me working here because he ain't surprised at nothing no more. He hurt his right hand someplace—and his left hand shaking so much I got to hold the cup for him. He really beat. He can't even hold a pen to write—that why later I print the note to Mrs. Elliot for him on Junie's set 'count of it fret him not to have her know he safe. He tell me he been to Westport with Miss Catherine—and he talk things over with her and Mr. Bede. They know you on the case and they all decide the best for him to do is come to you and explain he innocent and you going to take care of him. So he spend the night at Westport—and this morning Mr. Bede drive him back to the city and drop him near your police station. But when Mr. Bede gone about his business, Mr. Culhane get as far as the door and he just can't make his legs carry him through it. So after a while he walk away. He—"

"He stood outside the precinct and wasn't noticed?"

"That right, Mr. Grid-dely. 'Count of he don't look like no bad man, cops walking in and out pay him little mind."

Nelson turned away, not daring to look at her. Fiercely he kept telling himself that it was not a bit funny.

Sammy read anger in his averted head. Her deep voice was pleading. "I say to myself I tell you about it in the morning for true. It seem to me he ain't fit to bear no more misery till he have a night's rest. You ain't fixing to put him in jail right now?"

Nelson said coldly, "I presume you haven't finished your story."

She sighed. "He leave that old station. I think the way he feel about it got to do with where he raised and how the folk he raised with scared of having truck with cops. Well—he walk away. He don't study about where he walking or what he going to do. He shrink along small, hoping nobody notice—and pretty soon he come to Bryant Park and he sit on a bench and he feel safe in the middle of all the old men who taking the air. He sit there thinking and thinking a long time. He don't want to go back to Mrs. Elliot and start trouble for her. And then a notion come to him that if he find a drugstore and look up where you live maybe it easier to talk to you in your house. So that what he do—only he forgot his cash on the bureau at Miss

Catherine's and he got to walk from Bryant Park to here. Mr. Grid-dely—it ain't plotting against you—but when I see in the newspaper you can't wait to lock him up I got no choice but to keep him someplace till you find the dog who kill that girl. I sure you going to find that dog—"

"Of course," Nelson said. "And so you hide Kevin Culhane in my cellar and introduce him to Junie as the gas man. What could show more faith?"

"No call to talk to me out of the wrong side of your mouth. After the nurse came for his little friend, Junie catch me carrying blankets and stuff down the cellar and he creep behind me. I got to tell him something to satisfy him—"

Nelson had never seen tears in Sammy's eyes. He saw them now. She sat down suddenly. She said, "Mr. Kevin Culhane and Junie, they like each other fine. Weak as he is, he take Junie up and he sing him—and Junie listen like a angel. He can't get enough of them sweet songs—"

"Including 'The Rose of Tralee,'" Nelson said. "All right, Sammy. Go on ahead and tell Mr. Culhane I'm coming—and see that he doesn't change his mind again and try to skip."

"He got no skip left to him," she said.

"Aren't you going?"

"I going—but I got to say this first." She took a long breath. "Ain't necessary to resign your job. Who got to know he been hiding here? He get tired of running away is all and he come to tell you he innocent. Who blame you for that?"

"Thanks for your concern."

"Mr. Grid-dely—you acting plain ordinary."

"Isn't that what you expect of me?" He watched her depart, her head held high.

Chapter Seventeen

Downstairs, the voices that came from the living room sounded normal, and in the study the situation was as it had been. Nelson stopped to telephone. He spoke to Clevis, who had returned to the precinct, and gave him terse orders. Then he descended to the cellar.

It was as orderly and cleanly swept as everything controlled by Sammy, and she had made it as comfortable as possible for Kevin Culhane. He sat upon a cot, clothed in a pair of Nelson's pajamas. A robe of Nelson's lay on a chair near him. Culhane's blue eyes, so much like Bess's eyes, were dazed. The flesh was drawn taut over the bones of his face.

The two white-haired men looked at each other, one young and vital, the other older-seeming than his years.

Culhane said, "I hope you won't be harsh with Sammy. I'll get dressed as soon as she brings my clothes."

"Please get them, Sammy," Nelson said.

Her eyes were hurt and unbelieving. "He ain't fit—" She shrugged helplessly and went.

Culhane shivered. Nelson placed his robe over the thin shoulders. "Put that on until she comes back—and the slippers. It's not too warm down here."

"Are you saving me for the slaughter?"

"Did you kill Selene Rolfe?"

"No." He said it simply. "She was there—dead—when I went back to change my shirt. I'd been out to dinner—"

"Yes—I know about that. Was she lying on the floor?"

"On the bed—face downward. I didn't move her."

"Did you recognize her at once—not seeing her face?"

"Yes—I'd lunched with her that day—she was wearing the same clothes she'd worn then."

"Was the light on?"

"The lamp was on. The ceiling light had no bulb in it—but I had light enough to see all I wanted to see. I remember thinking it strange I'd left the lamp on—before I looked at the bed."

"There was a coat. Had she worn that at lunch?"

"I—no—she wore just the suit at lunch. It was a rather warm day."

"Had you ever noticed her resemblance to your wife?"

"Yes—she looked very much as Lisa did when I first met her. In fact, I had a moment's aberration and thought—but then I saw the clothes—"

"Why did you run away?"

"Blind instinct, I suppose—and reason returned too late to undo the effect of running away."

"Yet you tried to undo the effect by coming to me of your own free will."

"Not entirely of my own free will. The Mortimers persuaded me that you were a just man—that you would hear me out. But now I find I've little enough to tell except that I did not kill Selene. And although I've thought and thought, I see no way to prove it. I can't even believe that anyone hates me enough to have deliberately framed me."

"Weren't you afraid your wife would make trouble?"

"Not that kind of trouble. She got wind of the television show and wrote that her second marriage was a failure and that if she had money—or if I'd use my influence to get her on television—she could leave her husband and make a better life for herself. I had no influence, so I discounted that part of her letter, although I knew she'd always been stagestruck. I took the whole thing as a threat to my future—but that may have been due to my state of nerves. Lisa's not evil—merely perpetually discontented with her lot."

"What about her husband? Could he have seen you as a threat to his happiness—thought that she still loved you?"

Culhane shook his head wearily. "Lisa never loved me—and I've never met her husband. I understand from Alma that he's a decent unimaginative man. He'd have to be a psychotic to go to such lengths—and surely then it would be me he'd kill—not that poor child."

"There's Link Basset," Nelson said. "He was interested in Selene. It could have been jealousy that made him pick a fight with you in the restaurant."

Again Culhane shook his head. "I don't understand the nature of your questions. You might almost be a lawyer preparing a case for my defense. Unfortunately I can clutch at none of the straws you offer. Link Basset is not my enemy. I met him on the Coast and it was he who conceived the idea for the show and brought me to the attention of the network executives. He seemed sympathetic—anxious to give the series an authentic theme. He spent hours with me discussing such portions of my life as I cared to make public. I think that little passage in the restaurant was due to something that Selene Rolfe had confided to him. She thought she was in love with me—and seeing us together at Gully's, he may have believed I encouraged her. He's an odd brash young man who seems to fear that people will discover the good in him. At least that's my opinion. As for his feelings toward Selene—I think he took her out because he was sorry for her—I think love didn't enter into it." He huddled into the robe. "I've been over it and over it in my mind—but the only conclusion I can come to is that someone from outside wandered into my room and saw Selene—and tried to take advantage of her—and killed her in the attempt."

Nelson said, "When did you hurt your hand?"

Culhane pushed his right sleeve back to expose the neat bandage extending past his wrist. "That's an old story. I broke some bones in the wrist and fingers when I was a boy. I suppose they weren't set properly, because the strength never came back. I gave the hand a twist on the train and put off having it attended to—but Sammy taped it as well as a doctor could."

"What train?"

"From California. The porter brought me some iodine—"

Nelson said, "And you ran away!"

Sammy appeared with the clothes. Her manner was formal. "Miss Kyrie have company upstairs. I going to help her. I got nothing against Miss Kyrie." Her exit was queenly.

Nelson helped Culhane to dress, noting the freshly laundered underwear and shirt, the well-pressed suit. He said absently, "I saw Sammy ironing at dinnertime but was too preoccupied to notice what she was ironing."

"You won't let her suffer for her kindness to me?"

"She won't suffer." He was doing the suffering, he thought, because Sammy had placed his interests second to the cause of someone outside of what he considered to be her adopted family. Only it was not quite so simple. It was that he had been too smug about his place in her scheme, and that the awakening irked far more than her act. Whereupon he conferred upon himself the title of Grid Nelson, little tin god, deposed.

"I'm as ready as I shall ever be," Culhane said. He stood up. Looking at him, Nelson experienced pangs sharper than those inflicted by Sammy. He longed to reassure him, but could not. He said, "You'll stay under this roof tonight—but there may be an ordeal in store as trying as immediate arrest. The company upstairs consists of your former wife, your sister-in-law, your daughter—"

"My—?" Color flooded the transparent skin. "Do—do they know I'm here?"

"I don't think so."

"But why—?"

"It will all be explained. Can you face it?"

Culhane searched Nelson's face. He said, "Yes—anything—anything." His thin shoulders squared.

Kyrie heard them in the hall and came out. She said, "Grid—?" and stopped. Then she said, "Oh no—you can't take him inside. It's too cruel—"

Nelson muttered, "*Et tu*—"

But Kyrie's faith was shaken only for a moment. Her "I'm sorry" was for both of them. "You're Mr. Culhane, of course. I'm Kyrie Nelson and I—I'm glad to meet you. I just didn't realize we had another guest. Grid—Clevis is here. He's—"

"I'll see him in a little while." He led the way to the living room.

Link Basset sat on the sofa with Bess. Lisa sat there, too, a determined third. Alma Elliot stood at one of the long windows. Sammy was making the rounds with coffee and sandwiches. Sammy came to a full stop, immovable as a statue.

No one in the room stirred until Bess got up and went to her father. She put her arms around him and laid her cheek against his. Over Bess's head Culhane met the startled eyes of Alma Elliot, the open mouth of Lisa.

Lisa's voice broke the silence. "Kevin!"

Clevis shuffled into the room; a demoted Clevis wearing the blue uniform of a patrolman. He went to stand at Culhane's side. He did not touch him, but custody was implicit in his stance.

Bess held on. She said, "We're with you—we'll get the best lawyer—"

"Bless you." Culhane's voice was choked.

Lisa, who had been advancing toward the tableau, was halted by a muffled shriek.

The room emptied. Everyone massed at the study door. Clevis, now grasping Culhane's arm, used his free elbow to clear a path. He pulled Culhane with him over the threshold, the others crowding behind.

James Haskell rocked back and forth upon the couch. With manifest effort he lifted his head from his hands. He seemed to be striving desperately for orientation. He mumbled, "This isn't the restaurant where—"

"You're right, it isn't," Clevis said. "This is the residence of the acting captain of Homicide West."

Haskell rubbed his eyes hard. His large fists dropped, and one of them unclenched to pluck at the coat that was wound about his legs. He looked down at it with the eyes of a sick dog. Then he looked at Culhane, and from Culhane to the blue uniform. He said dully, "Why did you let them find you?"

"We always find 'em," Clevis said.

Lisa had come over to the couch. She said in tones designed to soothe, "James—you drank too much and I knew you wouldn't want to disgrace yourself by entering the Waldorf in that condition, so I accepted Mrs. Nelson's kind invitation. When you've had some strong black coffee I want to talk to you about a lawyer for Kevin. After all—he was my husband and we can't let—"

"Get away from me—"

"Why, James, you're still—I should have thought that nice sleep would—" She swooped suddenly upon the coat. "That's—that's my black cashmere. How did it get here?"

Nelson stepped forward. "Are you sure this is yours?"

"Of course I'm sure—there's my pin on the lapel—but I didn't bring it with me. James—?"

Clevis said in a bored voice, "Take it up later, ma'am." He tightened his grip on Culhane and turned him toward the door. "We got a place to go. I won't put the cuffs on you, Culhane, if you don't make trouble—"

James Haskell was off the couch. He was swaying, trying to block Clevis.

Clevis said, "Brush yourself off me, mister. I got no time for drunks. I'm a homicide cop—"

"No," Haskell said. "No—don't take him. As long as he was free I could live with it. But not this way—"

Nelson nodded at Clevis, who stepped aside. Nelson said, "I didn't think you could, Mr. Haskell. Do you want to make a statement?"

"I killed her. I can't even remember her name—but I killed her."

Clevis and Nelson cleared the study of a white and weeping Lisa, a younger, straighter Culhane, the rest. They fed James Haskell aspirin and black coffee, and Clevis took down his full confession. He unburdened himself with little prompting. The couch he rested upon might have been in the office of a psychiatrist.

"I'd never been married before," he said. "They say there's something wrong with a man who reaches fifty without marrying—but I got along all right until I met her. Maybe that's why I was hit so hard—it happening so late. I don't know. She seemed to love me too. She knew what she was getting into—the sort of life she'd have with me. I never painted it different than it was. But not much time passed before I discovered how she really felt. She'd been sure that when she had me tied she could persuade me to sell out and move to New York City. Me in New York!

"Short of that, I did everything I could—gave her everything money could buy—but still she wasn't satisfied. A couple of weeks ago I drove her to Boston. I thought that would please her—last her for a while—but we'd scarcely got back home when she began to talk New York again, and nothing would do but this trip. At first she said she wanted me along and teased me about thinking more of the horses than I did of her—but she was ready enough to take my suggestion that she go alone. That made me kind of uneasy she might have more than the trip on her mind. Still—I let her go. I put her on the train and when I came back the place seemed too quiet. If you knew her—really knew her—you'd think me crazy for missing her the way I did—but there it was, and I couldn't keep my mind on anything else. I went up to her room—not to snoop—just for company—and then I found the letter.

"It was signed 'Kevin' and it was on the Gretna Hotel stationery. She'd told me all about Kevin Culhane and the raw deal he was supposed to have given her, and I'd swallowed it whole until I got a bellyful and started to have doubts. Lately she'd changed her tune some, mentioning him as though she was comparing him to me—and not in my favor. That's what I thought of when I read the letter which said he'd received hers and would she wait another week or so until his affairs were in order.

"I wasn't angry. I just thought, But she's not waiting—she's gone to him and I don't want to lose her. I can get a plane to New York if I drive to the next town—and I'll get there in time to stop her. While I was thinking this I heard shouting and I went to the window. One of the stable hands was calling for me to come quick. I ran down and it was the red mare. My assistant was away. If I'd taken care, the foal might have had a chance—but it didn't—not the way I bungled the job. That was murder too—" He drew a handkerchief from his pocket. He dried his hands, which were either damp with sweat or with some fancied stain. He said, "I caught the plane and got to New York at seven-thirty. Her train had arrived at seven—which meant she'd time to get to the Waldorf from Grand Central and maybe change her clothes. Because whatever she did, she'd be sure to change her clothes for it—"

Nelson made the first interruption. "You brought her cashmere coat with you?"

James Haskell nodded somberly. "That's the kind of fool I am. She wouldn't take it because she said her bags were too full to hold it—and I knew the weather would turn cold. I had it over my arm when I asked the clerk at the Waldorf for her room number. He wouldn't give it to me so that I could go up. He said yes, she'd registered but he'd have to announce me—and when I said I was her husband he didn't say he doubted it. He just said he'd ring to see if she was in. She wasn't."

In his mind Nelson went over Lisa's account of her movements. She might have been in the bath and not heard the phone, or in the restaurant, he thought grimly.

"That was when I began to see red," Haskell said. "I told the clerk no message. I said I'd just remembered I was to meet her somewhere. I walked out of the lobby and I got a cab. I gave the driver a number in the West Twenties. I'd left the letter home and I couldn't think straight enough to remember the name of Gretna. The number I remembered wasn't right either, but it was near enough. I had to walk a few steps and I recognized the hotel name as soon as I saw it on the sign. I hadn't expected it to be so shabby. I thought, She must love him if she's willing to live like this—and somehow it made me madder than before.

"I went in. I asked for Culhane, and the clerk said the room number without even looking at me.

"The door was open. She was standing with her back to me. She was standing on one foot the way she—the way Lisa does sometimes when she's in a hurry. I thought, She never wore that suit for me—she must have been saving it. I don't know what else I thought. I could reach her from where I stood. I was still carrying the bag and the coat. I dropped them and I reached. She didn't have a chance to turn. She said, 'Kevin?' and I didn't let her say any more. We must have got tangled with the lamp cord. It was only when the lamp fell over that I stopped. I picked the lamp up. It was still on. I picked her up. The back of her head was bloody where it had hit her. And then—then I looked at her face—and she was a stranger—and she was dead. I carried her to the bed. I—" He was reliving it. His contorted mouth was out of control.

Nelson said, "You placed her face downward because you couldn't bear to look at what you'd done."

"Yes—I—and I took my bag and I got out of there. I forgot about the coat. I couldn't go back to the Waldorf. It wasn't possible. I walked and I thought about the girl I didn't know—and about Lisa—and Culhane—and myself—and what I'd done. And all of a sudden I thought about the coat—and I knew the coat would get me in the end. After a while I came to a flea-trap on Forty-second Street. I spent the rest of the night there and in the morning I slept a little. Then I went out and bought the papers. I read that Culhane had run away. It seemed like a ray of light to me. If they caught him I was finished—I'd give myself up—but if they didn't—if they never did—? I made myself believe that it could be—that I could go on as before. I made myself go to the Waldorf and join Lisa as though I had just arrived and nothing bad had happened."

Nelson waited. Then he said, "Do you want to say anything to Lisa before you go?"

"There's nothing more to say." He stood up. He said to Nelson, "How did you know enough to bring the coat and put it where I'd see it when I came to? Did—did she know? Was all this arranged—the restaurant—you being there—?"

Nelson shook his head. "It wasn't prearranged. She had no idea that you were involved."

"Well—well, I suppose that's something. Then how—?"

"You pointed to yourself by what you said in your cups about a dead filly—right after it had been explained that they were all called foals at birth. Taken with the rest of the evidence, it struck me that just possibly you might have been referring to Selene Rolfe."

James Haskell's smile was the smile he would wear in death. "Lisa needled me from start to finish. Sober, I could take it. The joker is that I'm not a drinking man—and I seldom lose my temper. But when I drink—and when I get mad—!" He shrugged. He said lamely, "I guess it all piled up in me—biding its time."

He did not change his mind about talking to his wife. Clevis and Nelson took him to the waiting police car. They left him in the driver's care for a few minutes.

Clevis said, "Well—I was right about it being a meatball—only I should have specified horse meat. How do you like me in blue? Prying that coat loose from the lab and bringing it here was your idea—the uniform was mine. I thought it would break him quicker than my regular togs."

"Maybe you ought to keep wearing it," Nelson said.

"Hey—I don't want that much appreciation."

Nelson went back into the house, envying Clevis, for whom a case was simply a case. Brooding upon this one, he thought of the people who were involved.

Selene Rolfe was dead. Her ambitious mother would now be forced to turn to honest work. James Haskell, stricken by the lethal combination of love and intemperate rage, would be convicted of murder. Bess Rohan would be all right. She would make Link Basset a good wife, and if not Link Basset, there would be someone else who cared enough about her to handle Lisa. But from all the signs, he thought it would be Basset. Lisa